"A magnificent novel with enormous
sweep and power . . . the crowning glory of
Ethan Canin's writing life."
—Pat Conroy

"Heartbreaking . . . beautifully written."
—USA Today

"A very ambitious take on the
great American novel about class, wealth,
politics, history, power, innocence, and
corruption. Beautiful, brilliant, complicated.
At times triumphant, at times sad."
—Linda Wertheimer, National Public Radio

"A superb achievement."
—Library Journal

"[A] splendid novel."
—Publishers Weekly

Praise for
America America

"A brilliant, serious book for serious readers."
—*San Diego Union-Tribune*

"A complicated, many-layered epic of class, politics, sex, death, and social history . . . Its reach is wide and its touch often masterly."
—JOHN UPDIKE in *The New Yorker*

"A sprawling, captivating, timely work of art . . . clearly the work of a writer at the top of his form . . . a novel that reminds us that fiction matters."
—*Houston Chronicle*

"As rich, ambitious, intelligent, emotionally satisfying and important a work of fiction as we're likely to get this year."
—RICHARD RUSSO, Pulitzer Prize–winning author of *Empire Falls*

"[A] satisfying, compulsively readable saga."
—*Entertainment Weekly*

"A glorious—and timely—meditation on American politics, both party and social. . . . Canin's rich, plangent prose is extraordinary. As a work of art, and as a history lesson, *America America* was a revelation."
—*Sunday Telegraph* (London)

"We've waited a long time for a worthy successor to Robert Penn Warren's *All the King's Men,* and it couldn't have arrived at a more auspicious moment."
—*The Washington Post Book World*

AMERICA
AMERICA

ETHAN
CANIN

 RANDOM HOUSE TRADE PAPERBACKS NEW YORK

AMERICA
AMERICA

A NOVEL

2009 Random House Trade Paperback Edition

Published in the United States by Random House Trade Paperbacks, an imprint of The Random House Publishing Group, a division of Random House, Inc., New York.

RANDOM HOUSE TRADE PAPERBACKS and colophon are trademarks of Random House, Inc.
RANDOM HOUSE READER'S CIRCLE & Design is a registered trademark of Random House, Inc.

Originally published in hardcover in the United States by Random House, an imprint of The Random House Publishing Group, a division of Random House, Inc., in 2008.

LIBRARY OF CONGRESS CATALOGING-IN-PUBLICATION DATA

Canin, Ethan.
America America: a novel / Ethan Canin.
p.   cm.
ISBN 978-0-8129-7989-3
1. New York (State)—Politics and government—Fiction.
2. United States—Politics and government—Fiction.
3. Working class men—Fiction.   4. Rich people—Fiction.
5. Upper class women—Fiction.   6. Character—Fiction.
I. Title.
PS3553.A495A83 2008
813'.54—dc22   2008002341

Printed in the United States of America

www.randomhousereaderscircle.com

9 8 7 6 5 4 3 2 1

Book design by Simon M. Sullivan

FOR MISHA, AYLA, AMIELA, AND BARBARA

AMERICA
AMERICA

ONE

I

2006

WHEN YOU'VE BEEN INVOLVED in something like this, no matter how long ago it happened, no matter how long it's been absent from the news, you're fated, nonetheless, to always search it out. To be on alert for it, somehow, every day of your life. For the small item at the back of the newspaper. For the stranger at the cocktail party or the unfamiliar letter in the mailbox. For the reckoning pause on the other end of the phone line. For the dreadful reappearance of something that, in all likelihood, is never going to return.

I wouldn't have thought, in fact, that I would be the one to bring it back now, after all this time. That I would be the one to finally try to explain it. What I know of it, at least, even if that's only a part. I can only guess at the other parts. But I've been guessing at them for half my life now, and I think I've made some sense of it.

Honestly I don't know what will come of this—who will find pain in what I say and who, in a certain manner, solace. It isn't only that Senator Henry Bonwiller is dead. His death was melancholy news up here, of course, but it's not the only reason I've set out to tell this. The other part is my children. That's something I'm certain of. We have three daughters, and one of them is just past the age I was when these events took place, and I must say I feel a certain relief that nothing similar has shadowed any of their days; but I also know that you never stop worrying that it will. After all, if children don't make you see things differently—first bringing them into the world and then watching them go out into it—then God help you.

The crowd at Senator Bonwiller's funeral was even bigger than I expected. Probably six hundred people at the morning eulogy—more if you count the uninvited crowd on the sidewalk in front of St. Anne's, standing under the shade of the sycamores and fanning themselves with their newspapers. And at least a thousand at the burial, which was open to the public that afternoon at St. Gabriel's Cemetery, not too far away and not much cooler than in town. St. Gabriel's is in Islington Township, and although no other famous men are buried there, Islington Township is where Senator Bonwiller was born and where he lived until ambition moved him along: I suppose it must have been his wish that he rest there in the end. It's also where his parents and brothers lie. His wife is buried a thousand miles away, in Savannah, Georgia, with her own parents, and there was no doubt some whispering about that fact. Henry Bonwiller was a complicated man, to say the least. I knew him to a certain degree. Not well enough to know what he would have felt about the grave arrangements, but more than well enough to know he would have been happy about the crowd.

It was a Saturday in late September. A heat wave had killed lawns all across the state, and the smell of rotting apples was drifting up from the meadow. The graveside service had just ended, and we were still crowded beneath the shade of the great bur oaks, whose grand trunks rise evenly across the cemetery lawn as if by agreement with one another. There seemed to have been agreements about other things, as well. *The New York Times* gave the news an above-the-fold headline on page one and a three-column jump in the obituaries, but their story only included a single paragraph on Anodyne Energy and not much more on Silverton Orchards. *The Boston Globe* ran an editorial from the right-hand front column, under "The Country Mourns," and ended with "this is the close of a more beneficent era." But it didn't do much more with either bit of history.

I didn't cover it for *The Speaker-Sentinel*, because I was at the funeral for my own reasons, but I helped one of our young staff members who did, the high school intern who arrived underdressed in her own ironic way and probably had no idea of half the personages she was looking at. Senator Bonwiller was eighty-nine when he died and hadn't been in the news for almost fifteen years, but the crowd included more than a dozen United States senators, two Supreme Court justices, the governors of New York and Connecticut, and enough lawyers and judges and state representatives to fill the county jail. I also saw what looked like an entire brigade of retired state police officers, decked out in their old satin-striped parade uniforms. But so many of them were leaning on canes or sitting in wheelchairs that you might have thought Henry Bonwiller had been a small-town slip-and-fall lawyer and not a man who, if certain chips of fate had fallen certain other ways, might once have been president of the United States.

The intern from *The Speaker-Sentinel* was named Trieste Millbury. Trieste and I have had our share of go-arounds since her arrival at the paper, and to tell you the truth I was wishing that afternoon that I worked at a bigger outfit—perhaps one where the publisher wouldn't find himself at a funeral with the intern. But that's the way *The Speaker-Sentinel* is: we like to send our own people on stories, even if the wire services have us bound and tied. We're the last of the local dailies not to have sold to McClatchy or Gannett or Murdoch, and though we recently stopped publishing on Sundays we still put out a very good morning edition the other six days of the week, a paper that we write ourselves and have for more than a hundred years. I'm proud of that.

Though I suspect that it, too, is coming to an end. That's just the way it is up here in Carrol County. It's been ten years now since the hardware store had the name Delaney & Sons on it and the bakery had the name Cleary Brothers, and fifteen since the Starbucks in Carrol Center convinced the descendants of Dutch root farmers to speak Italian at the cash register. Senator Bonwiller was the one who lured IBM up here in the first place, and once IBM arrived it wasn't long before DuPont and Trane and then Siemens followed. And that was the beginning of the way things have turned out now, with our Crate & Barrel and our Lowe's and the news of an Ikea opening by spring, all the way up here in what used to be lonely country. Plenty of people are grateful to Henry Bonwiller for that. And plenty are not.

Trieste Millbury's parents, I think, are among the latter. She lives with them in the failed farmland ten miles to the north of town, in a trailer on the edge of a drained bog that was allowed to refill in the 1980s after wetlands protection legislation went through—Senator Bonwiller's doing, again. That part of the county isn't as sophisticated as some of the areas to the south, which are dotted now with horse farms and gentlemen's estates and carriage houses painted historic red. But even so, there aren't many other trailers where the Millburys live. They're educated people—Trieste's father was once a chemist for DuPont—but Trieste, I believe, is the only one of them who goes to work in the morning.

Her job at the funeral was to help our reporter. The reporter was going to write the story, and Trieste was going to write the sidebar. Pick a subject, I told her when the committal was over, anything she wanted, and if she did it well I would run it Monday morning.

"I get a byline," she said, "right, sir? Just checking."

"If it's good," I said. "Yes, you do."

The air must have been close to a hundred degrees, and we were making our way to the refreshments. My wife and my father had been at the service, too, but they'd already headed into the stone entrance-house to escape the heat. At the table, a caterer was tearing open the wrapped bottles of spring water, and Trieste took one for each of us.

"If what I write isn't good, sir," she said, handing me one, "I wouldn't want the byline."

"I suppose that's true."

She smiled. "I can tell some of these men are famous," she went on. "But I don't know who they are."

"How can you tell they're famous then?"

"By looking at them. They're bigger than ordinary mortals."

I took a drink. "Powerful men are just like everybody else," I said. "They put on their pants one leg at a time."

She smiled again, a habit of hers and a useful quality in a reporter. "Is that something your father used to say, sir? I think I saw him at the service, didn't I?"

"It is, as a matter of fact."

"My father says it, too." She took a sip of water. "But my mother doesn't agree. She thinks powerful men have to put them on faster."

"Trieste," I said. "Senator Bonwiller was important in my life. I'm going to want to spend some time alone here today."

"I understand, sir. You see anybody in particular I'm supposed to recognize?"

"How about the governor?" I answered, pointing into the crowd. "That's a good start. And a whole lot of congressmen. But you're going to have to snoop around a bit on your own, Trieste. Find someone to ask. That's one of the things reporters do. More reliable than how big the people look."

"Got it. This water is nice and cold, sir, isn't it? Wakes you up." She looked at me. "But I should leave you alone now, shouldn't I?"

"Thanks, Trieste. That would be nice. And by the way," I said. "Look around. Everyone else is in a suit or a dark dress. This is a senator's funeral."

"I know," she said, moving off toward the crowd, "but this way, at least you can spot me."

ALL HIS LIFE, Henry Bonwiller had made powerful friends and powerful enemies, and as I made my own way into the gathering I saw that this is what the mourners were composed of now: a mix of both equally, united not by their fondness for the man or by their loathing for him, so much as by the fact that they all must have shared strong memories of what the country had been in the Senator's time, and also by the evident fact that life had now passed them all by. I've already mentioned the canes and the wheelchairs. When I was a boy I once heard Senator Bonwiller say that he liked his enemies best because he never had to doubt their sincerity; but walking through the crowd I wanted to tell him that maybe in the end that had been a misjudgment, too. The men and women who fought him—the ones who tried to pull him down with their editorials and their letters and their cocktail party whispers—they were here right alongside the ones who'd sent him Christmas gifts every year and checks every campaign, and they all looked equally affected by his passing. Somehow I sensed they'd all forgiven him. That they'd all forgiven themselves, too—now that the tumble was over.

But walking through the crowd I also saw that Trieste, who's been on earth not even as long as my youngest daughter, was exactly right: the men I recognized, the ones still in the thick of things, were just as she said—bigger than life. The senators and the governors, and even the members of the state House. There was something that still shone in them. Some light they cast that enlarged them for everyone around.

Dirk Bonwiller, the Senator's son, was making his way through the crowd. He'd spoken the eulogy that morning at St. Anne's, and it had only taken me a minute to realize that sometime soon he was going to run for office himself. As an orator he was as practiced as his old man—the same drawn pauses, the same basso whispers, the same poetic repetitions of the phrases—yet I must say that although the object of his eulogy had been the greatest liberal member of the United States Congress since Sam Rayburn and a defender of all the causes that poor people and working people and unions have ever embraced—I must say, you could easily have forgotten that he was also the speaker's father. There were policy points in Dirk Bonwiller's eulogy—three or four of them. That's how that family is.

Dirk is a handsome man in the same way his father was, too, a body of stature and an oversized, deeply expressive face that looks already lit for TV. Even now, after the homily and the prayer and the symbolic spadeful of dirt on the grave, that singular visage was already doing its work as it moved above the dark-hatted thicket of mourners. I used to be able to pick out Henry Bonwiller the same way, the shimmering features passing above the crowd like a bishop's miter above the congregation.

I'm tall myself, and when the Senator's son passed near me I pressed my way close to him and said, "Fine speech this morning, Mr. Bonwiller. Your old man would have liked it." I extended my hand above the crowd. "Corey Sifter—I'm very sorry about what's happened."

"Yes, I know, I know. *Speaker-Sentinel*'s a fine paper. Just about the last of 'em."

"Your people have prepped you well."

"Not at all. I know your work. We've always appreciated your support." He pulled down his glasses so that he could look over the lenses at me. "I hope we can continue to count on it."

Then he was hurried along.

Not exactly funeral talk, I have to say—but smooth enough. Our House seat has been held by a Republican for three terms now, as the western half of the state has grown more conservative, but still, Dirk Bonwiller has got to have at least an even chance at it. And after that, who knows what he'll do? He runs the Farmland Preservation Alliance in Albany, sits on the board of the Bronx Redevelopment Commission, and gave a main-stage address last year at the AFL-CIO convention in Rochester; he has a house up here and a brownstone in Brooklyn, too, and he vacations on Lake Ontario, near Sackets Harbor: it's no feat to see that he'd speak to all sides of the state Democratic Party when his time comes.

A preserve runs behind the cemetery, part of the tract that Henry Bonwiller helped legislate back into wetland once the biologists understood what the Dutch pioneers had done by draining it, and now, to get away from the crowd, I moved off in that direction. I'm not a loner—a loner wouldn't last a month in my job—but my wife had driven her own car and my father would be more than happy riding home with her. They didn't know the Senator the way I had.

When I reached the preserve, I saw that there were birds there now in good numbers, the land looking as though it had never been anything but what it had once again become: a low swamp of cattail and willow pocked by flats of water lilies and spent rose mallow. As the Senator's doubters say, it's taken us three centuries to get back to where we started. A sandhill crane was gliding low over the scrub. The entrance to the preserve itself is down a short, spined hill from the high ground of the cemetery, and behind me as I entered I could just see the tops of the buses as they turned from the lot onto the highway. In the hollow where I stood I could hear a lone bullfrog but couldn't see it anywhere in the spread of murk stirred by aquatic bugs and mysteriously swaying stems. Boardwalks skirt the edges of the marsh, rough-hewn planks of silvered cedar spiked together only a few inches above the water: I set out on one of them. The occasional catfish swifted itself into the depths. A quarter mile behind me a crowd of mourners was still about, but from the trough where I walked I could see none of it; I crossed the central bog, hidden to shoulder height by cattails, then climbed to the ridge that runs above the creek. At the top, I rested on a bench beneath a giant bur oak, wider than it was tall, its roots skeletonizing the long shoulder of earth that looks out over half of Carrol County.

What you aren't prepared for is the way children change your past, too. That's the thing. Everyone knows that they change your future, but to see them in their innocence—in their cribs and then on their bicycles and then in their cars, at their soccer games and then their recitals and soon enough at their graduations and their weddings—to see them through all of that is to know that everything you have ever done, every act you've ever had a part in, has another meaning as well, and that it is both greater and more terrible than the one you knew. Not just the meaning it had for you but the one it had for some-one's child, as well. That's what came back to me now, more than anything else. The unavoidable truth of that. That all one's deeds—those of honor and those of duplicity and those of veniality and those of ruin—that all one's deeds live doubly. I can only marvel at the for-bearance of my own parents and of others that are part of this story.

We're twenty minutes from Lake Erie here and not that much far-ther from Lake Ontario, and when you get up into the breeze, you're aware of the maritime lucidity in the sky and the feel of it in the air: a coastal hint to the winds even though we're four hundred miles from the Atlantic. My climb had taken a good quarter hour. To the east, I could see only a few cars left in the lot. Ahead of me, toward Masaguint, where Trieste Millbury lives with her parents, the first whiffs of a stratus layer were forming. Those clouds have always made the daylight heavens look even grander to me, lit from below at this hour like silver yard-marks but not yet dominating the eye as the more typical cumulus do here in the fall, with their mountainous white reach and pounding storms. I looked out on a full circle around. In a couple of hours the sky above Masaguint would be a dark gap in the horizon that's otherwise lit at night now all the way from Islington to Steppan. That's another thing this story is about, I suppose: how there's no going back.

I rose from the bench. Masaguint was behind me now, the ceme-tery ahead. I suppose the developers will get to the last of it soon enough. What remains, the part where Trieste lives, is embedded with car-sized boulders from the glacier; but these days that doesn't stop anyone. No doubt they'll call the subdivisions Granite Ridge or Boulder Brook Estates and turn the great, buried stones into pillars at the entranceways or fix them upright and carve them with the num-bers of the houses. Some think that's not coming for another decade; but I believe it's sooner.

On my return, the cemetery was nearly empty. A couple of mortuary employees in worn suits were stacking chairs, and from beyond the hill in the distance a tractor had appeared: the grave diggers. I had a good look, crossing the decks over the marsh. My last view of Senator Henry Bonwiller.

The mound of earth lay between us. The tractor slowed and a man jumped out of the scoop, and then the driver began pushing the pile toward the grave. I moved under one of the oaks. Even when they're burying a senator, grave diggers swear and spit and ash their cigarettes onto the grass, and that's what they did now as soon as they had filled the hole. Then they picked up their tools and proceeded to do a rather tender job of smoothing the contours of the dirt back into the lawn. Henry Bonwiller had always been a friend to the working man.

When they were done, they got into the tractor again and drove back over the hill, and it was then that another man appeared. With a hitching gait he stepped from behind a tree and limped across the grass toward the grave, one leg lagging behind the other so that he had to swing it around his cane. That's how I recognized him, in fact: the limp, and then the carved handle of the cane.

At the grave, he stopped and looked around, then bowed his head. He was as old as the Senator but even from a distance I could see that he still had that certain kind of roughly determined American face that you see less and less often around here. Not to be mercenary about it, but if he'd taken off his hat it would have made a front-page picture.

He was worn out, but the last one standing.

You could hear starlings now in the trees. But then in a few minutes the rumble of the engine returned, and after another moment the tractor appeared again over the berm, this time carrying the sod. It crossed the grounds and stopped within a few yards of the man's back. But he didn't even look up. I could tell that the grave diggers didn't know what to do. The driver turned off the engine. You could hear a boom box then, playing some kind of angry talk radio—it's going to be the death of newspapers like mine—until he reached down and shut that off, too. Then he sat there in the seat while his helper climbed out of the scoop and stood looking the other way. I suppose they were happy to have another minute to smoke.

Presently, the driver climbed down and the two of them went to work restoring the grass. They filled in down the length of the plot with squares of sod, carefully again, using buck knives to cut the last pieces to size. But it was only after they'd finished and set off across the lawn again in the tractor that the man finally looked up; and when I stepped out from behind the tree he finally looked over at me, too, but just for a moment. We must have been fifty feet from each other, but I'm sure he didn't know who I was. I had a decent look at his face, though, and then at the duck's head handle of his cane. I took a couple of steps closer and saw then that his wife was there, too, standing behind a tree. She looked wrecked, I have to say, and when she noticed me watching she gestured me away with her arm.

That's when I turned back and found that her husband had lowered himself onto one knee, and even from where I stood, I knew he was weeping.

That was it. The quiet end of all of it.

There was no one else alive now who knew.

II

1971

I was raised ten miles from that cemetery, in a town that was almost
entirely built and owned by a single family, the Metareys. The town
is called Saline, which if you're an old-timer rhymes with *malign*, and
if you're a newcomer, with *machine*. We're an hour south of Buffalo
in western New York State, in what used to be the territory of the Erie
and Seneca Indians. In 1881, a young boy named Eoghan Metarey
arrived penniless with his father in Fort Clinton, New York, having
endured half a year's voyage from their farming hamlet in the east of
Scotland, and the two of them made their way west together to our
low hills and hardwood forests. They shoed horses and shoveled barns
for their meals and passage, but by 1890 they'd saved enough money
to open a hardware store, and from there Eoghan Metarey launched
his empire. Within five years he'd bought his first large tract of land,
and within another five he needed a post to house all the woodsmen
and mill hands and quarriers he employed on it. He became the first
great capitalist in this part of the world and one of the first to found a
settlement for his workers; but unlike the other tycoons of his day, he

actually lived in the town he founded. When he first set to building Saline, a group of renegade Seneca was still roaming the woods; he wasted no time in dispatching them. A few were hired as guides and the rest paid to move south, so that by the turn of the century a visitor could take an Otis elevator to the top of Eoghan Metarey's six-story, granite-faced New World Bank of Saline, sit for a cup of Chinese tea, and enjoy a small, slate-colored view through glass at Lake Erie, twenty miles to the west, where those Seneca once fished.

Until the end of the Second World War, both Saline and the Metarey family prospered. The town's stately central square started at the wide marble steps of a Greek-columned library bearing Eoghan Metarey's name, and its walks were lit by cast-bronze gaslights bearing the name of his foundry. Across the street the public park was divided in two by the brook he had dug, its pumped water tumbling all spring and summer over a set of falls that had been carved from his granite. The downtown was six blocks long and by virtue of the Metarey quarries exhibited the elegant, stone-fronted façade of a good-sized city. From the peak of St. Anne's Hill, which started at the rear of the last commercial building, a visitor's eyes were drawn west toward Lake Erie, the same beckoning glimpse of water that could be seen from the top floor of the bank. At Port Carrol, Eoghan Metarey kept the largest yacht in the United States—or so it was said by Saline's old-timers. My grandfather was born in the Scottish Lowlands, but my father was born on Eoghan Metarey's property, in the house I grew up in myself, a tin-roofed clinker-brick saltbox that was split in two vertically: 410A Dumfries Street. 410B Dumfries was lived in by a man named Eugene McGowar, who also worked for the Metareys and who, like my father, always seemed grateful to have found himself ashore in a new world—even if it no longer thrived as it once had—in a neighborhood in which every block had been built by Eoghan Metarey and in which every house was the same.

Except for Eoghan Metarey's own, of course. By the time I was born, in 1955, most of the Metarey quarries and mills were silent and a good many of the Metarey workers had moved east, but the downtown still looked the same as it always had, and anyone who visited was still taken past Aberdeen West, the Metarey estate. Aberdeen West was a twenty-four-room brick and stone Edwardian manor that was by then occupied by Eoghan Metarey's youngest son, Liam, who had taken over the family enterprises. It sat at the apex of a hundred-thousand-acre triangle of land—almost a quarter of the county. Eoghan Metarey had been born to a village farrier, but by the age of thirty-six he'd already laid the railroad linking Albany with Washington and had mined the richest coal seam in Nova Scotia. This was at a time when coal powered most of New England's industry and would soon power all the new electric plants for New York's growing train-stop suburbs. Shortly before the first settlement boom in our part of the state, he'd built his three lumber mills between Saline and Lake Erie and bought the forests to supply them. And that wasn't even all of it: in an era when all the grand public buildings were going up in Albany and Buffalo and Manhattan, he'd dug limestone and granite quarries that cut great slabs of rock twenty-four hours a day, seven days a week, lit by Edison's amazing new invention, and laid them on flatbed Metarey railcars that rolled right up to his chutes. And a year before the onset of World War I, he'd made a partnership with John D. Rockefeller in oil wells two thousand miles west in Alberta, Canada. Like many such men, he always seemed to know what was coming.

During my childhood it was Liam Metarey who took care of the town. The fact that he so closely resembled his father didn't hurt his cause with the old-timers, either, who seemed to believe that God had offered special safeguard for them in the form of two nearly identical-looking old-world Scottish saviors. Both Metareys were tall, restless men with a narrow nose bent severely at the apex and Gaelic cheekbones pushing in on darkly staring eyes—eyes that still announce themselves in every photograph ever taken of either of them. It wasn't their color so much as their mood and the fact that their soulful look contrasted so strikingly with the martial cast of the cheeks and

nose. Both men, in fact, looked more like artists than industrialists—
at least they always have to me. More like those old photographs
of Kafka in Prague or Picasso in Paris than like any Rockefeller or
Vanderbilt.

And the Metareys always drove ordinary cars, too, and generally
wore the same clothes that are still worn today by the regular citizenry
around here. For Sunday dinners Liam Metarey's wife, June, shopped
at Burdick's Market herself, just as my mother and all the other
housewives did. All three of the Metarey children—the two girls,
Christian and Clara, and their brother, Andrew—attended Martin
Van Buren Elementary, then Governor Minuit Junior High, then
Franklin Roosevelt Senior High, like all the rest of us, and they all
walked home on the same path we did. At one point, just before John
Kennedy was inaugurated, Liam Metarey had worked for President
Eisenhower as the secretary of the treasury—I still have a fifty-dollar
bill printed with his angular, left-handed signature—but those few
months, as far as I know, were the only time the family had absented
itself from Saline. Otherwise, they lived all year on their estate and we
all lived on land that had once been their horse pastures.

By the time I was born, the Metarey holdings had already been in
decline for more than a decade; but even in that state they were magnificent. They still included brick furnaces, a paper plant, the New
World Bank of Saline, the iron foundry, a fiberglass boat works in Buffalo, the two remaining lumber mills, and coal seams and oil wells in
several Canadian provinces. The yacht was gone, but they kept a sailboat on Lake Erie and owned nearly three hundred houses in Saline
and Islington, which Liam Metarey continued to rent out at rates that
even the renters found reasonable. Two of their spent lime and granite quarries had been converted into lakes, which they stocked with
trout. Port Carrol was half an hour away, but if you grew up in Saline
you learned to fish and row and maybe drive an outboard on the old
Metarey Lime Quarry #3, and you learned to dive off the high rocks
at Granite Mine #1. My father and the other men from the neighbor-

hood took home quite a few nice browns from Metarey waters, just as they took home quite a few nice deer and pheasant from Metarey game lands in winter. For these and other reasons, Liam Metarey was well liked even by the men who worked for him.

My father was among those men. So had been his father, a miner, and his brothers, all five of them, who were construction laborers. With his oldest brother my father had run a sidewalk and foundation business, and one of my earliest memories is listening from upstairs to the slap of his knee-length rubber boots against the front corner of our stoop—*whap whomp, whap whomp*—as he knocked the mud and hardened bits of concrete onto our grass. When I heard that, I would run down to greet him. He would come inside for his bath, and my mother would hand me his glass of tea to bring up to him before dinner. For much of my childhood, a fine gray powder ran across our walk, climbed our porch steps, and collected in a pale ring on the woven mat inside our cramped front hall, which, like my father's skin and my parents' bedroom, always smelled of lime.

But my father studied every night in that tiny bedroom, and by the fall of my first year of elementary school he had earned himself a plumbing and pipe-fitting license. From the time I was old enough to care, that was what he was: a plumber. He joined a union, too, in the days when there was plenty of work for a union man. In our neighborhood, plumber was a high-ranking job—higher than what he'd been doing, certainly, and higher than his own father had ever reached. Most of his work—most of everybody's work—was for the Metareys.

He was a reasonably good electrician, too—that's how it used to work up here in the trades—and in later days he sometimes did both jobs on the projects that started going up quickly once Senator Bonwiller and the Metareys lured in IBM, in the sixties. The labor market was so good for a while that the Brotherhood of Electrical Workers looked the other way on those calls, and there are more than a few houses in this area where my father did all the piping and most of the wiring. There are even some where he did both those jobs and the foundation, too. If you look closely at the southeast corner of quite a number of forty-year-old basements around here, exactly at grade, you'll see the letters GCS—Granger Corey Sifter—scratched tidily into the concrete, just above the date. Corey was his middle name. Just as Granger is mine.

This boom was a new kind of development—houses built right along with the roads they sat on and owned by the families that lived in them—and those years were the beginning of Saline's second prosperity. In its newer form this prosperity lasts right to the present, with our electronics makers and box assemblers and now our chip suppliers coming into town—modern companies who bought the prime land where the Metarey mills and lumber forests once stood. These companies like the standard of living and the outdoor preserves and the plentiful high school graduates and the lakes so easily within everyone's reach—all gifts of the Metareys, in one way or another.

And of Henry Bonwiller, too. It might seem quaint today that a whole town thought of these men the way we did then—as benefactors and guardians, and even, if needed, as saviors. But that was what the town of Saline was like when I was growing up. My eyes are clearer now, and like everyone else I have my opinion about Senator Bonwiller, but I still believe that Liam Metarey was a generous, civic-minded, and altruistic patron of the whole community, even after his businesses had outlived their era. And even, I suppose, after what he did. That's a funny thing to say today.

I suppose it doesn't matter what his motives were, either—not that I could ever know them. All I'm talking about is the actual evidence of what he accomplished for the town—of what he accomplished for all of us in the area, and of what he tried to do, really, for the whole country. I know several facts: that Saline kept its population even through the itinerant years after the Second World War because Liam Metarey lowered the rents his father had charged; that Liam Metarey always made his lands available to hunters and fishermen; that he employed hundreds of townspeople in his mills and quarries when they were open, and dozens on his estate and in various smaller ventures after they were closed; that he awarded college scholarships to the children of local tradesmen; that he offered his employees health insurance and pensions long before the unions required him to; and that he paid the family of any man who was injured in his plants, on top of what insurance gave out. When I was a boy, a worker was killed by the gang saw in a Metarey lumber mill, and to this day the Metarey family supports the widow. And anyone who knows the history of the American labor movement knows how pivotal Henry Bonwiller was—and thus Liam Metarey—in a good many of its triumphs. It's easy to see what a force those men have been in our lives—it's easy to see why we revered them.

It occurs to me that Senator Bonwiller might even have thought of himself in some way as the moral heir to Eoghan Metarey. That is to say, as the man who would rebuild what the social moment had sent into decline. Even after he was elected to the Senate and bought his well-known apartment on Fifth Avenue, near the Plaza, Henry Bonwiller kept his house in Islington; and on weekends, even during the height of his power, he walked in Saline with his cocker spaniel, Uncle Dan, pausing to shop at one or another of the local merchants, the same way Eoghan Metarey had once done with his Scottish deerhounds. There are old-timers who still call the three of them, in fact, "the trinity," which implies, it seems to me, their faith that these men's legacy will be unified and everlasting.

And perhaps it will; but there were differences among them, too. When Henry Bonwiller stopped in to eat at Morley's Steak House, which was Saline's version of a fine restaurant, or at Flann's, across the street, which was the town's main pub, the union men made their way in to greet him. For Liam Metarey they might have tipped their caps through the window; and it's safe to say that for Eoghan Metarey they would have kept right on walking. Not out of enmity but out of deference. Liam Metarey worked much of his life, I think, to compensate for that deference; and Henry Bonwiller worked to harness it. By the time I was eleven, I'd already witnessed the Senator's shows of solidarity more than once: the men, my father included, taking off their caps to shake his hand, and now and then the Senator inviting a few of them to sit down at his table. His shining, well-pleased face glowed in the light of the bar lamps. The Labor Relations Act of 1966, as everyone knows, was almost entirely his doing.

To this day, the Senator's name will bring a nod of affection among the handful of old-time Local 68ers still drinking the free instant coffee at the back of Gervin's General Store. These men voted for Henry Bonwiller all their working lives. And like my father, they always understood that the Metareys were intimately tied with everything the Senator did. We all understood this. The Metareys were the ones who got him elected to the Senate, and they were prominent among the ones who ran him for president. But that's not even all of it. The closest of the Metarey businesses is now a hundred miles away, but the family still keeps dozens of townspeople employed—the kind who don't want to work for Ikea or IBM Assembly, or the kind who can't. Our own family, in fact—that is, the whole Sifter clan—has always been the particular beneficiary of their generosity, and there are plenty around Saline who'd say that I'm the one who's benefited most of all. Which is another reason for this story.

I WENT TO HIGH SCHOOL in the same building my father did, although in my father's time it was called Carrol County Senior High and not Franklin Roosevelt. And in my father's time, at least at Carrol County Senior, the sons of rock miners didn't take classes in algebra or American history or English. They took shop. This was 1942. Japan was winning the war.

My father and the other shop students maintained the grounds—it seemed to be their job. Not just at Carrol County but at the four elementary schools and the two junior highs and at all the other government buildings in the area—the post office and the town library and the public pool. As far as my father was concerned, it was a perfect education.

As soon as he turned seventeen, he was going to enlist. That's what he must have been thinking on the day in May of his junior year in high school when he was told to go up on the roof to repair the air conditioner. The Japanese had just taken Burma and Corregidor, and two days earlier they'd sunk the *Lexington*. But the U.S. Navy had stopped them short of Australia. That had been the headline on *The March of Time* newsreel that week at the Empire Theatre, another of Eoghan Metarey's gifts to the town. And that's when my father decided the navy was the branch for him.

He crawled out a classroom window onto the fire escape, climbed the ladder to the roof, and went over the parapet onto the top of the building. It was a hot afternoon and the tar grabbed his boots. In those days, air-conditioning was done with ice banks, and at Carrol County Senior the ice banks were mounted above the auditorium. When he crossed the roof, entered the mechanical shed, and pulled the manifold up onto the floor next to him, he discovered he was looking through a hole in the ceiling right down onto the stage. He saw the top of a girl's head.

She was dressed in a costume. Some kind of yellow dress. Suddenly she whirled and a wider yellow skirt flared around her. She was acting, he realized. Acting in a play. He'd never seen one. On the floorboards next to her was an X of dark tape, and she pulled a chair to cover it, then sat down, a little off to the right: now he could see a bit of the side of her face and part of her ankle. He dragged the manifold across the floor as quietly as he could, and when he'd set it against the wall he heard her deliver a line: "Thanks, Momma, I'm quite comfortable where I am." She rose from the chair and twirled again, the yellow skirt fanning out farther this time until he saw a hem of green. He set aside his wrenches and lay down to watch.

It would be a long time before he saw another play—more than sixty years, in fact. But that week he ended up seeing the one she was rehearsing—it was by Oscar Wilde. And a month later he joined the navy. Then he spent two years in the Pacific, maintaining the hydraulics of the cruiser *Louisville*. In the South China Sea near the end of his tour, a pair of kamikazes hit the ship, and what he found himself remembering as smoke filled the engine room was the view he'd once had through a rectangular hole in the ceiling, that girl's auburn hair against the green ribbon.

When the rehearsal was over he'd climbed down and come in the rear door of the stage. There was an electrical panel there. He stood in front of it, screwing and unscrewing a fuse, until finally she walked out of the dressing room. She was in her regular school clothes.

"Would you see me sometime?" he said.

She glanced at him. "Why would I want to do that?"

"Because you're beautiful."

"That's not a reason."

"Because I'm going over, then."

She pointed at his boots. "You're getting tar on the stage."

"Excuse me," he said. He bent down to clean it up. "Would you?"

"You don't even know my name."

"Would you tell it to me?"

"All right. Anna."

"Anna What?"

"Anna Bainbridge."

"Would you, then, Anna Bainbridge?"

"I have no interest."

"What if I came to the play?"

She looked at his boots again. "I don't think you'd like it."

"I might surprise you."

"Then come, if you want. It's a free country."

"Are you sure?"

"Yes, I'm sure." She pointed. "You didn't get all the tar."

He bent down again.

"I'm Grange Sifter," he said when he stood.

And a little more than a decade later, when my father had returned to Saline, Anna Bainbridge Sifter—after a stillbirth and a late miscarriage of twins—had me.

IT WAS AT THE GROTON NAVY YARD, where he was posted after his tour on the USS *Louisville*, that my father first gained the attention of one of Liam Metarey's foremen, and from the day he returned to Saline, his work was on Metarey rentals. The rentals were solid, handsome houses in a way that seems to have vanished today in all but the most genteel neighborhoods, with deep front porches shaded by red oaks, corniced eaves that formed rain shadows around the foundations, and signature brick steps in a diamond pattern bordered in herringbone. When I was a kid, those corniced eaves were still being built by one set of my uncles, and those brick steps were still being laid by another. The Metareys were able to go to great lengths to keep up their neighborhoods, in part because they owned the lumber mills and the brick furnace and the ironworks, but also in part because they employed men like my father and his brothers, who were more or less permanently at their call.

At the beginning of high school, I began carrying around the hand furnace that my father used for packing lead joints. This was my Saturday job. By 1970, you probably couldn't find a dozen lead-jointed pipes within fifty miles of Saline, but my father taught me how to pack them anyway. The furnace was a bulb of steel the size of a lantern, with a check valve and an air knob that mixed the gas into a hissing jet of flame. I scorched the lead in a melting pot until it changed from black to silver and finally to cherry red; then I poured it. He kept me well aware of the dangers: the fumes would addle me; the lead had to pour like soup or the joint would leak; a wet fitting could explode. I carried his caulking irons and packing, too, and the coils of oakum that left my fingernails reeking of tar. Before I left for school every Monday, I checked my hands for the smell.

There were new houses going up, too, in those days, but these were union jobs and the men didn't work on Saturdays. These houses were for the families who were moving in then a couple of miles to the west of us on the upward slope of Shelter Bend Hill, at the rate of a dozen or so per year: the new managers from IBM's expanding transistor plant in Islington. They were commissioning broad-chimneyed brick Colonials or turreted Queen Annes with brick for the first story and lapped cedar for the second. My father did the rough-in and the hookups. It was all still Metarey pipe, of course, and Metarey brick and Metarey lumber, too, and although the construction trucks said *O'Shaughnessy-Erie* in white script across their green doors, we all understood that this firm, too, was part of Liam Metarey's empire.

One day my father asked me to help on a sewer that had broken on the Metareys' own land. This was in the spring of my second year at Franklin Roosevelt High School. The sewer had been pierced by the roots of the estate's great bur oak, a majestic, horizontally drafted tree whose lowest limbs reached from the ridge of the main lawn all the way across the entrance road to the top steps of the porch. "You know what that means?" my father said to me at breakfast one Saturday.

"What?"

"It means we have to dig with a toothbrush." He took a sip of his coffee. "And we have to cut with nail clippers."

"Not bad money for cutting nails," answered my mother, who kept the family budget.

We had risen before dawn and she had cooked eggs and hash. On the stove ledge now she was fixing sardine sandwiches for my father and me and examining a sheet of stationery that had been engraved with the image of the same oak we were about to work under. I could tell she was reading the terms of payment.

"It's a ten-foot trench, I'd guess," said my father. "And in the heat of the day."

"Then you should be getting started then, shouldn't you?" said my mother.

"Right you are, love."

And that was what we did then, before it was even light. The drip line of the tree reached well past the sewer, and when we arrived at Aberdeen West my father set to work with a lantern and an iron spike, testing the ground for roots. The big house was still dark. My father was whistling "Roddy McCorley," but softly, and now and then he glanced up at the windows. When he was finished with the spike, we began digging, but before we were even down as far as our boots we had to switch from shovels to spades, wedging their narrow heads between the roots. They were everywhere. His whistling stopped. He gently pulled back the end of a tendril but as soon as he let go it dropped back into the hole. He stood looking at it in the rising light, which was still pale but already warm on my back. "What would you use here, Cor?" he finally said.

"Half-hitch?"

"Not gentle enough. Mr. Metarey's paying us not to hurt the tree."

"Two half-hitches and a round-turn, then."

"That's what I would use," he said. "Or a double-loop bowline."

It was almost noon before I could stand as deep as my waist in the short section that we'd dug. I hadn't seen Christian, who was in my class at school, but soon after we'd started, her sister, Clara, had come out and sat on the front steps, not twenty feet away from us. She was reading a book. Occasionally she would set it down, close her eyes as if to think about something, then pick it up again. I'd always been a hard worker, but I couldn't help being aware of her.

The pipe still lay another foot or two below us. Around me, a net of tendrils hung gently in the set of slings I'd been making from mason's line. A web of thicker, arterial roots still stretched across the channel, though, as intricately crossed as the tree's crown, and at this depth we had to bend over to dig in them. My gloves were already soaked.

As I took one off to free a root tip, I saw my father set down his shovel, and when I looked up Liam Metarey was standing next to the trench. "That's you men's secret," he said, jumping down between us. "Isn't it? It must be ten degrees cooler at the bottom here."

"God's air-conditioning," answered my father without a moment's hesitation—the kind of reply I was trying to learn to make. Then he began whistling "Roddy McCorley" again.

Mr. Metarey pushed his tie over his shoulder and knelt to examine what we'd done. "And I like the way you've secured those roots," he said. He lifted one of my slings. "Be happy to be treated that well myself by a Park Avenue surgeon."

My father smiled. "Ingenuity of the American working man," he said.

"Take it easy there, son," Mr. Metarey said as he climbed back out of the hole. I'd been wiping the sweat from my face with the dry end of my shirttail. He turned to my father. "Doesn't he know he's being paid by the hour?"

My father chuckled, more of a low shaking in his chest than a noise. "He's a good worker, all right." He was the steward of the plumbers' union local, and everybody liked him. "Beats me where he got it, though," he added.

"Perfectly clear to me where he got it," Liam Metarey answered as he walked back into the house.

Sometime past noon, as we were finishing our sandwiches, Christian appeared. She stepped over her sister and walked across to the trench, where she set a pitcher of lemonade on the planking. My father declined a glass—he drank tea even on the hottest days—but after a moment I accepted. I drank one glass and without asking she poured me another.

Clara put down her book now and was watching us from the porch. "Thirsty?" she called.

"He's just polite," Christian answered.

"Good. I like polite."

I drank my second glass, and Christian filled another. In school, we'd hardly spoken, but we had an English class together. "Drink as much as you want," she said softly. "Don't worry about my sister."

I watched her walk back across the yard. On the porch she had to step over Clara again.

"Careful, Corey," said my father.

At this depth, clay was veined into the topsoil, and I had to use a pick to pry it out. Around it the roots ran in many-stranded webs that had to be shaken free before they could be pulled. But even at that age, I liked work. I craved the discipline that settled over me and allowed me to escape my thoughts. By the time the sun dropped behind the high gable of the house, we'd freed a whole main trunk and all its branching; and soon after that, I pried a lump of clay from the far furrow of the ditch and came to the cracked sewer flange itself. As the trench moved into shade I dug away at the covering, chipping apart the clay hub with a chisel until I finally pulled out a long, fibrous lump in the exact shape of the joint.

That's when I heard Clara's voice again behind me. "You don't want this?" she said.

I turned. She had come down from the porch with the book in her hand. "You don't seem to be drinking it," she said.

"I'm trying not to drink it all at once," I answered, and I laughed. But she kept her eyes on me.

I picked up my shovel. "What are you reading?" I asked.

"You wouldn't know it." She made a face. "It smells like fish down here."

"Sardine sandwiches," I said. I smiled again, but she only looked down at me. I knocked the trowel on my boot. "Well," I said. "Back to work."

She held the glass of lemonade up to the sun. Droplets gleamed halfway up its side. "If you don't want it," she said, "then I think *I'll* drink it. Would that be all right? It's so hot out here." She took a long swallow, then set the glass back down. I blinked in the light, then nodded up at her, smiling again—that's the way I was. Finally, I looked away again and leaned back into the hole.

A few minutes later, I heard the sound of footsteps. This time, I didn't turn around. I was working at the bottom of the trench now, carving out along the length of the exposed sewer, and when the steps stopped on the planking I kept my head down. At the other end of the channel, I could see my father's legs. They rose, and his knees and boots turned. Finally, I heard Mr. Metarey's voice. "Here, Corey," he said, in what sounded like an amused tone. "I brought you another."

WHEN I WAS GROWING UP, our entire neighborhood, which had once been grazed by Eoghan Metarey's Clydesdales, was still dotted with his enormous oaks and sycamores and his grass-covered berms erected by human labor, all of it running inside a stone wall cut by hand. The wall was split in a meandering course by a brook that was narrow enough to jump and that we used to call the River Lethe—although I don't think even our parents knew what the name meant. The houses we all lived in were identical two-story brick saltboxes divided in half, the two sides joined by a common wall that was unusual for its time: the builder had been saving brick. During a brief period when Eoghan Metarey was in Europe after the First World War, a Dutch builder from Buffalo had double-crossed the family and set down row houses six to an acre. They were arranged in widening arcs around Aberdeen West, like fieldmen's cottages around a manor, ending near the Metareys' iron gate with its pillared entryway. That gate was Metarey iron, of course, and those pillars were Metarey limestone.

One morning as I was crossing near them on my way to school, Christian walked through. "I don't know why my sister's like that," she said.

"Like what?"

It was the first time she'd ever stopped to speak to me.

"You know—" she said. "Drinking the lemonade. She makes me furious. She makes *all* of us. I wanted to say I was sorry. To you and your father."

"You don't need to say you're sorry for anything, Christian. Neither does Clara. I already had plenty. I was glad to have any of it."

"You're sweet to say that."

"I *was*. It's the truth."

"It might be," she said. She set her books down beside the path. "Or it might not be. But either way, you're sweet to say it."

I shrugged.

She looked at me. "You're different from the rest," she said. "Aren't you.".

I looked away.

"You *are*. You're different from the other boys. I can tell that already." Then she took hold of one of the pillars and swung herself up onto the ledge. "Anyway," she said, "Clara's already in trouble."

"For the lemonade?"

"No. Not for the lemonade. Hand me my books and I'll tell you."

I did, and she put them underneath her to sit. "*Bad* trouble, too," she said. "Didn't even take her a week." She pointed behind us. "Look what she did to Father's shed."

I turned. On the far side of the row of spruces, two men were moving alongside one of the garages.

"Father's beside himself," she said, shaking her head. She threw her hair back over her shoulder. "She burnt it down."

"What?"

"Clear to the ground."

"On purpose?"

She examined me, the green of her Scottish irises flecked with the silvery glint I would later come to know. "Everything my sister does is on purpose," she said. She jumped from her seat. "Come on, I'll show you."

We crossed through the trees and on the other side of the driveway we found Gib Burl and Sandy Blount, two men my father knew, pulling down the remains of the building. Four black posts were all that stood, braced upright by bits of charred siding.

"She's going to reform school," Christian said.

A row of tools still hung on one of the posts, and as we stood there Sandy Blount took a jack plane off its hanger, looked around, and pretended to slide it into his coveralls. I realized he didn't know we were watching, and I stepped in front of Christian. The coal train blasted its horn. "We're going to be late for school," I said.

She only laughed and walked out into the clearing herself, where, when Sandy saw her, he set the plane in a pile with the rest.

EARLY ONE SATURDAY MORNING there was a knock on our door during breakfast, and when my father returned from answering it he said, "Well, that's interesting—it's Mr. Metarey."

"What?" My mother rose and stepped onto the back porch, where there was a mirror over the laundry sink. "*Here?* The sun's hardly up."

"He wants to see Corey."

She pulled her hair back into a bun, slipped a band around it, and pulled it tight.

"He wants *me?*" I said.

"On the porch."

"Go invite him in now, love." She leaned close to the mirror. "Granger—" she said.

"He doesn't want to come in. He said he didn't want to bother breakfast."

"He's not bothering us. You invited him in, I hope. How do I look?"

"You look beautiful, love," he said. "As always. I did invite him in. He didn't want to bother us."

"What should I do, Dad?"

"Go talk to him. He's waiting out there for you, Cor. Either go, or sneak out the window. Here," he said, moving to the glass, "I'll hold it for you."

"Granger," said my mother.

When I got to the porch, Mr. Metarey was standing on the lawn. "Sorry to disturb your breakfast," he said. "I told your father I'd be happy to come back another time."

"Of course not, sir."

"Your dad said it was grits."

"It is."

"Well, I certainly wouldn't want to keep you then."

"Thank you, sir."

He laughed. "You've had a good upbringing. Wish I could get my own children to treat me as well."

"I imagine they already do, Mr. Metarey."

He seemed to examine me then. I was wearing my Wranglers and a blue long-sleeved shirt, the clothes I wore every day.

"What are you doing this summer, Corey?"

"Working for my dad, I guess."

"I've spoken to your mother."

I looked at him.

"We need someone to work at the house."

"Yes, sir."

He crossed his arms and smiled, leaning back on his heels. "I'm offering it to you, son. I'm offering you the job. Working at Aberdeen."

"You're offering it to *me*?"

"Yes, young man. I already saw the way you work. Saves me the trouble of an interview. You could start tomorrow if you wanted. Would you like it?"

"Well, yes," I said. I thought of Christian. "I would, very much, sir. Thank you."

III

It's not that any part of Carrol County is still farmed. The farmers are long gone. Masaguint is the only bit in the whole watershed not yet taken by the suburb-makers who've long since claimed everything else. It's a wet, boulder-strewn downland: no good for a crop in the old days and no good for a development now. The Dutch Downs, as the old-timers call it. Bog from the time the glacier reached from Greenland to Pennsylvania. Our poor dike-building settlers at the turn of the eighteenth century thought they'd found a miracle soil. There was even a land rush. Muck farming, they called it—not having an appreciation yet for real estate terms. They drained the marshes and planted potatoes, sending to the Netherlands for their families to join them in the toil. But despite all their humble labor, despite all their Protestant prayers, they couldn't stop those marshes from eventually going completely dry. Near the end, the land grew so withered the topsoil began blowing away. First, gradually; then, ruinously. Up into the lake wind, then on in dark swirls toward the Atlantic. In the parched layer that remained, fires actually burned—underground infernos that poured smoke from the carboniferous peat. Imagine: the land itself in flames. God's displeasure. How could it have seemed anything else?

Soon the farmers gave up and left. Thousands of oxcarts moving west or north. That's considered a lesson in these parts: that the cropland around here, for all its gentle green cover in spring and its pleasingly hilly watershed, for all its sunny, cloud-tumbled horizon, will only fool you into optimism. Everything is hiding something.

For a long time after that, the commerce in our part of the state depended on lumber and mines. On men like Eoghan Metarey and his counterparts in the counties alongside. By the end of the nineteenth century, the remaining farmers had sold at rock-bottom rates to the mineral prospectors and the railroads; pits were dug and track laid. When I was a boy the coal train still blasted its two-note whistle at eight, four, and ten, approaching the drop-gate on Bridge Street, and you could board a passenger train at Saline Station and not get off till Baltimore. But five years ago the last of the rail bed was converted to bicycle path, and all the mines are long sealed. For most of the seventies and eighties, the economy around here provided wood and coal and rock, but not much else. People scraped by.

Which is one reason, I think, that Henry Bonwiller was so loved, even though he was a social and economic liberal in a county of close-lipped lowlanders. But the politics of Carrol County aren't easily apparent, and to those who don't live up here they must be an absolute mystery that is further veiled by a habit of silence. We don't like to talk much, or to argue at all—we just think there's too much work to be done. And we certainly don't like to talk politics, especially with a stranger—which, in these parts, means anyone you haven't known since elementary school. And in fact this taciturn habit of ours might be the very thing that saved Henry Bonwiller when all his troubles began. For thirty years he protected the people of Carrol County. And the people protected him in return.

Even today, there's still a lot of work to do around here, which is the way we all like it—too much to do to waste time with Washington gossip or tax code riders or a president's private philanderings. At primaries time, when the candidates swing through on their fifteen stops of the day in the western half of the state, I think the people here are more interested in getting through the grocery line at Burdick's without having to talk about whether it's the government's business to rule on what you can say in a biology textbook, let alone what goes on in a citizen's bedroom. Those kinds of divisions embarrass us. I've known people for fifty years and I still can't guess if they're Democrats or Republicans. And the people who know me—friends of my parents and my own friends from the old days, as well as the newcomers who've found their way up here for the air and the water—certainly a few of them could identify my leanings if asked, but I'm certain they don't care.

This puts a newspaperman at a disadvantage, actually—figuring out how to break through that wall of industrious lowlands silence. It's also been the primary influence on the editorial policy of The Speaker-Sentinel, which I've had the privilege of helping form over the fifteen years I've been at the paper. Our readers—the blue-collar descendants of farmers and mill workers—might not agree with all our editorials, but at least we can count on a few items that can still rouse them, if only a bit: corruption, misuse of our land by downstate interests, and the morals of our kids.

There are three community colleges within fifty minutes of Saline, I'm proud to say, and Eoghan Metarey's library in town gets its new bond approved overwhelmingly every four years by a group of voters who almost never go in there—except perhaps to vote—but who probably hope their children might. Or even their grandchildren. That's a nice population to share a county with. On most days I'd take this place over the big city, hands down, even though in towns like this there's always plenty to miss about the old times.

In any case, I'm at the age when a wistful melancholy is a rather pleasant way to spend an afternoon. That's what I was doing over lunch the day after Senator Bonwiller's funeral, in fact—thinking about the old times—when Trieste Millbury appeared in my office. "I just wanted you to know," she said, "that I'm all over it."

"Over what?" I asked.

She spooned some yogurt into her mouth and took a seat on my windowsill.

"The Bonwiller story. When he ran for president in '72, I mean. His campaign was run by Liam Metarey, sir."

"Everybody older than my daughters knows that."

I opened my sandwich. Corned beef. That morning before dawn I'd trimmed the fat from it and put it on whole grain, no mayo. This contributes to my wistful melancholy.

"And Nixon's men were in on it," she said.

"Oh," I said. "Better. Nixon won that election. If you remember from your reading."

"I mean more than that. I mean Nixon was in on it from the other side. Silverton Orchards. Anodyne. All that stuff."

"Where'd you read that, Trieste? Some blog?"

"I Googled it, sir."

"Did you find any evidence?"

"No."

"Then what kind of credence do you give it?"

She took another spoonful of yogurt. "Okay, then," she said. "There wasn't great evidence. But yes, I give it credence."

"And how's that?"

"Sir," she said. "I'm like all good reporters."

"Which means?"

She looked at me with her curious eyes. "Which means I go with my instincts."

IN THE SPRING of 1971, near the end of my sophomore year in high school, I went to work for the Metarey family. It was a life that took me by such swift surprise, I now realize, that within a very short period of time I'd lost track of where I'd come from. And because of the Metareys' generosity—I call it that, though I could as easily call it their *peculiarity*, or, as my wife used to say, their *nasty sport*—because of how the Metareys let me into their existence, I think I first took it inside myself, at the age of sixteen, that such an existence might someday be mine.

I worked as the groundskeeper at Aberdeen West: trimming the great bushes of gardenias and roses in the three oversized gardens, raking the pods that fell from the groves of sycamores and the husks from the walnuts, watering meadow after meadow of feed grass. The Metareys grew a thousand acres of hay that they sold to stables in the area, and my first job every morning was to water them. I drove their old Massey-Ferguson tractor, hauling the big pipes behind me on metal wheels big enough for a covered wagon. The main pipes were three-inch-diameter tubes of cast iron, forty feet long, that were coupled together with huge, greased compression nuts—a system most farmers had abandoned half a century before. But every morning before school, and one morning on the weekends, I pulled them behind the Ferguson, maneuvering them into place on their giant wheels and linking them together with a wrench as long as my arm. By the time the sun crested the oaks, I was sweating through my clothes.

Liam Metarey didn't bury his watering system like the other gentleman farmers because even at the height of his fortune I don't think he ever thought of himself as a gentleman; he must have still heard the voice of his own father—the Scottish blacksmith's boy who had stepped penniless from steerage at Fort Clinton. To the main-line hubs, which probably weighed three hundred pounds each, I coupled vertical steel sprayers twice as tall as I was. When I opened the flow valves, their spray heads gurgled for a moment, then stirred. Finally they lifted their long, flat arms, rising to throw out stuttering half-moons of water forty yards in either direction—great rainbows of mist that shimmered on one side of the pipe, fell in a heap of gems, and in a moment reappeared on the other. I was back home just in time each morning to change for school.

I have to say, I felt lucky. It was solitary work, but I liked being alone in the fields, especially as the sun came over the oaks; it was strenuous, too, but I liked that, as well. All spring and summer as I moved about the Metarey land, I felt I was being shown a secret, some riddle of possibility. And somehow, as well, I had become friends with Christian. Her friendship was as bewildering as any of it and had come upon me the most mysteriously of all. Part of the puzzlement I felt was the knowledge, really, that I didn't deserve it. I didn't deserve any of it. I didn't belong here, not on this land or with these people. There were grown men in Saline who would have been very glad to have my job—quite a few of them, in fact—and there were plenty of seniors at Roosevelt who would have walked all the way across town to exchange one sentence with either of the Metarey daughters. Yet somehow, it had all come to me.

One Saturday morning, not long after I'd started, a biplane appeared over the east end of the property and flew low over the house. I'd been moving pipe in the high fields at the top of the land, and below me I watched it break course and head in my direction. It looked like a crop duster, dark red with an open cockpit between the wings and a windshield that flashed in the sun as it started up the long hill. Halfway across the meadow it nosed up, dipped suddenly, and flew straight over my head, not a hundred feet above.

I turned the tractor around. Over the far western border of the land, it began to ascend again. A moment later the rising whine of the engine reached me as it climbed nearly to a vertical; then, at the top, it paused like a roller coaster, crested the arc, and passed backwards into a banking, upside-down descent. Just above the treeline it pulled out, its engine roaring.

I moved the tractor under the boughs of the Lodge Chief Marker, the great Norway pine at the top of the Metareys' property, and shut off the engine. The Lodge Chief had been planted three hundred years ago by the Seneca as a beacon for lake travelers, and in its deep shade I sat looking over forty miles of tree and meadow. In the distance the bi-plane made loops, then figure eights. Then it performed a frightening maneuver in which it climbed swiftly, then slowed and nearly stopped in the air, canting backwards at the peak before spiraling down, the engine suddenly roaring again as it pulled out of its fall. Then it headed straight out over the woods again and returned. It would head out and return, head out and return, sometimes moving so low over the fields that I was sure it had set down in them. There was a landing strip, I knew, at the east end of the estate, a long stripe of concrete with a wind sock and two aluminum pole hangars. I'd watered near it once.

Behind me, a voice said, "See you're watching the show."

I turned. It was Gil McKinstrey, the house carpenter, straddling a bicycle. He was the one who gave me my orders.

I started the tractor again. "Just for a second."

"Don't have to do nothing on my account," he said. "Far as I'm concerned anyway." He hopped off the bike and let it fall. "I'd do it too if I was in your shoes."

"I wasn't watching any show. I was working." The plane was already small in the distance. I reached behind me into the cart and searched for a fitting. A compression ring came up in my hands. "I was looking for the wellhead."

He wedged open the top of his boot and pulled out a half-smoked cigarette, then smiled and pointed it at a row of raspberries. "It's in the same place every week, though, ain't it?"

"Sometimes it takes me a while to find."

He pointed again. "Like I say."

The plane came in low over the trees now and passed over the far end of the field.

"Aberdeen Red," he said.

I nodded. "That's Mr. Metarey in that thing, isn't it?"

He looked at me. "You're close," he said. The plane turned a loop in the distance and he traced it with his cigarette. "You tellin' me you really don't know?"

"No, sir."

He laughed. "It's his wife, kid."

I looked at him, then reached for a nut to match the compression ring. "It is?"

The sound of the engine rose again, and when I looked up the red fuselage was coming in for another run. It angled diagonally above the meadow this time and tipped its wings. Gil McKinstrey hardly looked up. At the end of the field it turned and climbed again, closer to the estate now, passing below us over the sycamores by the garage. There it banked, smoothed into a shallower ascent, and, as it crested the roof of the main house, suddenly rolled over and flew upside-down half the length of the entrance drive. At this even Gil McKinstrey let out a laugh. I tried to make out Mrs. Metarey's figure in the cockpit. When the plane disappeared, I hopped down from the Ferguson and walked back to sift through the cart.

"She been to the South Pole in that thing once," he said. He struck a match on his boot and lit the cigarette. "Or maybe it was the North Pole. But I know she's been to some pole or something. Get cold, though, wouldn't it? Freeze your nuts clean off."

The compression ring in my hand was rusting. I reached into the bucket of grease. "There's a lot around here you could just stare at all day," I offered.

" 'Stead of working."

"Maybe so."

"Even more to look at inside the house," he said. He winked.

"I wouldn't know."

He turned to watch the plane, but I could tell he was smiling.

"I never work inside the house," I said. "I work out here."

"Learned it out some ranch in the West," he said finally, turning again to regard me. "Her daddy's land, I guess. Montana or some-place. When she was a little girl, I heard. Before she met Mister Metarey."

"She's good, isn't she?"

"Guess so. Least that's what folks say who ought to know." He wiped his face with a rag from his pocket. "Christ," he added, "hot enough to boil rats out here." He looked at the ground. "But you're a cool customer, ain't you?"

"Just trying to do my job."

He folded the rag and set it back in his shirt. "I only come out for the ball-peen hammer anyways. Left it in your cart like an ass." He pinched out the cigarette, replaced it in his boot, and looked to the west, where the biplane was descending now over the strip. "Didn't mean to spoil the show."

"I wasn't watching a show," I said again. "I was working."

He was shifting parts now in the bottom of the cart. The ball-peen hammer was on the far end, underneath some quarter turns, but I didn't say anything. "Sure," he said at last, pulling it out and testing its blow a couple of times against his palm. "I know you were, kid. You're doing good enough."

BEFORE LONG, Christian and I had begun meeting on weekend afternoons when my shift was over. Back up at the house, I'd find her waiting on the cool limestone porch or under the shade of the bur oak in the driveway—the one my father and I had worked under—where we'd sit down together and talk about what we'd done during the morning. My own mornings were always the same, and I made an effort to make them seem commonplace, even though they still weren't—not for me. Hers consisted of riding lessons, which her father paid for in return for chores in the stable, or reading, or trips with her friends to the quarry lakes. She laughed sometimes at small things I said, and her laugh did something to me. Soon I found that these interludes were marking my days—the ones when we saw each other, and the ones when we didn't. If during one of our visits Mr. Metarey had asked me to go back out and work, I would have obeyed him instantly—and I would never have sat with his daughter again. And I suppose I was expecting that he would. But he didn't.

So we kept it up. That job was the first I'd ever had in any way independent from my father, and I remember those mornings in the high sun as the first times I was aware that there were borders around my life. This was a strange sensation to a boy not prone to contemplation, a boy not yet even aware of himself as anything beyond what everyone else assumed he was. I was sixteen and until then was seeing girls from school, just as all the rest of my friends were, taking them onto the grass hillocks built by Christian Metarey's ancestors, kissing them under the oaks her grandfather had planted at the end of the last century. Whenever I saw Mr. Metarey, I nodded, and he nodded back, but we didn't speak much more than that.

I'd been inside their house a few times now, too, but Christian hadn't let me see much of it. We'd always go quickly upstairs to the library, where she would pull the record player out onto the balcony and we would sit there listening to the Beatles or James Taylor or Boz Scaggs, talking about the same things we talked about outside. Through the open doors I could see the maids working in the halls. The bookshelves behind us closed with glass doors hinged from above, and on each wall a slanted wooden ladder moved on rubber wheels. Next to the long table the leaves of an oak nearly entered through the side window. I had the idea that she was testing me, somehow, showing me just a little to see whether I would want to see more—the inlaid walnut border of the wainscoting, the Oriental rugs on the floor, the beveled window glass that broke the sunlight into three-colored stripes on the walls. There were other times, though, when she quieted, and her face took on a look, and I thought that maybe she was waiting for me to do something else: to take her hand, maybe; to lean toward her.

One evening near the end of May, the phone rang at my own house and my father answered it in the kitchen. From the living room, where I was reading about what was already turning into another losing year for the Cleveland Indians, I could hear him talking jovially, and presently he came in and stood before me. "Well, captain," he said. "Looks like you're going sailing tomorrow."

My mother looked up from her knitting.

"What?" I said.

"If you want to, that is. That was Mr. Metarey. They've got that boat at Port Carrol. They invited you. Memorial Day. Hope you didn't eat too much dinner."

"Goodness," said my mother, getting up.

And the next morning, for the first time in my life, I was sitting with the whole Metarey family. It was just after dawn, and I was in the backseat of their Chrysler, between Christian and Clara, holding the pie my mother had woken up early to bake. I didn't even know whether I was coming along as Christian's friend or as the family's hired hand, but when Mrs. Metarey turned from the front seat to greet me, I offered her the tin. It was still warm.

"Why thank you, Corey," she said.

"You're welcome."

"He baked it himself," said Clara.

"I did?"

Their brother, Andrew, who was home on leave from the army, sat on the far side of Clara, his fatigue cap pulled low over his eyes. "You don't have to listen to her," he said in a calm voice, then leaned his head against the window and looked out at the sky. Mr. Metarey was driving; next to him, their dog, Churchill, an English setter—Christian had told me—pressed his face against the windshield. As we left the gates, he turned to look back at me and let out a short bark.

"That means hello," said Clara.

"Hello, Churchill," I said back.

"That's Corey," Mrs. Metarey said. "He's very polite." Then she added, "Liam, you're sitting on his tail."

Mr. Metarey shifted in his seat, then glanced in the rearview mirror. "Guess it's clear who the beloved one is around Aberdeen West," he said. " Isn't it, Corey?"

I laughed so he could hear me.

"I doubt you've had a chance to do much sailing," said Mr. Metarey, catching my eye in the mirror. "Is that right?"

"Yes, sir. I mean, no. I've never been."

"But he knows all the knots," said Christian.

"Is that right?" said Mrs. Metarey.

"My dad's taught me a few, ma'am."

"Corey's dad was a navy man," said Mr. Metarey. "That's as promising as anyone could want."

"Only if he was in the navy in the eighteenth century."

"That's enough, Clara," said Andrew.

"You're in Christian's class, then?" said Mrs. Metarey.

"Yes."

"Of course he is, June. He's Grange Sifter's boy. Corey's family's lived in the neighborhood all their lives, dear. He and his dad were the ones who cleaned out the main line, and they didn't put one scratch in the roots." I saw him smile in the rearview. "I checked," he said. Then he turned to his wife. "The driveway oak, dear. The bur. Your dad's the best pipe fitter in the county, Corey."

"Thank you, Mr. Metarey."

"That's nice," she answered. She tried to light a cigarette but the match broke and she tossed it out the window. "Well, what do you think of President Nixon then?"

There was silence.

"Were you asking me, Mrs. Metarcy?"

"No," said Clara. "She was asking Church."

The dog barked.

"Clara," Andrew said without lifting his head from the window, "watch that mouth."

"Father doesn't like Nixon much," Christian said. "Nixon's an internationalist, all right, but he's a throwback. Isn't that right?"

"That's about right," said Mr. Metarey.

"Mother hates him, too," she said. "Mother thinks he slithers."

"To put it mildly, dear," said Mrs. Metarey.

"Are you a Democrat?" asked Clara, looking at me.

"Clara," said Andrew.

"What?"

"It's none of our business."

"I'm not really anything, I guess," I answered.

"Corey's a freethinker," said Christian. "Aren't you?"

"Is that how you'd describe yourself, Corey?" asked Mr. Metarey.

"Yes, sir, I guess it is."

He chuckled for a moment and then pointed the mirror toward me. "Please don't call me sir," he said. "Makes me think my old man's in the car."

Mrs. Metarey slid up her window—I'd never been in a car with power windows before—and succeeded in lighting her cigarette. Then she lowered the glass a little until the smoke was sucked out through the opening at the top. "If your father was in the car, Liam," she said, "we wouldn't be sailing on a workday."

"Memorial Day weekend, dear." He pointed the mirror at Andrew this time. "In honor of the soldiers."

"Father's a Democrat," said Christian. "But he's a freethinker, too, really."

"He just doesn't like people to know it," said Mrs. Metarey.

Andrew lifted his head. "Christian always says that," he said to me. "About Dad being a freethinker. Everybody knows he worked for Eisenhower."

"That only proves it more, Andrew. You're a Democrat, aren't you, Father?"

"Of course I am, honey." Mr. Metarey opened his window and nodded at the cumulus clouds that were bundled on the horizon. His wife's cigarette smoke changed course and snaked backwards through the car. "South wind coming up in the afternoon," he said. "I hope you all took your Dramamine."

"You've crewed before then, Corey?" said Mrs. Metarey.

"I thought he just said no," said Clara.

"Never on a sailboat, at least," said Mr. Metarey.

"No, he hasn't, Mom," said Christian.

"Good," said Mrs. Metarey, "then he doesn't have any bad habits." She took a long draw on her cigarette and tossed the rest of it out her husband's window.

"Bad habits indeed, June," said Mr. Metarey.

Andrew looked up again from where he'd been resting, somewhat alarmed it seemed to me. "Don't worry," he said across the seat. "I'll teach you."

So it turned out in the end that I was a guest. The boat was berthed at the near end of Port Carrol, ten miles north on the lake, and while Mr. Metarey and Andrew went about setting up, Christian took me up the dock to show me the spot where Franklin Roosevelt had moored the *Potomac*. Churchill barked and tugged on the leash as we walked. Christian pointed over the water and explained that a series of locks separated the lake from the Saint Lawrence Seaway, so that a ship laden with ore could bypass Niagara Falls down to Lake Ontario and from there find a deepwater passage to the Atlantic. The dog bounded ahead, pulling Christian wherever he found a scent among the pilings. It was still early in the morning and nobody else was about, and finally Christian unlocked a gate so that we could walk out onto the long section of slatted dock where the slips were. Only the Metareys' held a sailboat. It was called *The Adirondack*. Onboard, Andrew and Mr. Metarey were taking care of various tasks, moving nimbly about the deck, and even though I was fairly certain by now that I wasn't supposed to be working, it still seemed to me I should have been helping them. Christian was carrying my mother's pie, and when we finally boarded she went inside the cabin and set it on the table.

"Corey Sifter," she said as I followed her into the low, dark room, where the porthole gave us a view of Andrew threading rope through a pulley outside, "you *are* different from the rest."

I picked up the tin. "I really didn't bake it, you know."

"That's not what I mean."

We emerged again onto the deck just as Andrew hopped down onto the pier, untied the lines, and walked us backwards out of the slip, leaping back onboard at the last moment. Then we were backing out of the marina and motoring along the narrow straits of the channel. I watched everything. *The Adirondack* was a beautiful boat, built of varnished mahogany with a trim of redder wood where the cleats and hardware were bolted, and the folds of the sails and even the coiled rope shone like washed laundry in the morning light. Mr. Metarey was at the wheel. Andrew moved around the deck uncoiling lines from cleats, checking them and recoiling them again; Christian moved up to the front by Clara, and the two of them lay down against the side handrails at the front quarter of the hull, where Churchill made a place for himself between them; June Metarey retreated to a folding chair by the door of the cabin, where she sipped from a tumbler as her husband studied a chart spread under glass below the wheel. We motored clear of the last pilings and turned out toward the breakwater. Ahead, the marina's entrance flags were whipping. Mrs. Metarey zipped her jacket and leaned forward into the wind. I knelt down against one of the rails midway to the rear, nearer to Andrew and Mr. Metarey. Then suddenly Andrew was pumping his arms and the sail was up and the boat lurched forward and surged out into the strait.

We carved through the water. Near the wave-break, he pulled on a rope and we rose steeply up on the keel. I climbed the deck, and when I took hold of the rail on the high side I saw Christian and Clara laugh together. I couldn't hear it but even with their heads turned I could see it in their shoulders. Mrs. Metarey was smiling, too, her chin thrust forward into the wind. Christian and Clara remained at the forward tip, both of them barefoot, Clara's arms draped into the frothing wake where the prow sliced the water.

"He's just sensible!" I heard.

It was Mr. Metarey shouting from the rear.

"I can already see that," he went on, shaking his head. "Unlike you girls!"

Andrew came up to the high side and stood next to me.

Mrs. Metarey sipped from her tumbler. "We're eminently sensible," I heard her reply.

For a short distance we moved along the beach, then turned west and headed out into the darker water. The boat tilted one way and then the other. It wasn't a feeling I liked, but before long I'd relaxed enough to come down and stand in the middle of the deck while the hull shifted with each tack. The harbor was in a small east-pointing finger of the lake, and soon we had moved out from its close shelter. The open water was breathtakingly large from this vantage, the shore more and more distant until eventually I could see only the flagpole at the breakwater and then nothing but the far-off stripe of the trees. At the crest of Pond Hill, long in the distance, the Lodge Chief Marker made a dim point against the sky.

At noon Mr. Metarey turned the boat into the wind. Andrew lowered the sail, and Mrs. Metarey came up from below with sandwiches. We ate with our legs dangling from the deck. Churchill sat where his leash had been tied to the cabin door, pulling apart two pieces of bread to get at the roast beef. I had never drunk beer at lunchtime, but this was what Mrs. Metarey offered. "Law of the sea," she said, handing me a bottle. "Jack Kennedy would say so."

"Could make you seasick, Corey," said Andrew. "You don't have to drink it. There's water, too."

"Jack Kennedy wouldn't drink on the water," called Mr. Metarey from the rear.

"That's why he didn't sail much, dear," said Mrs. Metarey. "And besides, Andrew, it *helps* seasick."

"In that case I'll have another one," said Clara.

"You share one with Christian or me," said Andrew.

"I would deem that unlikely."

"Now we're going to have Corey's delicious pie," said Christian.

"Corey baked it himself," Clara said again.

Christian glanced at her, and I did, too. She seemed to be angry at me, and I didn't know why.

"He's learning to cook," she went on. "He burned the first one."

"Well, let's hope this is the second one, then," said Mr. Metarey.

"What kind is it again, Corey?" said Clara. "Father chokes if he eats boysenberries. It happened at the McNamaras'."

"Actually, I can't remember what's in it," I said. "I don't remember boysenberries, though."

"That's a boy, Corey," called Mr. Metarey. "You're going to go a long way around here."

"Andrew," said Clara, "I said I'll have another one."

Andrew sat down on the ice chest. "You can share it."

"Mother!"

"Enough!" said Mrs. Metarey. "First we're going to finish our sandwiches. Then we're going to devastate this delicious pie, whatever it is. Then we're going to sit down and find out all about our guest."

But nobody ever asked me any questions, and after we had finished the pie, which turned out to be strawberry-rhubarb, Andrew raised the sail and we picked up and headed farther out into the lake. The beer had eased my legs, as Mrs. Metarey said it would, and after a time I noticed that I had relaxed. We moved in long, easy tacks now toward the shore, which had come into sight again to the east. Andrew and Mr. Metarey had changed places, and in Andrew's hands the boat moved more calmly through the long, low swells that had come up in the steady wind and were large enough to have been on an ocean. Clara and Christian knew they could no longer tease me by lying close to the water, and Christian had sat down at the lunch table, where she was reading. Mrs. Metarey had gone below, and through the door I could see her lying on one of the cabin beds trying to kick off her shoes. The straps had caught around her ankles. Through the round window I watched her two calves work against each other, trying to free themselves, then kick furiously until one of the shoes finally fell off. I looked away. Clara had changed into a long skirt and stood at the rear rail now, watching our wake.

"Basically," Andrew said when I wandered down close to the wheel, "there's a few knots you need to know—but it sounds like you already know 'em. And a few fancy words, to use around the bar. *Port* means left and *starboard* means right and *sheet* is a kind of rope. Not a sail, which a lot of people think. Or you can say *line*." He rolled his eyes. "*Sail* is still sail," he said. "There's no special word for that."

"You're a soldier," I said.

"I guess I am."

"How long you back for?"

"They gave me a week."

Later, when I was in college, some of my classmates talked about their older brothers living in Canada. For the kids I grew up with in Saline, though, Canada wasn't an option. Certainly not for the son of Liam Metarey.

"That scare you?" I asked.

"Scare me?"

"Being in Vietnam."

He laughed. "I assumed you meant being back here." He unrolled a chart onto the stand and examined it. "I'm assigned to the Roads and Grounds Section of the Post Engineers," he said. "C Company. Fort Dix."

I looked at him.

"New Jersey," he said.

"Oh."

"They don't send guys like me over to fight."

"I didn't figure, really."

He looked at me appraisingly. "You want to know what I do?"

"If you can say."

He laughed. "I pour asphalt. Set a few fence posts. Pull a tractor mow. Not too bad." The edges of the chart began to flutter, and he turned his head and looked to the west. "Although I suppose a post could fall on me." Then he patted me on the shoulder—something his father would do many times over the years. "But yeah," he said, "I'd be plenty scared if they shipped me over."

He gripped the wheel with two hands and turned it, and in a moment the gust was on us. Then it passed, and I watched the craze of ripples skip away over the water.

"You remember everything I told you so far, Corey?"

"Port, left," I said. "Starboard, right. Sheet, not rope."

"Perfect. Now you can drink at the captain's club."

He turned to look ahead of us, where a Great Lakes freighter had come onto the horizon, and for some reason I turned the other way, where Clara, facing us now in her skirt at the rear railing, knit her brow at me and then slid off the deck into the water.

"Hey!"

I shook Andrew. Churchill ran to the stern, barking. The boat broke to the left and bit into a turn and I saw Clara kick out of the wake and throw back her hair and plunge under. Then Mr. Metarey was beside us. He took the wheel and turned the boat sharply into the wind so that the boom came around and the mainsail flapped thunderously above us. The hull went dead in the water and then bumped as the wake ran under it. Clara was already thirty yards back, her hair a black pelt in the dark water.

"She can swim," said Mrs. Metarey, reaching her head out of the cabin.

Mr. Metarey looked back.

"Don't go around for her, Liam. She'll catch up."

But Andrew had already gone forward to lower the sail and in a moment I heard the rumble of the engine from below. The boat swung in a broad arc and when we pulled alongside Clara she came shivering up the folding ladder onto the deck.

"How was the water, dear?" said Mrs. Metarey. One shoe still dangled on her ankle.

"Splendid, Mother." She was staring furiously, at her father it seemed to me.

Mr. Metarey went below for a moment and returned with a towel, which he tried to wrap around her; but she shrugged him away and draped it herself around her shoulders. Churchill was sitting calmly now. Andrew took off his sweater and put it over her, and then she stood there looking at all of them, her dark eyes passing from her mother to her father to Christian.

"Well," she said finally, "I fell in."

"Please," said Mrs. Metarey.

"Andrew came up short on a tack. I wasn't expecting it."

"Churchill deems that unlikely," said Christian.

The dog let out a bark.

"I never changed tack," Andrew answered.

"I seem to remember it the same way," said Christian.

"Well, I'm the one who fell in. You were all below."

"Nobody was below," said Mrs. Metarey. She reached and yanked off her shoe.

Clara looked around furiously. "Corey saw it, didn't you? I fell in when Andrew veered."

"Ah, but we know Corey is a diplomat," said Mr. Metarey.

"Didn't I, Corey?" Clara said, and she turned and fixed me in her stare, a stare that I had no power in those days to resist, nor even to comprehend.

"You fell in," I finally said.

"Corey Sifter!"

"You're boring all of us, Clara," said Mrs. Metarey finally, starting for the cabin again. She leaned her head back out the door. "Except, obviously, for our guest."

"LORD KNOWS you probably do enough around here already, Corey," Mr. Metarey said one afternoon not long after, "but I wonder if I could ask just one more thing."

"Yes, sir." I rose from the walk where I'd been having an iced tea with Christian after work.

"We're having a little affair Tuesday night," he said. "God knows why—" He picked up a few pebbles from the walk and tossed them into the bushes. "You'll have to ask my wife about that one. In any case, just a little party. A gathering. One of the bar-backs just called in sick and Mrs. Metarey thinks we could use another hand."

"Yes, sir."

"It starts at eight. If you could come by six-thirty, I'll pay you till eleven." He looked down his glasses at me. "But you can leave at ten."

He gathered another handful of pebbles and tossed them into the bushes. "Because it's a school night."

"You don't have to do that, Mr. Metarey."

He laughed. "What would your dad say if he heard you asking for a lower wage?"

"It's my mom who wouldn't like it."

"That's right. And you should heed your mom. And on top of that," he said, "you can tell her I'm paying you double." He smiled. "For the short notice."

He looked out at the far end of the fly pool, where in the distance the casting targets bobbed in the wind. "Tell you what—if I hit one first try, that's what I'll pay." He picked up a stone from the drive and weighed it in his hand. "If it takes me two tries, I'll pay triple."

"You'll break it if you hit it, Mr. Metarey." A set of the targets hung in the work shed where I parked the Ferguson. They were the diameter of basketball rims and carved from thin flats of cork with an aluminum cup that held the flag.

"Three tries, quadruple," he said.

"Daddy was a star pitcher in high school," said Christian.

"I didn't know that, sir."

"I wasn't a star pitcher," he said. "I wasn't even a very good one." He shook out his shoulder. "Not much of a curve."

The targets were twenty yards away. Three of them, like floating golf holes with their short flags. He was left-handed. "This is for double," he said. He brought the stone behind his ear and took a short step. A splash jumped in one of the rings.

"Looks like that's what it'll be," he said, "Double. Sorry about that."

"Nice shot, Mr. Metarey. That's more than generous. And I won't tell my mom."

"I appreciate that. We need her on our good side."

After he'd left, Christian said, "He really was a star pitcher, you know. He's always modest like that. His team went to the league championship."

"I like your dad," I said. "He's never asked me to work in the house before."

She looked at me. A drift of wind touched us. She leaned forward. This was another of those moments: I thought she might have wanted me to kiss her. Above us a door slammed, and she leaned back again. "Join the club," she said. She looked toward the house. "I mean, about liking my father."

Later, as we were walking back toward the patio, she said, "You want to know who the party's for, Corey?"

"Sure."

She stopped and looked at me. "Morlin Chase."

I looked back at her.

"I guess you're the wrong person to try to impress with that, aren't you?" She laughed. "He was most of the brains behind Kennedy," she said. "A lot of people thought *he* was the one who should have run for president, Daddy included. And now he's thinking of running for governor. That's why Mother wants to have the party for him. He's been other things, too, like ambassador to Russia. He's very well connected in the Democratic Party. Oh," she said, looking at my face. "Don't be nervous—he's friendly. I've met him."

"I *am* nervous," I said.

"Don't be. Mostly, Mother thinks he can help with Henry Bonwiller."

"With Senator Bonwiller?" I knew his name, of course—everyone did—but that was the first time I'd heard it spoken at the Metareys'.

She smiled at me, reached up, and kissed me quickly on the cheek. "Oh, Corey," she said. "You're going to have an interesting summer."

THAT SUNDAY MORNING, as I was washing the Massey-Ferguson in the big garage, a rusty yellow Corvair pulled in behind me and a man began to struggle out. He had to shove his cigarette into his mouth and lean both hands on the door to get his legs free from the driver's seat, but then without turning to look at me he tossed his keys backwards over the roof into my hands. I noticed they were on a Buffalo Bisons ring.

"Hear you're an Indians man," he said in a short-of-breath voice. When he finally stood, I saw how fat he was.

"Yes, sir."

He stopped and looked behind himself theatrically, as though I'd been speaking to someone else.

"Bisons fan myself, kid." He slapped his huge belly. "If that's not too ironic." Then he limped around to my side of the car, tugging at his sweaty shirt. "Born and bred Buffalo." He bent forward to draw on his cigarette. "You watch, though. Bisons'll be an Indians farm club before too long."

I set my sponge down on the Ferguson's muddy engine case. "Not for a while, anyway."

"Johnny Bench was a Bison originally. Before the team went Canuck."

"I know that, sir."

Again he looked around theatrically.

"You know who I am?"

"No, sir."

"Then *that's* why you're calling me that."

"Excuse me?"

He leaned forward and peered at me. "You don't even realize it, do you? Remarkable." He stood again. "I'm the bottom of the fish tank, kid." He stuck the cigarette in his mouth and held out his hand. "Glenn Burrant. *Buffalo Courier-Express*. Politics beat."

"Corey Sifter. I help out at Aberdeen West."

"Washing tractors?"

"And grounds work, sir."

"You ever hear of the *Courier-Express*, Corey?"

"Of course, sir."

"Mark Twain's old paper."

"I wouldn't know, I guess."

"I wouldn't expect you to." He looked at me closely again. "I hear we're going to have some news out of here any day now," he said. He raised his dark eyebrows and jiggled the cigarette with his jaw.

"I wouldn't know that, either."

"I guess you wouldn't then, would you? Say," he went on, "you read my roundup yesterday on the possible Dem contenders?"

I didn't know what to say.

"Oh, I see. So you're just like every other kid in this town." He ran his hand along the door of the yellow Corvair and a smudge of black came up on his fingers. "Don't read no *news*paper, I guess."

"Not much, sir, I guess. I'm sorry. I can wash your car for you if you want."

He laughed. "Not enough water in the well."

"I can do my best."

"The whole aim of practical politics is to keep the populace alarmed," he said then. He leaned down to the side mirror, wiped it clean, and ran a comb through his hair. "By menacing it with an end-less series of hobgoblins." He set the comb in his pocket. "All of them imaginary."

I looked at him.

He stood and tugged at his shirt again, then snorted. "Mencken."

"Yes, sir."

He peered at me. "God damn," he said. "You don't know who Mencken is."

"I guess I don't, sir."

"H. L. Mencken. Henry Louis. Most famous man ever to pick up a pen in my business. Too bad, kid. I suppose, anyway. But guess I can't blame you. You ever hear of Ed Muskie?"

"I think so."

"Humphrey?"

"Yes."

"How about George Wallace or Gene McCarthy?"

"Who?"

"Maybe you ought to find out, then." He sniffed. "Before you end up in a jungle somewhere."

He turned away gruffly. But just before he disappeared out the door, still tugging at his shirt, he turned. "Listen, comrade," he said. "Go ahead and wash it. But not *too* clean." He winked. "And if you find a ham and provolone sandwich under the right front seat, send Jeeves inside to fetch me."

I watched him limp across the driveway to the house, where he slowly climbed the stairs, gathered himself at the door, and, to my surprise, went in without knocking.

And it was that morning, while Glenn Burrant was inside the Metareys' house, that for the first time in my life I picked up the front section of a newspaper. It was the *Courier-Express*, and it was under the front passenger's seat, just where he'd said the sandwich might be. His article was right there at the top of page one, below the headline "Early Field Takes Shape," and I remember the feeling that came over me as I read it. Under the headline, in good-sized type, was his name—Glenn Burrant—and seeing it there gave me a sudden and unfamiliar thrill almost as deep, I have to say, as if it had been my own.

"PUT ON A TIE, COREY!" my mother called from upstairs. It was Tuesday evening, and I was checking my clothes in the front hall mirror before I went back to the Metareys' for the party.

"Nah," said my father from the couch. "Don't waste one."

He was reading the baseball scores in the living room with our neighbor from next door, Mr. McGowar, who was listening to his portable radio. Mr. McGowar spent his days digging up the never-ending supply of rocks that poked up in the gardens along Dumfries Street—a service that was much appreciated by the gardeners, who were also the housewives—and his evenings in our half of the duplex, listening to baseball on his radio while my father read the sports pages. Neither of these activities involved speaking, which is why Mr. McGowar liked them. He'd long ago lost his voice from half a century at the stone saw in Metarey Granite Mine #2.

"Mr. Rockefeller's been governor since Corey was in diapers," my father said. "Isn't that right, Eugene?"

Mr. McGowar looked up quizzically.

"Just saying," my father said in a louder voice, "MR. ROCKE-FELLER'S BEEN IN THERE FOR AS LONG AS ANYONE CAN REMEMBER. Isn't that right, Eugene?"

Mr. McGowar pulled the flesh-colored radio cord from his ear. "Since," he rasped, taking a deep breath. "Fifty." He coughed. "Eight." He cleared his throat, and I could see him concentrating. He was as tall as the doorway and as vigorous a man as I've ever seen, but it was painful to watch him speak. "Yan-kees. Braves."

"I don't see why they're even bothering with this other what's-his-name," my father went on. "And who starts a campaign this early, anyway?"

"Morlin Chase is his name," I said. "He's very well connected in the Democratic Party."

My father looked up. "Well, Cor, don't be too impressed by any of it."

"Christian Metarey said Governor Rockefeller's vulnerable because he spends so much time thinking about being president. So Morlin Chase could beat him. He's supposed to be very smart, too. That's all I'm saying. I'm not impressed, Dad, I'm only telling you."

"Nelson Rockefeller wouldn't get out the front door against Nixon," my father answered. He laughed. "I'll give you five bucks on that one. Right, Eugene?" He looked over at Mr. McGowar. Then he put down the ball scores and picked up *Lou Gehrig: Pride of the Yankees*, which he'd been working on for as long as I could remember.

Mr. McGowar raised his finger in the air. "Nixon's got—" He tried to stifle another cough, but couldn't. When he was finished he raised his finger again. "—Rock-e-feller's. Balls." He thumped himself on the chest. "In his. Sock drawer."

At that one, Mr. McGowar himself let out a laugh, which sounded like a tire deflating. His laugh continued until my mother appeared on the stairs.

"You just never know," she said. She was holding my father's blue tie in her hand. "You just never know who's going to be there at the Metareys'." Then she added, "And you never know what's going to happen."

"Who could be there that's going to matter to Corey?" said my father. "Rockefeller's going to be governor till the day we all die."

"That's what *your* father used to say about FDR," she answered. "And look at you, Corey. Just like your father. You look like a cabbage. Do you two think your shirts iron themselves?"

As I unbuttoned my shirt, I could see Mr. McGowar's long rib cage still bouncing from his laugh. When my mother had disappeared back up the stairs, he held up his finger again. "He was," he said, "almost—"

He coughed.

"Almost what, Eugene?"

"—almost—" he rasped.

He took a whistling breath.

"—almost. Right."

My father looked at him over his glasses.

"—Your father," he managed to get out, "—about FDR."

He coughed for a good while then, before he put the earpiece back in.

By then, my mother had reappeared at the bottom of the stairs with my ironed shirt and my father's tie over her arm.

"Oh, all right," said my father, getting up at last from the couch. "At least let me tie the condemned man's noose for him."

As the sun was setting that night over Aberdeen West, the guests began to arrive, and by dark they'd overflowed the patio onto the lawn. Behind a long mahogany table Gil McKinstrey had set up the bar. Not long after the party had begun, I was unloading a case of champagne when a courtly-looking man walked up in front of me and ordered a rye whiskey on the rocks. His nod to Gil was courtly as well, and he wore a stiff black suit that gave him something of the demeanor of a priest; but when Gil handed him the rye whiskey he tossed it straight back, then put his hand out for another.

If I'd known who Morlin Chase was, of course, I'd have been too nervous to even stand that close to him. But I wouldn't know about any of these men, really, until many years later. Not about Chase. Not about Henry Bonwiller. Not about half the figures I would come across that year, from Averell Harriman to Arthur Schlesinger, and not even about the Metarey family. I've thought about that summer for many years now, and there will always be parts of it I don't understand. Chase, I discovered in college, was the son of a railroad baron himself, and he'd been as close to as many presidents as anyone in the history of American politics. But the governor's election was still four years away.

That night my duties were to stock the liquor and the ice for two hundred guests and to collect dirty dishes and glasses, and although two other bar-backs from town were working as well, I barely had a moment to look at anybody. The first time I pushed open the swinging doors to the service kitchen, I was surprised to see a room the size of a tennis court, with a whole row of stoves and sinks dividing it up the middle and two spray hoses on runners that were being yanked back and forth by the maids preparing the dishes for the sterilizer. It was as busy as a tennis court, too, with maids and cooks hurrying across the floor. I stayed in a line between the door and the pantry.

As I was fetching a case of Scotch a few minutes later, I ran into Clara standing at the door by the sinks. She pointed to my tie.

"Oh—" I said, "do you like it?" I'd tucked it into my pants so that it wouldn't dip in the glasses.

"Did I say that?"

"I guess you didn't."

"But I have to admit, it's an interesting way to wear one."

With the Scotch in my arms, I made my way down the narrow pantry. "Where's Christian?" I asked when I reached her. "I haven't seen her."

She regarded me but didn't answer. She was standing in my way. "Morlin Chase is just a sucker," she said without moving. "Do you know that? This is all just a big act to flatter his family."

"I don't know anything about any of it," I answered. I had to stop and lean the box against the jamb. "That's the truth. I just need to get this over to Gil before he runs out."

"That's right," she said finally, taking a step sideways so I could pass. "That *is* the truth. You don't know anything about any of it."

At the bar again, I put the bottles down on the floor. Morlin Chase was standing outside on the patio now, between two leaded ballroom windows that cast a yellow aura on him like a pair of stage lights. As he spoke he gestured around a circle of onlookers, which included Mr. and Mrs. Metarey. I could see that they were listening closely to him.

"You watching the show again?" Gil said.

"I'm waiting for orders."

"Then here's one," he said, slapping a tray onto the bar and setting a tumbler on it. With a flick of the scoop he filled it with ice; then with a tilt of the wrist he measured it with bourbon. "This one," he said, "is for that sorry bastard out there."

I looked at him.

"The Hunchback of Times Square," he said, out of the side of his mouth. He tilted his head toward the patio. "Mr. Metarey likes to keep his joints oiled. Trawbridge is his name. The real heavyweight in the crowd. Not Morlin Chase." He thunked another tumbler on the tray and measured off a double whiskey. "And this one's for Chase. Five bucks he'll be standing near Trawbridge."

On the patio, I zigzagged through the crowd with the tray of drinks, and only when I stopped behind Morlin Chase did I understand. Mr. Metarey had somehow disappeared already, but standing directly across the circle from Mrs. Metarey was a man whose back was bent almost double, his hands resting on a pair of canes nearly at the height of his shoulders. As I stood there, Morlin Chase addressed him, and he stiffened his arms with a trembling effort and looked up, like a man climbing a ladder out of a hole.

Saline is a suburb now, but it was a lumber and mining town then, and like all such towns we had more than our share of the injured. But still I couldn't help staring. He wore a pair of oversized black spectacles and a dark red bow tie that had been knocked at an angle, and his unruly brown mustache hid his mouth; yet the thing that struck me was the great decency of his expression. I felt a kind of instant kinship with him, too—perhaps because I could see how diligently he was working for his place in the crowd.

As Mr. Chase scanned the group he kept pausing first on Mrs. Metarey and then on this man Trawbridge. And occasionally, in response, Mr. Trawbridge would give him a small nod; he gave the same one to me when I finally moved over to take his empty glass from the side table and set the full bourbon in its place. He had to shift one of his canes to pick it up.

All the while, Morlin Chase was holding court. Other guests were leaning in close to hear him, and I could see them smiling, but I could tell that they were looking at Trawbridge, too. So was Mrs. Metarey. After a time I moved over until I was holding my tray with the last drink on it right next to Mr. Chase, but even then he didn't stop speaking. It was only after Trawbridge lifted his tremorous head and made a gesture over his spectacles that Mr. Chase finally reached out and without breaking rhythm exchanged his empty glass for the full one on my tray. Then he went on with what he was saying.

Later that night, as I was fetching ice for Gil McKinstrey, Christian appeared in the rear pantry. She sat down silently on the low bench next to the ice machine and curled her legs under her, the way she did sometimes. She watched me fill the pewter bucket.

"Who's Trawbridge?" I finally said.

She looked out the small window to the patio, where the party was. "Oh," she said. "Isn't that sad? He's an old friend of Daddy's. From Yale, I think. He's here because of what Daddy might do tonight."

"What's your dad going to do?"

She looked up again, and this time she kept her gaze on me as I worked; but she didn't answer, and she didn't really seem to be watching, either. I knocked a row of cubes off the dripper and scooped them into the bucket. The look on her face was half ebullience and half consternation, as though she were trying to remember some blissful thing that eluded her. "Okay," she finally said, more sharply.

She rose and took my arm and pulled me down the side hall to the front doors of the house. They were partway open, and when we stepped behind them I could see Mr. Metarey standing by a car in the entrance circle. We stood like that in the foyer, her hand on my arm and her gaze focused out the crack in the door. I set down the ice bucket and looked up. Beyond her on the wall was a large oil painting of her grandfather, Eoghan Metarey, and I noticed for the first time that his eyes looked the way Christian's own had a few moments before. Darkly shadowed yet with that curious energy. They also seemed, by a trick of technique, to be staring directly into my own. "I need to bring the ice to Gil," I said.

"Do you see Daddy?" she said. "Go out there and stand near him."

"What?"

She opened the door wider. "Go make yourself visible. Like you want to be useful."

"I do want to be useful."

"Then go out there."

"I can't, Christian." I glanced behind us. In the ballroom I could see people gathered around the bar. Mrs. Metarey was among them again. "I'm working."

She turned and looked at me that same way; then, so resolutely that I didn't try to stop her, she took hold of my arm and pulled me onto the porch. In a moment we were down among the front walk hedges, making our way toward the garage. At the end of the turn-around Mr. Metarey was leaning into the backseat window. He didn't look up. Christian kept tugging on my hand, and in the dark we crossed the driveway and ducked inside the feed gate of the horse barn, where Mrs. Metarey's gelding, Breighton, looked up in the dim light. "Shhh," Christian whispered, and patted him. He snorted softly and went back to eating. Then Christian crouched and brought the gate shut, and when she pulled again on my hand I squatted next to her, both of us looking out through the slats now. The car was a Cadillac, an Eldorado. Mr. Metarey still hadn't looked up.

"Gil asked me to get more ice," I whispered. "I just left the bucket in the front hall."

"Oh, stop it about the ice—Gil can wait."

In the dark the garage lamp cast a cone of pale illumination, and below it the inside of the car was obscured; but then the rear door opened and a man in a dark suit got out. He was even taller than Mr. Metarey, strong-featured and dominating even in the half-light, and I don't know why I should have recognized Henry Bonwiller, but I did.

He stood surveying the scene around the side of the house, where the farthest-out clusters of guests were standing on the lawn in the flicker of the citronella torches. We were not more than twenty-five feet from them. He put his hand on Mr. Metarey's shoulder and spoke into his ear.

"They're deciding," Christian whispered. She turned and looked at me, her eyes shining. "Senator Bonwiller's deciding tonight if he's going to run. I think he is. Look at him."

"What about Morlin Chase?"

"I'm talking about president, Corey. President of the United States. Look at them. I think they've decided."

Mr. Metarey was leaning forward now to speak, and as we watched him the light suddenly brightened on the gravel and a moment later Clara emerged from the house. She'd changed her clothes: I could see the black silhouette of a dress now. She looked both ways along the turnaround, then stepped down onto the walk. She was carrying the ice bucket.

"Shoot—" I said.

"Oh, don't worry. My God, Corey—look!"

Mr. Metarey and Senator Bonwiller were patting each other across the shoulders now, and then they gripped hands. As they did, Clara crossed the drive and walked up next to them, and Mr. Metarey leaned down and kissed her on the cheek. He was smiling.

"They're going to do it!" Christian whispered.

Henry Bonwiller took Clara's hand then and leaned down to kiss her on the cheek as well. She set the bucket on the gravel.

"Oh, I knew it!" she said. "I knew it. Daddy's going to do it! Corey Sifter, you're looking at the—look, Corey! Look at what you're seeing!"

Clara turned and craned her neck toward us.

"Shhh!" I said. "I really should be getting the ice."

The two men turned then and started back toward the house, and when they were past us I stood, mostly to see what Clara was going to do with the bucket. But she just stayed there with it, watching her father and the Senator make their way around the willow to the party in back.

It was then, as I leaned into the slats of the feed gate to watch her, that a hand touched my neck; and when I turned I felt Christian's lips. Her tongue tapped quickly against mine. Then she pulled back.

"Oh," I said.

"I can't believe we saw that together—" She leaned toward me again, and this time she pushed her tongue between my teeth.

I dropped to my knees and pulled her down next to me in Breighton's bedding. Her mouth tasted of mint. Her hands were warm, and her hair smelled of the hay and something else. Roses, I think. Perfume. Hay and mint and perfume.

Her mouth lifted. "I like you in a tie," she whispered. Then her lips moved to my neck. "You should wear one *every* day."

"I'll see what I can do," I whispered back.

"Oh, Corey," I heard, as we rolled sideways.

That's when the light came on.

"Well, well—" said Clara, and a flashlight moved to Christian's face. "Look who's found the Easter egg." Then it moved back to mine, and in a moment down to my shirtfront. "And look who's gone and ruined his tie."

LATER THAT NIGHT, there was rain. Sometime well before dawn the sound of it grew louder and woke me in the blackness. Then I realized it wasn't rain. Someone was tapping on my screen. "Come out," I heard Christian say.

"Shhh—" I climbed from bed. "How'd you get up here?"

"Flew." She flapped her arms and jumped on the metal roof.

"Shhh," I said again. "Come in—come inside."

"No, you come outside." She shone a flashlight in my face. "You were asleep," she said. "I should have known."

"What did you expect me to be doing?"

"Thinking. Like me."

"About what?"

"The world. Everything. *You*, I guess." Then she said, "All I can say is you better hurry—we'll lose the moon." She leaned in closer. "You'll need your shoes."

I lifted the screen into the house. She took my hand, pulled me through the open window, and led me straight to the edge of the roof, where the cedar reached over the eave. My parents' room was around the corner, and Mr. McGowar's was right behind us. She took hold of a branch and swung toward the trunk, then scrambled down through the boughs.

In a moment I was next to her on the ground. She took my arm and pulled me across to the alley. I was holding my shoes in one hand until

I hopped for a few steps and slipped them on. She wasn't going to let me kiss her again. That's what it seemed like to me. Not here, at least.

In the distance a dog barked.

"Church," she said. "Quiet."

Then she was off. She moved quickly, down Dumfries onto the grounds of the estate, turning at the far side of the lower stand of birch, then heading up into the pines. I followed. The footing changed to soft needles, then to packed dirt along the grade near the highway. Then the mulch of the upper oaks, and at last tall grass. We were out onto the unmowed field at the top of the property. Across the dark expanse, the huge Lodge Chief pine stood out against the purplish sky; Christian stood below it, the flashlight high above her head.

When I reached her she was still standing like that, at the base of the great tree, her head tilted back. The flashlight was on the ground now, casting light through the grass.

"Westinghouse threw the first switch here," she said.

"The first what?"

"George Westinghouse. Westinghouse Electric. Grandfather knew everyone. Westinghouse wanted to beat out Edison, so he wired it for Grandfather and threw the first switch for the lights. In eighteen-ninety-something. Christmas Eve. People thought it was going to explode."

"I love the lights," I said.

"There's a story to them like everything else. Grandfather never paid him. He just threatened to hire Edison instead."

I waited.

"You coming?" she finally asked. "It'll take your breath away. Come on, Corey." She moved in among the roots, grabbed hold of the lowest bough, and without saying anything more pulled herself up into the branches. The needles swayed, then stilled.

I must say, I could barely keep close. Above me, she rose like a creature of the jungle. The great pine's limbs were evenly spaced most of the way up the trunk, but I was more cautious than Christian. I'd picked up her flashlight and wedged it into my pocket. Inside the tent of needles the night was black, but I could see her white shirt above me, a pale shape in the moonlight.

When I reached her at last, she was leaning back against the trunk. We might have been sixty feet in the air. Through the dense needles the lights of the entrance lane cast a faint channel above the trees.

"You know why we came?" she said.

I took a spot a couple of limbs down. "I can't say I do."

She pushed on a branch and a triangle of sky opened up. "For the view."

"Okay."

"Look at it."

"I am."

"No. Really—*look* at it."

There it was. The purplish band at the horizon. The blue-black slit of the distant lake in the moonlight.

"It's beautiful," I said.

"It is. I could see why they thought it would explode."

"What would explode?"

She didn't answer. "That was nice," she said instead. "In the barn."

"It was."

"But it doesn't mean anything."

I looked up at her.

She shook her leg and a patch of sky moved sideways, then closed. The needles rustled again and a moment later a smaller patch opened above. "It doesn't mean it'll happen again, you know?"

"I know."

She moved around her new perch above me. After a moment, she said, "Then felt I like some watcher of the skies—"

This was from a poem we'd read at school.

A breeze rose and the trunk swayed.

"When a new planet swims into the ken," she said. Then she stopped. After a time, she added, "I don't know—it's probably silly."

"It's not silly."

"I feel like a balloon that's ready to burst," she said. She shook her head. "With happiness." She shook it again. "No. Not happiness. That's going to burst with ecstasy."

I looked up again.

"I'm all blown up," she said. She reached out her arms. "I'm ready to burst."

"I'm glad we did this, Christian. I'm glad we did all of this. I'm glad you came to get me."

"Poof."

I reached up and touched her arm. "We can go down."

"Don't," she said. "I'd rather go up."

She started moving again.

"Christian, it getting thin up here."

"See the moon?"

"Let's sit."

"Oh, come on, Corey! Not you! Come up with me. See the moon?"

I climbed a few feet. In the distance I heard Churchill again. "We're pretty high up already," I said. I could see the tops of the other trees below us now. The moon was setting over them, orange and big. The trunk here was no wider than my leg, and it was swaying as she moved. I climbed slowly until I was able to reach out and touch her ankle.

"Oh, stop," she said. She moved out farther. "Corey Worrier!" She laughed. "You have to trust."

A break appeared in the wall of needles.

"Trust who?"

"That's funny. The gods."

"Okay. Maybe we can just sit here and trust them?"

"Corey," she whispered, "today we witnessed something we'll never forget." She looked down at me. "Something *historic*."

"We did," I answered.

Then she was quiet. How long we sat like that, I don't know. But every few minutes she would find a bit of new energy and move up a limb or two. And I would follow. We must have been eighty feet up

now. The early morning wind had picked up and the trunk was swaying steadily. The needles making their sifty murmur. I was looking
through them to the west, toward the house. A light had come on
downstairs.

After a time, she said softly, "I don't know—sometimes I have it in
my hand. But then I get scared."

"Like now?"

"And I ruin it."

"You haven't ruined anything, Christian."

I moved out toward her again, keeping my eyes on the house. She
let me touch her arm. It was shivering.

"Christian," I said. "It's me."

"Corey, it's indescribably beautiful up here."

"I know. You look scared."

"*You* look scared."

"I am."

The needles shook and then dipped farther, and then I was aware
that the branch was moving in a different way. She was shuddering.
The gap widened and that's when I saw another flicker of light, in the
trees at the bottom of the hill.

"Let's just stay here now," I said.

Another one appeared next to it. Two lights: moving toward us.

"I know you're different, Corey. I know you believe it, too."

"I never know what you mean—"

"Go to hell."

Behind her, I took the flashlight from my pocket and blinked it on
and off. "That's something your sister would say."

"Damn you!"

"So's that."

I blinked it again. Then I peered into the darkness. One of the
other lights was on the hill now.

"We stole this from the Seneca," she said. "All this land."

"Your grandfather built it, Christian. From nothing."

"Damn you, Corey."

"Come back this way. We can sit if you want. But come in closer."

She was two branches above me, and we sat like that for a while, silently; then after a certain period she turned and climbed down to me. I reached for her arm and held it. And presently, after a few more minutes, I could feel her relax. "God," she said at last. "You must think I'm crazy."

At the time, I think, I didn't. I was driven only by fear—not just that harm would come to her in that tree, but that harm was about to arrive for both of us, in the form of those two lights that were approaching; but by the time they arrived and we heard Churchill's steady barking, we had both started the long climb down the trunk. And by the time Mr. Metarey's flashlight was shining among the branches, we were almost at the bottom. I held Christian under her shoulders as she let herself drop into her father's arms. He spread his coat over her, then took her hand.

"I can explain, sir," I said when I was on the ground.

Gil McKinstrey stood off to the side with a hurricane lantern.

"You don't have to," Mr. Metarey answered. "I imagine I know."

"It's not what you think, Mr. Metarey."

"Don't worry, Corey. I know it's not. I suspect I know what it was. I'm grateful, that's all." He looked down the hill. "Thank you."

Then they started across the meadow, his arm over her shoulder. I stayed back a distance, near Gil. Churchill was barking happily as he ran in and out around us. Mr. Metarey was walking slowly and when we reached the stand of Scotch pines that made the deepest woods on the land, Gil moved in closer and lifted the lantern over his head so that it cast its light down the trail ahead of them. And that's how he kept it until we reached the lower run of oaks and saw the dawn coming through the trees.

THAT WEEKEND, as I was leaning down over the back-cart of the Ferguson, a voice close behind me said, "Work will set you free."

I stood. "Yes, sir."

"You're taking good care of that, I see. Which knot is that you're using?"

I'd just tightened a rope around a handful of pipe bends. "A jamming hitch, sir."

"Looked like a taut line. But not quite."

"Little sturdier, Mr. Metarey."

He nodded at me and smiled. I didn't know how long he'd been standing there. The field around us was painfully bright, already dry after its morning watering. I picked up the sheaf of pipe and dropped it back into the cart. The knot held. "Easy to lose one on a bump," I said.

"But I know you won't." In the distance Aberdeen Red was curving through long figure eights, and he leaned back and shaded his eyes to watch. I had the impression he wanted me to look, too, so I did, but I stayed bent over the cart. I was wondering if Clara had said anything to him about finding us in the barn.

"Things are going to change around here soon," he said. "I just wanted to let you know that."

"You won't need me anymore, sir? I understand."

He laughed. "I won't tell your mother you said *that*, either," he said. "It's the opposite, actually. It's going to get a fair shake busier, as a matter of fact, and we're going to be needing you *more*. There's going to be some news about Senator Bonwiller."

I took a chance. "In that case, sir, I should tell you—I already know. Christian mentioned it to me. People say it's the right time for Senator Bonwiller to get into the race, too."

He looked at me.

"I mean, with all the demonstrations in Washington. I read Mr. Burrant's article, sir."

"You did, did you? Well, very good. Then you know all about it."

He patted me on the shoulder. "And you'll be reading plenty of others now, I suspect."

Aberdeen Red whooshed in over the field, then angled into a climb.

"She's good," he said. "You have to give her that."

I was quiet.

He pointed to the plane. "My wife, I mean."

"Oh, yes, sir. It's amazing. I see her do it every morning."

"That's because we only let her do it in the mornings." He chuckled, a little stiffly. "I also wanted to tell you that I appreciate everything you're doing for us. It can't be easy, with your schoolwork, too."

"School's over this week."

"And both my daughters like you, too. That's a good sign."

My hands were caked in mud, and I leaned over the cart to wipe them on the grass.

"I guess what I really want to tell you is that I appreciate what you did for Christian."

I looked up.

"The other day," he said. "Sometimes she gets like that. I'm glad she was with someone levelheaded when she did. That's all I mean."

"We were just—"

"You don't have to say anything, Corey. I'm grateful you're both all right. So's Mrs. Metarey."

He picked up a stone and threw it at the split-rail fence. Over the trees the plane was skimming low now.

"I've been thinking things over," he said then, "and I've arranged a chance for you." He climbed up onto the tractor and shut off the engine, then climbed back down next to me. "I spoke to a friend of mine named Tom MacDonald. A fellow's going to be up here next week to speak to you about Dunleavy."

I nodded.

"Dunleavy," he said.

"Yes, sir."

Aberdeen Red was marking off the corners of the landing strip now. We watched Mrs. Metarey make the final turn for her approach.

He smiled. "I guess that was silly of me. You don't know what Dunleavy is, do you?"

"No, sir."

He patted me on the shoulder again. "It's a school," he said. "Dunleavy Academy. You'll know that soon enough. It's a very fine and exclusive school. I went there myself. And so did Andrew—for his first couple of years, anyway. If you impress this fellow next week," he said, "you'll have a chance to go, too."

"I will?" I bent to the grass and wiped my hands again. Aberdeen Red had distracted me. At first I thought he had said *task*. I've arranged a *task* for you.

"And don't worry," he said. "I'll give you a few pointers before you meet with him. Just so you know what to expect." He tossed another stone. "You certainly deserve it," he added, "as much as anyone."

IV

On a ravishing summer afternoon in the second half of that month, with three TV cameras, a dozen radio microphones, and two rows of print reporters in front of him, and his wife and two teenaged sons next to him, Henry Bonwiller, chairman of the Senate Appropriations Committee and senior member of the Armed Services Committee, announced to the country that he would seek the Democratic nomination for president.

Now, of course, the Senator is known for what happened later; but this was early on, well before Anodyne Energy or anything else, and I can only say that in the days that followed he seemed to light the air he walked through. When he arrived in the morning, I could see the staff standing at the windows to catch glimpses of him. When he walked in town in the afternoon, stopping for kids to pet Uncle Dan, a policeman had to keep the traffic moving.

His ring of influence immediately grew wider. Early in the summer, President Nixon announced that he was going to allow trade with Communist China, and not even a full day later, there was Senator Bonwiller speaking about it to CBS Evening News outside the Metarey work barn, where he and Eric Sevareid stood next to a new John Deere combine. And there they both were again that very evening, on my parents' television set, while Mr. McGowar and my father watched from the living room couch and my mother looked in from the kitchen, a dishrag and a wet pot in her hands.

"China—" Mr. McGowar coughed. In his hands was an apple-sized hunk of quartz that he was cleaning with his handkerchief. "That's—" He took a long breath. "That's—" He coughed again. "—Trouble."

"Nah," said my father. "For the unions it's great. Think of all those millions of Chinese." He took a drink from his Pabst Blue Ribbon. "Buying our stuff. They'll buy Deere and New Holland by the thousands." He took another drink. "They don't have that kind of thing over there, Eugene." Then he whistled the opening of "Cockles and Mussels."

Mr. McGowar looked pained but didn't answer. He just waved one hand at the TV and with the other went on polishing.

"Hmm," said my mother from the kitchen doorway, "you know, Senator Bonwiller's a handsome man on camera. Did I see you for just a sec in the background, Cor?"

"No, Mom. You didn't."

At the end of June, the Supreme Court ruled that *The New York Times* and *The Washington Post* could publish the Pentagon Papers, and President Nixon called for the arrest of Daniel Ellsberg, who immediately went into hiding. That Monday, Henry Bonwiller stood up on the Senate floor and called Ellsberg a national hero. He read page after page of the Pentagon Papers into the *Congressional Record*, recording for posterity that the government had bombed Laos and attacked North Vietnam and yet had denied both to the public. The Senate chambers were thrown into commotion and he was nearly shouted down. The incident didn't make it onto the evening news but I knew about it because it was covered in the *Post* and the *Times* themselves, and in the *Courier-Express*, all of which I'd begun to read now on my own.

I'd been reading newspapers now, in fact, ever since the morning I'd met Glenn Burrant. In those days Liam Metarey subscribed to dozens of them, which I picked up for him every afternoon from the Saline post office and arranged on café sticks in the library. Since school had ended, I'd started full-time at Aberdeen West, and my last job every Friday afternoon was to bring all the old papers over to the Saline Public Library. But every day now, after I was done with my shift, I would sit down on the side porch and read one or two of them myself. They were still last week's editions, most of them, because they had to be mailed to us; but I found that I consumed them eagerly. I liked it, somehow. This was a surprise to me, that I took this kind of pleasure from knowing about the world. Around my parents I felt I had secrets.

By then I'd also taken to watching for the arrival of Glenn Burrant himself, who'd been visiting the house almost every day since the news about the Senator. Anytime there was an important meeting now, or a position statement coming out, or an appearance by Henry Bonwiller, the yellow Corvair would sprint down the entrance drive, squeaking and bouncing on the gravel. Perhaps because of the proximity of the *Courier-Express*, Glenn obviously had a privileged relationship with Aberdeen West, and he was allowed to wait outside while the meetings took place. I'd made a point of letting him know that I'd read his article, and though he changed the subject I could tell that he was pleased. He would wave at me as I went about my work. While Liam Metarey and the campaign staff deliberated inside, Glenn would rest on the iron bench in the shade of the bur oak, one leg up beside him on the seat like a packed duffel; and when the meetings broke, he was first to get the scoop. I liked the way he stood when he was summoned—as though he were these men's unlikely equal—pulling a reporter's notebook from his back pocket and a pen from behind his ear as he labored up the three steps to the porch, pausing at the front door to stomp out his cigarette and then to comb his hair in the glass. Much of what impressed me was his brusque manner and how big he was—when he zipped his nylon Windbreaker it bulged like a sausage casing; but it was also because he greeted me with a conspiratorial intimacy whenever he gave me the beat-up old Corvair to bring down to the garage. No other adult took me in like that.

I'd been given the job of parking cars now, too. And among the cars that were appearing at the estate, the Corvair couldn't possibly have been more of an aberration. It sprang up like a jack-in-the-box whenever Glenn stepped out of it, and the driver's seat was squashed so flat I felt like I was sitting on the floor when I drove it. But even among all the Cadillacs and Lincolns and Mercedes-Benzes, Liam Metarey gave it a high priority. There was an order I had to follow when I brought all the cars out after a meeting broke up, and he asked me to always keep it among the first few that I delivered, its windshield washed and a new booklet of state toll coupons clipped behind its visor.

Glenn would accept my shutting of his creaky door with an elaborate flourish of his mitt-sized hand—the hand that wrote for the *Courier-Express!*—then crank down the window on the passenger side—his own was stuck shut—and streak up the curved driveway, the chassis listing to the left. At the bend under the sycamores, the listing would level off momentarily, and a split second later his cigarette would fly out the far window onto the gravel. I would walk up to collect it.

I mention Glenn not only because he was the one who first started me reading the newspaper, but also because he was as astute as anyone who ever knew the Bonwiller campaign, from inside or out. Yet I still don't know how he figures in what happened. Was he in the end a friend to the Senator and to the Metareys? I don't even know *that*. Or was he in fact a friend more to the truth—a moral man who, like many such men and women, gave little such impression? If I look too closely at all of it, in fact, the whole thing begins to shimmer—and

Glenn Burrant, as much as anyone, remains a mystery. After all these years, I don't know what I would have done if I had known, or at least suspected, what I think he knew.

But that house: it was irresistible. On the one hand, here was Henry Bonwiller, striding across the magnificent bluegrass lawn to a microphone set up on the great porch, while TV reporters milled in the drive: on the other, here was my mother, sitting at the kitchen table re-sewing the seams in my father's work apron. Here she was, beating the rugs outside our back door or hanging sheets from the line. And here was I, driving Averell Harriman's Aston Martin with its mahogany gearshift down the short gravel lane to the garage. Taking a set of lambskin-covered keys from Tom Watson, the chairman of IBM. Lining up Henry Bonwiller's set of dark leather valises on luggage stands in the guest cottage and unzipping them halfway. I hung his dark suits in the closet and propped his hand-sewn Maine shoes on the wooden tree. The shoes of the man who was going to be president! The Senator's own house was only a half hour away, in Islington, and his wife and family were there, but he had permanent quarters now at Aberdeen West. Two other guest apartments had been set up for his advisors now, as well, men who arrived at all hours from cities on the coast, their black cars wheeling up the drive or their planes touching down behind the trees. Senator Bonwiller's rooms looked out on the riding ring and the two oblong casting pools behind it, and before going home every evening I made sure a bamboo fly rod was hung by the coat rack and a corkboard of flies was on the sill.

And yet even as it was happening, it was all half unreal to me. I was still surprised, I have to say, every time his dark blue Eldorado rolled down the garden turnaround, still relieved every time Henry Bonwiller emerged from it, shaking hands with Liam Metarey and handing his briefcase to his driver. I suppose from my upbringing I expected some disappointing news to be at hand, some inevitable punishment for this kind of ambition.

One evening, on the library balcony where Christian had invited me after my shift, she said, "Daddy's going to be secretary of the treasury again."

Clara snorted. "Daddy's going to be secretary of the pub."

The three of us were sitting on iron chairs, looking down over the band tent, where a campaign party was being held. It was the first time Christian had invited me anywhere since the night in the tree, an episode that I still didn't understand, and I was wary. She wasn't outside on the bur oak's iron bench anymore when I finished work in the afternoons, and she wasn't anywhere in the house—at least, not that I could see—when I arrived in the mornings. But sitting now on the balcony, she looked the same as she always had. And to my relief she acted the same, as though nothing had happened.

Below us, a couple of hundred guests stood on the grass drinking cocktails, and under the entrance awning a jazz trio was playing. Senator Bonwiller and Liam Metarey were speaking privately underneath the stretched guylines outside the tent, and I could see that there were other men waiting nervously to join them. Churchill lay across Christian and Clara, stretched out on their laps like a white stadium blanket they were sharing.

Christian said, "Daddy said Treasury or maybe Interior, Clara."

"Church agrees with *me*," said Clara. "He thinks the interior of the pub." She was drinking something with liquor in it. She kept offering it to us, but since Christian refused, I did too. Gil McKinstrey tended bar at these parties.

"Not at all," said Christian. "Daddy says Senator Bonwiller will win Iowa or maybe finish second there."

"Glenn Burrant thinks he has a good chance in New Hampshire, too," I added. "Even though it's a conservative state."

Clara snickered. "We've been talking to Glenn Burrant, have we? What Senator Bonwiller has a good chance of finishing," she said, "is ass-up on the lawn. Tell Glenn Burrant *that*. I know the kind of man Henry Bonwiller is. He's going to be dead last in Iowa. Right, Church?"

The dog raised its head.

"He can see the future, you know," Clara said, tilting her glass to her lips. She patted him on the snout. "Can't you, sweet?"

Churchill whimpered and licked Christian's hand, then Clara's.

Christian said, "However, the dog is too great a politician to commit at this point."

"Okay then," said Clara. "In that case, Corey will have to tell us. Tell us, Corey. Tell us what *you* think, not what Glenn *Burr*-Ant says. Henry Bonwiller's going to finish ass-up, is he not?"

Her eyes were shining. Christian's eyes gazed sensibly into mine.

"Clara," Christian said quickly, "you're drunk. Here, give me that." She reached for the glass. "You give me that."

"And that's if he's *lucky*," Clara snorted. She pulled the glass away and held it above her head. "He's got less of a fucking chance in Iowa than *I* do," she scoffed. She shook the ice cubes, then leaned forward and threw them over the rail into the crowd.

ONE MORNING SOON AFTER THAT, I carried a clean shirt and a pair of long pants with me to the Metareys', and at lunchtime when I came in from the grounds I showered in one of the guest rooms and changed into them. When I was done, Mr. Metarey came downstairs to take a look, and he returned a moment later with a tie. I hadn't mentioned anything to my parents.

When we emerged together, June Metarey and Christian were in the hall. "Needs a woman's eye," Mrs. Metarey said. "Let's have a peek." She was wearing heels—she didn't look like someone who could fly a plane.

"You look very nice," said Christian.

I smiled and touched the tie.

"Liam—" said Mrs. Metarey.

"He's been working," answered Mr. Metarey.

"Wait right there, young man."

I heard her quick footsteps on the stairs, and when she returned a few moments later she was holding a pair of shoes.

"Mother."

"They're Andrew's," June Metarey answered, holding them up. "He won't mind."

"I don't quite believe this," said Christian. She touched my elbow. "Your shoes are fine. Andrew would tell you to wear whatever shoes you want."

"And Andrew didn't fit in at Dunleavy," said Mrs. Metarey. "Did he?"

She examined them, then quickly brushed their tops and set them down next to me. They were loafers—not new, but buffed to a dusky brown that made me embarrassed for my own black school boots, which I had just wiped in the guest room with a washcloth.

"A little big," she said, "but they'll work." She reached inside one. "Decent pair of socks, too."

"Oh, please, Mother."

"Corey's got socks, June. He doesn't need And's."

"Liam."

I sat down, took off my boots, and pulled Andrew's socks on over my own. They matched the loafers, and two pair made a decent fit.

"Shoes make the man," Mrs. Metarey said then. She knelt down on one knee and brushed the shine again with her sleeve.

"Oh, nonsense," said her husband.

"It's something Daddy taught me," she went on, speaking to me. She was leaning on the dark red Persian runner that ran the length of the hallway. "In his business, he had to be able to judge character." She looked up at my face. "That's always what he looked for. The details. Cheap shoes to give away a decent suit."

"More nonsense."

"I appreciate this, Mrs. Metarey," I said. The only other time she'd spoken to me had been on the sailing trip.

"God bless him," she answered.

"Thank you."

She looked up again.

"I meant Daddy," she said. She rose from the rug. Then she added, "But God bless you, too, Corey."

Then Mr. Metarey stood before us. "Just answer all his questions with the truth," he said. "You have a lot to be proud of, and that will be evident. Your dad's quite a tradesman. He was an enlisted man in the U.S. Navy. You've done well at school and certainly for me. I even hear you're a good soccer player. Now, that's an unusual game."

"I learned it in the neighborhood."

"Indeed you did. Indeed you did."

"Look at you," Christian said, stepping back. "You'll do great."

At precisely one o'clock Liam Metarey led me into a side room. There, the man from Dunleavy was sitting in a dark blue blazer at a large desk beneath a landscape oil of the Carrol Valley. His loafers were just like the ones I'd borrowed from Andrew. He motioned me into the chair across from him, and when Liam Metarey had left the room, he filled his pipe, tamped it down, and said, in a way that made me think he was amused, "Welcome to school."

I needed no scholarship, as it turned out. Mr. Metarey was going to pay my way. And Mr. Metarey was the one who must have told my parents, for when I came home that day, my mother already knew. It surprised me that she seemed pleased. I think I'd expected her to forbid the whole thing when she heard it. My father, too. But neither of them did. Instead, when I came in the door that afternoon in my muddy field pants, holding the duffel at my side, my mother greeted me in her apron and said, "First thing, I'll take you to Brownlee's for a set of new clothes."

"We'll all go," said my father.

And so my life, as though it hadn't changed enough already, changed again.

V

"I HARDLY EVER SEE YOU ANYMORE," my mother said.

She had come up to my room after my father had fallen asleep in his chair with *Pride of the Yankees*. Now she was sitting at the end of my bed as I read the scores.

"A baseball widow," she said.

"What is it, Mom?"

"We don't talk anymore."

The Indians were having another sub-.500 season. There was the usual grumbling about Alvin Dark and the usual talk about pitching, but this year even Sam McDowell was losing. Ever since I'd switched from the Mets to the Indians, he'd been doing that.

I looked up from the desk. "That's because I'm working," I said.

She smiled. "How's Ray Pinson doing?"

"*Vada* Pinson." Vada Pinson was my great hope. He'd been a dynamite center fielder for the Reds, and I had dreams that he could get the Indians winning again. "You're thinking of Ray Fosse," I said. "The catcher."

"How's Ray Fosse doing?"

"He's hitting .270." I glanced down. "Pinson's hitting .265. That's not good for either of them."

"You're over there so much, Cor."

I looked at her. "I'm earning money every minute of it, Mom."

"I know. I'm not complaining. It's just that—" She rose and went to the wall, where my Buffalo Bills pennant was hung. I had a knack for losing teams. "Well, it's just that soon you won't be with us—I don't know—you won't be with us much at all."

"I can come home every weekend if I want."

"I know, I know. And it's not for a while yet."

"I can always change my mind."

"I wouldn't want you to, sweetheart." She fingered the Buffalo at the crease between its red felt shoulders. "Forgive your tired mom," she said softly. "I've been under the weather."

"I forgive you then."

"Thank you." She smiled. Then she touched the side of her head, and a pained look came across her features. I could tell she was thinking.

"Mom, Dunleavy's a hundred miles from here. I can come home whenever I want. There's a bus. Or a train."

"I know, I know. It's all a wonderful thing for you. We're all grateful." She pulled down the pennant and straightened it against the edge of the desk, then set it back against the wall and pinned it. "Corey," she said, "what's Senator Bonwiller like?"

I set down the paper.

"Your father wouldn't want me prying," she said. She glanced at the door. "But I'm curious anyway. I don't know—is he really all that different? Doesn't he seem just like anybody else?"

"Dad's met him."

"I know. I'm wondering what *you* think."

"When you're near him," I said, "he's the same as a lot of people you see over there. In a crowd he's different."

"How's he different?"

"I don't know. He's brighter or something. Like he's got a light on him. You can see it."

"Have you been near him?"

"I take in his bag sometimes."

"And how does he treat you?"

"He shakes my hand every time."

"Does he really, Cor? Does he recognize you?"

I looked at her. Her fingers were clasped together and she was leaning forward in her chair. I picked up the sports section again. "He knows I'm almost old enough to vote," I said.

She separated her hands. "Corey," she said, "don't be like that."

"Like what?"

"Disrespectful," she said.

I turned the page. The Indians had been at the bottom all summer. Maybe that's what had put me in a mood. They couldn't even beat the Brewers. "Christian calls it *realistic*," I answered.

"Does Mr. Metarey ever speak to you about him?"

I turned the page.

"Sweetheart?"

"Not to me. Of course not."

"Your father thinks he has a chance to win."

"Everybody thinks that, Mom. That's why they're doing it. They're gearing up for Iowa in January and then New Hampshire. Then they're going to see. Muskie's the front-runner, but they like it that way."

She looked at me.

"Senator Edmund Muskie, Mom. From Maine."

"Oh," she said. "Your father took me to Bar Harbor for our honeymoon." She smiled. "What about Mrs. Bonwiller, Cor? Is she ever around?"

"Not yet. But she's going to be later when the days get heavy. The southern swing."

"The southern swing?"

"She's from Georgia," I said. "She can help down there. The

southern swing starts in May. No Democrat's ever won without the South." I paused. "Some people say that's why he married her."

She looked at me.

"Where did you learn that?" she finally said.

"What?"

"That kind of talk."

"From the Metareys. From Christian."

"I don't know, honey."

"What don't you know?"

"Whether any of this is good for you."

"You just said you were grateful."

"I am. But still." She touched the side of her head again.

"Mom," I said. "I'm just a groundskeeper."

"You're not. You're more than that."

"A little more," I said. "That's true."

She got up from the chair and went back to the wall. "Tell me the order of the cars again," she said.

"Why?"

"Because I think it's interesting."

I glanced at the Brewers-Yankees score. Dave May had homered in the ninth for the Brewers, but even with the loss, the Yankees were still three games ahead of us in the East. I turned the page to the Mets-Dodgers.

"Cor," she said. "I'm your mother."

"All right," I said, looking up. "Senator Bonwiller's is first, of course. Unless the governor's there, which he was the other day."

"You drove Governor Rockefeller's car?"

"His driver did, Mom. I just gave him the signal to get it from the garage. After the Senator, there's a few judges. Then the newspaper owners. Then the police."

"Police come?"

"State police," I said. "Then the reporters. Yesterday one of the reporter's cars wouldn't start."

"What did he do?"

"Actually, Mr. Metarey ended up starting it."

"Mr. Metarey did?"

"Something was wrong with the carburetor. He taught me how to fix it. You unscrew the cover and spray gas into it."

"Mr. Metarey helped you do that?"

"He didn't help me do it, Mom. He *did* it. Did you know that in a Corvair the engine's in the *trunk*? I didn't. But he did. That's the way he is. He does everything himself."

"Hmmm," she said, and the pained expression crossed her face again. She sat down on the end of my bed, contemplating.

It was true about Mr. Metarey. If anything broke, anywhere on the estate, he tried to fix it himself; and if he couldn't fix it, he dismantled it, salvaging it for parts, which he filed in the work barn in a ceiling-high collection of labeled drawers—themselves salvaged, it seemed, from some country auction. It was as though he were two men: the Liam Metarey who owned a third of Carrol Township and spoke with the governor just about every week, and another man entirely—a determined, hardscrabble Scotsman trying to scrape out a living on rocky land. His toolshed looked like the barn of an ingenious and frugal farmer.

"What was he wearing?" my mother said.

"When he fixed it? A suit. What do you think? He'd just gotten out of a meeting. I held his jacket. He showed me what to do if it happens again. That's what he always does."

"Well, good," she said. "I like him."

When I heard that, I felt somehow that a door had been opened; but I was sixteen years old, and at all times something was preventing me from talking too eagerly to my mother, or from appearing to listen to her too closely. So I just turned another page in the sports section. I wish I hadn't been like that, but I was.

"In that case," she finally said, "I guess this is the view I'll have to remember." She rose and moved toward the door. "The top of your sweet, uncombed head."

"WELL," CLARA SAID TO ME, "did you have a good time at that latest fiasco?"

I looked out from under Mrs. Metarey's Galaxy, where I'd been lying on a slider changing the oil. "At the latest what?"

"Fiasco. My father's little fête for the candidate."

"Did *you*?" I asked.

"It was interesting. I wish I'd hit him with the ice."

"Oh, that," I said. "I wasn't sure you'd remember."

There was a pause. "I asked if you had a good time."

"I thought it was very nice."

"Very *nice*?"

"Yes," I said, and I slid under the chassis again. I was hoping the clatter of the wheels would hide my words. From the first time I'd met her, Clara had seemed to be my accuser. She said something I couldn't hear.

"Hmm?" I answered, making some noise with the wrenches.

"Stop it!"

"Stop what?"

Another silence.

"My sister's not good for you, you know."

"I can't hear you," I said. I slid the oil pan under the drain.

"You know what you are, Corey?"

I angled my head out. She stood at the open door of the garage; I reached under the chassis and unscrewed the plug, then slid back under to watch the oil run out into the pan. Another silence followed. In it I heard Breighton stamping in the stables and Gil McKinstrey hammering shingles on a roof. I turned my attention back to the work. The oil was still a clear amber: the car hadn't been driven more than a few hundred miles since the last change.

"You know what you are?" she said again.

By the door I could see the toe of one shoe scratching the strap of the other. "No," I answered.

"What did you say?" There was irritation now in her voice.

She was forcing me to emerge. I did, finally, sliding out until she could see my face. I wondered if there was oil on it. "I said no."

She tilted her head sideways. "You're my grandfather."

"Your grandfather? You mean Eoghan Metarey?" I wiped my hands on my pants and slid back under. I was thinking of the portrait in their entrance hall. Even in a painting, the man had a predatory face. It was softened by the brooding eyes and the luxuries of the scene—the velvet chair-back and the gold-studded walking stick—but it was predatory nonetheless. Next to his shoulder a yellow canary stood on a perch, its dark irises painted so that they caught the viewer's own in the same tenacious way its master's did, as though everyone who entered that house was observed by two unsleeping sentinels from the past.

"What was your grandfather like?" I said from under the car.

"What was he like? Well, he got all this because he wanted it so fucking much, for one. That's what he was like." She clicked her tongue. "And don't tell me you haven't heard about him."

"Of course I've heard about him," I said, sliding my head back out—but she was already gone.

IN JULY, when the campaign began to pick up advisors from all over the East Coast, I was promoted to driver. This meant mostly that I was doing errands for Mr. Metarey around town, but on weekends, now, it also meant that I was driving Senator Bonwiller. This would have been a remarkable turn in any boy's life, but it was even more remarkable for the fact that I'd only had my license for a few months. Before he'd asked me to take on the driving, Mr. Metarey had sent Gil McKinstrey to check out my ability, and Gil and I had spent an afternoon bouncing around the estate and then wandering through town in his rusted old Ford pickup. Gil was a man who rode through life as though the horse had already bucked him, but when he saw that I wasn't fully confident with a stick shift he took me up to the Lodge Chief hill to learn. He sat next to me smoking his hand-rolled cigarettes as I learned to start on the steep rise, gravel flacking the chassis when I popped the clutch. "Got to think the paint don't like that," he said, then added, " 'Cept there ain't no paint!" and laughed ruefully. But he let me practice until I got it right.

Driving the Senator was of course the highlight of my job. In the blue Eldorado, I drove him to his weekend lunches at Morley's, and if they were on Sunday I would bring him back afterwards to his house in Islington, even though he hardly lived there anymore. His wife was in Atlanta now, helping organize the southern campaign, and usually when the Senator was in town he slept at Aberdeen West. But he still liked to speak to reporters from the front steps of his own house, an old yellow four-square with a white picket fence and a good-sized yard that he mowed for the photographers at his Monday press briefings, or whenever a Senate vote was in the news. And so once or twice a week, I drove him.

The rest of the time my errands were in Mrs. Metarey's Galaxy, either to pick up newspapers or groceries, or sometimes liquor, and once a week to drive June Metarey herself to her beauty parlor appointment in Steppan, a trip that she spent in the backseat flipping through a flying magazine called *Wheels Up!* And now and then I even drove Mr. Metarey, in his Chrysler, usually to Gervin's for hardware. He'd always buy something, even if it was just to take it apart on a handkerchief and study it on the front seat of the car between us.

I don't know why they all needed drivers. They were all certainly capable of driving themselves. But I think my job was also, in part, a nod to what the citizens of Saline expected of the men and women of that station: that not only did Metareys and Bonwillers require servants, but that they kept all ranks of townspeople in their employ. In comparison, those days were simple ones, especially politically, and I suppose it was a mark of that simplicity—or perhaps merely of the innocence of that place in particular—that a teenaged boy who had just learned to drive would be entrusted with the care of a senator; but I was. On the other hand, I have no doubt that Henry Bonwiller also knew my father was a union steward, and in Carrol County alone the unions could deliver five thousand votes. It also hasn't escaped my attention that I might have been intended as the Senator's protection.

In any case, after Henry Bonwiller had declared his candidacy, there seemed to be a rule that nobody was to go anyplace alone. I should add that now that I was driving the Senator, I was by necessity hearing snatches of his conversation, and I felt I could no longer be candid with my mother. Nobody had said anything to me about it, but I had picked it up, anyway—maybe from watching his regular driver, a light-skinned black man from New Orleans named Carlton Sample, who'd been his chauffeur since Henry Bonwiller had first been elected to office, in 1950, as state attorney general. One of the things I noticed about Carlton Sample was that he always appeared friendly but rarely said a word, and in short order this became the personality I tried to maintain around the Senator myself. Carlton Sample had other habits that I emulated as well, like using the inside of his sleeve to shine the door handles after he shut them. And when I opened or closed the Cadillac's convertible roof I stood off to the side the same way he did, my feet together on the pavement and my hands folded neatly in front of me. I took all my tasks seriously, for I was a boy raised not only with the creed of hard work but with the almost religious understanding that only discipline and diligence brought reward. My grandfather had been a miner; my father was a union tradesman; and now here I was, driving a man who could be president.

The Bonwiller Cadillac Eldorado was midnight blue, so dark it looked black in the shade, and sometimes on the forty-mile drive to Islington the Senator would have me pull over more than once, just to open or close that ingenious roof. When I opened it, the car— already large—felt colossal. He would move up to the front seat and don his dark glasses, then sit with his back half-turned as he wrote notes on a stenographer's pad on the armrest. Or sometimes he thumbed through a book of Walt Whitman that he kept in the glove box, pausing now and then to look out at the horizon. We didn't talk. The wind leaped over the windshield, pressing my forehead like a warm hand if I straightened my back, filling my shirt like a pillow if I set my elbow at a certain angle on the door ledge. It was hard to believe I was being paid.

To close the roof, he liked me to park where people could watch. First I unbuckled the vinyl cover that was tucked behind the rear seats; then I reached in the driver's door and engaged the control. At this point, I stood back and folded my hands, the way Carlton Sample did. A humming would begin and the stored roof's shiny fabric would fill, then bulge in its housing, then at last break free, its two metal arms rising suddenly into the air like a man throwing off his chains. People on the sidewalk moved closer. At the apex, the whole cloth-covered arrangement bent forward at the elbow and began its descent toward the windshield, unfurling as it went. As soon as it touched down, I latched the closures, and we were ready to go.

"You're taken with that, too?" Henry Bonwiller said to me one afternoon as a pair of young mothers watched us from the sidewalk, their babies in strollers. I'd picked him up in Islington and we were on the way into Saline for his Saturday lunch at Morley's.

"Yes, sir, I am."

"It's brilliant, isn't it?" He slapped his hand affectionately on the hood. "That's American engineering, son," he said, in his carrying baritone. "Best in the world." He turned to the two mothers, tipping his Yankees cap and smiling. Then he added, "Cadillac puts together those roofs now just downstate."

What am I to make of those comments today? Were they purely for the benefit of our onlookers? Senator Bonwiller didn't speak much to me, not in all the time I knew him—I didn't expect him to—but did he really care that working men and women from New York State made those convertible roofs? That American labor was ingenious?

Did he really think that American engineering was the best in the world? Or were those young mothers just two more voters—that is to say, two more of the quarry on the other side of his power? He no doubt had a Japanese TV at home and probably an Italian sports car in his garage. Was this just the accepted palaver of an elected man? A powerful aristocrat's obligation that was no different from his elaborately deferential sirs and ma'ams when he spoke to voters on the street? Or the red-white-and-blue straw hat that he wore to the Metarey barbecues? He was one of the last great liberal leaders of the Senate, in a period when such men commanded wide-ranging power, but he was also without doubt one of the landed gentry, just as Liam Metarey was.

But these are afterthoughts. I've since looked carefully at his voting record, and I must say he seems to have lived by his words: he did support workers; he supported civil rights, too, and, although he was just a bit slow to pick up on women's issues, he became a champion for them when they eventually became part of American politics. And nobody else fought as hard against the war in Vietnam. But did he really believe all of this, or was it all just part of the persona that gave him purchase and distinction and renown? I spent many hours with him, in his car and in the Metarey house, and I've thought about him for a number of years now, and I'm still not sure I know.

At the time, of course, I was nothing but proud. When we reached Saline that afternoon, I opened the roof again, and as I steered the Cadillac slowly up Ontario Street, stopping well ahead of pedestrians and offering deferential courtesy to passing motorists, I could feel on me the eyes of a whole town, eyes that knew me for who I was and that no doubt marveled at this upgrade of my fortunes. (There were, of course, my schoolmates from Roosevelt, too, who no doubt scoffed; but they were behind me now.) I drove carefully, and with pride.

In the backseat, Uncle Dan was running from side to side, barking excitedly as we passed groups of pedestrians on the sidewalk. Henry Bonwiller waved steadily at them, his pleasure washing over both of us. Though we were still over a year away from the general election, men even came out of the shops to greet us. "Senator Bon!" they called, waving—the populace, as all New Yorkers know, has always called him that.

He had taken off his glasses, as he always did when he was in public, and now as we passed the set of iron benches in front of the post office, he said in a low voice, "How many?"

He always asked me this, how large were the groups of onlookers—or, as he called them, *voters*. "Twenty, sir," I answered, although I could see that there were actually closer to fifteen. "More from inside the shops, too."

"Nice, nice," he whispered, waving back without turning from the sidewalk. "They're thinking about the election now. Wallets are getting thin." He held his hand high and saluted, then added, in the same low rumble, "Bad for them. Good for us."

He was referring to the economic figures that had been on the front page that morning: stagflation. I was pleased to understand the reference.

As we passed the corner I could see women pointing us out to their children, turning back to watch our car move up the block. But when we reached Morley's and I pulled over to park, his face suddenly darkened. "Go around the corner," he said. "Damn it."

"Yes, sir."

I drove past the restaurant and turned at Siding Road. Now we were hidden from Ontario Street. We continued halfway down the block.

"Stop," he said. "Close the roof."

I did. He ducked quickly out of the car and moved back to the rear.

"Now," he said, "take me around to Morley's again."

This time when I pulled in front of the restaurant and stepped out to open his door, he stopped me with his hand from the backseat. "I'm not going in," he said.

"Yes, sir."

"You go in by yourself. Order me a Coke from the Irishman at the bar register and bring it back out."

"Yes, sir."

"Speak in a loud voice. Go in there. Walk slowly. Go up to the bar and say you'd like to buy a Coke for your employer who's too busy to come in at the moment. Say it in a loud voice. Don't shout it, but just say it louder than you usually do."

"Yes, sir."

"And take Uncle Dan with you." He handed me the leash.

"Yes, sir."

"What's your name again, young man?"

"Sifter, sir. Corey."

"You've always done an admirable job, Corey. Now close the door."

When I entered Morley's it took a moment for my eyes to adjust to the dimness of the dining room, but when they did I saw that Glenn Burrant was in there. He was eating by himself, a steak and two baked potatoes. He didn't look up when I entered, and I didn't say anything to him as I passed his table. He was looking down at his plate, working at his steak like a man digging a hole in the ice, and drinking from what looked like a tumbler of Scotch. Morley's was also an inn, and there was one other diner in the restaurant, a young woman in a flowered hat and dark glasses who looked like what I imagined a schoolteacher on vacation might look like, sitting at a table in back near the house stairs with some wine and a pad of paper in front of her. She nodded slightly as I passed, and when she saw the dog, she smiled.

I walked quickly to the bar and said what Henry Bonwiller had asked me to, in a voice that I raised a little from my normal one. The bartender poured the Coke for me. He poured it in a real glass, even though I told him I was taking it out, and the woman at the table looked up as I protested. But the bartender dismissed me with a wave, and the woman looked away. On the way out, she glanced up once more and smiled, as though she meant to help me, and she reached to pat Uncle Dan's head. I stopped for just a moment, then said excuse me and gave a quick tug on the leash. Once I was past the tables,

Glenn Burrant finally looked up, a fact I know because I was watching the mirror by the coatracks.

At the car I handed the Coke to Senator Bonwiller, who promptly moved across the backseat and emptied it out the far door onto the pavement. Then he handed me the empty glass and let Uncle Dan leap in next to him. On our way back to his house in Islington, he ordered me to stop at Ferland's, where I bought two roast beef sandwiches—one was for the dog—and at McBride's, where I picked up a bottle of French wine. Then I drove him home.

There are several different ways you can interpret that afternoon now, but none of them leads you anywhere clear. It might have been a coincidence that Glenn Burrant was in there. Or it might have been that he was there because he wanted to find out what was going on in Henry Bonwiller's private life. But of course it hasn't escaped my attention that he might also have been there to warn the Senator away.

And to this day, people occasionally ask me if during my time at the Metareys' I ever met JoEllen Charney. It's not a question I like to answer, for inevitably it leads the conversation in a direction that I don't want it to go. So usually I tell them the literal truth, which is that I never did.

TRIESTE MILLBURY HAD TO BEAT OUT quite a bit of competition for *The Speaker-Sentinel*'s internship. Carrol County has four high schools now and plans for a fifth, and for that single opening we received more than a hundred applications. But Trieste's stood right out. She was the youngest of six sisters and brothers rotating through the four bunks and the queen-size pullout in their trailer, their father an obviously brilliant man whose brilliance caused him to reject both a job and the social order. Trieste was considered a townie. This was unusual, since her family had been in the area only half a generation. But they had nothing to do with the engineers or the middle managers or even the professional office staff that the locals now call the newkies; and so by default they were townies. For money the Millburys grow raspberries and blueberries. Their trailer is parked along a marsh—someone else's marsh—and they sell their berry crop from the back of their hand-painted station wagon.

Trieste's mother is evidently quite an artist, and the quarter panels of that car are streaked with French Impressionist strands of yellow and green so that they look just like the field of overgrown grasses in which it's parked most days, next to their trailer—which is itself painted to look like the sky. On summer Sundays I used to see Trieste standing beside the station wagon at the intersection of Ontario Street and the highway, working a scale made from a pole and plastic milk jugs. This was our hand-selected intern and our best local candidate for the Ivy League in the last five years. I'd bought berries from her before we hired her—before I had any idea what she was like—and even then I could hear in her northern hillbilly voice what I later came to learn was her father's social opposition. A thin flow of bile mixed with a radical amusement and a fierce, uncooked intelligence, nourished over decades of contemplation. Class upon class.

As I grew to know her, Trieste told me of her father's experimentation: he'd been a chemist at DuPont before switching to berries. He and Trieste's mother had schooled all six children themselves, in the trailer—which was divided, like the parents, into arts and sciences. The part near the ladder door was her father's; the part near the pullout awning, her mother's. They had begun from what Trieste called God's Principles. When I questioned her further I found out that by God she meant the sun. The Sun. This is what the Millbury family had decided was God.

"It satisfies all the criteria," Trieste said, looking at me challengingly her first day in the office.

"Such as?"

"Such as, it gave us life. It sustains life. We can know it only in death."

"How do you mean, only in death?"

"I mean the source of its energy. Two protons. Nuclear fusion. The hydrogen bomb. The death of mankind."

"Ah," I said.

So, you see. That is the kind of girl Trieste is. At seventeen, brighter—far brighter—than I will ever be. But dressed in the same flimsy, imitation wardrobe that I used to wear, and slowed by the same awkward stride. She wore boys' clothes, as a matter of fact; but there was always something—a daisy in a buttonhole, a painted rock on a string at her wrist—that winked at you.

We've become friends of a kind. Or that is to say, when she's not bothering me, I like her. I don't know how she feels about me, on the other hand, because her demeanor toward adults, at least toward all the adults I see her speaking to, is cryptic. Curious. Diligent. Attentive. Often oddly polite; but always cryptic—as though she is one line ahead of you in the joke.

She also has the aspect of one who will eventually tell you the joke—just not for a while. I've grown used to her curious questions and the traces of her needling smiles. And to her strange way of moving from opposition to cooperation, too, or the other way around, in an instant. All of it, I have to say, I find charming. But what could I teach her? For her first feature story, two weeks into her new job, she proposed a piece on the Shelter River, which forms the eastern border of Carrol County and used to be the roadway on which Eoghan Metarey floated his fortune to the mill.

"It's carcinogenic," she said.

"What is?"

"The water." She stood before my desk, drinking from the bottle of milk she brings in every morning. "Actually," she said, "it's mutagenic."

"Mutagenic." I was going over the figures for our most recent month of advertising. Like every other paper, *The Speaker-Sentinel* offers a Web edition now, so the numbers were decent—we were in a solid enough position in spite of the current state of the independent press in America.

"There's a difference, sir. I can't say whether it's actually carcinogenic. Not all mutagens are carcinogens—of course." She was using a patient voice. "But it's still alarming."

"Of course, Trieste. And how do you know all this?"

"I tested it."

"You tested it."

"Yes."

I took a drink of my skim-milked coffee and looked at her. Her expression was flat; yet there was that particular humor in the features. "You tested it yourself?"

"Of course."

"And how did you do that?"

"With an Ames test."

"Ah," I said. "Your father." I smiled equally patiently. "The chemist."

"My father had nothing to do with it."

"Trieste," I said. "Sit down."

She did. Her pants, a pair of chinos with a tiny yellow flower embroidered at the ankle, were nearly worn through at the knees. She'd come to work in them every day so far.

"Trieste," I said. "What did you say the name of that test was?"

"The Ames test, sir. Bruce Ames invented it. A biologist." Then she added, "Not a chemist."

"Fine. But let me explain—what the reporter does is interview the scientist who's performed the Ames test. The reporter doesn't perform the Ames test herself."

"Why is that, sir?"

"I suppose the first reason is because we're not experts."

"It's a petri dish, sir, and a culture medium and some histidine-deficient salmonella in growth conditions. You don't need to be an expert."

"Obviously not," I said. A couple of reporters behind her were trying not to laugh.

"So then why shouldn't I do it myself?"

"Because you might get it wrong, for one."

"But nobody else is doing it."

"That's right," I said. "And that's what you write your story about. You get me? That nobody is testing our river water. And you interview people who'll tell you that."

"But that's dull," she said.

"Pardon me?"

"That's dull. And staged."

"Perhaps, but that's the function of the press."

She looked at me with her needling smile. "In that case, then," she said, "I'll look forward to trying it."

And she did. She poked around the biology department at the community college, and one thing led to another, and she made a trip to Buffalo, and then one to Albany—hitchhiking—and two months later the same result was announced by the EPA in New York City: dioxin from the Cold Creek paper mill ten miles upriver. It was the first feature she wrote, and it made the front page. The other reporters weren't laughing anymore.

But even after her big success she was still appearing at our offices at dawn. We're a morning paper with a nighttime deadline, and it's safe to say that at dawn most of our other reporters are still settling in for their best sleep of the night. I'm an early riser, myself, and I've always worked hard. But every morning when I arrived I would find Trieste's bike already leaning up against the post of the arched footbridge that crosses the gulley in front of our grounds, its handlebars gleaming with dew. One morning shortly after that first article, in fact, I showed up a few minutes later than usual and found her lying down on the span.

"There you are," she said, yawning.

"Right you are," I answered, "here I am. Were you sleeping?"

"I try not to."

"You try not to sleep?"

"Sleep is a waste, sir."

"That's a very ambitious statement, Trieste."

"It's a very miserly statement, sir. Ambition is something else."

"I suppose you're right, I suppose you're right."

Well—what else do you say to a seventeen-year-old girl who talks like that? The sun, though not much higher than the treetops, was already shining powerfully. I pointed. "Were you worshipping, then?" I asked.

Her face had a pained look, as though she expected me to differ utterly from the commonplace, even as her employer; but she didn't answer.

"Good thing I wasn't driving across, kid," I offered. This was the kind of mildly threatening sarcasm that at first had taken me aback in my own teachers at Dunleavy.

"I'm shorter than an axle, sir. You could have missed me and still been on time." She glanced at her watch. "Almost."

"Ah—but your cranium is broader than half a wheel." I don't know how this kind of repartee has come to me, other than from those days at Dunleavy.

"In that case, you would no doubt have enjoyed waking me."

And I don't know how it has come to her. I laughed at her comment, and after a moment she laughed at mine. But just as I laughed at much of what she said over the time we knew each other—and just as she laughed in response—I nonetheless had the feeling that there was much more to it than we ever talked about. That all the inconsequential lines she muttered that year, and all the small talk and asides that she parried my needling with, were in fact deadly assessments of both of us.

My wife says all of this is in my imagination. That Trieste knew me no better than any other seventeen-year-old knows a middle-aged figure of authority—that is, only in regard to herself: as protector, employer, parent, maybe as teacher. Anything more was simply my invention. And my wife is a clear-eyed judge of character. But I disagree with her here. Trieste was very bright—exceptionally bright, I would say—and the truth, I think, is that she recognized me even before I recognized her.

IN MID-AUGUST, five full months ahead of the earliest primary, the papers first reported Henry Bonwiller's lead. It was a Harris poll, and the margin was narrow; but it was there. Four percentage points. The economy was flat, inflation was rising, and President Nixon, in a tight corner, had announced wage and price freezes. But they weren't enough, said editorial writers all across the country. By now there were peace marches in every big city, too. "We are in urgent need of change," wrote *The Washington Post*, "and we believe either Senator Muskie of Maine or Senator Bonwiller of New York is in the best position to provide it."

That weekend, the campaign threw a party. Six hundred people were invited; I would estimate that almost a thousand arrived. Gil McKinstrey drove downstate to pick up five butchered hogs and twenty turkeys. One of the house cooks made a glaze from maple syrup and Coke, and by the time the work crew arrived to set up the tent, the hogs had turned a cracked, molasses brown over the spits. June Metarey herself was in charge of the preparations. By noon there seemed to be nothing left to do but refill the ice chests and wait under the awnings in our party clothes.

Early in the afternoon, from above the stand of Norway maples to the south, the first plane came in, a sleek white private jet so close to the ground I could read its tail numbers. It banked over the tent, crossed above the work barn, and disappeared over the sycamores toward the strip. Not a minute later, another appeared. The noise shook the ground and by some oddity of the hills seemed to precede the planes from the direction they were heading. Soon enough, a half dozen more had come in, shaking the poles as their shadows streaked over the vaulted canopy.

Mrs. Metarey had hired real barmen to help Gil McKinstrey for the evening, four Scottish brothers from MacGladdie's Tavern in Islington who had closed their own business for the day—this gives an idea of the Metarey wages—and were already working steadily by three o'clock, before the party was even officially scheduled to begin. The barkeeps stood in their tuxedo vests and folded-back shirtsleeves, handling the bottles by their necks and mixing the drinks with both hands while the early, boisterous crowd of rich Scots and Italians and Irishmen pressed in on them. Henry Bonwiller hadn't yet arrived, and in his absence, a number of men had gathered around Liam Metarey, who was standing on the lawn outside the tent.

A short time later, when the crowd had filled in close to its full strength—Gil McKinstrey had had to set up two more bars—I heard a more familiar drone. I went to the edge of the tent and looked up just in time to see Aberdeen Red appear over the sycamores. It was flying so slowly that by the time it had descended over the entrance drive and crossed toward the riding corral and the fly pools, the crowd at the periphery was coming outside for a view themselves. A biplane can maneuver so well that from certain angles it can appear to almost stop in the air. That's what it did now, and as it crossed in front of the tent we could see two figures in the double open cockpit, one behind the other. Both of them were wearing leather helmets, and when a cheer started at the edge of the crowd and hands went up, Henry Bonwiller pulled his off and waved it in the air. Mrs. Metarey banked the plane in front of us, pulled off her own helmet, and waved to the crowd, too, and I realized from the initial silence, then the pointing and the murmuring and the gathering cheers, that most of the guests didn't know she could fly. She circled the tent and banked for her approach, and I don't know why—it might have been the boldest thing I'd ever done—but I ran out to the newly mowed grass at the far end of Breighton's corral, where I'd realized she was going to land.

When she touched down, she let Aberdeen Red run up to the hillock by the stables. This gave the Senator a stage, and when she finally stopped I was right alongside them, in view of the whole tent. Even as a boy I had the sense not to try to help Senator Bonwiller climb down from his seat but went straight to the pilot's berth and helped June Metarey instead, although we both knew she could have done a cartwheel on the wing if she'd wanted to. She cut the engine and let the propeller wind down, and then she allowed me to hand her onto the grass. Henry Bonwiller himself had climbed out onto the lower wing, like a barnstormer, and he leaned from the struts and waved. Voices were shouting—*Senator Bon! Senator Bon!*—and when I turned toward the cheering I missed the sight of him jumping onto the grass. But in a moment I felt his leather helmet sliding down over my head and then my hand being pulled up in the air. I wondered if Christian was watching.

"How many?" he said in his low voice.

"Twelve hundred," I answered, without turning my gaze. Press photographers were raising their cameras on poles. "Maybe thirteen."

"Good, son. Good."

All afternoon, clots of men circled him. Nobody who knew him well ever called him Senator Bon, but I heard all kinds of men do it that day, raising their drinks and shouting it over the top of the crowd, shaking his hand jovially and smiling broadly as they exclaimed it with a head leaned forward, as if in some kind of intimate congratulations.

For his own part, Henry Bonwiller looked like the groom at a wedding: a garrulous and self-deprecating haleness to his expression, the great jaw tilted back in laughter at the remarks of a patron, then the outstretched hand drawing another suitor into the coterie, the nods and animation of the reddened face slowed and deepened by the imminent satisfaction of what even a teenager could see was a profound and long-standing ambition.

At one point late in the afternoon, as I was setting up a keg of beer on the bar stand, a man's voice behind me said, "Old son of a bitch would turn in his grave."

I knelt and hooked up the coupling. As soon as the tap was flowing, Glenn Burrant leaned down on the ice barrel and filled his glass.

"Who would?" I said.

"Eoghan Metarey. Fellow who built this castle." He was panting from the effort of leaning. "Biggest skinflint this side of the garment district. Old bastard wouldn't stand it half an hour." He rose again and surveyed the throng. Next to us, Gil McKinstrey was mixing and pouring and shaking drinks, handing them across the bar two at a time in each hand to men in expensive suits. At the buffet beyond him, a hired boy was carving the roast pig as fast as his arm would move. Plates were being filled up and carried back into the crowd. "There are two things that are important in politics," Glenn went on. "The first is money." He blew the foam off his beer. "And I can't remember what the second one is."

"You can't?"

He grimaced. "That's a line, kid. A famous one." He leaned down to fill his glass to the top again. "But it says it as well as anything."

"I guess so, sir."

"Every other generation," he went on, sipping the beer down from the rim. "One makes it." He found a chair and leaned back to take a longer drink. "One spends it."

"Did you know him?"

"Know who—Eoghan Metarey?"

"Yes."

He laughed. "How old do you think I am?"

"I don't know."

"I'm thirty-six, kid. The old man's been in the ground since I was on my momma's knee." He drank again. "Good thing, too," he said.

"Why's that?"

He looked at me. "You don't want to know," he answered. "Not from me, at least." He raised the glass again and tilted it high on his lips. But in the middle of drinking, he suddenly lowered it and peered around me. "My God," he said. "Look at that."

"What?"

He pointed. Behind me was an opening in the crowd, and at the far end of it stood the stoop-backed man with the two canes: Trawbridge.

"Looks like the *Times* is following old Glenn Burrant around," he said.

"Sir?"

"George Vance Trawbridge," he said, pointing again. "G.V. to you and me. Most famous political writer in America." He wiped his mouth with the back of his sleeve and straightened his shirt. "And best one, too, in this reporter's opinion. Chief correspondent for *The New York Times*. Eating roast pig in Saline with the rest of us. Can't get his coat off the hanger by himself but he's got as much to do with picking the American president as anybody in the republic."

"Hunchback of Times Square," I said.

He almost spat his beer. "Where'd you hear that?"

"He's been here before."

He looked at me closely. "And he'll be here again, comrade, if your man Bonwiller is lucky."

With that, he set down the glass, rose with some effort, and moved into the crowd, where he approached G. V. Trawbridge and extended his hand. Trawbridge took it, shifting his canes and raising his strikingly large head to say something that was evidently funny. Glenn leaned forward with his palms on his knees to laugh, and G. V. Trawbridge let his head fall again until it bounced up and down on his chest. Then the throng closed in front of them.

By now it was almost dark and the citronella torches were being brought out from the shed. The bartenders at Gil McKinstrey's direction had begun watering their shots, and the band crew had moved onto the platform. I stepped to the outskirts of the tent and began walking the periphery, making sure the rolling carts of china were stocked and all the plates were taken from the chairs and tables. But really, I was there so I could get a better look at the crowd. I still hadn't seen Christian.

At ten o'clock, the local string trio stepped down and the great Ray White Blues Quintet took the stage. The tall torches were lit and the shadows of the pole streamers began to writhe on the striped ceiling of the tent. By then, I'd already seen half a dozen guests go around the bend. In the light of the path lamps I saw a man walk into one of the fly-casting pools and start a thrashing stroke across; then another man waded in to pull him out. Everywhere around the tent, there was shouting and hand-slapping and a frantic liquor-fueled strategizing among the Senator's courtiers. Even I could see it. It was the first time

I'd witnessed the making of a politician: how the ritual of deference precedes the auction of influence, and eventually the orgy of slaughter.

But it wasn't until almost midnight, when Ray White himself jumped up on the piano bench and took off on a baritone sax solo, that the energy of the crowd came to a boil. Couples were dancing now in a clearing by the stage. Past them on the lawn, a fistfight erupted among three guests in the parking area and was over in a few moments. They got into their cars. At the stroke of the hour, fireworks came up from the west, above the Lodge Chief Marker, covering the sky in showers of red, white, and blue, and the crowd surged onto the great lawn to watch. By then, I'd lost track completely of Henry Bonwiller. The throng seemed actually to have grown larger, and the barmen from MacGladdie's had gone over to filling their shots without taking the glasses out of their customers' hands. I could barely make my way around.

That's when Christian found me. She didn't say anything, merely came up from behind, took my hand, and led me out to the lawn. I turned to watch the colors in the sky, but she pulled me along the stables toward the back of the house. I'd had a bourbon on the rocks a few minutes earlier, handed over without a word by Gil McKinstrey, and as I followed her around the corner of the main house the liquor began to sing its little tune. The stomping of the quintet quieted, and by a trick of acoustics the entire party seemed to disappear. I could hear the sounds of the land again—our footfalls on the round river gravel of the walkway and Breighton's neighing from the barn. Christian still hadn't spoken. When she was intent on something I knew by now just to follow, but with the liquor and the sudden quiet her bearing had the effect on me somehow of a premonition. We flushed a pair of rabbits from the bushes and in the wavering blue and red light they bounded before us under the steps.

She led me onto the porch, then along the inside staircase to the rear balcony. We stood at the far edge now, overlooking the backyard. From around the corner another sound had come into our hearing: a popper landing in the fly pool. Someone was casting. I could hear the tiny slap of the landing, then the pluck of retrieval. She moved to the far corner; from there we could see the oblong lagoons shimmering in the colored light, and the pale rings of the floating targets. "Do you know who that is?" she said.

I leaned out. "Your father?"

"Look closer."

I did. From this vantage I saw that obviously it wasn't Liam Metarey. A man was casting wildly in the direction of the buoys, each throw fed by two or three whipping false casts in the air behind him. Liam Metarey's own left-handed cast, which I'd seen in the early mornings through the windows of the toolshed, was methodical and unhurried, a pitcher's delivery evident in the three gearlike steps of its unfurling. But whoever this was seemed to be trying to hurl the popper all the way to the end of the pool by sheer force of muscle. Then the silhouette split and a slighter figure appeared in the shifting light. "Looks like there's two of them," I said.

"Yes," said Christian. "One of them's my sister. Now, who's the other?"

I looked closer. It did appear to be Clara's slender posture now standing next to the boulders beside the pool. The man before her was still casting wildly. It was impossible to trace the path of the line, but from his movements the popper might have been landing in the driveway twenty yards beyond the water.

"It's Gil McKinstrey—" I said.

She laughed. "You're too sweet for your own good, Corey," she said. Then her look darkened. "And you still don't know my sister, do you? Look a little closer."

I did: I couldn't discern the profile. And then, while I was waiting for the figure to move out of the shadow of the boulders, I think I saw Clara raise her head and look up at the balcony where we were standing.

"That's why he's never going to win," said Christian.

"What?"

"That's why he's never going to win. The party's still going on. Do you think anybody knows he's out here?"

"It's Henry Bonwiller?"

"My father's out front handling the party for him. He *threw* the party for him. Daddy's making friends for him. He's setting everything up. The head of Goldman Sachs and Lazard Frères are in that tent. So's Elysis Vanderbilt and Vance Trawbridge. Henry Bonwiller for president. And what's Henry Bonwiller doing? He's back here with my sister, drunk, throwing a sopping fly. Look at him out there. He's going to break my father's heart."

How long Mrs. Metarey had been standing behind us, I don't know. But now she said, "Don't worry, sweetheart. Nothing could break your father's heart."

We turned. She was in the open doorway of the house. Behind her a hat-check girl was rolling a rack of coats onto the service elevator. "It's a little heart made of clay and water," Mrs. Metarey said, as she stepped out onto the balcony, nearly tripping in a broken heel as she crossed and lit another cigarette from the spent one in her hand. "It's a little tiny heart all mixed up in a mixing bowl with sugar and flower petals and celery stalks and—Oh, my God! That's Clara!"

I thought she had seen at the outset.

"Clara can take care of herself, Mother."

But Mrs. Metarey was already stumbling back to the door. "Liam!" she shouted into the hallway. "Liam!"

Even now I think about those days, and there are times I wish I could have them back, to live them again, not because of the exhilaration or wonder they held for me, but only because I think I would have taken something different from them now, with what I've learned. We have our own three daughters, and the youngest, as I've mentioned, is now just a little older than I was that summer, and I see in her everything from my wife's nervy wanderlust to my father's politeness to my mother's diligent faith in the future; but as I stood on the balcony that night with Christian, watching Mrs. Metarey call frantically through the house and stumble first one way and then the other past the lighted door on her broken shoe, I had no reason to look at the situation from the perspective of a parent. What did Mrs. Metarey mean by calling her husband's name? At the time I assumed she was calling him to do something, that she was summoning him from the party to go out to the pond and bring back their daughter from the inebriated influence of Henry Bonwiller. And as an assistant in that house I felt the urge to take a stand myself, to go fetch Clara because that's what Liam Metarey would have done if he had been there.

Behind us, the hallway lights went on. I pulled my hand from Christian's and moved a few steps toward the door, but she knew enough about the situation—she no doubt understood far more than I did—that she followed me across the balcony and took my hand again. From inside I could hear Mrs. Metarey still calling her husband's name, her voice hoarse now as it came out first through one window on the stairs and then through the next, heading down. I don't think it was until my first daughter had turned fourteen, though, and had snuck out one weekend against our wishes, taking a Greyhound bus to the Syracuse football game when she had told us she was sleeping at a friend's house, that I realized why Mrs. Metarey was staggering through the halls shouting her husband's name: she was blaming him.

From the railing I could see that Clara had sat down again at the edge of the fly pool. My hand was still being held, and I understood from the firmness of the grip that I was not going to be saving anyone. Then, as we watched, Henry Bonwiller set aside the fly rod, pulled Clara up by her two hands, and turned toward the boulder, where the two silhouettes came together in the darkness.

That's when Christian turned and kissed me. I must say, this time I was ready. I reached and pulled her in. Where we stood now, closer to the stone walls of the house, the music had somehow reasserted itself, a distant, tamped melody as though mutes had been placed in the horns and the lid on the piano closed halfway; but the surprise of her mouth this time, even with the liquor and the music and the smell of the gunpowder and citronella mingling inside me, could not overcome what even in my heightened state seemed like something forced to the wrong conclusion. She was awkward but not hesitant. She pulled me in harder. But even then it didn't seem like Christian I was kissing. The Christian I'd kissed before—that time too, I realized, we'd been watching Clara—*that* Christian was amused and slightly hesitant; not from fear, but from some suggestion of experience that seemed to make her wary. Like a queen wiser than her subject. But now there was no hesitation. I wondered if Gil had mixed anything for her. Again she pulled me tighter. After a time, I opened my eyes over her shoulder and saw that Clara and Henry Bonwiller— if that's who they were—were a single shape against the glittering flats of the casting pools.

That's when we heard the impact. It was a tremendous sound—the house itself shook—and after a moment of confusion my mind went with terror to the planes.

We ran down from the balcony. Already guests from the party were running, too, over toward the barn, although I could see others moving elsewhere in the periphery of torchlight from the tent. Churchill was barking. Several men had gathered near the stables, and one of them sprinted across the riding ring, jumped the split-rail fence, and continued west through the fields in the direction of the landing strip. All this took place under the shifting red and blue light from the fireworks on the hill. Someone else was making his way with a lantern around the parking circle at the front of the house. Several of the maids had appeared on the balcony, at the spot Christian and I had just left, and were standing at the rail looking toward the barn. At the same time the party continued. Guests were dancing and the band was playing and a crowd pressed as it had all night against the torch-lit bars. I held Christian's hand as we made our way through milling bodies toward the casting pools: that's where I thought the sound had come from.

To be looking for two such different things while in a state of agitation and mild drunkenness, and to be holding Christian by her warm hand at the same time, to be running in a crowded night full of distant music and the quiet thud of fireworks, to tell the truth, had filled me not with dread or duty but with a deep and unexpected longing that seemed to live like vapor in the warm air itself. I gripped her even harder. We ran onto the grounds and made our way through other running figures. Flashlights darted.

What we found finally was Clara standing against the dislodged post at the corner of the work barn, smoking a cigarette, and Henry Bonwiller pulling on the door of Mrs. Metarey's car, which rested halfway through the collapsed wooden wall of the building. He was trying to open it to get to her. Mrs. Metarey sat motionless in the driver's seat, her eyes closed, leaning back against the headrest under the yellow glow of the dome light. Churchill was barking frantically and circling. The collision had pulled the siding down around the Galaxy like a curtain, and Henry Bonwiller pushed his way through a gap in it as he crossed to the other side and tried the passenger door, which wouldn't open, either. Mrs. Metarey wasn't moving.

"Mother's missed the garage door going in," said Clara. She took a drag off her cigarette. "Which Church and I find rather amusing."

"Though rather surprising," said Christian. "Seems she missed the garage itself, didn't she?"

"For Christ's sake, both of you," I said. "Is she all right?"

"Perfectly," said Clara. "Seems she thought the door was on this side. Church thinks she might have got the buildings confused."

I went around and tried the passenger door, also, and when it wouldn't open I looked in at Mrs. Metarey sitting perfectly still with her eyes closed and her head resting back. By now a group of onlookers had arrived, and someone switched on a light. Mrs. Metarey's chin was pointed up at the roof, her neck lit at its obtuse angle. I sniffed for gasoline, then tried to get my hand in above the rear-door window, which was open a couple of inches.

Clara went to the windshield and rapped on it. "Mother, unlock the door."

She did then, dreamily, as though half waking from sleep, and

Henry Bonwiller finally opened it. But Mrs. Metarey refused his help. She merely stood, brushed her dress, and headed out across the lawn again, toward the tent. Then the garage was filled with dozens of men, guards and tent workers and aides of the Senator, and in a moment Mr. Metarey himself was there, surveying the damage with what looked like a slight smile on his face before he took Henry Bonwiller by the arm and led him back toward the party.

ONE WEEKDAY AFTERNOON, my wife and I were driving into town in a downpour when we came upon a woman walking ahead of us on the road. The rain was drenching, the kind we get up here on the eastern shore of the lake, but her stride looked leisurely, as though she were out on an unhurried afternoon stroll. Only as we pulled closer did I realize who it was. Trieste has a distinctive, pulled-in stance to her shoulders that makes her look just slightly embarrassed—even though embarrassed is the last thing she is—and from fifty yards back I could see those shoulders cutting their determined way through the weather. She was wearing a dark slicker, and as we drew behind her, I saw that it had been made from trash bags.

Two were taped together for the body, two more for the sleeves, and a third pair for the pants, which flared over her shoes. On top of it another had been fashioned into a broad-brimmed rain hat, with flaps like a sheik's that came down to her shoulders. All in all, it was quite an impressive outfit. My instinct was to congratulate her—but that isn't the way we've come to speak to each other. As I pulled up alongside, her obtuse smile appeared.

"Testing the rain?" I said.

"Very funny," she answered. "Actually, I was testing the coat."

"Would you like a ride into town, Trieste?" said my wife.

"No thank you, ma'am," she answered. She held out her arm and drops splattered off the sleeve. "But if either of you wants to walk with me, I'd be honored." She pulled a roll of unused bags from inside the jacket. "I can make another of these in two and a half minutes."

"Are you sure we can't take you somewhere?" asked my wife.

"I'm sure," she answered. "But I'd be happy for company. If you don't mind the puddles, it's quite beautiful out, actually."

"I think we'll keep testing the car," I answered.

"So, COREY," Mr. Metarey said as I was running the sander over a coat of Bondo on his wife's car, "I see you're getting the hang of it."

"Almost done, sir."

I was the one he'd asked to repair the damage to the Galaxy. It wasn't serious. She'd merely driven through a wall of cedar siding that had probably been drying there for fifty years. By the next afternoon, Gil McKinstrey had replaced the broken boards with a set that looked just as old as the originals and had already been painted the same fading, farm-machine green. The only significant damage to the car had come from the knee-high standpipe along the wall, which had left a foot-long crimp in the front fender. Other than that, you couldn't even tell it had been in a scrape. Liam Metarey had rigged up a dent puller in his metal lathe, and I'd spent most of the afternoon fixing the damage. I'd filled the screw holes with Bondo, and was getting ready to prime it. There was a shop in town that would do the final painting. The shop in town would have fixed the dent, too, if that had been the way Mr. Metarey worked.

"Good, good," he said, running his hand over where I'd feathered out the Bondo into the gloss. "You've got mechanical talent, like your dad." He patted me on the back. "And on top of that, you like to read the newspaper. That's a rare mix. When it's ready to be final painted, by the way, perhaps you'll tell my wife."

"Yes, sir."

"She's in the library." He pulled a cigar from his pocket, sniffed it, and bit off the end. "Unfortunately," he said, lifting a match to it, "she's not in there reading." He smiled through the smoke. "I'm afraid she's not in the mood to hear much from me at the moment, either. But you'll do better. She'll want to choose a color, I suppose. Might as well get a new color out of all this."

"I'll tell her."

"Thank you, Corey. That would be a favor." He leaned closer to the car. "Nice job with the sanding especially," he said.

Late in the afternoon, though I wasn't sure exactly what I was supposed to do, I entered the house and asked the cooks if they'd seen Mrs. Metarey. They told me she was still in the library. I wasn't used to going up there without bottles and glasses for the balcony bar in my arms, or at least the morning's newspapers on their sticks, but I climbed the steps anyway to the landing, composing my words.

I found her sitting at the long reading table, looking out the window. "Excuse me, Mrs. Metarey," I said from the hallway. "Pardon me. We were wondering what color you'd like the car painted."

"Sorry?"

I stayed in the hallway. "Mr. Metarey and I were wondering what color you'd like us to paint the car."

"Well," she said. "What color is it now?"

"*Your* car, I mean. The Galaxy."

"Yes, I said—what color is it now?"

"Well, it's black, Mrs. Metarey."

"Then paint it white."

"Yes, ma'am."

I turned to go.

"Wait a second," she said. "Come in here."

She gestured me in, and I entered. "Oh!" I said. "Hi, Christian."

"Hi, Corey." She was sitting on the floor in the corner. On the reading table was a tumbler and alongside it one of Liam Metarey's decanters.

"How old are you, Corey?" said Mrs. Metarey.

"Sixteen."

"A good age to learn then."

"Mother—"

"Those people at the party, Corey—all those men who flew in from Albany and Boston—they're nothing but sharks—"

"Corey's fine, Mother."

"And we all know what Henry Bonwiller is. Don't we now?"

"You don't know that, Mother."

"Please, darling. I'm only stating the obvious." She turned to me. "I'm sure Corey would agree?"

"Well—" I said.

"And don't let me forget New York City. *Especially* the ones from New York City. And the reporters, too." She took a drink. "*Especially* the reporters. Vile animals, every one of them."

"The reporters are fine, Mother."

"They're all here drinking our bourbon and eating our food, but what they're really doing is circling Henry Bonwiller," Mrs. Metarey said. "They're smelling for his blood." She sniffed the air. "And for my husband's, too. You understand?"

"Well—"

"Corey doesn't need to hear any of this." She turned to me. "Corey, you don't have to stay in here. You must have plenty to do outside."

"But they don't want to destroy him," Mrs. Metarey went on. "Not yet, at least. You know why they want his blood?"

"Mother—"

"*Shhh!*"

"No, I don't," I said.

"So they can control him."

"Wow," said Christian. "A revelation. Really, Corey. You don't have to listen to this."

"I see," I said.

"You understand the difference?"

"I think so."

"And Senator Henry Bonwiller is letting them smell plenty of it, isn't he?"

"Mother, please!"

"My husband would be the first to tell you. If he wasn't so damn loyal, that is. Loyal to his own enemies. Loyal to the sharks." She drank again. "Come here, Corey."

"And now," said Christian, standing, "the curtain opens."

Mrs. Metarey stood and walked to the back of the room, where she leaned against one of the tall wainscot panels until a hidden door abruptly slid open. She crossed inside and beckoned me after her. I glanced in. The space seemed to be a small office, with a desk and a telephone and shelves lining the walls. But the shelves weren't filled with books. They were filled with wrapped parcels of all shapes and colors. "Now tell me, Corey," she said, "what in her majesty's ripped slip do you think all of this is?"

"It looks like an office."

Christian crossed the room and stood behind me. "It's the dungeon," she said. "Those are the chains."

"That's right," said Mrs. Metarey. "It's an office." She pointed to the rows of boxes. "And do you know what all these are?"

"No."

"They're gifts."

"I see."

"From *well-wishers*," she said. She reached over and retrieved a large box, wrapped in gold paper. "This is from Dale Vinson. Dale Vinson is the biggest oil and gas man in New England. Do you think Dale Vinson wishes Henry Bonwiller or my husband well?"

"I wouldn't know."

She laughed. "Dale Vinson does not wish either of them well."

"Mother, you don't know that."

She looked sharply at Christian. "Sweetheart, Henry Bonwiller doesn't need to give any more help to his assassins."

"They're not all his assassins, Mother. You're making too much of this."

"Am I really?" she raised her eyebrows. "Corey, do you know what well-wishers are?"

"I think I do, Mrs. Metarey."

"Well-wishers," she said, "are people who wish you'd fall down the well."

I laughed.

Christian looked at me. "Grandfather used to say that," she said.

"That's right," said Mrs. Metarey. "And don't you forget it. None of this would be here without your grandfather. Corey, do you know who Eoghan Metarey was?"

"Yes," said Christian, "he does."

"He was a great man," said Mrs. Metarey. "That's what he was. He dug the coal mine and laid the railroad. He knew what the world needed and he knew how to get it."

"Corey knows all about him—"

"He wasn't anything like the Henry Bonwillers of the world," she went on. "You can bet on that. He did what needed to be done. He took care of the people who helped him. He was tough and he was disciplined and he was principled."

"Henry Bonwiller is principled," said Christian.

"Please—"

"In all the important ways, Mother, he is. I believe that."

"Oh, God—please don't get me started."

"You already *have* started, Mother," she said. "Corey, really—you don't have to stay here and listen to this."

"One of the reporters was just talking about him," I offered. "I mean Mr. Metarey's father, Eoghan Metarey."

"You think those are reporters, Corey?"

"Mother, now I really think you've said enough."

"Not nearly enough, sweetheart." She pointed at me with the wrapped box. "I was asking our guest a question."

"Who?" I said.

"Those bottom-feeders, Corey. Those bottom-feeders who come around for their bits. You think they're reporters?"

"I know Glenn Burrant is," I said.

"Glenn Burrant," she said, rolling her eyes as she said it. "Glenn *Burr*-ant," she repeated, giving venom to the name. She nearly spat it. "You think Glenn *Burr*-ant is a reporter?"

I looked at Christian. "Isn't he?"

"Glenn *Burr*-ant writes what he's told to write. Didn't you know that, Corey?"

"No, ma'am. I didn't."

"Do you think Glenn Burrant might be looking for a job in the new Bonwiller administration?"

"I guess I don't know the answer to that, Mrs. Metarey."

"I can pick up the phone right now and call Glenn *Burr*-ant and he'll write exactly what I tell him to in tomorrow's paper. Can't I, Christian?"

"Mother, you've had quite a bit now—"

"Shhhh! I haven't had nearly enough, is the problem." She pointed out the door at her tumbler on the library table and snapped her fingers. "Call me a friend of Glenn *Burr*-ant's," she started singing in a loud, tuneless voice. "He's had some problems with closing his pants—"

Then without warning she bumped down into the chair, laid her head on the desk, and began to sob. I stayed where I was by the door. The two of them seemed frozen, Christian standing by the shelves and Mrs. Metarey slumped in her chair, her tears gradually waning until finally she roused herself and dried her cheeks on her sleeve.

Then she lifted her head and picked up the phone. Midway through dialing, she paused to point at the tumbler again and snap her fingers at her daughter. Christian didn't move. She snapped again, so I went and retrieved it and set it in front of her. Christian wouldn't look at me.

Over the years, I've thought quite a bit about what happened next:

I think, finally, that Mrs. Metarey didn't have anyone on the other end of that line; that she merely wanted to pretend, even if just for me—a lackey in their house—that she was in command of what she alone must have realized was going to happen. I don't understand exactly how she knew it, or why she felt the need to do anything for my benefit, but I can't get around the fact that what she did next, she seemed to do for me. I don't think she was doing it for Christian. Years later, I found out that Mrs. Metarey's father had been a salesman in a men's clothing store in Arizona—it wasn't what I'd imagined—and I wonder if that might have been part of what she saw in me: that same under-stature of our backgrounds. Otherwise, I don't know why she would have cared.

I also don't know what it means about Glenn Burrant. Was he really a flunky? Or did he engage her fury because in fact he wasn't one at all? I grew up to do the same thing for a living that he did, and it's clear to me now that an undifferentiated silt-panning for truth serves the citizenry only slightly better than a crooked disregard for it. Glenn didn't teach me that, but I think he lived by it, and I come down in the end on his side. He must have known things about the Bonwiller campaign that set the family on edge; and he must have chosen to keep those things to himself. Where it went from there is anybody's guess. As I've said, it all begins to shimmer.

When she'd finished dialing, Mrs. Metarey said softly, "It's me," and picked up the tumbler.

"Here," Christian said, "give me that—"

Mrs. Metarey didn't bother to cover the phone. She gestured at the decanter. "I'll give it to you when I need it filled again, dear."

"Mother—"

"I want a story in tomorrow's paper," Mrs. Metarey said into the receiver. "That's right. Tomorrow's." She took a drink. "Then extend it. You heard me—*extend* it. A piece about Henry Bonwiller and Anodyne Energy. Mm-hmm." She shook her head.

It was the first time I'd heard that name—Anodyne Energy.

Then Christian said, "You're not really doing this, Mother." Those were her words. She turned to me and said, "She's not really doing this."

"Aren't I?" said Mrs. Metarey. "No," she said tersely. "Nothing that specific. Just insinuation." Then she hung up. She set both hands calmly on the desk and looked across at both of us. "Tomorrow," she said, "is the beginning of the end. A two-bit shill of a company called Anodyne Energy. You heard it here first. Did you hear it here first, Corey?"

"I did, ma'am."

"Good," she said. "Now, then—" she went on, snapping her fingers. "Now I'll take that refill, darling."

"SHE CALLS YOU DARLING?"

"She was talking to Christian. She calls me Corey. If she calls me anything."

"What happened after that?"

"I finished the car."

"Oh, Corey. You're seeing quite a circus over there—oh, look, here's a pair of size thirty-two chinos. I can shorten them."

We were in the back of Brownlee's department store in Islington together, leafing through the rows of pants on the sale racks. It was the first time in my life I'd heard the word *chinos*.

"Mrs. Metarey's usually not like that, Mom. She was upset about something."

She looked at me skeptically, then held the pants to my waist. "I know it's exciting, honey. But it's also so—so, oh, I don't know."

She waited.

"Cor, sweetie—" she said. "Pay attention. Let's see if these fit you."

Now, of course, Brownlee's is long gone. Like everything else around here, it's been upgraded. For a while in the eighties it was a

Dillard's, and then briefly a May's, and in 2003 the building was torn down and a Nordstrom went up, with underground parking and an indoor atrium that has real trees and grass in it. These days you can buy a green-tea chai downstairs, and if you prefer your Lake Erie sweatshirt to be made of organic cotton, that's not a problem, either. But in my childhood, for my family, Brownlee's was a very fancy place.

It was a three-story stone building with an elevator, and at every landing there was a refrigerated water fountain that made a humming noise when you pushed the button. The top floor was men's, the middle floor was women's, and the ground floor was everything else, from fishing rods to curtains. There were always bowls of mints at the cash registers, too, and as you stepped from the elevator into the men's department, a suit salesmen would greet you offering a glass of lemonade or a cup of coffee. Before we left the house that morning, my mother put on lipstick.

"I'll take the coffee," my father said as we stepped into the air-conditioned entranceway, "unless you have tea."

"I should have known, Granger," said the salesman—it never surprised me when anyone knew my father—"I'll make you a cup of tea." He turned. "And for Mrs. Sifter?"

"Nothing for us," my mother answered, glancing at my father. I knew her thinking, of course.

She took my elbow and started me toward the far wall, where the sale clothes were. This part of the store was empty. There weren't even any salesmen in the aisles, but as we walked along the racks she lowered her voice anyway. "We're going to get you what you need for school," she said. "Don't worry. But I'm sure two pairs of pants will be plenty. For a start, anyway—you're still growing. Your father will want to get more. I don't want you to listen."

"I won't," I said. "Two pairs of pants are fine with me."

"He'll want to buy the first things he sees, but if we wait a little, he'll leave us alone."

"Okay, Mom."

"And you'll have to learn to iron a shirt, too. I'm not going to be there to do it for you. Your father still hasn't learned to iron *his*, you know."

"He doesn't have to, Mom."

She eyed me. "All right, wise guy," she said. "If you get a stain on one, just soak it in the sink. Cold water. You'll need undershirts, too."

"Fine," I said. "I'll do that." Then I added, "If they have loafers, I wouldn't mind a pair."

We began sorting through the rack. Most of the sale pants were light summer wear, but after a few minutes of searching we'd found a couple of pairs of chinos and a few made of heavy wool for me to try on. She glanced between the rows of racks. "Okay," she said. "Quick. Let's go."

The door on the dressing-room stall went only as high as my neck, and when I looked over I could still see my father, all the way at the other end of the sales floor, leafing through a display of shirts near the register. From the tilt of his head I could tell that he was whistling, but I couldn't hear him. As I watched, the salesman approached with his tea and they stood there talking.

"What do you think of Mrs. Metarey, then?" my mother asked in a quiet voice.

"She's fine."

She stood and looked over the stall door. "I'm your mother," she whispered.

"I just told you a good story about her."

"What do you *think* of her, though?"

I buttoned the first pair of pants and opened the door. "She's all right."

"Those are too small. Try the next ones." Then, in a whisper again, she said, "Does she always drink like that?"

"I don't know."

I opened the door.

"Those are better," she said. "But they need to be bigger. They should be a little too big."

I went back in and pulled on a pair of the chinos.

"Does she scare you?" she whispered.

"Mom."

"It's okay. We're the only ones here."

I opened the door again. This was not the way my mother acted, certainly not in public.

"She seems unbalanced," she went on. "That's all." She crossed her arms and examined me. "Those are good. Set them aside." Then she added, "Or not very trustworthy, at least. Maybe that's it."

"She's adventurous, Mom. She flies a plane upside down."

She regarded me again.

"Now, Liam Metarey—" She whispered this even more softly. "Now, *he* seems trustworthy."

"He is."

She waited while I went back in and sorted through the rest of the pile.

"Corey," she finally said. "It wouldn't kill you to talk to me a little."

"I *am* talking, Mom. What's gotten into you?"

"I'm just curious about your life. We won't have many more chances."

"Okay," I said, pulling on a dark wool pair. "I can count on Mr. Metarey, I guess. You always know what he's going to be like. Christian's that way, too. Usually." I opened the door. "Clara's like her mom."

"Does Christian spend time with you?"

"What do you think of these?"

"They're good. But try the others."

I went back in.

"I'm just asking," she said.

"I know you're just asking. I guess I'd say yes, we like to spend time with each other."

"Well that's nice, at least."

"Thanks."

"What's that like for you?"

"What do you mean, what's that like?"

"What you're doing. Your father works on their houses. Her father's running for president."

"He's managing a campaign."

"You work on their land."

"We're in school together."

I opened the door again.

"No good," she said.

When I was back inside, she said, "Is there anything between you two?"

"Mom."

She waited.

"Well, maybe there is. *Maybe.* Something—I don't know. I'm not sure."

"That's nice, Cor. That's good. Don't think I object."

"Mom, I didn't think you'd object."

"But be careful."

"I am."

I opened the door.

"Okay," she said. "But try the last one. She was over at the house late at night once, wasn't she?"

I closed the door.

"A couple of months ago," she said.

"Oh—" I said. "—*That.*"

"Your father saw her go off the roof."

"I thought you were asleep."

"We were, until your father saw her go off the roof."

"Oh, well."

"The prices are better on the light ones," she said, "but I guess you need a dark pair, too." Then she added, "What about Clara?"

"Clara's never been over."

"I'm asking what's she like. I see she never went to reform school."

"Well, she doesn't like me, for one. I know *that.*"

"How do you know?"

"You don't have to be a genius."

"Why doesn't she, then? Did you not treat her well, Cor?"

"I don't know. I've never done anything to her. I just leave her alone."

"Maybe that's why she doesn't like you."

I glanced over the top of the slats. She was drinking from one of the cups next to the water fountain.

"Because you leave her alone," she said, looking up.

"Thanks for the advice."

"You might want to listen to me."

When I stood in front of her again, she said, "Oh, now those are nice."

We went to hang all the other ones back up, and on the way back to the register, she said, "This is more than you've ever told me, Cor."

"It's more than you've ever asked."

"From now on," she said, "this is how we're going to talk. Okay? Now that you're going away."

"Mom, really. It's ninety-four and a half miles. Mr. Metarey's timed it. I'll be home all the time."

"I know," she said. "But it will be different. You're heading off into a fancy new world and you're not going to need us anymore. But that's fine, really. I'm happy you're seeing the world. You'll find out one day yourself, Corey. I'm happy about it. And those pants are perfect."

"Then why are you crying?"

"Oh," she said. She touched her cheek.

"It's okay, Mom."

"Uh-oh, Cor," said my father, appearing now out of the aisle with a shopping bag in his hand. "Did you take something from the regular rack?"

"Oh, quiet, Granger."

"I think Mom's upset about me leaving, Dad."

"It's just that it's happening so soon," said my mother. She wiped her eyes and started half to laugh and half to cry—one of the things she did that always reminded me she'd once wanted to be an actress. "Oh, it's nothing," she said, sort of cheerfully gasping. "It's silly." Then she sat down to compose herself, drying her face with a tissue from her purse and puckering her lipstick. My father sat down next to her and put his hand on her leg. When he did that, she leaned forward and looked into his shopping bag. "Oh, no you don't," she said.

"He told me he wanted a pair," he said.

She looked at me.

"I just mentioned it to him, Mom."

"He needs them," said my father. "He needs a good pair."

"His black ones are perfectly fine, aren't they, Corey?"

"They're fine," I said.

"Nonsense, Anna. A man needs a good pair of shoes no matter what he's doing. Cor, your mother's afraid that if we buy a pair of shoes we won't have enough to eat."

"If your father did the shopping, we *wouldn't*."

"I don't need the shoes, Dad. I really don't."

But it turned out my father had already paid for them. They were a buttery dark brown; and that night after dinner, while he was in the living room listening to the Yankees game with Mr. McGowar, my mother finally said, "Oh, all right—come here then, and let me see those fancy things."

But she was the one who had already risen and stepped around to my side of the table. In retrospect, of course, I realize she probably knew already what was coming. She tapped me on the shoulder, and when I rose she circled me in her arms. We stood there. Soon I gave up and wrapped my arms around her, too. But I could tell she wasn't even looking at the new loafers. Her eyes were closed, and we just stood there like that. After a while, I let my hands fall, but still she didn't move. She rested against me with her arms around my shoulders and her head against my chest, until the teakettle began to whistle, and then finally to shake. If it hadn't, I don't know how long she would have stayed there like that.

ON THE MORNING I LEFT for Dunleavy, my mother woke me early and brought me out behind the kitchen to the laundry porch. "Okay," she said. "You're only going to get one lesson, so pay attention."

Her ironing board was set up in the corner and one of my Sunday shirts was lying on top of it.

"I thought I packed that," I said.

"If you planned on wearing it at school like that," she said, "think again." She picked it up and flung it open, then set it back down inside out. "First you have to find out what it's made of," she said.

I looked at her.

"The shirt," she said. "What material is it?"

"I don't know—cotton?"

"Cor, look at the label."

I did.

"Okay," she said. "Good. For cotton you set it on high. Wet your finger and touch the bottom to make sure it's hot. Like this."

"Ow," I said. "Hot."

"Now, start with the collar. And don't let the iron sit on it. You'll burn a hole."

By the time my father came downstairs for breakfast, I'd learned the technique: collar, cuffs, sleeves, back, front, in that order—all but the sleeves inside out. My mother stood there watching, offering encouragement every few moments as though what I was doing was astonishing. I still iron my own shirts this way, as a matter of fact, and I like it. And I can still see the way she stood that morning, looking out into our backyard, her fingers at the side of her head, while I worked and reworked the sleeves.

Finally, near the hour of our departure, there were footsteps on the porch and a knock on the front door.

"Why Eugene," I heard my father say. "You look like you're running for office."

Mr. McGowar walked into our living room wearing a suit. It was black and close-fitting, and his shirt, I noticed, was well pressed. I wondered how he had ended up with a set of clothes like that and had the brief thought that he was planning to drive to school with us. Then I remembered his wife's funeral, ten years before.

From his lapel pocket he pulled out an envelope. He stepped into the kitchen and handed it to me. My name was written in capitals across the flap.

"Thank you, Mr. McGowar," I said.

He nodded and pointed.

"He wants you to open it," said my father. "Voice is in a bad spell. Right, Eugene?"

Mr. McGowar nodded vigorously.

I opened it and read what was inside. When I'd finished, I said, "Thank you again, Mr. McGowar."

He pulled another sheet from his lapel and wrote:

YOR WELCM

He reached out his hand then and shook mine—his palm always felt to me like a dried-out baseball glove—and then turned around and headed back onto the porch. That was the end of our formal goodbye, and by the time we were ready to load the station wagon with my father's navy bag and my boxes of belongings, he had appeared again on the steps in his usual white undershirt and stained quarry pants, the radio earpiece trailing into his pocket. As my father did some final arranging of the boxes in the back of the car, Mr. McGowar set to work digging out a rock from our front garden. I watched him. There was something about him I was going to miss.

He was working hard with his pry bar, but even in the heat he was as dry as a cactus, the way he always was. Finally, he gave a massive pull and the rock came up in his hands. From the backseat where I was sitting, it didn't look much bigger than a grapefruit, but my mother leaned over and honked the horn anyway as he held it up over his head. He waved as we pulled out. We turned onto Dumfries and he followed us, hurrying along on his spidery legs most of the way down the block, still waving and smiling, his long arms swinging in the rearview mirror until we turned the corner at Kirkcaldy.

"Well," said my mother from the front seat. "That was a nice goodbye. What did his note say?"

I took it from my back pocket and leaned across the seat.

COREY HAV A GUD YER AT SCUL

"Thoughtful of him," she said.

"That kind of man," said my father, taking the turn at Glenford, "makes for the right kind of neighbor."

"He spelled my name right, too."

"That shows extra effort," said my mother.

Our first stop was at the Metareys', who had asked me to say goodbye on our way out of town. It's hard to remember now exactly what I was feeling, sitting in the backseat of the Plymouth as we crossed the short streets of our neighborhood and entered through the stone columns onto their driveway. I'd been thinking about what I was leaving. My mother's conversations. Mr. McGowar and my father with the ball scores. My mother humming in the kitchen while she scrubbed the black and white checkerboard floor. The crowds on Ontario Street as Henry Bonwiller waved from the Cadillac. Liam Metarey at his shelves of parts. Christian.

I saw the beauty of the land now as we drove, too. The sway of the high grasses at the edge of the estate, browning after the summer; the bursts of yellow-orange in the hills where the first maples had already begun to turn; the rustling poplar leaves, glinting now like nickels. I was wearing my new chinos and loafers, and my mother had put on perfume. I could smell it from the backseat.

Then, as we came out of the woods and saw Christian waiting for us on the front porch of the estate, my feelings cleared for a moment and I had the brief sensation that although my future was still open to me, it wouldn't be for long. That this was where my life was going to divide.

As we entered the gravel roundabout by the bur oak, my father turned around and said, "Don't worry, Corey. You're doing the right thing."

I don't know how he knew to say that.

Then we were at the top of the parking circle, and Christian and her mother were coming down the steps to greet us. My bus was leaving from Islington in a little more than an hour. June Metarey shook my father's hand and she reached around to pull my mother into an embrace. That surprised me, and I could tell it surprised my mother, too. Then she came to the back, where I had gotten out to talk to Christian, and she hugged me, too. I eventually came to know her, and for all her complications she was the one in that family, I think, who felt things most powerfully. Mr. Metarey appeared with Clara then at the front door, and he left her on the steps and came forward.

He was holding a duffel bag across his shoulder. He shook my father's hand and then my mother's, and at last came across the driveway and stood before me. "Here, young man," he said, sliding it off his arm. "A gift. From all of us."

"Really?" I said.

He nodded. "It was mine at Dunleavy. Back before you were born."

"Thank you, sir."

"You're very welcome."

"My goodness," said my mother.

"Thanks to all of you," I said, though Clara still stood behind us on the steps. My mother turned and waved up at her. "Thank you," I called, as Churchill came bounding around the corner of the house.

"And look at this," said Christian, turning the bag over in my hands. "Just so you don't lose it."

On the leather panel where the two hand-straps met, my initials had been sewn.

"Thank you, Mr. Metarey. Thank you, again. All of you. I won't lose it, don't worry."

"Church says you'd *better* not," said Christian, and the dog barked.

"Our pleasure, Corey," said Mrs. Metarey.

"And one other small item," said Mr. Metarey, unzipping the duffel in my hands now and showing me a package inside. "But this you're to open at school."

Then he went around to shake my father's hand again, and when he had stepped behind the car Christian pulled me quickly to her. "I'll miss you," she said.

"I'll miss you, too."

"I wish you weren't going."

"So do I."

She glanced behind her. "Thanks for spending the summer with me," she said. "Bye, Corey." And then, although we were still in view of Clara and probably her parents, she went up on her toes and kissed me on the lips. I walked around to the front, shook Mr. Metarey's hand one more time, patted Churchill on his warm head, and took my place in the car.

One of my own daughters is married now, and all of them are grown, and despite what a father is supposed to feel on the day a child takes a real place in the world, what I felt more than anything else on the Saturday morning when my own daughter stood at the altar was loss; not loss that she was leaving exactly but loss that we had come as far as we had. That I could, in fact, let her go. As a little girl—when she was our only child—she used to wake before dawn, pad over to the room where my wife and I slept, and wake me by tickling my face with my socks—which she insisted I leave every night on the table next to the headboard. Then she would hand me my shoes. With giggling delight she would watch as I put them on, as though they were her own marvelous invention. My loss on her wedding day was simply that we had traveled so far in the world that I was now ready to give her away without tears. I can only imagine what my parents were feeling as they readied me to go away to a place neither of them could have begun to imagine, or to understand.

I also think about Liam Metarey. He was many things, of course. He was a capitalist and a man of great influence—not just in Carrol County but in Albany and Washington—and he had the strength and the imagination to make an attempt that few would ever make; yet I also think that he was kind at heart, and that as a father he must have felt for his own children what I still feel for mine. I wonder to this day why he took it in his head to help me the way he did. I wonder why he sent me off to Dunleavy, and then did everything else for me after that. Was it just his democratic urge? And if it was, why did he not send Christian and Clara to a similar school? In those days, Dunleavy didn't take girls, but there were other schools that did—several within a day's drive of Saline.

And, of course, why had he let Andrew come home after his sophomore year? I know that Andrew had never liked school nor taken to it. Was that his reasoning? Was he merely an efficient spender of his fortune? Did Mr. Metarey somehow see scholastic potential in me, or at least drive, that he didn't see in his own son? Any of this is possible; and it's made more complicated, too, by the desires of his wife, who I don't think would have taken easily to sending their children away.

But there are other possibilities, also: Was he, as I sometimes wonder, trying to make me of a rank with his daughter? Or was it, as I think at other times—how could I not?—was it that he was trying to separate me from her?

But these questions didn't come until later. When I got back into the car, I felt an unfamiliar kind of courage, a courage that had been produced, almost entirely, by his gift. I held the bag's leather grips in my hand. They were trimmed in a tightly woven cord of black and dark orange and were sewn into the sides with triple rows of stitching. And beneath them, mixed among my cursive initials, I now saw the faint, needle-pocked outline of Liam Metarey's own. There was something about that. I ran my other hand over the end pockets, which were sewn from darker leather panels and the same woven cord. Then I realized I was being watched, and I looked back up and waved. Everyone but Clara, who was still standing on the porch, waved back.

I must say, I felt encircled by goodwill. Sitting in my father's Plymouth with the bag's stout grips in my hands, I thought for the first time that I might actually be ready for a place like Dunleavy; that the new life that had been given to me—thrust upon me, really—was not a test, after all, not a severe and mysterious probation of my character but an open arena of chance in which I might in fact prosper. The bag somehow gave this to me. And I believe that Mr. Metarey, who came down now and stood with his hand on the roof of the Plymouth as if he were the hireling and my father the master, understood exactly how I felt. He reached through the back window, smiled his amused half-smile, and ruffled my hair.

"We'll repack into the duffel at the bus depot," my father said, glancing at his watch. "Thank you, Mr. and Mrs. Metarey. You've been very good to my son."

All the while, Clara had not come forward from the steps, but now she walked down and greeted my father in the driver's seat and my mother next to him. Then she came around to the back, where I sat by the open window in my new clothes, my hand still around the handles of the bag. She looked in at me appraisingly. At the last moment, she leaned in the window—I had the sudden thought that she was going to check my shoes—and when her head was inside she whispered, so softly that I don't think either of my parents could hear, "I know what you're doing, Corey Sifter."

TWO

I

My confidence about Dunleavy, as it turned out, was fleeting. By the time we reached the bus station in Islington, in fact, it was gone; and it was not even a memory by the time I was picked up at the outdoor Greyhound stop in Highton, New York, just two hours later, by the Dunleavy school van, a dark, wood-paneled station wagon driven by some kind of groundsman with what I mistook for an English accent. By then I felt dreadful.

I'd begun my slide down into the state of introverted self-consideration that would hinder me for the next two years—for the next six, even—a halting apprehension that settled over me the moment I set foot in the peculiarly echoing hewn-stone halls of that school. Over my entire first year it would find expression in what I would soon begin to think of as my masquerader's hitch—a hesitation that gripped me whenever I spoke or even moved in the presence of my classmates. It only loosened its hold when I was on the soccer field—I discovered there that I was one of the better players at the school—or on my long vacations home, when, as I stepped off the bus in Islington each December and May, it slid from me again, like a cloak I'd forgotten I was wearing.

Imagine the cold immensity that a boarding school can seem to a newcomer, let alone a boy from a different world. The mysterious traditions. The haughty upperclassmen. The buildings themselves, which at Dunleavy were built from coarse-split, dark gray stone that rose four stories in a show of institutional imperviousness. Imperviousness to effort, to brilliance, even to surrender. In the hot fall the walls were cool and in the winter they were ledges of ice. The interior of my own hallway ended in a circular run of stairs that was faced inside with the same dark stone, and the tens of thousands of boys who had descended the steps over the decades had blackened the casework with their handprints and worn the footway as though by a steady flow of water. This willingness of the school to bear only the imprint of the multitude of us, never of any single one of us, might have been the bleakest facet of the whole place; and although it took me years to understand this, I also think I was in some way aware of it from my first moments on the grounds, standing by myself at the head of the semicircular entrance drive of the headmaster's house as the groundsman drove away behind me. I still remember the feeling.

On the fields beyond, the football team was drilling; at the edge of the woods, the track team was running laps in a single mass; through an open window I heard what sounded like an orchestra playing, and I could see the movement of bows. I don't think I'd ever felt so truly alone. Even today, with our interns at *The Speaker-Sentinel*, I try to remember the sensation. Dunleavy's refusal, thirty years ago, to take away any portion of our manic hope or our private suffering, while at the same time showing us daily the magnitude of our storied antecedence, must be every bit as much a problem today for any kid whose ambition takes him beyond his rank—for all the Trieste Millburys out there, and all the Corey Sifters, too—no matter how gamely they hide it.

At the main building, a secretary came outside, ushered me in, and showed me into the waiting room; after quite a few minutes there at the window, watching the football team run blocking dummies backwards across the end zone, I was finally called in by Mr. Clayliss, the headmaster. He pointed to a chair across from him, then pulled a file from a stack. "You're Liam Metarey's boy," he said.

"Well," I said. "I work for him."

He blinked at me across the desk.

"He's not my father," I explained. "If that's what you meant."

"No," he answered, looking back down at the file. "I know he's not."

"I'm grateful for what he did."

"Young man," he said. "I don't have any reason to think you're not. However, we'll see about that. You're starting here as a junior. We'll see how well Franklin Roosevelt did in preparing you for that." He shuffled the papers together and closed the file. "Mr. Metarey's got himself involved in politics now, I see."

"Yes, sir. He's one of the men in charge of Senator Bonwiller's campaign."

"Don't see why he'd want to do that." He looked across the desk at me, blinking again. "You're in Wilcott," he said at last. "Third floor south. You'll be rooming with Highbridge. Doors lock at nine. Not ten after nine. Not five after nine. You're caught smoking—cigarettes or *anything else*—you're on your way home." He stood. "That's what happened to Highbridge's first roommate, in case you're wondering. Clear enough? A boy'll take you up there now"—he gestured at the door. "Welcome to school, Sifter."

Highbridge's first name turned out to be Astor, a combination I couldn't have made up myself but that I read on the nameplate a few minutes later as I stood outside 318 Wilcott. I peeked through the narrowly opened door at a set of pale, noble features gazing up at the ceiling from the pillow. Astor Highbridge. He hadn't seen me yet. I stepped back until his chinos came into view, then his boat shoes, sprawled from the end of the mattress. He wore them without socks: I realized I hadn't even considered all the ways I wouldn't fit in at Dunleavy.

In the hallway, although I could hardly bring myself to do it, I bent down and scuffed my new loafers.

Behind Astor were two small windows looking into a tree, and between them a poster of Carl Yastrzemski waiting for a pitch. I was glad to recognize Yastrzemski even if I despised the Red Sox. I looked closer. The background was out of focus but a left-hander in a blue cap was on the mound: it might have been Sam McDowell. The Indians had no doubt lost that day. I stood at the crack in the door surveying what I could of my new room: a dark green rug flecked with gray and gold, a dull brass trash basket, the corner of a desk piled with books, the toe-ends of a pair of cleats. I turned around. In the hallway behind me, all our names were cut into black laminated stock in orange letters above the doors; I don't know how long I must have been standing there, gripping Liam Metarey's duffel and studying the names, before I heard, "You must be Corey, man."

The door had opened and he was offering his hand.

"And you must be Astor Highbridge."

"*Astor*'s plenty, man," he said. "Come in. Nicer in than out." Then he added, "Barely."

I held the duffel in front of me. The room was just large enough for the two of us to move past each other. One of the beds had no sheets.

"That's yours," he said. "In case you were wondering."

"I figured."

"Kind of bleak, then, huh?"

"I guess so."

"It gets better, man. Don't worry. I've done two years already. Not eligible for parole."

And that was my introduction to Dunleavy.

Later, I understood that he'd even left me the good bed, hidden from the door and closer to the windows; but at the time his generosity was lost on me. My mind was too raw. His white shirt was old and worn, and the sleeves hung loose around his wrists, but when he reached to open one of the windows I saw that the cuffs were embroidered with the tiny letters *AH*. I turned my own duffel so he could see the front. I didn't want to unpack it, of course—not in front of him or anyone else. I only wanted to be alone.

Astor sensed this, I think. He said he was just setting out on a walk. A moment later, he returned to tell me that bedding was distributed from a closet near the dining hall and that he would be glad to collect mine for me—the first of hundreds of kindnesses he would show me over the year. I didn't want to tell him that a good part of my duffel was taken up by the sheets my mother had washed and ironed that morning, so I asked him to take me along. As we walked the stone path toward the linen commissary he said hello to half a dozen other students, who appeared to be older. His brother, he told me, was a senior.

"Clayliss give you a nice welcome?" he said to me as we made our way across the grass quad.

I looked sideways at him.

"Oh, sorry, man," he said. "Only kidding. Don't worry. That's how he is with everybody."

"He mostly warned me about stuff."

"Not five after," Astor said. "Not ten after."

"A cigarette and you're on your way home."

"A cigarette *or anything else*, man."

We both laughed.

"That's what happened to Sturgeon," he said.

"Sturgeon was your roommate?"

"Yeah, Sturgeon hated it here. He *wanted* to go. It's cool. I respect the man for it. And I'm glad to have *you* instead."

"Thanks, Astor." Behind Mr. Clayliss's office was the laundry—in the distance I could see a line of students stretching out the door—and I wondered suddenly if there was a charge for picking up our linens.

"Actually," I said, "I've got my own sheets. My mother, like, might have even ironed them."

"Oh, just use the school's, man. They use bleach to kill the fleas." He chuckled. "Kidding," he said.

"I figured."

"But at least it'll save you the trouble, right?" Then he patted me on the shoulder and said "Clayliss," again, chuckling dismissively. We walked past the administration building and he nodded toward the window. "Clayliss is a real throwback, man."

"Like, five hundred years back," I offered.

"Yeah," he said. "Like, five thousand five hundred."

We were at the laundry shack now. I took a place at the end of the line, my hands in my pockets.

"Got to take off now, man," he said. "But you're cool from here." He stepped closer. "And don't worry," he said quietly, "tuition covers everything."

THE HEADLINE DIDN'T COME the next morning, as June Metarey said it would; but it did finally appear, two months later: The *Buffalo Courier-Express*, October 3rd, 1971. SENATOR-ANODYNE TIES PROBED. A short piece buried at the end of the news section, which I found in the Dunleavy library's week-old copy of the paper. The page trembled in front of me, while outside the window my classmates filed across the frost-tipped grass to the breakfast hall. A single paragraph. All it said was that the state's attorney general had summoned a grand jury to investigate Senator Henry Bonwiller's ties to a Wyoming oil drilling company named Anodyne Energy. That was it. There was no byline. Nothing to make me think Glenn Burrant had anything to do with it. As I stood there, I heard the door open behind me in the library. I closed the paper quickly and walked out into the chilly morning.

I WAS ON THE SIDE LAWN of the house, setting up folding chairs for Senator Bonwiller's press conference in the morning, when Christian appeared on the gravel turnaround, out of breath.

"There you are!" she gasped. "Come on, Corey, hurry! We're going up with Mother!"

"We're going where?"

"For a spin. In Aberdeen White! Come on, Corey—run!"

This happened over Columbus Day, when I was home for the first time from Dunleavy. For the whole weekend I'd been working at the Metareys', and at night I'd been sleeping in my own bed, and it was such an unexpected relief to be doing both things that a kind of giddiness had entered me. It was the anniversary of the UAW strike against General Motors, and in the morning Henry Bonwiller was going to be speaking about his labor record; it wasn't going to be much of a press conference, but under the small tent in the side yard I was snapping open quite a few rows of chairs, anyway, just in case more reporters showed up than Mr. Metarey expected.

"Oh, please, Corey!" Christian panted. "That's enough. Leave them for later. Mother's going to take off without us!"

Aberdeen White was Mrs. Metarey's second plane, a big, twin-engine Beechcraft that she used for bringing in guests from the coast. When I told my parents about it later in our kitchen, my father set down his can of Pabst Blue Ribbon and went to the window, where he pulled up the shade and looked out at the sky; my mother, who'd been washing dinner dishes at the sink, stopped scraping and rinsing. Finally she moved next to me at the table.

"Do you think you might have called us before you went along?" she asked.

"He didn't have time, love," said my father.

"And why did they decide to take you so suddenly?" she asked.

"I don't have the faintest idea," I answered.

And that was the truth. I had the impression, actually, from the way Christian yanked my hand as we ran all the way back along the two-track, then pulled my arm firmly as we crossed the landing strip, then stopped and turned around at the top rung of the plane's boarding ladder to smooth my hair—I had the impression that my coming had been an item of contention. But I didn't mention this to my parents.

Aberdeen White's steps shook suddenly and an engine came on. Christian took a deep breath and settled her skirt; then we ducked inside.

June Metarey was in the pilot's seat. She turned and smiled quickly at me, then went back to studying a clipboard in her lap. Mr. Metarey was next to her, and he welcomed me with a nod, then a wave. I closed my eyes to adjust them to the dim light, and when I opened them again I noticed how utilitarian everything looked. The walls were unfinished, just white metal panels punctuated by bolts and welds. This seemed like a secret to me, suddenly, some interesting and unpredictable aspect of the Metareys' private world that I'd been unexpectedly allowed to see. I don't know why: I suppose I'd expected luxury. But the seating was hard and it rode in rows of metal track, and the chairs had tall backrests with a system of clips and hooks for the seat belts. Behind her mother, Christian was already working expertly with hers. She pointed me to the place across the aisle, and I made my way toward the front. Beyond us was a third row, and where the sixth seat should have been was an empty section of floor, covered by a blanket. Next to the blanket sat Clara with Churchill on her lap. She was holding him down, but even in the shadows I could see his hindquarters shaking.

"Don't worry about Churchill," Mr. Metarey said. "He's just excited. My wife thinks he's scared, but I know my own dog."

"He's frightened as all get out," said Mrs. Metarey without looking up.

"Okay," he said, "but he's worse if we leave him. You know that, dear."

"Were there seat belts?" asked my mother.

"Of course. Really good ones. Shoulder belts, too. From both sides."

"The dog must have been scared, is right," she said.

"That dog has seen more in his life than most grown men," said my father, sipping his beer.

"You sit there," said Mr. Metarey, pointing where Christian had.

"You'll get the best view on the way in." He pointed to the bank of clouds shadowing the land to the west. "Looks like just a bit of cover on the way out."

When I looked through Clara's window I saw Aberdeen Red, so close that its double wing nearly touched our own. Its color looked duller than it did in the sky, like a fish that had been pulled from the water. After struggling for a few moments with the complicated arrangement of clips on my seatback, I allowed Mr. Metarey to turn and fasten my shoulder belts for me. The plane bucked, and off to my right the second engine came on.

Mrs. Metarey made some notations on her clipboard, spoke a few words to her husband, who checked a clipboard of his own, and then, with no more ceremony than she might have displayed backing the Galaxy out of the garage, she pushed gently on the throttle and we taxied out of the hangar, rolled through a turn, and then without pausing sped off down the runway.

First the dark grass sprinting below. Then the broad limbs of the oaks. Then their tops, stretching in a rust-colored lake punctuated by the brilliant maples and the tallest white pines. Then the hills. Then the blue, blue sky. My chest dropping inside me. The propellers roaring. The plane banking and heading west, the turn I had seen Mrs. Metarey make a hundred times from below in the fields. We leveled off and I managed to calm myself. The propellers quieted a notch. Ahead of us the estate was in shadow. Everywhere else it was ablaze with light, and the wings were even more brilliant than the land. We bumped slightly and their ends bounced. The metal dark, then light again. A moment later wisps like tracer bullets over the tips. Then gray sky again and everything was gone.

"Clouds, Corey," said Mr. Metarey.

Oblivion now. My eyes found nothing to hold on to. Churchill barking. We bumped hard, then smoothed out. Then bumped again. The plane rumbled with the low churning of the engines, and underneath it came the steady yapping of the dog. Out the window, depth disappeared and the double panes confused me. Tiny droplets shimmied between the layers of glass; I'd mistaken them for trees in the distance. Truly nothing for the eye. I could barely make out the propellers. We bumped again, harder this time. Then again. Churchill let out a low howl. I held my seat.

"Now get ready," said Christian.

And then we were through, out into sun that lit a sea of white to the horizon. I have to admit I think I shouted.

"Oh, no," said my mother. "What did you shout?"

"I don't know. 'Wow,' or something."

Mrs. Metarey turned and smiled. She made a whoop.

"Women's lib," said my mother.

A sea of brilliant white now. Again Mrs. Metarey whooped, then dipped the plane back. A moment later, out again. Then in. Then out. Our startling shadow gamboling on the cloud tops. Churchill was barking steadily now, twisting madly in circles on his bed of blankets behind me. Mr. Metarey himself laughed, his head thrown back. He turned, smiling broadly at me, and slapped me on the knee. "Hey, Mr. Sifter," he said, "not bad, is it?"

"Is that what he calls you?" asked my father.

"He calls me Corey."

"It makes you believe in Almighty God," said Mr. Metarey, throwing back his head again and laughing, "*doesn't* it now?"

Then June Metarey lifted the nose, and my stomach dropped out. We headed straight up and at the same time turned back, settling flat only after I was sure we were going to flip. My vision spun and straightened. Out the window the horizon leveled again, mercifully, and it was blue, and then we were beyond the cloud cover once more, heading east toward the Metarey estate over open land that at last I recognized again. The River Lethe and Little Shelter Brook curving languorously below. Our shadow preceding us to the northwest, leaping over the stream banks and rushing headlong through the treetops. Soon I saw the shapes of the fields I knew, the matching red wind vanes spinning atop all four of the Metarey barns, the double streaks of blue sky that were the fly pools, suddenly splintered by a covey of landing ducks. The white top of the press tent where I'd been arranging chairs that morning for the Senator.

Mr. Metarey must have seen it, too. "Don't know if we're going to get anybody showing up tomorrow," he said, turning back to me. "But we sure want to get out in front with the unions." He smiled. "Never hurts to get your name in the papers, anyway."

"Yes, sir," I said over the engines. "Especially with the president going to Russia." This was only a rumor, but I'd read about it at school.

He smiled. "I see you're getting something out of that education, at least."

"I'm grateful, sir."

Mrs. Metarey turned in the pilot's seat. "Do you want to take it?"

I thought for a moment that she was speaking to me, but Liam Metarey answered. "Only if it's okay with our guest."

When I realized what they were talking about, I said, "Of course, Mr. Metarey, it's fine."

"What *were* they talking about?" asked my mother.

"About taking the plane. She was asking if he wanted to fly it."

"He knows how to do *that*, too?" said my mother.

My father looked up. "He probably built the thing, love."

Mrs. Metarey unclipped herself from the belts, then rose and moved between us to the back. I looked over the seat and saw that her husband had taken over from a second set of controls. Then I looked over at Christian, who seemed unconcerned. And to tell the truth, so was I. Mr. Metarey was as capable a human being as I've ever met, before then or since, and though it's ridiculous to say it, I think even in that situation I trusted him as much as I trusted his wife. Perhaps more. I leaned as far as I could to the side to watch. He drew back on the wheel with his finger, and I felt us bank to the south.

"Back pressure," Mrs. Metarey said from behind me. "Left rudder to start."

"At your service."

"Nose up. Steady. Now bring it through."

Mrs. Metarey was behind me now, and when I turned I saw that she was trying to calm the dog, who was barking plaintively. When she succeeded in closing his snout, the barks became pathetic whines through his teeth. She held him close about the neck, burying his face in her chest so that he couldn't see. For a moment, this would stop the barking and whining; but then he would struggle out, and as soon as his eyes were free he would begin again, thumping his tail and stamping in place and whimpering. At last Mrs. Metarey seemed to subdue him in her grasp, and he lay down against her, still sighing occasionally but finally burying his head in the crook of her arm.

"So," Christian said, "you want to try it, too?"

Clara pointed to the empty pilot's seat. "Flying a plane's easy," she said.

"They wanted *you* to fly it?" said my mother. She glanced at my father.

"She was kidding, Mom."

"Good thing," said my father, taking another sip of his beer. Then he added, "I thought it might be something they teach you at boarding school."

"It's *landing* that's the trick," said Clara, from behind me. "I've heard that a million times."

"That's right, Corey," said Mr. Metarey from the front seat. "Flying is easy. Taking off's nothing. And there's plenty of room up here." He gestured out the window. "It's *landing* that's the trick. Flying in clear weather? I bet you could do it right now without a problem. You're welcome to give it a spin while we're up here."

"No, thank you."

"Smart kid," said my father.

"Shhh," said my mother. "Let him finish."

Presently Mrs. Metarey stood, and Churchill began whimpering again, curled on his rousted blankets with his tail beating rhythmically on the floor. Clara was patting his head now as Mrs. Metarey passed between us and took her place again at the controls. I must say, I saw a look of relief pass over her husband's features when she had belted herself in again and taken hold of the wheel by a single finger at its edge. She pulled the plane up, then edged gradually to the south and began to descend. Over Little Shelter Brook, on the far third of the property, she brought us down low so that we skimmed the treetops, passing over the pool the beavers had damned years ago, a motionless azure mirror that suddenly showed us in our entirety, streaking west.

She gained altitude again and pointed us toward the landing strip, which she then angled in on from all the cardinal points of the compass, turning at the three corners of a rectangle until she finally brought us down aside the long edge, a little more steeply, pulling up gracefully just before we landed so that the wheels barely bumped on the tarmac. The descent had been so steady that I hadn't been scared at all, but the sound of the engines idling down as we rolled up the runway filled me with a relief that was almost as powerful, I think, as my ecstasy had been when we first broke through the clouds. She brought us to a halt alongside the hangar.

"Good dog," Christian said, and reached back to pat Churchill. He whimpered again and rose next to her, pressing against her leg. "Watch this, Corey."

Mr. Metarey came around between us. "Now hold him," he said to Christian.

He first reached back to touch the dog's brow, which instantly quieted him; then he turned to unlatch the door. He was swinging it out when a pale blur flashed in the sunny opening. By the time Churchill's paws touched the ground he was already sprinting madly for the woods, his forelegs appearing through his hind ones until he was nothing but a pale, undulating ghost, bounding through the trees.

"Well," Mr. Metarey said in a philosophical voice, rising and letting down the steps for the rest of us, "I guess he didn't like that, after all."

My father set down his beer. "Not one bit," he said.

"Oh, Corey," said my mother. "That poor dog." She laughed gently then, but something crossed her expression and she sat down at the table, touching her head the way she did in those days, and turned to look out the window.

IT'S DIFFICULT TO SAY how much of my life has turned on the kindness of Astor Highbridge: having a friend at Dunleavy was what allowed me to stay and to do everything that followed. He was on scholarship, himself, as it turned out, the son of a schoolteacher—the monogrammed shirts were hand-me-downs from an uncle. As the term went on he couldn't have been friendlier; but even his friendship could barely ease the disquiet I felt nearly every moment I was awake. For a month I flinched at every shadow that came swooping over the grass from the shrieking mass of crows in the oaks across the quad. In class I said nothing beyond the obligatory.

But then I began to study. That's how I buried my fear.

I suppose it's predictable, that the ones who become the best students are the ones who feel the least qualified—for that's what I felt, and that's what I became. My inborn talent was surely near the bottom of my class, but from the outset my grades were near the top. There was a boy my year who could multiply three-digit numbers in his head; another who knew the details of every battle of the Civil War; and a Korean kid from Brooklyn, my only better in grades, who memorized everything we read. But my marks were almost as good as his, and better than the others'. If Mr. Burrows, our history teacher, mentioned the Second Battle of Manassas, I wrote it down and went straight to the library to read about it—and about the first one, too; if Mrs. Merrilews, our English teacher, quoted a line from Emily Dickinson, I set out to read every poem she wrote. This wasn't as difficult as it sounds. I'd found that by some natural aptitude I was a fast reader, and all my life I'd been a hard worker. Now I was working at my studies.

By the time the library opened at seven in the morning, I'd already spent an hour with my books in our room. On my way out the door I would shake Astor's shoulder to wake him, then pass by the cafeteria for a slice of toast on my walk to the stacks. I had a half hour then before the first-period bell rang, and this bit of time was my only indulgence of the day. I would sit by the window and read from the shelf of newspapers that was kept there, as outside on the grounds the school began to come to life before me. The teachers with their briefcases, hurrying on the paths; the delivery men at the cafeteria doors; my classmates in their rowdy flocks. There was something in all this that gave me peace, somehow. And something in reading the papers that allowed me to think I had a hand in a distant world; that I was beyond everything here.

Every Monday, Glenn Burrant would publish his political column in the *Courier-Express*, and two mornings later that column would appear in the Dunleavy library. On Wednesdays I felt a particular anticipation as I crossed the empty quad, not only because the week was finally tipping toward its end, but because Glenn's column so quickly carried me to that distant world. The *Courier-Express* was a liberal paper, and Glenn was allowed to cover the issues of the day with remarkable latitude. My first September at school, he editorialized on busing, on the peace marches, and on the Attica prison riot, and at the end of the month, he updated his summary of the Democratic candidates. That article, of course, almost seized me with excitement.

At Dunleavy, classes started at seven-thirty and went until four-thirty, so I didn't have time to read more than a single paper each morning; but because of the long school day our vacations were long, too—five weeks at the turn of the year, another two in midwinter, and a summer break that began in May. I'd encountered this charitable schedule one night early on when I looked through the school calendar, circling every vacation. It was a surprise and a relief—I well remember the feeling—and about the only optimistic bit of news I found for myself in those first, whirling weeks.

My days were like nothing I'd ever known. Our morning block of classes went until nine-thirty, followed by a half hour's break in which most of the students, by school tradition, went to the dining hall for donuts and coffee. But I went back to the library instead. From ten till twelve-thirty, we had our long period, and then lunch. I took my plate and went up to our room. From one-thirty to four-thirty we had math and science, and at quarter of five was sports. I played soccer, and when practice was over we were given another half hour's break before dinner. I was able to spend most of that time with my books. And after dinner was when I truly began my work. All my life I'd not needed much sleep, and it was not uncommon for me to look up from my books and see the watchman's lantern outside our window as he made his sweep of the dormitory doors at two in the morning.

When I look at Trieste Millbury today, of course, I see my own past; but I also know that I was different from her. She has a gift—some fortune of gene that has endowed her with both a hard head and a hard intelligence, and she feels no pull, at least none that I can see, toward the conventional comforts. Ease. Plentitude. A bit of luxury. I was, and still am, far from that. My head may be as hard as hers but my intelligence—and by that I mean whatever small power I have to see things for myself—is diminutive in comparison, and the quality of mind that allows her to think so fiercely—ambition, I would call it, of an intellectual kind—is only sputteringly apparent in my own consciousness. Which is to say, I have since my first days at Dunleavy been a learner—and an eager one—but she, already, is a discoverer; and the discoverers are the ones who shoulder the burden. I've been happy enough myself for most of my life reading the well-trod classics of my generation, and I'll readily admit that the thought of a glass of wine with my wife on our back patio, where on most afternoons we can watch our downhill neighbor sweeping the deck around his swimming pool, is generally sufficient to get me through a day. I suspect that such bourgeois rewards are nothing to Trieste; but still, I do believe I once felt what she now feels.

In class I spoke only when I had to—and even then with my plaguing hesitation—but it wasn't long before the faculty realized that I could be relied upon for an answer. This wasn't what I wanted, of course, because it brought attention. So I responded with as few words as I could and tried to acknowledge as little as possible any compliments my teachers gave me in class.

"Man," Astor said to me one night, "you're a mystery. You know that?" He was lying in bed, almost asleep, and I was studying at my desk.

"How's that?"

"Like, if I knew all those answers—if I knew *half* of 'em—you wouldn't be able to shut me up."

"You know a lot more than you think, Astor."

"That's a cool thing to say, man"—he yawned—"but it couldn't be farther from the truth. I'm just passing the time. I'm a waste of a bed."

"You're the most popular guy in our class."

I heard him turn over.

"But you, man . . ." he said, his voice fading. "You *love* to study." He bunched his pillow under his head. "You're like some mysterious monk," he mumbled, and then in a few moments he was snoring.

At that point in my life, I have to say, this was exactly what I wanted people to think.

Yet such were the overwhelming sensations of my earliest days that it was not until a Saturday afternoon midway through November that I looked out the window at a boy carrying a duffel bag into the gym and realized I'd forgotten all about the gift Mr. Metarey had handed me. Astor was at a football game and I'd been studying in the room. I set down my trigonometry book. Out the window beyond the buildings I could see a group of kids playing lacrosse, jabbing their sticks in the air and sprinting between the sidelines. I went straight to the closet, opened the bag, and took out the package from where it lay folded in my ironed sheets.

Later, after I was married, and even after we'd had our daughters, I would become familiar with such moments, moments in which the world seemed to withdraw and yet at the same time to grow closer. Listening to the clack of the lacrosse sticks and the shouts of the players, along with the occasional rumble of the work vans that were going and coming on the gravel drive, all the while holding my forgotten present from Liam Metarey, I was struck both by my remove from the commerce of that place and at the same time by a certain peace in somehow being part of it. It was close, I suppose, to what I felt reading the newspaper. On the other hand, perhaps it was just one of the few hours all month in which I wasn't reckoning with being an outsider; or perhaps it was merely the package itself in my hand, which seemed to carry with it a measure of Liam Metarey's own being, or at least of the generosity he'd always shown me.

It was bigger than a book, but lighter, and soft. I unwrapped it. Inside was a second layer of tissue, and when I opened this one I found a square of dark terry cloth, the same hunter green as the paper. A bath towel, folded tightly. The gloomy idea crossed my mind that this was some kind of insult, and despite my recent cheerfulness my thoughts went straight to Clara. She might as well have been standing in the room with me. I saw her skeptical eyes.

It wasn't until I'd turned to the closet, though, to hang it on the hook, that I unfolded it and discovered that it wasn't a towel at all, but a robe. A fine-looking one, in fact. I shook it out. It was long, with a belt and full sleeves tipped in leather, and a hood that drew with a cord. All of it sewn from some kind of rough, sturdy terry that I haven't found again in all the years since.

But: a bathrobe. I was still puzzled. The duffel I could understand, and the fact that it had belonged to Liam Metarey himself—when he was living in these same halls—had immediately given it the qualities of a talisman. But a robe? Even if it was made of such fine cloth and its belt tipped in leather, even if I'd not opened it till now, under these circumstances of my first real ease, I have to say that its presence nonetheless set in my gut a stone of disappointment. And I still couldn't shake the feeling that there was some reference in it to my own worthiness. Again I thought of Clara.

My wife tells me I overthink. I don't think it's possible to do that, but I do admit that my tendency has always been to go first to the dark interpretation. Sometimes I attribute this to my mother's influence, despite her avowals of the opposite—for doesn't insistent optimism imply what one is all the time combating? My father, on the other hand, was inclined by nature to see the world as benevolent, which is why a good-humored pessimism was the mark of his bearing in the world. I guess, when it comes down to it, that I ended up more like my mother. I was wrong about the bathrobe, as it turns out. But I don't think I'm wrong about the other things.

II

The *Buffalo Courier-Express*
Monday, January 17th, 1972

Police have released no new information concerning the body discovered over the weekend on the grounds of Silverton Orchards in Saline, pending an investigation. The frozen corpse, an unidentified adult female, was found early Sunday morning near a drainage ditch bordering Route 35 by workers making road repairs south of the Saline-Steppan interchange, according to sources. Anyone with information is asked to contact Commander Larry MacKenzie of the New York State Police Office in North Islington, or this newspaper. Nighttime temperatures over the weekend reached nine degrees below zero.

III

1972 WAS A YEAR OF CHANGE for the Democrats. The Chicago convention in 1968 had left its bitter memories. Mayor Daley's cops swinging truncheons in the crowds. National Guardsmen pointing grenade launchers off the Congress Street Bridge. But none of it would have mattered if it weren't for the election results themselves: Hubert Humphrey, the candidate chosen by the party establishment, went down in a watershed drubbing.

301 to 191. That was the electoral count. Richard Nixon was in the White House. Robert Kennedy and Martin Luther King were dead. The country was in the hands of others.

That's the stage Henry Bonwiller walked onto when he started campaigning in earnest, late in that fall of 1971. As a senator, he'd made his share of enemies, of course, but from the very first he'd been able to win a crowd merely with the stirring note of his voice. That deep, woody cadence, like a cello speaking. It was this voice, I think, more than anything else, that suited him to the new politics. In 1972, for the first time in history, a candidate didn't have to be likable in person: he just had to be likable on TV.

It's easy to think it's always been that way; but it hasn't. That was the year the king-making was brought for the first time into public view. The historic moment. The primaries rather than the backroom deal. Not the party bosses but the people, now—especially the people from Iowa and New Hampshire—the people, now, would choose the candidate. It was a watershed change in the rules.

And the Democrats needed a new kind of man for it. Edmund Muskie of Maine was far from charming but he was straightforward in front of a camera; by early winter he had regained the lead. George McGovern, from South Dakota, was still on the periphery. George Wallace, who'd won 13 percent of the vote in 1968, was no longer a marginalized southern segregationist, and Humphrey himself, despite his first trouncing, was in the running. So were Eugene McCarthy and Shirley Chisholm, the long shots. And Scoop Jackson, who was convincing in person but didn't have the charisma, in Liam Metarey's opinion, for a national run. It was Muskie onto whom the country seemed to settle its hopeful gaze—stolid, serious Ed Muskie.

Lou Harris's polling firm had been engaged by the Bonwiller campaign to find flaws in Muskie's reach, and in the strategy sessions it was a given now that Henry Bonwiller could at best fight Muskie to a tie in the Northeast; but it was in the South, especially the urban South—Virginia and North Carolina and Georgia and Florida—where we might take him. That's what I learned from my visits to the meetings upstairs when I was home from school, every other weekend or so. I wasn't around often enough to do my regular jobs anymore, but I was carrying up drinks and hors d'oeuvres now to the strategy sessions in the library. It was Muskie that we had to get past. And it was Muskie that the campaign was going to focus on. You didn't have to be around the estate long, especially as the vote in Iowa approached, before this paramount fact became clear.

ONE AFTERNOON A FEW MONTHS AGO, my wife and I were looking for garden supplies at the country outfitter in Islington Center when I stumbled across a sale on an oilcloth duster—the kind of raincoat worn up here at the horse farms and riding stables. It was the last of the smallest size, and the wet season was ending, so it had already been marked down more than once. I paid for it and slipped it into the car trunk, which was so full of flower pots and trays of budding annuals that I don't think my wife even noticed.

Although dusters have clearly become a status item around here lately—you see them in the backseats of plenty of Toyota Highlanders parked at the upscale malls—they're also as utilitarian a piece of clothing as has ever been stitched by man. The cut covers you from neck to heel, and the oilcloth material sheds water as though it's allergic. In a wet March snowstorm you can walk ten miles in one and not feel a drop of damp—and because they were designed for horsemen, you can even ride a bike in one. But they're not cheap. That night at home I took it out of the box and thought about roughing it up to make it look used. I even thought of just leaving it anonymously on Trieste's desk at the paper. But she's the kind who would ask about a lost and found.

Instead, I called her into my office for the conference we have with every intern midway through the term.

"Nice job on the dioxin piece," I said.

"A waste of time," she answered. "But thanks."

"The assignment, you mean? Or what you did with it?"

"The former."

"And therefore the latter."

"Well, it turned out all right. But I could have told you all of it without having to hitch to Albany."

Without saying more I reached behind my chair and brought out the copy of the front page that I'd had framed. I'd had the whole staff sign it, too. "Well, we're glad you did it, anyway," I said, presenting it to her over the desk. "Your article made a difference to a lot of people."

"Whoops, Mr. Sifter."

"That's okay. I appreciate your honesty." Then I took out the box from under the desk and handed it across to her, too. This she accepted without a word. She opened it, removed the duster, and tried it on. It fit.

"Oh, I see," she said, smoothing the long panels. "I guess you figured I could use one." She smiled her enigmatic smile.

"Next time you hitch to Albany."

"Very funny, sir," she said. But then she pulled the button loops tight and looked over at herself in the window, and I could see that it had touched her. "Thanks, Mr. Sifter," she said softly. And then she added, "I'm grateful."

"Makes you wish it wasn't a Saturday night," Liam Metarey said to me. "Not a farm supply open in the state."

We were out by the work barn standing alongside the old Massey-Ferguson, which had broken down in the snow. It was the beginning of Christmas vacation. The snow had been falling heavily since morning, and now, past dark, it was just beginning to taper. Earlier in the evening, I'd driven the tractor down from the garage to plow, but when I'd tried to push it into low, it had made a snapping sound and stopped dead. A gearbox cable. That's what Mr. Metarey told me as he pulled a small mirror from under the crankshaft and screwed closed the engine housing. Already there were two inches of white on the seat. "Broken clean through," he said. "Time for the shovels."

"Our neighbor's got a New Holland," I said. "Eugene McGowar. I can call."

"Oh, no," he said. "The trick's to see the opportunity. That's what my old man would have said. Come on—let's pull the damn thing back into the barn and then we can get to shoveling by hand."

It seemed odd, of course, to start such a task in the dark; it seemed odd, in fact, that he wanted to do it at all. But as I've said before, I've always enjoyed the feeling of physical labor. We looked out together over the turnaround and the drive sloping uphill to the sycamores. There must have been two feet of snow in the yard already, and the drifts on the north-facing slopes of the drive were as high as my shoulders. Mr. Metarey went into the barn for a moment and came back with a pair of chains.

"Isn't it funny," he said, gathering one over his shoulder. "How everything will eventually reverse itself on you?"

"How do you mean that, sir?"

"Reverse what it needs and what it offers. You and me pulling the old Ferguson, for example." He handed me the other chain. "But it's true for all kinds of other things, too. One of God's lesser-known laws. The law of comeuppance. Come on, Corey," he said. "It'll be good for us. Here's your end."

He clipped both chains to the plow stay, and then I gathered mine over my own shoulder and we leaned down into the load, pulling steadily until the tractor's inertia suddenly broke and it began to creep up the hill behind us. We kept our steps short in the slick footing, guiding the wheels back up their deep tracks until at last we had succeeded in pulling the huge machine up the slope and levering the rear axle over the threshold into the barn.

"Nice work, young man," he said.

"Thank you, sir."

"Now," he said. "The shovels."

I mention this incident not to illustrate what a ferocious worker Liam Metarey was—although he certainly was *that*—but to show what I think must have been the precarious state of his mind around that time, which I believe was when he ended up making his fateful decision for the Bonwiller campaign. He was, as I later came to understand, bedeviled by a generational curse—the very curse that had made his family what it was. And now I wonder if on that evening it had hold of him.

I have to say, the task seemed impossible. Before us, the snow stretched two feet deep for almost a quarter of a mile before it finally thinned under the dense branches of the sycamores. But he merely said, "Two hundred yards to the trees, knee-deep most places. How many shovels is that, Corey?"

"A lot."

"By my figuring, thirty-two hundred. Sixteen hundred each. That is, if we keep up with each other." He smiled and pulled down the two widest snow shovels from the wall, then hung his coat from the peg. "If we clear one lane, I mean. We can clear the other way in the morning."

"Are you sure, sir? I can call our neighbor."

"Seneca Indians used to do this sort of thing when they wanted a vision. The Great Chief Sagoyewatha."

We began with the turnaround. Before long I'd taken off my coat and then my sweater. Next to me, Mr. Metarey had rolled up his sleeves. The shovels had wide blades and short handles that were meant for pushing and not throwing, and the snow was wet; but still he worked like a piston. He was thirty years older than I, but before long he'd built a lead on his side of the drive. When he saw it, he crossed over and began shoveling on mine.

After a few minutes he looked up. "Been thinking about the presidents," he said.

"Yes, sir." I was glad for the break.

"You ever hear of a man named Isaiah Berlin?"

I stood from the snow and leaned against my shovel. "Not a president," I said. "He's a singer, I think."

"I suppose you mean Irving Berlin. The composer." He bent to his shovel again. "I'm talking about Sir Isaiah Berlin, the philosopher. He was the one who noticed that there are two kinds of thinkers, the monists and the pluralists—that's what he called them." He was working now again, lifting and burying his shovel as he talked, tossing the load into a gathering ridge at the side of the drive. "Let's see— otherwise known as hedgehogs and foxes. You heard of any of this?"

"No, sir."

"The fox knows lots of things. The hedgehog knows only one thing but he knows it in his bones. I've been thinking. Been thinking about which one Senator Bonwiller is." He stopped working for a moment. "Fifty," he said as he resumed. "You know your presidents, Corey?"

"Yes, sir, I think so."

"Who was the first?"

"The first president?" I looked at him. "Washington, sir."

"That's right. Washington was a monist. A hedgehog. A charismatic one, too. Those are the great leaders."

We were fifteen yards up the drive now. Both of us sweating.

"A republicanist in the true sense of the word, I should add. Voluntarily gave up command of the army. One of the great acts of any world leader. 1783, that was—and the statement still holds. Back to a life in Mount Vernon. Stunned old Europe. A true hedgehog. Beat Adams, Jay, Harrison, Rutledge, and Hancock. And soundly, too," he said. "Next?"

"Sir?"

"Next president."

"John Adams."

"Pluralist. A fox. Beat Pinckney, Burr, and his own cousin Samuel. Not to mention Jefferson—barely. Nothing of Washington's charisma but a student of the world. Saw both sides of everything—a hindrance if there ever was one. Defended British soldiers at the trial for the Boston Massacre—how's that for an unpopular stand? Just because he saw it that way. 1770. And *still* won. Lived by the mind. Took notes on everything he saw, all his life. A fox through and through. No doubt on that one. Hindered him in the end, of course. One hundred. Always does. Next."

"Jefferson."

"Pluralist. Greatest fox of them all. Philosopher. Paleontologist. Violinist. Architect. Mathematician. Cryptographer. And wrote some of the most brilliant words ever written. Still took him *three* tries to win." He stood and looked downhill at the blunted house and the land running into blackness behind it. " 'We hold these truths to be self-evident'—listen to this, Corey—'that all men are created equal, that they are endowed by their Creator with certain inalienable rights.' *Certain inalienable rights*," he said, bending back to the shovel. "What words!" He was breathing steadily from the effort. " 'Life, liberty, and the pursuit of happiness.' " I heard the rhythmic scrape of the blade and the soft landing of the snow. " 'That to secure these rights Governments are instituted among men, deriving their just powers from the consent of the governed.' From the consent of the governed, Corey! All Jefferson. One-fifty. We live in what he invented. A pluralist at the exact moment when the country needed one. The greatest in history. Wouldn't survive now six months in politics. Not with Nixon on his tail. Next."

"John Quincy Adams."

"What're they teaching you at that school of ours?"

"Madison?"

"Right. And then Monroe. Then Quincy Adams."

All the while he was shoveling, and the black of the road was appearing again beneath us. We had gone perhaps forty yards now. I won't record everything he said, but two hours later when we reached the trees, he'd covered every president through Lyndon Johnson and had shoveled his own half of the trail and probably a third of my own. I'd never seen him like that. He knew the losing candidates in every election since Washington's, and he knew the tally of the electoral votes. I'd never realized the extent of his knowledge nor the concentration with which he obviously executed his job—indeed I'd never even realized that he was a man of books, on top of everything else he was. He didn't show that side to me ever again.

I can only tell you that as we made our way up the driveway, him counting off every fiftieth shovel stroke in a rough cadence and me dropping behind by four or five at every interval, I too began to feel the euphoria of that kind of hard work in that kind of cold weather. Of that kind of discipline against what the inner voice says is insurmountable. When we reached the cover of the sycamores where the snow thinned to a depth that was passable for cars, he set aside his shovel and we sat down together on the asphalt, both of us exhausted, and he said, "Henry Bonwiller's going to win this goddamn election, Corey. I've figured it out on the graphs of history. I've had my vision." The snow had stopped now but the veil of flakes drifting down from the canopy caught the light of the lamps like a gossamer stage curtain behind him. "That's what I'm trying to show you. The monist tends to win against the pluralist. And most so amidst uncertainty. That's the mathematical lesson of history. And those forces are coming together for our man right now—the intersecting graphs of discontent and optimism. By November Nixon's going to wish he'd never heard of Henry W. Bonwiller, I guarantee you that! And Muskie, too. God damn him to hell! We're standing at the crossing point of the great unchallengeable historical vectors. And they're on our side, Corey! You mark my words. They're on our goddamn side! Goddamn right we're going to win the thing! You mark my words!"

HERE'S WHERE IT GETS COMPLICATED.

It was a week into Christmas break now, a little more than a month before the Iowa caucuses. Mrs. Metarey had taken Clara and Christian skiing in Idaho, and Aberdeen West was quiet, especially in the mornings. Very early one of those mornings, just after light, while I was sweeping snow off the front walks, Henry Bonwiller arrived alone at the estate. He didn't even have Carlton Sample with him, and instead of giving me the Cadillac he parked it himself in the garage and went quickly up the stairs to the house. He looked ashen. Weather had come in the night before—a warm snow that was pleasant and hushed when you were out in it, as I was, but that was getting thicker. Liam Metarey was in the horse pasture helping Breighton walk off a sprained foot. I ran to tell him the Senator had arrived.

"He looks worried," I said.

"Christ," he answered, "it's the weekend. Isn't one injured animal enough?"

"Sir?"

"Did he say what he wanted?"

"He didn't even say hello."

He looked startled. "Walk him," he said, handing me Breighton's reins. He glanced up at the house. "Henry Bonwiller would say hello to the hangman."

I think I was aware through these years—and by that, I mean the time from the summer I first began working on the Metarey estate until the fall I went away to college—I think I was aware through these years that they were already apart from my true life, from my *own* life; and it's because of this, I think, that they have become the substance of my most formidable memories. That must be why I still see the events of that time with such clarity, when otherwise my childhood is just a wash of ordinary sensations: wet ball fields, the ringing of school bells, the smell of lime on my father's clothes.

Liam Metarey and the Senator spent the whole morning in the downstairs study. I could see them talking at a table. At one point I looked in from the corral and saw the Senator stumble as he rose from his seat, and then Mr. Metarey take his elbow. The snow was getting heavier and I'd had to shovel a track for Breighton, who was skittish from his injury, before I could lead him back to the stall at lunchtime. By then, Mr. Metarey and the Senator were in the upstairs library.

That afternoon I was summoned there to build a fire, and when I came in with an armful of walnut their conversation stopped. They watched me as I set up the wood. On the table in front of them sat a pot of coffee, and in the few minutes I was in the room Senator Bonwiller finished a full cup and poured himself another. Then they both sat back against the cushions. By that point in my work at the Metareys', my presence was rarely noticed, but now the two of them were clearly waiting for me to leave. The snow was thick outside and the room had taken on the stony chill that the house emanated in the darkest days of winter. When I stepped back into the hallway and closed the door, I heard their conversation begin again.

A few minutes later, I saw Liam Metarey go outside to the work barn and emerge driving the Ferguson. He headed up the driveway on it, vanishing into the falling snow.

That evening, near five, which was my hour to go home, he found me in the toolshed. "We need a driver into Buffalo," he said. "An errand."

"Yes, sir."

"I'm sorry if it means you'll miss dinner at home—but Gil's out and there's no one else to do it. We'll eat in Buffalo, all of us together. You can give your parents a call from inside. But hurry," he said, glancing at his watch, "we're late. And big snow's coming tonight. We'll take the Senator's car." Then he looked at me. "There's trouble," he said. "I'm sorry."

I don't know, and I suppose I never will know, exactly what Liam Metarey thought of me, or what I was to him. But he looked at me openly now. "We couldn't be in a bigger mess, actually."

"I saw the headline," I said.

He looked startled. "Which headline?"

"The grand jury," I said. I considered whether I might have overstepped. Finally I added, "Anodyne Energy."

"Oh, that—" he said. "Well, I wish that was all we had to worry about."

"You can count on me, sir."

"I know," he answered, "I know." Then he reached across and ruffled my hair the way he did sometimes. "Let's go, I suppose. I'm sorry."

Of course he didn't tell me what the errand was, and of course I didn't expect to know—it was only years afterward that I pieced together what might have happened. I called home and a moment later came outside to find the two of them already waiting in the idling Cadillac. It was almost dark now and all the porch and garage lamps were off, but the car's inside light was on, and I recall clearly how they looked as I hurried from the house. Henry Bonwiller gestured as he spoke from the backseat and Liam Metarey nodded as he listened from the front, both of them illuminated so starkly that they seemed to glow. The driver's door was already open, and I quickly took my place at the wheel. I didn't take any kind of close look at the car; there was no reason to. A thin layer of melting snow whitened the carpet by Mr. Metarey's shoes, and when I glanced to the back I saw snow there, too, on the floor and on the ridge of the seat, but I didn't bother to think about how it might have gotten in there. "I can sweep the snow out," I said.

"No, no," said Liam Metarey. "Don't bother with it."

"There's no time," said the Senator. "Just drive."

The car was warm. With the sides of his shoes, Mr. Metarey was brushing the snow to the edge of the carpet, and I could hear the Senator in the backseat doing the same. As I rounded the curve by the house the front wheels slid in a drift, but I turned the wheel toward the skid and we straightened. I fixed my concentration on the road.

"Rough weather," said the Senator.

"We should be thanking God for that, Henry," Liam Metarey said sharply. "And thanking God," he added in a gentler tone, "that we have someone like Corey to drive in it."

The air had turned noticeably colder in the afternoon. There were several inches of snow on the pavement now, but it was dry and the car's heavy tires threw it out of the way. I made a point of driving particularly cautiously, but if they asked for speed I was ready to supply it. It occurred to me that they might need to resume whatever conversation they'd been having that day, so I turned on the radio, which was set to a jazz station, and let them see that I was listening to it. The sun was almost down. We turned from the gravel traffic circle of the courtyard onto the long driveway, which ran through the rows of sycamores and the dense woods of oak and Scotch pine. Here the road passed nearly into its full nighttime dark, and the snow lay thinner where it was shielded beneath the limbs.

As we passed out of the lane where the sycamores met overhead, into the longer, open stretch of lower trees, Liam Metarey leaned forward, turned off the radio, and said, "Look at that—a hawk." He pointed out my corner of the windshield toward the sky. "Hunting on our land. That's got to be a sign."

"A redtail," Senator Bonwiller said quickly from the backseat. "That's an auspicious omen."

"Do you see him, Corey?" said Liam Metarey, leaning low on the seat toward me and craning his neck so that he could point at the sky through my window. His head nearly rested on the steering wheel. "Do you see his regal tail?"

We were in the middle of the forest now. "I can't look, sir, at the moment."

"Spectacular," said the Senator. "Look at him."

"I can't yet, sir. But I've seen them before. I've lived here all my life." Instantly I regretted mentioning anything about myself, even a fact so small—not because of modesty, but because I knew that Henry Bonwiller wasn't the least bit interested. In order to move the subject back to the hawk, I said, "I'll see him at the turn, sir."

"He'll be gone by then," said the Senator. "It's nearly dark. Take a good look at him now, son."

I slowed the car.

"Don't stop," he said. "For Christ's sake. He's right overhead in the gap. Just open the damn window and put your head out."

I lowered the glass. It was snowing heavily here at the break, but I leaned out and looked up toward the sky. In order to please the two of them, I made a show of getting my head most of the way out of the opening. Big flakes landed in my eyes. I saw no hawk, only the froth of descending white against the blackening clouds.

It's impossible to reconstruct everything that happened next. I remember feeling stuck. I think my arm must have been pinned against the top of the door. I lifted my hips to free it.

I heard Mr. Metarey say, "Sorry, son."

That's when the steering wheel jerked in my hand. We left the road and in an instant were sliding down the steep embankment. I felt Mr. Metarey's strong arms pulling me in, then the violent bounce at the bottom of the gulley. We skidded on the riprap and pushed sideways through a drift, then ran headlong across open ground, plowing snow over the hood, until we hit.

A sledgehammer. Followed by silence. Then hissing. I opened my eyes. A good-sized oak rose from the corner of the hood. Mr. Metarey reached and switched off the engine. The hissing stopped and we were surrounded by an eerie quiet until after a moment I heard the almost imperceptible pattering of snow on the roof. He was rubbing his forehead.

His voice sounded strained. "Well, Corey," he said, "I guess we're not going to see that hawk tonight, after all." Then he began brushing at the snow around his feet again.

"Ah, but he was something," said Senator Bonwiller, in an almost jovial tone. "Believe me."

"Are you all right, Senator?" I said, turning to the backseat.

"I sure hope so, boy."

He laughed at that, and he seemed to be fine as he unstrapped his seat belt and climbed out. He stood at the tree inspecting the damage. "Both left quarter panels," he said. "Front one just at the point."

Mr. Metarey got out, too, and ran his hand over it. "Both'll have to be replaced," he said. "Simple. Done by tomorrow night, Senator."

When I finally joined them outside, Henry Bonwiller greeted me with a slap on the back. "That was a fine piece of driving, there," he said. "Both of you."

That's what he said. I remember it.

"I'm sorry, sir. Are you all right, Senator? I'm sorry, Mr. Metarey. I can run back to the house. Is everyone okay? I'll run back and get another car. I'll be right back. I can get someone. I'm sorry, Senator. I'm very sorry."

"No," said Liam Metarey, looking up the road to the north. "Wait here with us."

"Should I get the Chrysler?"

And as though to answer me, at that very moment a pair of lights appeared at the north entrance. They flickered in the distance, then swung around and steadied toward us. At the time, I thought it was our great good luck.

"You'll wait here with us, boy," said Henry Bonwiller.

We had all turned to look now. It might have been a dream. The distant headlamps zigzagging through the black woods, causing long tracks of luxuriously swirling flakes to materialize out of the dark. The beams grew brighter, moving slowly around the curves, and when they rounded the last bend I saw that they belonged to the maintenance station wagon. Gil McKinstrey was at the wheel. I scrambled up the embankment, my legs plunging in the drifts.

"Calm there, Corey," Liam Metarey called. "Calm is ninety percent in a situation like this."

The car slowed and Gil shouted out the window, "Anyone hurt?" He held a hurricane lantern.

"Nothing a hot toddy wouldn't cure," the Senator bellowed back.

"I'll see if we have one around then. Yes, sir."

Then, before the station wagon had even stopped, the back doors swung open and three men emerged clutching rescue equipment. Oh, how new I was to that world, and how naïve. It was all strangely incomprehensible until they were most of the way down the embankment and I finally understood what was happening: it wasn't rescue equipment at all—it was camera equipment. They were press photographers, climbing down with their gear.

I'd seen them before, I realized, at the Metarey parties. One was from *The Sentinel*, I think, and one from the *Courier-Express*, and one was just a man they hired for handshake shots. Henry Bonwiller clapped me on the back, and although he was dressed in his usual dark suit and suspenders, he hopped right up and sat on the wet front of the hood. And after that, there seemed to be nothing but frivolity. He took off his coat and offered it to me—my pants were covered to the knees with snow—and then he gestured with his broad hand for me to sit next to him. I did, and he placed the coat over my shoulders. The *Sentinel* photographer, who had already set up his tripod, looked down into his camera and began to count backwards for the flash.

Over the years I've thought about this incident, probably more often than about any other bit of this story, and I still can't say if what Mr. Metarey and the Senator did was an intelligent gamble or merely the product of ambition, delusion, and the frenzied velocity of the campaign. In a drawer of my desk at home, I still have a framed picture of the Senator and me sitting on the hood of that car. It's the original of the print that I believe they were keeping in case they needed it to run somewhere. I suppose they had their reasons to do it that way—it would have provided what they needed, if it ever came to that. And they could have spread it a lot farther than the *Courier-Express*, if they'd had to. But they never did.

I've never known another politician, and have never again in my life come so close to a man of history like Senator Bonwiller, but at the time I must have supposed that such experiences would one day become common for me. I took every incident as a fable, every milestone as a fortuitous lesson on how to act in this new and public world. The Senator sat on the hood with me, and although he'd begun to look uncomfortable, he started to tell jokes then, anyway, the way he often did when photographers were around. In front of us they clomped around in the deep snow, lugging their tripods. I must say, not one of his stories struck me as funny, but I remember that I was laughing anyway—loudly enough that he would hear. It shames me to admit that now. In retrospect I'd say that I didn't like him much, even then, but I suppose in those days there was nothing I wouldn't do for him. Or for Mr. Metarey, either. Flashes were going off now in quick succession. When the Senator indicated that he wanted another shot from a wider angle, the men picked up their gear and lugged it farther into the woods. I rose from the hood and leaned against the tree on which I'd just ruined his car, smiling for the cameras.

As for Liam Metarey, something bleak had entered him and suddenly he seemed to want nothing to do with it anymore. He walked up to stand behind the tripods in the dark. Each time a flash faded away, I could see him leaning against a tree, near Gil McKinstrey, who was watching us from alongside the station wagon.

"That's plenty of pictures," Mr. Metarey finally called down to us. "Let's go now, before any tears are shed."

"Cold enough to piss icicles," came Gil McKinstrey's barely audible voice.

"Ready tears are a sign of treachery," Henry Bonwiller called back in his operatic bass. "Not of grief." He was speaking now as though addressing a crowd, looking left and right while one of the cameramen exploded a last flash from deep in the trees. With his chin the Senator gestured at me cloaked in his elegant jacket, and with his broad hand he pointed at the folded bumper of the car.

"They can also be a sign of cold," said Liam Metarey, coming down to toss me a blanket from the back of the station wagon. I guess I must have been shivering. I should say that still nothing anybody was saying struck me as funny—it all seemed like some kind of mannered English stage play instead, acted not just by the Senator but by the photographers, too, who continued to laugh heartily as they began to pack up their instruments, and watched by Liam Metarey and Gil McKinstrey and me. I could make no sense of the mood. All I knew was that I wanted to be part of it.

"I'm not blaming you, Gil," I finally called out, in a voice so loud that to my own ears I sounded drunk. "But you were the one who taught me to drive."

Henry Bonwiller let out his booming laugh. You can imagine how that felt. And I could hear the photographers chuckling, too. But then my eyes went to Gil himself, standing at the edge of the lantern light in his slouched posture by the door of the car. He merely raised his head a bit and looked at me.

THREE

I WENT TO COLLEGE at Haverford, just west of Philadelphia. A month after my eighteenth birthday the draft ended, and in September of 1973 I stepped off the R5 Paoli Local at Haverford Station with Liam Metarey's bag over my shoulder. By then, the country was already turning away from its anger. Kent State was in the past. SDS had disappeared. Nixon was on the run then, but we were out of Vietnam and the feeling across the country on the day I stepped off the train and made my way across the street to find a taxi to take me to college was that the years of unrest were over. The trees were turning. By the cab stand, a brilliant cardinal was whoop-whooping in the top of an elm.

When I think back on those days, I realize that they were the fulcrum I used to lift myself away from my upbringing; to finally push myself, really, by dint of education, into a social class that I at last belonged to by accomplishment, even if not by wealth. I'm not proud of that and I'm not ashamed of it. It's just a fact, which with the years behind me I can see. I loved college. Haverford was dotted with the same kind of students I'd seen at Dunleavy, the offspring of privilege who fancied themselves rebels according to the amount of dope they smoked or the numbers of classes they missed to play Frisbee on the rolling lawns by the duck pond. I won't deny that I felt superior. A strange thing to say for a boy who'd spent the previous two years feeling like a charlatan, even among Dunleavy's laggards, but either I was growing up by virtue of years or by virtue of the things I'd seen at Aberdeen West. Those things had toughened me faster than most kids get toughened, and made me wiser, too. One night in the Metareys' dining room I'd seen Melvin Laird—Nixon's relentless attack man against Henry Bonwiller's opposition to the war—enjoying a long and jovial dinner with the Senator. I'd seen plenty of other things, too. It was difficult for me to get excited over the prospect of missing classes.

So I did just what I'd done at Dunleavy. I studied. Right off the bat I met a girl, from Bryn Mawr. I was living in a dorm, a four-story stone building with old wooden windows that had to be slammed with the butt of a hand to open, but that looked over a plush lawn, dotted with oaks and maples, running down a long slope to the duck pond. You can imagine what took place around that pond among a group of nineteen-year-olds who'd just found out they wouldn't have to go to war. At a barbecue there one night, when most of the crowd was drinking spiked punch out of quart mason jars, I met Holly.

Holly Steen. She was like me. A freshman, too, and the first in her family to go to college. She'd already declared an English major, with the idea of going to law school when she was done. She was from Memphis. Her father was a mechanic at the Ford dealership and her stepbrother was a long-distance trucker. She worked in the dining hall for her student aid, and I worked in the library.

The two of us, in our earnest ways, set out to separate ourselves from both our classmates and our backgrounds. Kids then were listening to the Who and Jefferson Airplane, but Holly and I made a point of taking the train into the city to hear the Philadelphia Orchestra. I'd never been inside a concert hall before in my life. When the rest of campus was crowding onto buses to go to Lancaster to watch Haverford play baseball against Franklin and Marshall for the league title, we were on the same train into the Philadelphia Museum of Art to look at the oils of Thomas Eakins. You can't underestimate the determination both of us had. These days, of course, I'm reminded of Trieste—although her resolve is in the form of vigorous originality, and ours, if I have to put a word on it, was in the form of *hunger*. We wanted the things that the kids around us had by birthright, kids who'd grown up in the ivied suburbs that we could see from the windows as the train swayed and clacked its way into Philadelphia. I'd seen those things at the Metareys', of course, but I'd had to leave home for good, I think, had to travel not just the hundred miles to Dunleavy but the full length of a state before I felt free enough—and deserving enough—to try for some of them myself.

Those weren't easy times to go against the crowd, but I should add that we weren't alone. There was a group of students at Haverford and Bryn Mawr and Swarthmore then who ran contrary to the common attitude, and soon enough we'd found one another. That fall we decided to form a group, united by the fact that we took our studies seriously. Over my time there we reliably numbered about thirty, and we met at night in one of the campus houses over apple cider to talk about art and music and history; we staged mock debates between nineteenth-century philosophers and presented oral reports on our visits to museums and monuments. We invited professors to speak to us. I think most of us were deeply grateful—I might even say giddy—to find ourselves among libraries and pianos and unabridged dictionaries on stands. Those were the things we wanted.

Holly was our leader. She was a small girl, and I remember her smallness as important. She wasn't slight, but she was compact, and when she spoke she lifted herself just perceptibly on her toes and tilted her head up, and there was such sincerity and eagerness in her pose that I believed any man who spoke to her for any length of time would fall in love with her. This put me in a constant state of urgency. When I'd met her myself for the first time, at the barbecue alongside the duck pond, and she'd raised herself on the front of her feet in that particular way, I understood instantly that I'd found what I was looking for.

AFTER THE ACCIDENT in the Senator's car, sleep ran away from me. Every night I lay in my childhood bed waiting for it, and every morning my eyes twitched open still in darkness to the memory of frantically steering as we plunged down the hill. We were halfway through the Christmas break now, and in two weeks I would be heading back to school. There was something about returning to Dunleavy that seemed particularly final to me; but even so, I hadn't yet begun to steel myself for it. And I hadn't yet called my old friends from Roosevelt, either. I was beginning to realize that I wasn't going to. They weren't going to call me, either. Maybe not ever again.

What was odd was that nobody at the Metareys' had said a word about the accident. Clara would certainly have chided me if she'd been there, and Christian might have comforted me, but they were both still skiing with their mother. Every day, I was going over the incident in my mind, and perhaps as a result, the specifics had already become a jumble. Obviously it had been a mistake to lean out the window, but Senator Bonwiller had ordered me to—hadn't he? Also, it had warmed briefly in the morning before cooling again: there might have been ice under the snow. On the other hand, the car might easily have flipped when it came over the lip of the embankment; but it hadn't. This could have been because I was driving so reasonably when we went in. But the truth was, if somebody had told me a twelve-point buck had hit us, it wouldn't have been long before I believed it. That was the kind of condition I was in.

More than anything, I wanted to be working again. Work was a cure for anything. But as Christmas neared, Aberdeen West seemed to go into a sort of hibernation—a peculiarity of the Metareys that I would come to know later—the house emptying rather than filling, and all the busy commerce of the place slowing nearly to a halt. And although serious tests were coming for Senator Bonwiller in little more than a month, the campaign appeared to have moved elsewhere, as well. The whole estate was quiet. Since the day I'd crashed the car, I'd only been called to work a couple of times, once to cart in a cord of firewood and once to fix a gate hinge that had come loose in the barn.

Beyond that, there seemed to be no jobs for me. I spent my time in the overheated front room of my parents' house, trying to study for the exams we would take when we returned. Every morning I called the estate to say I was available. Sometimes I called again in the afternoon. I always hoped to reach Mr. Metarey, of course; but I never did. Although I knew he was home—I'd seen him in his upstairs study— after the accident occurred he'd seemed to withdraw from public; at least, he withdrew from me. This was unsettling.

Whenever Gil McKinstrey answered, I tried to ask in my usual, offhand way if he had anything for later, or for the next day. But so far, he had almost nothing. And for the rest of the time at my own house, really, all I did was wait for the phone to ring. I guess what I wanted was to prove myself again. To prove that I wouldn't let them down.

Two days before Christmas, Mr. Metarey himself finally did call, asking me to come over and help Gil with the lights on the Lodge Chief Marker. These days, of course, the big tree is lit by Thanksgiving; but back then, they waited until Christmas Eve, a ritual guided not just by Liam Metarey's frugality, no doubt, but by the frugality of the whole county as well. I hurried over. Among the townspeople, the lighting of the Lodge Chief could not have been more elemental to the family's renown. Eoghan Metarey himself had started the tradition sometime around the turn of the century—that's when he'd hired Westinghouse—and a good many of Saline's older families still made the trip out on Boxing Day to sing carols under the lights. I should add that I've seen similar situations since then—the way workers or townspeople or even the most miserable inhabitants of third-world shantytowns will cleave to some slight gesture of cordiality from the capital class, as though it superseded all questions of rank and wealth and justice. Sometimes I think Mr. Metarey thought so, himself. Clara later told me that he had to be reminded every year to light it. I think he felt the paltriness of the ritual and was embarrassed at how important it had become to the citizens of Saline.

Nevertheless, he lit it every year. It wasn't until late afternoon, though, that he finally called, and by the time I made my way on foot through the woods I found the tree already ringed with its mantle of lights. Gil McKinstrey was at the top, finishing up. I walked over and stood on the far side of the underbranches. I'd seen these same decorations every year of my childhood, but never from so close: now I saw that the insulation around the plugs had been repaired over and over, and that whole stretches of cord were wound in electrical tape. Maybe a fifth of the bulbs were burned out, too. Of course, this was characteristic of the Metarey thrift that I was now so familiar with. But the tree itself, despite the raggedness of its wrapping, had already begun to glow, its lights twinkling faintly in the waning light.

The truth was that I was afraid of seeing Gil. I knew there was a reason he wasn't calling me. From behind the branches I watched him. The great pine was twice as tall as the house itself, and now he was within his own height of the top. He gripped the narrow trunk with climbing spurs and leaned out into the air. He swung a short coil of lights a couple of times in his hand, then lobbed it to the end of a drooping limb, where it caught. From where I stood, he looked like a fly fisherman casting a luminescent jig into the heavens. Finally, I shouted up to him.

"Get on out of here," he called back. He clapped his gloves against the trunk and a cloud of frost drifted into the air. "Colder than a well digger's balls up here."

"You sure you want to be working with the stuff plugged in?"

"It'd be a relief is what it'd be. Warm me up half a degree."

"Mr. Metarey sent me out to help."

"Don't need you."

"I'm happy to do it."

"Don't need you," he said again.

The next day, I knew, he would stand there at sunset while the townspeople gathered in the descending dark, waiting for Mrs. Metarey to flip the oversized throw switch that was banded to the trunk. He was just testing everything for now. The wind had died down, as it always does here after sunset, but still it was blowing a bit, and I can only imagine how cold it must have been in the top of those branches: I wonder what thoughts went through his mind, too, as he leaned out eighty feet in the air to do the hard work that someone else, the next day, in a fox-fur winter coat, would get credit for.

"You sure?" I called up.

But either he didn't hear me or he didn't bother to answer. I turned and walked back home through the trees to my parents' house.

At that time of year, my mother made samplers for all her sisters and their families, and that evening after dinner she sat down on the couch across from me with her embroidery needle. "I know what you're thinking," she said.

"Please."

"You're thinking that you missed us at school. But now that you're home, you realize that you miss being at school." She smiled at me. "Isn't that right?"

"It's nothing like that."

"I see."

After a few moments, she said, "You can talk to me about your life, you know, Cor. I won't bite."

"There's nothing to say, Mom."

She picked up her handiwork then. And I'm ashamed to say that the sight of her there in her thick slippers, holding the needle at arm's length so she could see the threads as she embroidered *Peace on Earth,* was more than I could take. I was already in my undershirt, which was as far as I could go in our house, and I'd already called the Metareys' once that day, but I opened the back door anyway, pulled the phone out to the stoop on its long cord, and dialed again.

It was probably just after six now. But the midwinter darkness made it seem later, and the temperature was well below freezing. In my undershirt I leaned back against the door and waited for the connection. The number I used rang in the long mudroom behind the kitchen, where Mr. Metarey liked to tinker and where Gil McKinstrey did his inside work. I assumed Gil was still out at the tree or putting things away in the barn, but if he answered, I would just ask about tomorrow. And if Mr. Metarey did, as I hoped, I had several new ideas: they hadn't yet split a pile of walnut behind the barn, and I'd seen a beam in the garage that was starting to rot. I even considered offering to replace the burnt-out bulbs in the tree, despite the fact that I didn't know how to use climbing spurs and even though I knew it was something Mr. Metarey would never do. I could see my mother watching from inside.

But it was Christian who picked up the phone. "Good," she said right off, "it's you." Before I had a chance to say anything else, she said, "We're having a dinner tonight. Are you free?"

For some reason I was embarrassed to tell her we'd already eaten. "I thought you were skiing," I said.

"We just got back. Can you make it over?"

"A dinner?" In all the time we'd known each other she'd never invited me for a meal in their house. It seemed like a line between our two families, drawn by both of us. "What kind of dinner?" I said. I knew they ate late. It was something my mother had commented on.

"It's Andrew's birthday."

"Oh. He's back, then?"

"No."

"Oh."

"Actually . . ." she said. She hesitated.

"Yes?"

"He's been shipped out."

"He's what?"

"He left Fort Dix. Day before yesterday."

"He did? Where to?"

"Where do you think, Corey?"

I was quiet, thinking of him on the sailboat.

"Sorry," I said.

"It's all right."

Through the door, I saw my mother set down her work.

"Are your parents worried?"

"He's not going to the jungle," she answered. "He's going to a medical base. He'll be a long way from the fighting." In a low voice she said, "I think my father did that."

"That's good."

I pushed on the door to make sure it was closed.

"But still," she said.

"I know."

"Anyway," she said after a moment, "Mother wants to have a little party for him."

"Well, I don't know."

"He'd want you here."

As soon as we hung up, I hurried upstairs to my room and put on a pair of corduroys and my good shirt, which I found ironed on a hanger. As it happened, I'd bought a Christmas present for Christian at school, and one for her mother, too. I went to the back of the closet to get them out. I don't know why I'd bought one for Mrs. Metarey— I doubted I'd have the courage to give it to her—but at the time I'd found it, in a gift shop near the Dunleavy train station, it had somehow seemed right. And now, of course, as I dressed, I saw that it was prophetic: a medallion of Saint Sebastian. The patron saint of soldiers. I took it from the box and shined it between my fingers. Sebastian was tied to a tree, but the arrows hadn't yet hit him. That was a relief. I thought she would appreciate the fact. Christian's present was a pumpkin-colored scarf that Astor's older sister had pointed out to me one afternoon in the same store where I'd bought the medallion.

By the time I arrived at the estate, they were already at the table. Much of the staff must have been on vacation, and at the door one of the cooks let me in. He took my coat, which had the presents in it, and hung it. Things seemed odd immediately. It was a birthday party for someone who wasn't there; that was one thing. The conversation at the table paused as I crossed the atrium from the front door. I could actually hear my steps on the marble floor. Christmas was only two days away, and still there was no tree in the house. That was another. At least no tree downstairs, and no presents anywhere I could see except for one wrapped box at an empty place at the table, which I saw when I reached the dining room. This I understood was for Andrew. I took the seat across from it, which was set with a dish and a wineglass.

"Hello, Corey," June Metarey said right off. "You'll see that my husband doesn't believe in Christmas."

"He does believe in it," said Christian. "Just not the modern version. Hi, Corey."

"Welcome," said Mr. Metarey.

"Hi, everybody."

"Hark the herald angels sing," said Clara.

That's when I realized I hadn't brought anything for *her*.

"I was just saying that Christmas is a commercial profanity," said Mr. Metarey. "I've always believed that."

"Lovely," said Mrs. Metarey. "Wine, Corey?"

"And I'm saying it doesn't have to be," answered Christian.

"That's right," said Mr. Metarey. "It doesn't. And we all do help out, don't we? Christian's going to her cousin's in New York City, for example." He filled his wife's wineglass. "To work in a soup kitchen." He looked at Clara. "And Clara's going to volunteer next week at the old people's home."

"Volunteer?" said Clara.

"And Mrs. Metarey's already raised a nice amount for St. Jude's."

"To hopeless causes!" said Clara, tilting her glass.

"By the way," said Liam Metarey. "Thank you for helping with the tree today. I hope Gil appreciated it."

"You're welcome, sir. I wasn't any help."

I should say that the mood didn't seem at all caustic, even though it might sound that way. Everyone actually seemed rather jovial— especially considering the circumstances. Except for Clara, who seemed to have keyed herself that night to some mysteriously taut emotional pitch. The others were speaking in something like amused voices, and Churchill sat on the carpet near the door with a red ribbon tied around his neck. Every now and then Mr. Metarey's fingers reached up behind his wife's chair to play with the ends of her hair. The cook who had let me in stood just outside the dining room door, in the hallway that led to the kitchen. I could see him whenever I leaned back in my seat.

"Corey, do you drink wine at home?" asked Mrs. Metarey.

"Churchill deems that unlikely," said Clara.

"Well in either case you're welcome to have some," said Mr. Metarey. Then he added, "Or there's juice."

"I can bring juice," the cook said from the hallway.

"I think he'd prefer wine."

"Then would you pour him some Bordeaux, please, Clara?"

"Here," she said, handing me the bottle.

At that point in my life, I'd only drunk wine from a jug, at the lime quarry. I must have poured it very close to the rim.

"That's nice," Clara said, looking over at me as soon as I'd finished. She lifted her own glass. "To getting your money's worth."

Christian cleared her throat. "And Dad's been working with orphanages in Southeast Asia."

"To hopeless causes again!"

"In Vietnam and Laos. It's terrible," said Mr. Metarey. "Worst for those kids. They need anything we can give."

"That's right," said Mrs. Metarey.

"This is what we try to do around Christmastime," he said. "Rather than just buy more things for one another, we try to spread around some of the good fortune we already have." He looked around the table, and when his eyes came to mine he winked. "And I do give some presents, too," he said, "despite what they say."

"Small ones, Daddy," said Christian.

"Not all of them," he answered, looking at me again.

Then we ate. It was a prime rib, carved by the cook. There were brussels sprouts, too, and potatoes cut thinly, and some kind of greens I'd never seen before. It didn't stop me that I'd already had dinner. Whenever I finished something, the cook moved up behind me and placed more onto my plate. He also poured more wine. Near the end of the main course, Churchill rose, strolled over to my seat, and sat down at my feet.

"It's okay," said Christian, "you can give him something."

"He wants his Christmas gift," said Mrs. Metarey.

"Has he done his volunteering?" said Clara.

"He wrapped all the presents," said Christian.

I could see the dog looking up at me from next to the chair, his pale eyes troubled by desire. I cut a small piece of meat and held it below the table.

He thumped his tail on the rug but didn't rise.

"He likes it cooked a little more," said Christian.

"Two thumps means a well-done slice," said Clara.

And that's what Churchill did then: he thumped his tail twice.

Growing up, I'd never had a dog. I didn't know what to do with the meat I was holding alongside my seat, so I just held it there a few inches in front of his snout. "I'm not sure I have a well-done piece," I said. With my fork in the other hand I lifted the prime rib on my plate. "I don't," I said. "All I have is medium rare."

"Church," Clara said, lowering her head, "would you think of taking one medium rare?"

Again, two thumps.

"Oh, well," said Clara. "You heard him."

"Church is a little picky," said Christian. "But I suppose it's about time you saw what he's really like."

"Ah," said Mr. Metarey, "and at last you see what my two girls are really like."

I looked over at him. "Sir?"

"Take it, Church," he said.

In an instant the meat was plucked from my palm. Then the dog ambled over to the door and sat licking his chops.

"Ah," said Clara. "At last"—she sipped her wine and bumped the glass down on the table—"at last you see what my father's like."

Mrs. Metarey let out a laugh like a sneeze.

"Touché," said Mr. Metarey.

After the main course, the cook brought out a salad. And after that he brought out a tray of figs, which I'd never seen before. The Metareys' ate them with strange distaste, like vitamins, and when they were finally done, or at least when their haphazard eating seemed finally to have petered out, Christian set down her glass. "Three thumps," she said, "means it's time to give And his present."

"Four thumps means he'd like Corey to do it," said Mrs. Metarey.

We all looked over at the dog, who did nothing.

"Indeed," said Mr. Metarey. "Corey, would you be kind enough?"

He pointed at the wrapped box across from me. I'm not sure how much Bordeaux I'd had by then, since the cook had kept my glass full, but I rose from the chair and went around the table to Andrew's seat. I'm also not sure how I knew what I was supposed to do, but without hesitation I unwrapped the present and set aside the paper. Inside the box was a leather jacket.

"My father's," Mr. Metarey said. "He used to wear it crossing the Atlantic."

"Oh, sweetheart," said Mrs. Metarey.

"I thought And should have it."

Again, I knew what was expected of me. It fit, although a little tightly across the shoulders. The material was a soft leather, finely cracked in places but still dark brown and supple, set with rows of tarnished brass snaps. I stood so they could all look at it. Then I took it off, hung it over the back of the chair, and went back to my own seat. The family continued to gaze across the table at Andrew's place. Mr. Metarey nodded his head.

"Happy birthday, Andrew," said Christian.

"Happy birthday, Andrew," we all said.

"May the wind be always at your back, And," said Mr. Metarey.

"Hear! Hear!"

We sat then in silence. Churchill rose, padded across the room, and lay down next to Andrew's seat.

"Isn't Vietnam tropical?" Clara said at last.

Mrs. Metarey said, "It gets cold there at night. He can wear it then."

Suddenly I said, "I brought something for you, too, Christian."

"How nice of you," said Mrs. Metarey.

I wasn't exactly drunk, but I wasn't exactly sober, either. I went quickly to the hall for my coat. "For *you*," I said, taking the slim box from the pocket and sliding it across the table toward her.

Christian looked around. I could see that she was embarrassed. But when she unwrapped the scarf and held it up, I had the feeling that she was happy with it. She held it to her neck.

"Ravishing," said Mrs. Metarey. "Truly."

"Beautiful," said Liam Metarey.

"It is," I said. She'd wrapped it now so that it crossed in front of her clavicle.

After a moment, Clara said, "Who helped you find it?"

"Clara—" said her mother.

"I don't know if I'd answer this one, Corey," said Mr. Metarey.

"Don't you think I could have picked it out myself?"

"Well, actually—no." It was Christian speaking now. "Now that you mention it—no, I don't think so." She held up her own glass for the cook to refill and looked at me around the side of it. "But thank you anyway. It's lovely."

"To a job in the Bonwiller administration!"

"Clara," Mrs. Metarey said again.

"Let Corey be," said Christian.

"I could say the same for you, Christian."

"What's that supposed to mean?"

Clara turned to me. "Didn't you bring anything for Father?"

"Clara Metarey!"

Clara, strangely, came near to tears then. I don't know why. I saw them gather in her eyes.

"Both of you," said Mr. Metarey in a low voice.

That's when I took the other box from my pocket. I don't know how much this gesture ended up meaning in my life. "And this is for Clara," I said, pushing it across the tablecloth.

She looked at me, blinking.

"How kind of you, Corey," said Mr. Metarey.

"I'd say diplomatic, Daddy," said Christian.

Clara picked it up. She smiled nervously. The shine was still in her eyes. Then she pretended to weigh the box in her hand. Finally, she opened it. St. Sebastian lay on his cotton bed. But the surprising thing was that when she lifted the clasp so that the pendant slid down the chain into her other palm, the tears welled over and came down her cheeks.

"We're all tired," said Mr. Metarey, rising and moving around the table to put his arm over her shoulder. Churchill got up, too, and pressed himself against her. "We're all worried about And. But he's going to be fine, sweetheart. And'll be right back here next Christmas."

I was still looking at Clara. She wouldn't look back at me, but the tears were still there. I realized I didn't know the first thing about her.

"Andrew will be just fine," said Mrs. Metarey.

Clara sobbed once, softly.

"There, sweetheart," said her father. "There now, come on now."

When I looked back, Christian was watching me, that striking silvery glint in her eyes. The cook came up behind her to take her plate, but she didn't move aside for him.

THE POLICE SPOKE to all four body shops in the area, and the fact that they turned up nothing has bolstered the conspiracy theorists for years and given support to those who still perk up at the suggestion of wrongdoing. But the simple truth was that Liam Metarey and I were the ones who repaired Senator Bonwiller's car. The damage wasn't as bad as it seemed. The hood had actually popped open and not even been chipped. The hissing had been from the radiator cap, springing its safety. There was no crack in the radiator body, nor in the block.

We didn't have to pull out the dents. Waiting for us in the barn the next morning, wrapped in kraft paper and wound with gaffer's tape, was a brand-new quarter-panel set, along with the chrome bumper and double headlamp. When I came in just after dawn, three large packages and two smaller ones were sitting on a pallet by the workbench, and when I unwrapped the quarter panels I saw that they'd already been painted midnight blue. All Mr. Metarey and I had to do was bolt them onto the frame. We had to replace the signal-light covers, too, and their lamps, and the chrome trim-stripe behind the wheel cutout, but all these parts had been delivered as well, and we didn't need more than an hour to attach them. I don't remember what Liam Metarey did with the old quarter panels, which had been crimped pretty seriously by the impact, and I suppose that's one of the questions people want an answer to. But it's not one I can help with. At the time, he and I worked silently together, and quickly. He was normally affable, of course, but today he worked without speaking. I took my cue from him. We exchanged almost no words at all. Only late in the afternoon, without thinking, did I say in an offhand way, "Hard to believe the parts got here so fast."

He looked over at me. "Ingenuity of the American working man," he answered.

That was our only conversation. At the time I simply understood that we were two members of a team with an important job to do; and for a while I flattered myself by thinking that he'd chosen me instead of Gil McKinstrey because, for that single morning at least, as I held up my end of the panels and handed him bolts and machine screws and his old Rockwell impact wrench, I might have been the last person left in the world that he trusted.

Later on, of course, I realized that his silence had been meant to protect me.

ON THE EVENING of January 25th, I walked into the Dunleavy commons lounge and found Mr. Clayliss looking up at me from the couch with his chin thrust forward pugnaciously. "Sorry to break it to you, Sifter," he said, putting on a mock hillbilly accent, "but your dog's broke a leg." He laughed, and so did a couple of the teachers sitting around him on the couches. But not all of them, and not the two other students in the corner by the door. I joined them there. Mr. Clayliss's chin gestured toward the TV set. "Broke bad, I'd say."

A moment later Walter Cronkite came on and announced in his imperturbable rumble that Edmund Muskie had trounced the field in Iowa. Henry Bonwiller had finished fifteen points back, barely ahead of McGovern. Mr. Clayliss stood and strode to the door. The rest of us remained where we were, and a couple of the teachers looked over at me. After a few moments, I turned and walked out. I made my way along the walk onto the playing fields beyond the creek.

It was a clear night. Bitterly cold but bright with a rising moon. I walked well beyond the track, out into the deep drifts behind the stacked soccer goals and almost to the woods. Ahead of me the slender silver lines of the birches marked the break. Behind them the school was just a set of faint yellow windows through the branches. Most of my classmates were barely aware that a presidential race was being run. In Wilcott I could make out a group of them jostling back and forth in the hall, flinging something.

My link with everything bigger than myself was ending. That's what I realized at that moment. That everything that had allowed me to ignore the unease I felt here, that everything that had lifted me away from it, was over now. From here forward, if I was to make something of my days in this place, I would have to lift myself. I turned and walked farther. The paths glittered with ice.

FOUR

I

The Islington Speaker
Saturday, January 29th, 1972

> *DIED.* JoEllen Charney, 26, of Steppan. Miss Charney was raised in Albion and worked at the law offices of McBain & Sweeney in Steppan, where she also served as President of the Carrol County Optimists' Chorus and a school volunteer. A graduate of the State University of New York at Buffalo, she was the recipient of a Rotarian Scholarship and the winner of the 1969 Miss Three-Counties Beauty Pageant, as well as a semifinalist in the Miss New York State competition of the same year. She is survived by her parents, George and Eunice Charney, of Albion. Private services have been held at the Third Lutheran Church of Islington. Donations may be directed to the Carrol County Optimists' Chorus.

II

Every year in late summer, the Speaker-Sentinel Foundation holds a dinner for its benefactors. These are the people who help us with our internships—we offer more than just the one at the paper—and the other projects we sponsor in the community. This year we held it at the estate of Clive Wantik, of the grocery family—Find What You Want at Wantiks!—who has been more than generous with us over the years. For these dinners we invite all the interns we can find, past and present, so that the contributors can see exactly what their money is buying.

The Wantik property is magnificent—horse stables, a dark-bottomed pool, a main house built from stone that looks as though it was brought over by ship from an English manor with the moss still on it. It's even more impressive at a glance than Aberdeen West used to be. Even at its apex, the Metarey estate maintained all the equipment and services of a working piece of land, while at the Wantiks' you'd be hard-pressed to find a stack of firewood. Let alone a metal lathe. But you could no doubt take your choice from a shelf of extra-plush towels in a variety of colors if you wandered into one of the pool cabanas. And all of it is owned by a man who's risen in thirty years from stock boy in a town grocery on the Jersey shore. For the dinner we sat at round tables set in linen. Trieste was seated at my own, making pleasant enough conversation every time I looked over, with Isabelle Wantik herself, who I suspect is the one who writes the checks.

We'd stumbled on a splendid night. The dinner was held outdoors on the brick of the rear patio, which also held a twelve-piece brass orchestra on a bandstand, a wooden dance floor, and a raft of Polynesian-looking torches whose flames were doing a nice job of keeping the mosquitoes to the other half of the yard. Each intern was at a table with a benefactor, and I must say I was proud that Trieste was at mine. The tickets cost fifteen hundred dollars each and the dress was black-tie. Most of the girls looked wonderful in their long dresses—it's a graceful age—and most of the boys wore sport coats.

And that's what Trieste was wearing, too—a sport coat. Herringbone. In the heat it stood out even more, and it actually pained me a little—but it was a fine evening and full of good feeling. And to tell the truth, I hadn't expected her to dress up at all. We'd been served gazpacho while the horn players snapped their way through "Pennsylvania 6-5000" and "Tuxedo Junction." As the gazpacho was being cleared, Isabelle Wantik rose and crossed to the bandstand, and I saw Trieste reach over and borrow her soup spoon. She set it over her own to make a maraca, which she sat lightly tapping on the table as our hostess waited for the beat of Glenn Miller's memory to wind down. The band finished and in another moment the guests quieted. The afternoon had been hot, but now the heat had softened into a mist of lilac and citronella, and the season's last fireflies were dancing. Isabelle Wantik made the usual pleasantries and acknowledgments, then bowed slightly as her guests applauded. My wife was between Trieste's seat and mine, and I saw her raise her eyebrows.

When the chairman of the foundation then stood to make a toast, my wife looked at me dead-on. Then she inclined her head a little toward Trieste. I looked over. She was holding the maraca in her lap. A waiter appeared with a tray to collect the dishes, and as he leaned over her I saw her drop one of the spoons into her pocket. Then she handed her bowl to him, cleared her throat, and looked up expectantly as the board chair began his toast. My own spoon was still in my hand. Even in the low light I could see it was silver.

"Well," she said, a half hour later, when we were away from the tables. I'd approached her next to the shellacked wood stage. "Find what you want at Wantiks!"

She was smiling. There were, as there always are, any number of ways to interpret that smile. I wasn't exactly at a loss, but I was certainly wary of tipping my hand. Actually, I had no intention of accusing her. Near us, the trumpeter slouched in his folding chair and beat out a mournful solo through his mute, sweat shining on his bald head. Trieste leaned against the bandstand, both hands in her pockets, and looked frankly out at the guests. At that moment, I must say, she seemed much older than she was.

"You enjoying yourself?" I asked.

"Do you ever just want to steal from these people?" she answered.

"I see."

"All this money—it makes me want to steal sometimes. Doesn't it ever make you?"

"I suppose I've never thought of it that way. They've been very generous with us."

"Haven't you? For some reason I think of it every minute." She shrugged her shoulders, which were a little tight in her herringbone coat. "I was just wondering if maybe you do, too."

She'd had some wine, I realized. That explained it. There was something undone in her voice.

"Maybe I've thought about it, Trieste," I said. "But I've certainly never acted on it."

She looked at me. There was a pause, and then she laughed. "Not bad, Mr. Sifter." Then she looked away. "I had a feeling you saw. That was very observant."

"Why don't you return it?"

She thought about that. "Just mail it back with my thank-you note?"

"Trieste."

"Yes?"

"Just walk over and put it on the table."

"I need it for my collection."

"Your collection—"

"My little—I don't know—my little nostalgic collection. My little jewels of revenge."

"Revenge for what, Trieste?"

She looked at her fingernails. "I've been taken to more than my share of these parties, sir. There's something about me, I guess. People like to feed a stray."

"You sound like an ingrate. These parties help a good cause. They help *your* cause."

"Ingrate?" She smiled to herself. "I don't know if I even believe in good causes," she said, gesturing at the tables. "And what's charity? I don't think there's any such thing. Or public service, for that matter. Do you?"

"Let's stick to the spoon."

She opened her palms. "Are you going to turn me in, sir?"

"I don't know."

"I hope you don't. It would only confirm what they think."

"Not everybody thinks that way."

She laughed quietly.

"Why do you care, Mr. Sifter?"

"Because I suspect I know what the world is like for you. It was like that for me, too, Trieste. Sort of."

She gave me a slight, teasing smile. "What goes around, comes around, I guess." Then she turned to watch the trumpeter, who seemed to share a knowing look with her as he tapped out the melody to "Baby Mine." I watched, too.

"Ingrate?" she finally said, looking out over the milling crowd. "I'm surprised that *you* would say that, sir."

THE SHARPNESS OF THE KNOCKING startled me from sleep. Early morning, the day after the Iowa caucuses. Still dark. From my bed I watched Astor shuffle across the floor in his pajamas. He straightened, then stepped aside. Mr. Clayliss's head appeared: "Phone, Sifter," he said gruffly.

"Sir?"

"*Phone*, I said."

"Yes, sir. Is it my mother?"

In the hallway he was already striding ahead. "No, boy, it's not." He didn't turn around. "And this isn't a farm, either. Get your shoes on."

I did, then followed him across the quad and through the covered portico to the administration building. He had to punch the buttons on the main lock, and when I came up behind him he shielded me from the combination. Then he roughly pulled open the door. Inside his office, he handed me the phone and said, "When you're done, I need to talk to him."

I put the receiver to my ear. "You heard the news?" said Liam Metarey.

"Yes, sir. I'm sorry. I was going to write you a note this morning. I'm sorry about it."

"Sorry?" He cleared his throat. "Corey—it's good news."

"Sir?"

"We couldn't have gotten better news."

"We couldn't have?"

"God, no. Second place in the first primary. Don't be sorry at all. He's done better than anyone thought he could. And that's how they're covering it, too—thanks to a little effort on our part. Forgive me," he said. "I thought you knew. I'm sorry if you didn't. That's probably my fault."

"No, sir, it was my fault. I haven't had a chance to look at the papers."

"Hell, he beat Humphrey and McGovern. Think of it. Muskie's been the nominee now for months, if you follow the polls. And he's still a tough steak to cut. But I'll tell you, they're the ones who're worried now. I'll tell you that. Second place in a state that wouldn't eat lunch with anybody east of Indianapolis! It's the war, Corey. That's what's getting people out. And it gives us a real honest-to-goodness chance. We're gearing up."

"You are?"

His voice quieted. "Those graphs, Corey," he said. "History. Foxes and hedgehogs. History's on our side."

"Yes, sir."

"I talked to your parents. They say it's fine for you to come back weekends."

Mr. Clayliss was frowning.

"To work with the campaign," said Mr. Metarey.

"And it's all right with school?"

Mr. Clayliss rose from his chair and began sharpening a pencil at the corner of the desk.

"I'll *make* it all right," said Mr. Metarey.

I remember wondering then why he did that. I was useful around the house, but there were plenty of other boys in Saline who could do just as much. Most of what I did for the campaign was drive Henry Bonwiller around—and even this was only when Carlton Sample wasn't available—and now and then wash a few cars. Anybody could have done those things, and anybody could have set the *Globe* and the *Post* and the *Times* on their café sticks in the library, and anybody could have made sure the bottles of Glenlivet and Glenfiddich hadn't run low in the pantry. Did Liam Metarey know how unmoored I felt in my new life at Dunleavy? Did he feel he had done that to me? Was that why he was offering me the chance to come home?

"I'd be honored to do it, sir."

"Good, then," he said loudly. "Let's consider it done." Then he lowered his voice to a whisper. "Now give me back to the imbecile."

"Yes, sir," I said. "Just a moment. He's right here."

"IT HAD NOTHING to do with him feeling sorry for you."

"How would you know that?"

"He wanted you close by."

"That's flattering. But I don't know if it's true."

"In case the cops came in on it, I mean."

"That's one possibility, Trieste."

"One *strong* possibility, Mr. Sifter."

We were the last two in the newsroom. A Sunday night. Closing on our Monday edition, the biggest of the week. "He was a very decent man, Trieste."

"So are you, sir."

"I don't know."

"A decent man is all you can hope for."

"Liam Metarey made some big mistakes," I said.

"I said *decent*, sir. Not perfect." She smiled.

I took a drink of coffee. "How do you come to such strong beliefs, Trieste? At your age."

"My father," she answered, without a moment's pause. "Where I live, if you don't have strong beliefs, you're eaten for breakfast."

"And *you're* not going to be eaten for breakfast."

"No, sir," she said. "I'm not."

AT HAVERFORD, Holly and I were spending almost all our days and nights in each other's company, and our sophomore year we finally took the bus to Memphis for me to meet her family. This was over Easter break. By that point, I should add, I hadn't been home for any length of time since the summer I graduated from Dunleavy. I'd come back from Philadelphia at Christmas my first year of college, but only for a few days, and I'd spent that summer in an apartment at school, working in a bookstore and continuing the weekly discussion meetings Holly had organized around campus. Saline was simply too fraught for me by then, not only from what had occurred there, but also because of what I was trying to make of myself at school.

The Steens lived in a small brick house in a tidy block on the western edge of the city. The neighborhood ran down a hill onto flats that ended at the Mississippi, and when we stepped out of the dilapidated cab that had taken us in from the bus station, the smell of river mud was in the air. There was something about that. Holly sniffed, too, and made a face. Then she gathered herself and we walked up the concrete drive to the door. She knocked. There was no answer. I was holding both of our bags, and after a while I set them down. Then the door opened.

It was Mrs. Steen. "Lordy, Lordy," she said. "They have arrived!" She was solid looking. Not fat, exactly, but stout, and no taller than Holly. Much of her appearance was softened by her puffed cheeks and an elaborately set hairdo, but she had a broad, eager face in which I immediately saw Holly's own—especially the eyes, with their darkened, excitable stare. They were animated in the same way as Holly's, too, glancing here and there across the porch but then fixing intently on my own, just as her daughter's had at the duck pond. The same forceful brown irises, too. I must say the resemblance was disconcerting. Mrs. Steen coughed loudly into her elbow, then stepped out the door and hugged Holly. When that was done she took another step onto the porch and hugged me, too. She smelled of cooking. "Come in," she said, "you poor tired souls. Come in. Come in." Before I could stop her, she had picked up both the bags.

Inside, she handed me a glass of lemonade that she'd already poured—maybe this was why she'd taken so long to get to the door—then without asking proceeded to show me through the whole house, which didn't take long. It wasn't much different from the one I'd grown up in myself. A tidily kept living room. Work boots by the back door. A TV in the den with two recliners in front of it, one a little nicer than the other. A framed piece of needlepoint above the kitchen sink that said "Welcome To Our Home." A set of bookshelves that held photographs and dishes but not books. The bedrooms were down a hall, and she set down my bag in the one that had belonged to Holly's stepbrother. There was nothing in the room but a bed and a dresser. No chair. No rug. No shade on the window.

All the way down on the Trailways bus, Holly had been warning me: her parents hadn't had an education; they didn't listen to music; they didn't read. Her father could be gruff; her mother could be simple. Now I washed up in the tiny bathroom and came back out to see them, and when I arrived in the kitchen her father was there, too, standing halfway in the storm door with a mug in his hand. He was red-faced and bald, wearing coveralls with oil stains on them. The room stunk of cigarettes. He turned to Holly and said, "He ain't so tall as you said."

"Clem, this is Corey Sifter," said Mrs. Steen.

"Nice to meet you, sir."

He gulped from the mug and set it down hard on the table. "Like-ways, I guess," he answered. Then he said, "Back for supper," and continued out the door.

I knew at that moment how difficult it was going to be. The door snapped shut on its closer, and when I turned and looked I saw the typical, charming determination in Holly's eyes. She blinked a couple of times and then smiled. Her mother began tidying up the kitchen, which was already clean.

If we'd gone to my house instead, things might have been different. My father didn't read books, either—not in those days, at least—and he was always running out the door to jobs; but even then he could talk to people who did read, and there was a fundamental openness to his disposition that I've since found again and again among those who make their livings with their minds. The next night at dinner, Holly mentioned the Eakins show that we'd seen in Philadelphia, and Mr. Steen looked up from his mashed potatoes and said, "I don't know what the hell you're talking about."

That was by far the worst moment of our trip. When I snuck into her bedroom that night to see her, I found her sobbing quietly in her childhood bed. I doubt my own father knew who Eakins was, either. But I know he wouldn't have said that.

The rest of our time was pleasant enough. On the Saturday before Easter we went to the Peabody Hotel for tea and to see the ducks, and in the afternoon we walked along the river. Mr. Steen didn't appear that evening for dinner, and when it was time to go back to school on Sunday, it was Holly's mother who took us to the bus. Just before I boarded she drew me to her in a hug and said, "We're so glad to have you in the family."

"Thank you, Mrs. Steen," I said.

For a few weeks, Holly and I made a joke about it. When she accidentally knocked a paperweight off our history professor's mantle one night during a seminar, I said it to her—"We're so glad to have you in the family"—and when I overwatered the potted ficus in her dorm room so that most of its leaves fell off, she said it back to me.

"Thank you, Mrs. Steen," I replied.

THE *CHICAGO TRIBUNE* IS A REPUBLICAN PAPER—Dewey Defeats Truman!—but one Saturday when I came in with firewood I found Liam Metarey reading it, and I must have realized something from his expression. This was soon after I'd started coming home from Dunleavy every weekend to work. In my days in that house I'd had plenty of opportunities to see items of confidential importance, but that afternoon, for the first and only time in my life, I took advantage of one of them. I came back after lunch, when he was out walking among the oaks, and I took a look at his desk.

The piece wasn't on the front page, but the headline was: NEW YORK SENATOR IN STATE PROBE. The article itself was buried in the national section, and it said nothing except that sources from the New York State Police had revealed that Senator Bonwiller was to be questioned in a local highway incident.

Then the story disappeared. I looked at every copy of the *Tribune* that month, and at every copy of all the New York papers and all the

California papers, too, but I didn't see it again. With my parents—and then later in the teachers' lounge at school—I watched Walter Cronkite every night; but nothing was mentioned about it there, either. It certainly didn't make the *Courier-Express*, which I read all the way through in the library now, every morning. The story simply vanished.

"SON?" I was being shaken awake. "Son?"

It was Mr. Clayliss again.

"Son. A phone call for you—I'm afraid—another call."

"What time is it?"

"It's late, son. Come on. Shhh. Come."

He had a coat for me this time. "Here," he said. "It's cold out." We descended the main stairs and crossed the commons toward his office, our steps clicking on the ice, but then we continued beyond it all the way around to the rear of the main building, where the headmaster's residence stood. My feet felt heavy. At the door I brushed my shoes on the mat. But he urged me on. Inside, his wife was in a robe at the kitchen table. She had a pot of tea in front of her, and when I came in she slid a steaming cup across to me and pointed to the opposite chair. I sat down. The cup was china and there was a silver spoon in the saucer. Mr. Clayliss brought the phone over from the counter, holding out the earpiece. I picked it up. The wall clock, an alpine scene with pine trees for hands, said 4:32. I suppose I'll always remember that.

"Cor?" I heard my father say. His voice was thin. "Cor? Are you there?"

FIVE

I

I CAN PICTURE HIM, earlier that night. Out on his call, running an auger in a waste pipe. He whistles as he works—"My Darling Clementine," maybe "Bridgit O'Malley." Carting up the motor and the heavy winder from the basement of a Metarey rental, turning to smile as the family thanks him on the stairs; then out to the side yard where the shared main line continues through to the street. " 'Tis a Bright Golden Day on the Meadow." A bite of cold in the air. There's a cleanout here, too, and he knows he can do a better job by running the auger again to ream the long roots that are in every pipe in the neighborhood. So he does. It's dark now. A dusting of snow picking up the moon. He sends the blade out forty feet to the drip line of the big Norway maple at the road. An extra few minutes but worth the effort. At this hour he gets time and a half anyway—but he would do it even if he didn't get a penny. That's how he is. My mother will have a bath ready for him when he gets home, doesn't matter what time— so he might as well do it right. "Danny Boy," maybe, because it gives him a sweet melancholy. When he's finished, he stops at Flann's for a pint of bitters—the song's put him in the mood—and he talks to the bartender he's known all his life and to a table of union men happy over their new contract, then goes to the pay phone at the door. A little late: he's always courteous that way. He's feeling something. The brace of the winter air. The tinge of the melody.

It rings in the kitchen, but no one answers.

He hangs up, drops in another dime.

THAT EVENING she's had the first inkling. The usual headache—she's used to them by now—but this time it's on her the instant she gets up from her nap. Maybe it even wakes her. There's something different to it now. Hard to describe. The pain's gone lower, come up underneath, closer to the side of her head. Has it done that before? She stops and looks out the kitchen window, toward the east. That's where her son is at school. How can she put it? Her body doesn't feel exactly hers: things at a distance. The moon rising now behind the house. The leprechaun clock above the door. Even looking at the hands she can't say what time it is. That's funny. Her arms half-given to someone else. More the right than the left. She shudders for a moment. Lifts them both. Yes—more the right. Opens and closes the fingers. That's better. Puckers her lips. Says aloud a piece that comes to her somehow out of thin air, from her high school play. Gwendolen Fairfax. *Oh! I hope I am not that. It would leave no room for developments!* Her drama teacher, Mr. Ferrari, standing at the stage edge, imploring: *You ARE! You ARE!*

Makes her laugh. She even remembers Donny Tarlow's part, the fat boy with his piercing crush on her, always moving closer than he had to. His jeans that smelled like a barn. Turned out he became a veterinarian. *I am in love with Gwendolen! I have come up to town expressly to propose to her!*

A vet!

She wouldn't have been able to stand the smells.

Then comes the first blow. The feeling in her arm dropping away. A shudder over the shoulder and scalp. Then the swooning. The floor pitching. She tries to right herself. Grabs the counter. Use the other arm, silly. Lift! Silly girl! Up, Anna Bainbridge. Up! The floor, wrapping her. All over, how can it do that? Cheeks on the cold linoleum. Funny, funny! God, it's turning me over. The black and white. The squares. A wave turning me over.

THE FUNERAL WAS HELD in St. Joseph's parish, and the reception was at the Metareys'. I'll always be grateful that they did that. My mother's sisters had spoken in the church, and so had my father, and I'd sat in the first row with a hundred friends behind me, thinking not of how I'd lost my mother but of how I'd lost all of *them* now; of how their lives at Roosevelt, and in the lime quarries, and at the beaches on the lake, were nothing at all like my new one at Dunleavy, and would never be again. Odd thoughts, I suppose.

But all I know is that I felt no grief. Not then. I felt only their eyes on me.

Glioblastoma multiforme. Those were the words for it. That morning I'd found a page about it, sitting on our counter. I don't think my father had even read it.

A brain tumor.

Under *symptoms*:

> Headache
> Personality change

It had bled finally, sometime in the evening, while my father was out on his call. That's what Dr. Leary told us. It wouldn't have taken long. Maybe a few moments. And she wouldn't have felt much pain.

"I want you to know that," he said. "Granger. Corey. I want you both to know that."

He was at the reception, and after he said this he moved away, vanishing into the crowd of jackets.

Clara and Christian were next to me. Clara kept going to the food table and bringing me plates of little things—crackers and cheese, tiny shrimp on toothpicks, ginger cookies. It was the first time she'd ever been kind to me. Both of them stayed at my side, and Mrs. Metarey acted the way my mother herself would have, leading me from one group to the next in the drawing room, touching me low on the back whenever the conversation faltered, moving me along. My mother had lots of friends, and they all were there, too, setting their cakes and roasts on the long table. Men from the union were there with my father. That's where Mr. Metarey was, too, I could see—he was never far from Dad.

Late in the afternoon, when the crowd had finally thinned and Christian and Clara and her mother had left me alone, I stepped from the house and walked down to the fly pools. The grounds were almost empty now. A skin of new ice lay over the water, as clear as glass, and when the back door opened I followed the reflection of a man in uniform walking down from the house. He stopped a few feet behind me on the gravel but didn't say anything. I had to turn around.

"Wow," I said. "You're back."

"Special delivery." We shook hands.

"How'd you get here?"

"C-130. Nha Trang to Fort Drum, with a stop to pee. Five-day R and R. Happened to be stateside when I heard, so I came right down." He lowered his head. "I'm really sorry, Corey."

"I appreciate it. I appreciate your coming. Giving up a day of leave."

"It's good to be back. Just nice to be chilly again, tell you the truth. Sorry it had to be like this." He cleared his throat. "My sisters still taking care of you?"

"They are."

"Nobody jumping in the water?"

"Nothing like that."

"Nobody gouging any eyes?"

"Eyes are still fine."

"The other word for right?"

"*Starboard.*"

"Well, good," he said. "You're ahead of when I left you then." He shook his head. "I didn't know your mother, Corey. But she had to be a good woman. Anybody can see it."

"Thanks, Andrew."

He looked down.

Up at the house, I saw Mr. McGowar's stone-colored face watching us out the window.

"And what's it like where *you* are?" I asked.

"Oh, not terrible. Not terrible." He looked across the ice. "Long way from any action, at least. Rear medical base. Some bad-off guys in the beds but by the time I see 'em they're cleaned up and stitched up. And drugged up. Army Medical Corps now." He shrugged. "Things are going to hell in that country and everyone knows it—but all I see are white sheets. All the blood's up front."

Later on, of course, I found out that he wasn't telling me the truth. Or that he wasn't telling me all of it, at least. Maybe because of the occasion.

Finally, he shook my hand and took his leave. The door closed behind him at the house, and a moment later it opened again and Mr. McGowar appeared. He was in his black suit. I started up to him but he waved me back with his long hands, then started down himself. He walked as high-legged as he always did, throwing his comically long arms this way and that for balance as he chose his steps in the thin snow, like a daddy longlegs coming down the hill. Then he was on the gravel. It was an awkward hug.

"How are you, Mr. McGowar?"

He opened his mouth and a breathy sound came out. He pointed to his throat and shook his head.

"That's okay, Mr. McGowar. Nice to just stand out here for a minute and look at the land. Beautiful, isn't it?"

With his foot he was pawing at the egg-sized face of a rock that was coming up through the gravel. He took out his pad.

YOR MOM WUS BUTFL TU

I had to laugh. And why that suddenly made me cry—for the only time in a decade, as it turned out—why that made me cry for the only time until I was a father myself, I'll never know.

ITS OK

He set the pad back in his pocket and then stood there in his funeral suit, patting me on the shoulder and working at the rock with his shoe.

"MAY I ASK YOU SOMETHING, TRIESTE?"

"Of course."

"You're not going to give it back, then?"

"Oh—you've been thinking about that."

"As a matter of fact, I have." I was going about my words carefully. "Do you ever think it might make me wonder—well—do you ever think it might make me wonder whether I can trust you?"

"On the contrary, sir," she said without hesitation. "It ought to show you that you *can*."

I regarded her. She had that look again—the one-line-ahead-of-you look. We were alone in the office. It was after seven and she still hadn't finished her piece. Now she was tapping the space bar on her keyboard.

"If I gave it back, sir," she said, "you wouldn't—" She looked up, almost impatiently. "Well, I mean you wouldn't *have* anything on me."

"Oh, I see," I said. "That's interesting, Trieste. Interesting logic."

"I've been thinking about it."

She went back to typing.

"Trieste, may I ask you something else?"

"Fire away, sir."

"What do the other kids think of you?"

"Which other kids?"

"The kids at school. What do they make of someone like you?"

"The kids at my school are my brothers and sisters, Mr. Sifter."

She typed a few more words.

"How do you mean that?"

"Literally."

I regarded her.

"I'm homeschooled," she said. "Remember?"

"Oh, right. I forgot. Well what's *that* like then?"

"Homeschooling?" She took a sip from her carton of milk. Then she wrote some more words. "It's using the whole buffalo."

"Okay."

"You eat the meat. You make clothes out of the hide. You make glue out of the hooves. You make a necklace out of the teeth. That's homeschooling."

"Interesting."

"To a point."

"And what about—well—a social life?"

"You mean—*boys*?"

"Well, that's one thing. Yes, boys."

"Not ironic enough. At least not the ones around here."

"What does that mean exactly? Not ironic enough. My daughters say it, too."

"Means they're cutting with the dull edge of the knife, Mr. Sifter.

Rooting for the Bills. Trolling for the prom date. I've given up on boys. At least till college."

"Ah," I said. "So you do plan to go?"

"To college? Of course."

"Well, I was worried."

"Why?"

"I guess I thought you always took your own path. In everything."

"God, Mr. Sifter," she said, "why would you think that?" And although the same enigmatic smile teased her lips, I realized she wasn't kidding at all.

PICTURE ME: a resolute young man but quiet. Nineteen years old. I have no money for clothes but I wear an old suit vest over my shirt because Holly thinks it makes me look serious. I'm tall and thin, and my hair, like everyone else's, comes almost to my shoulders. Other than the vest, my only affectation is an old Sears pocket watch, whose chain I finger when I search for words. Holly looks up at me expectantly when I do. No one besides my mother has ever listened this carefully to what I have to say. For over a year now we've been sleeping together. The world recedes. We can't believe our good fortune. In the top of my bureau drawer I keep one of my old shirts that she likes to sleep in, and in the morning if she's not in my room—she's the only person I've met who wakes earlier than I do—the first thing I do is rise and smell its collar. Sometimes there's a note in the pocket. We're taking two classes together, a history lecture and a seminar on European politics; in that one, Holly is the most diligent student in the room—she seems to have read more than the professor. After class, we go for a walk, and the world then is not much more than distant sounds. I still think about my mother nearly every day, and she seems somehow to be there with me most acutely on these walks. I look over at Holly next to me and am aware of something. Her words

and the way her hand touches me on the shoulder or the arm. We follow the edge of campus, staying in the greenery behind the track and
the baseball field. She talks about Henry James's *The Portrait of a
Lady*, or why Schopenhauer despised Hegel, while I nod thought-
fully and look for weak spots in her argument. I'm not exaggerating—
this is the way we are. The shouts of the track team drift past. When I
stop to look at the leaves of a bur oak she stops alongside me, and
when I tell her that these are the grandest of God's trees she takes a
leaf and sets it in her pocket. My mother would have done that, too.
We kiss a little under the boughs. Then we walk on talking about
philosophers. She wears a denim dress and another of my old shirts,
the cuffs folded to her elbows. Her eagerness and grace are apparent
to me in every step she takes, but what I'm really beginning to notice
is her determination. And for all of the intoxication and outlandish
good fortune that I feel, I'm also, behind it, becoming slightly afraid.
As we descend over the furrowed incline of pine needles and pale
green forest grass, I feel that we are in a boat together, somewhere
where nobody can find us. More accurate—I feel that she *is* the boat,
and in my paling moments I sense we are a long way out to sea.

One morning that spring, I'm reading in the stacks of the library
when from behind I hear a whisper: "Trying to get ahead of me?"

I haven't heard her coming. My first instinct is to hide what I'm
looking at, but instead I tilt my chair back and merely slide the books
to the far corner of the desk. They're a small armful of library-bound
volumes that I've pulled from a single dusty row, all of them treatises
on the American industrial magnates of the nineteenth and early
twentieth centuries. The history class we're taking together is on the
westward expansion, and I know this is what she thinks I'm reading
about; so I don't say that what I'm really looking for is Eoghan
Metarey's name. She's devoutly interested in almost everything, so
why don't I tell her that? Why, instead, do I lean back and kiss her?
And when her eyes are closed, why do I reach across the desk to place
my notepad over the books?

II

THEY WERE STATE POLICE. I don't know why, but they were. And that was a relief: the state police, at least up here, had always been friends of the Senator's. I'd seen several of them before, in fact, at the big campaign parties and occasionally at the meetings, and I'd even parked a few of their cars. I knew their dark uniforms, the pleated shoulders and double-creased hat, the darker, velveteen stripe on the leg. The officer who questioned me was my father's age. He leaned against the counter in the toolshed, put one boot up on a chair, and carefully took off his gloves. He gave me a long look.

"You're familiar with the Senator, then?"

"Yes, sir."

"How well would you say you know him?"

"Not real well. I drove him sometimes. Weekends, usually. But some other times, too. We didn't talk much."

He took a pad from his pocket. "And was there anything unusual about him that day?"

"Which day?"

"The one we're talking about."

"I saw him in the study for a few minutes in the afternoon. With Mr. Metarey."

"Anything unusual then? Agitated? Strange?"

If my mother had been alive, I don't know how I would have answered. Since the service, the Metareys had invited me up to the house every afternoon. "He seemed the same as always," I said.

"Was he drinking?"

"Alcohol?"

"Yes, alcohol."

"I never saw him drink alcohol, officer. Mostly coffee."

"You drove Henry Bonwiller for—how long was it?"

"About six months, sir."

"And you never saw him drink alcohol."

Out the window, Gil McKinstrey was chiseling sheets of frozen mud off the Ferguson's big rear tires. I was heading back to Dunleavy when the weekend was over.

"You never saw him drink alcohol?"

"No, sir."

"I see." He swung his foot down from the chair. "I hear you're an Indians fan," he said.

"I guess I am."

"Mostly Yankee guys around here."

"I guess so."

"What do you think of their chances?"

"Of whose chances?"

"The Indians'."

"Well," I said. "They lost a hundred and two last year."

He let out a small laugh and put away the pad. "Mistake by the Lake," he said, shaking his head.

"You can say that again."

He shook it another time. "They need pitching, is what they need. Another Feller. You're too young to remember Feller. A Feller and a Lemon. I'm from outside Sandusky. Only been up here ten years."

"They need hitting, too. Another Shoeless Joe. And I know all about Bob Feller, sir. And Bob Lemon."

He smiled.

"Might be other officers asking you these same things," he said, carefully putting his gloves back on. "You know? You gonna answer them how you answered me?"

"Of course, sir."

He stopped in the doorway. "So he seemed his usual self and wasn't drinking—least not that you know of."

"No, sir."

"That's all the questions I got for you then, son."

"AND NOW YOU WISH you'd answered him differently."

"No. I don't necessarily think I do."

"Does that mean you really don't think he did it?"

"Ah," I said. "That's the question, isn't it?"

"Indeed."

"Well, let me ask you this," I said. "If he *did* do it, how do you think he could have kept on going the way he did? How do you think he could have kept on operating? He didn't show the least bit of remorse. Not that I ever saw, anyway. Wouldn't it have changed him? Wouldn't it at least have slowed him?"

"From the way you describe the man, sir, he was—I guess you could say, egomaniacal."

"He was a politician."

"And that's one of the job requirements."

"All you can really say, Trieste, is that the whole thing never made it to a courtroom. You can wonder about the reasons. But one of them might be that they've never been able to build a case against him."

"Another might be that he had a lot of friends."

"He had a lot of enemies, too."

She considered that. I took out my half sandwich. Skinless chicken breast. Mustard, no mayo. That morning at the QuickStop I'd bought a chocolate-pecan brownie, too. It sat there at the bottom of the bag, like a cyanide capsule.

After a time, I said, "All I mean is that no matter what kind of man he was, no matter how great an actor he was, he still would have shown something. Don't you think? Maybe not remorse, but what about guilt? What about fear?"

"Fear of what?"

"Fear that it would catch up with him. That everything was going to end."

"So you're saying that because he didn't seem afraid and because he didn't show any remorse, you don't think he had anything to do with it?"

"Actually," I said, "I'm not saying that at all."

"Then what are you saying, sir?"

"That perhaps he didn't *remember* having anything to do with it."

She turned and looked out the window.

"Oh, please," she said. "How could he not remember?"

"When I saw him at the house he could barely walk. It took him all morning to sober up."

"You don't know that."

"Trieste," I said, "have you ever been drunk?"

"Not *that* drunk."

"Well, it happens. It happens all the time."

"I guess I didn't think of that," she said finally.

"And I have no idea if it's true, just like I have no idea if any of this is what actually happened. But I do think it's a possibility."

She took out her own lunch—a cup of homemade maple yogurt and a sliced peach—and set it up neatly on the desk. Inside the bag I fingered the brownie in its plastic wrap. She was watching me.

"Go ahead and eat it, sir."

"I'm trying not to."

"I know." She smiled. Then she started to eat. After a moment she said, "May I ask you about something else, Mr. Sifter?"

"Of course."

"Why are you telling me all this?"

"Why?"

"Yeah. I'm just a kid."

"An unusual kid."

"Thank you. But why?"

"Senator Bonwiller's gone."

"And you can clear your conscience?"

"My conscience doesn't need as much clearing as you think. He did a great deal for people like you. How old's your dad, did you say? Fifty?"

"Fifty-two."

"Then you might not even be here if he hadn't been elected to the Senate."

"You mean what he did about Vietnam?"

"That's exactly what I mean."

"And you might not be here, either, sir."

"I was too young for the war. I was lucky."

"I'm talking about what he and Liam Metarey did for your father, sir. Not to mention for *you*."

———

ONE SNOWY WEEKEND, Holly and I went up to New York City to see the ballet. In those days, they played two shows on Saturday, and the early one was discounted for students. We took the train in, and in what had become a small blizzard we walked uptown toward the State Theater. The snow had quieted everything and the city was in a meditative mood. Traffic was light—on Broadway barely a cab moved—and the usual boisterous commerce of the west side had vanished. The storm was windless but an endless column of feathery snow descended steadily between the buildings. I couldn't see more than half a block. By the time we reached Forty-fifth Street, businesses were closing their doors. Soon it became obvious that there wasn't going to be a ballet. But we went on anyway. Holly was wearing a hat fringed with rabbit fur and had pulled the lapels of her coat up around her cheeks. Still, I could see the eagerness in her step, and between the two flaps of wool I watched her face. She looked beautiful.

It's daunting for everyone, I suppose, to realize how chance can rework a life. At Sixty-third Street, we found a single guard rubbing his hands and stamping his feet in front of the hall. The performance had indeed been canceled. I still remember the way that guard looked. An exaggerated, almost zoological face; a cigarette-stained smile and a mustache above it like a frozen strip of fur. All of it narrowed by the earflaps of a Russian-style cap. A Pole, maybe. Or a Slav. An unlikely angel. He pointed us around the corner to the single business that remained open: a coffeehouse, named Linden's.

So many things had to be right. It was a large place, maybe fifty tables, and a corner position that looked out on both streets. We arrived just as a couple was getting up from a booth. At first, Holly took the seat that faced the counter and I took the one that faced onto Broadway; but in a moment she got up and asked me to switch so that she could watch the snow. We changed places. I was looking at the counter now, where knots of customers were taking off hats and coats, stamping boots, and shaking out umbrellas. A squad of waitresses passed close in front of me every few seconds carrying dishes from the kitchen. The busboys were moving, too, hauling big wash trays back in the other direction. But then for some reason there was an exodus: the door opened, a cold breeze washed through the place, and for a moment or two all the standing coats and hats disappeared; and at the same time the waitresses paused in their continuing bustle from the kitchen. For a brief instant I could see all the way across the dining room.

It wasn't that I recognized her immediately—she'd changed enough that I really didn't—but my glance lingered anyway. She sat in a booth by herself at the far window, half-turned away from me. She was starkly different. Her cheeks looked either bruised from tears or overly made up, and her hair was short. Still, I had only a moment to look at her, but even before the band of customers regathered at the counter and blocked my view again I had understood with a start who she was.

I remember my reaction. It was shame. I was ashamed to be sitting there across from Holly Steen with her rabbit fur hat and her eager expression. Her thrift-store gloves and her easily given enthusiasms.

We'd ordered omelets, and when Holly finished hers she stood and said she had to use the bathroom. I reached to take her hand, and when my elbow knocked her cup, she said, "We're so glad to have you in the family." Then she made her way through the crowd.

When I reached the other side of the restaurant, Christian didn't even seem surprised. All she said was, "Oh, no—I'm a wreck, aren't I?"

I stood there looking down at her. She was searching in her purse for something. I only had a few moments. "You look beautiful," was what I said.

"I'm having a hard day, actually." She pulled out a book of checks and tore one off.

"Are you all right?"

"Do I *look* all right?"

"I can't imagine what you must have gone through."

"I guess it's been a hard couple of *years*, actually—if you really want to know. I guess I never knew how it felt. Did you?"

"You can't," I said. "Nobody can."

"But we're having a party this weekend." She handed me the check. "You ought to come, at least."

The address was on Eighty-sixth Street, on the west side. "A party?"

"Remarkable," she said. "But true."

"No, it's just that I'm afraid it would be hard. I'm still down in Philly."

"Who are you here with then?"

I guessed she'd seen. "A girl," I said. Then I added, "from school. She's in the bathroom now. How's Clara?"

"She's good. She's about to get engaged."

"Who to?"

"To a guy she doesn't want to marry."

"Oh, I see. In that case, I guess—well, give her my best."

She looked up. I waited for her to go on.

Her hands were resting in her lap, and she lifted one and set it on top of mine. Then she looked away. "Well," she said after a moment, "you'd better go back to your table, then."

ONE NIGHT I WALKED DOWN TO the dining hall for dinner and found it empty. This was my first Saturday back at Dunleavy after my mother's funeral. Maybe it was because of this that on my walk to dinner that evening I hadn't noticed that the paths were empty. And the dining hall itself was abandoned. I checked my watch: six o'clock. The usually boisterous front room was vacant and no places were set at the tables, but instead of looking for someone and asking where dinner was, I walked back to the dorm by myself and up to our room. I'd always been beleaguered at Dunleavy by the sense that I'd failed to grasp something—something important that was the birthright of all my classmates—but that night, perhaps because of what I'd just gone through, I seemed to have been released somehow from my usual apprehensions. I ate some crackers from the drawer and went to the end of the hall for water. That was my meal. No one else was upstairs, either. I sat down at the window in our room.

I hadn't been there long before I began to hear sound. It grew louder, then softer. Some kind of music. It would appear for a time; then vanish. I stayed there at the window, listening, thinking about my mother, until I realized it was coming from the heating duct. I squatted by the register and listened. A chorus. A chorus of voices.

Presently there was a knock on the door.

"Wow, man," Astor said. He always knocked, even at our own room. "You think it was angels?"

"I knew it wasn't angels."

That made him laugh. "Nobody told you, I guess?"

"I guess not."

"It's every Saturday night now. Spring semester, man." He rolled his eyes. "Glee club—instead of dinner. We eat downstairs and not in the dining room. And we *sing*. Dunleavy tradition." He rolled his eyes again. "But everybody's got to do it, man. O'Breece just asked me where you were. It's not bad, though—really. You might like it. I kind of do, even. I know all the words, too, from my brother. You can have my lyrics book. Mr. O'Breece used to be some kind of opera singer or something. The seniors call him *Mr. Obese*."

"You're in your bathrobe," I said. He was. It was blue with white stripes.

"Oh, yeah," he answered. "Don't ask me why. We sing wearing them. Another tradition, I guess. I've got an extra for you, man, if you need one."

"That's okay. I have my own."

So, you see, it's not hard to imagine what someone in my position would have thought about Liam Metarey—it's not hard to imagine how continually grateful I was to the man whose sturdy hand had once again reached out to help me.

But it was that night, too, that I first had an inkling about my mother, as well. As I stood in the basement commons in my leather-tipped robe with the fifty other boys in my class, working through the tenor part of "Didn't My Lord Deliver Daniel," my mind went incessantly to her. Had she had a part in this, also? I saw her, as far back as I could remember, sitting by the window with her fingertips against her head. Had she, in fact, long known? And if she had, could she actually have gone to Mr. Metarey herself? The Metarey family had always taken care of the citizens of Saline, especially any who were in need. She was certainly aware of that. Was that how all this was set in motion then, from the very beginning?

I don't think she would ever have asked Liam Metarey for anything directly, but she knew what a word to a man like him could do. And it occurred to me that night that all of it could have been arranged— that all of it *must* have been arranged—without my father even knowing. My father was a proud man, more in his silences than in his words, and the most ardent expression of his pride was his self-sufficiency. That's why my mother might have been forced to plan her contingency in secret, telling only Mr. Metarey and not her own husband. First my job at Aberdeen West, then my job in the campaign, and finally my departure for Dunleavy, all of it might have been plotted because she knew what was coming—even if she didn't know when—and the deliberate arc of it might have been kept secret so that it evaded my father's natural resistance. That's what my mind kept returning to, as I stood midway back in the rows of giddy juniors wearing robes over their clothes. If she'd asked my father about it in its totality, I have no doubt he would have refused. But it was set in motion one part at a time, and he—like me—was swept along.

That semester, I discovered that I liked to sing. I found that I was decent at it, too—good enough, at least, that I fit in with my classmates. But there was something more to it; something about standing in that cool, low-ceilinged room, where against the four rock walls our voices built themselves into a torrent of sound, something about letting my own voice rise into that stirring mix that seemed at last to set me free.

THE HOUSE HAD BEEN CLEANED. That's what I saw as soon as I opened the door. The rugs were vacuumed, my father's boots were sitting on a tray in the entry hall, and all the flowers had been removed except for a vase that had dried at the center of the dining room table. After I brought my bag upstairs to my old room, I came down to see him. He asked me to sit, then disappeared into the kitchen. The flowers were roses, dried papery thin. It was the first time I'd been back. Your childhood home without your mother is no longer your childhood home.

He came out carrying the salad bowl. "You know," he said, "Mom did this every day."

"What?"

"Made a salad. Have you ever made a salad?"

"A couple times."

"You wash the lettuce. Then you have to dry it. If you don't dry it, the dressing comes out watery. I hate drying it. But I do it. On a paper towel. That's the way she showed me how. She showed me a lot of this stuff, you know."

"And then she would dry the paper towel on the windowsill," I said, "so she could use it the next day."

"That's right. So I do it now, too. Come look."

He went back into the kitchen.

When I came up behind him, he said, "There it is," and pointed to the sill.

There it was. Damp. Folded over the top stile of the sash to catch the sun.

"I've used the same one every day now since — since it happened," he said. "She'd like that. Dries good as new." He pulled the roll from the shelf. "They're Scott, see? She always bought Scott. So now I do, too." Her apron was still hanging on the stove handle, and after he set the towels back he reached to straighten it. "Wish I could tell her."

"You seem to be getting along all right, Pop. Place is clean."

"Her friends do that. She had a lot of them. I'm realizing that. Never knew it before, I guess. A different one every weekend. They clean the place."

"Not a bad deal."

"I don't think they really need to do that. I can clean for myself. Gives me something to do, if you want to know. When I'm not working."

"Who does the cooking?"

"I do," he said. "Yours truly. Most of it, at least. I'm learning. It's not so bad. No worse than pipe fitting, anyway — and I'd rather be cooking, to tell the truth. I made real string beans. You know what you have to do to make string beans? Pull out all the strings — or whatever you call 'em. But first you have to cut off the ends. Every single string bean. You know, two ends. Chop, chop. I made about thirty."

"That's a lot of chopping."

"That's right. Makes you appreciate every bean. And your mother did it every night."

"She did, didn't she? And she washed all our clothes, too. And if I needed my good shirt she ironed it."

"Mine, too." He lifted a pot lid, and steam licked the window. I could tell he was fighting his thoughts. "Then you boil 'em," he said gamely. "I get the water on the stove before I start."

"And add salt."

"Right. She always added salt. Everything she cooked tasted good."

"It did."

"I miss her, Cor."

"Of course you do, Pop. So do I. But I missed her before. Ever since I went to school."

"I miss her every day." He reached his arm to the stove and smoothed the hips of the apron. "Jeez," he said. "Listen to me." He blew his nose on a handkerchief. "But this is going to be just like hers." He reached for the box of salt. "You won't know the difference. I found her cookbook. It's all I need. I read the whole thing."

"You read her whole cookbook?"

"You know," he said, "I kind of liked it. Just sat down one evening and read it."

"It's hard to picture, Dad."

He pinched a fingerful of salt and dropped it into the pot, then sat down on the stool by the stove. "What else am I going to do?" he said, reaching the top off another pan. Two pork chops were sizzling in it, like a pair of Africas. "And I brush 'em with her sauce."

"Brown sugar and canned tomatoes."

"That's right. And a little garlic."

"She used to can the tomatoes herself."

"Well, I don't know if I'll be doing that."

Back in the dining room, he served me, then walked around the table, set his own pork chop and string beans on the plate, and sat down. "Those are her roses, too," he said.

I touched the vase. "I saw them, Pop. They're very nice. They're beautiful. Who are they from?"

"From *her* actually."

I looked at him.

He put his napkin on his lap. "From your mother."

He was arranging everything around his plate in the predictable way he does, as though preparing to solder a pipe, moving his glass close to his right hand, straightening his spoon and his knife.

"Say that again, Dad."

He looked out the window. "She just bought them herself," he said. "For no reason. Day before it happened—sweet woman. Just to have them. Bought the vase, too. Funny. I was thinking about it the other day. She was starting to do things like that. Your mother, the lady who reused paper towels."

"Doesn't seem like something she'd do."

"Never bought a bouquet in her life, that woman. But that day, she did. Roses." He lifted his glass of water. "To her," he said.

"To Mom."

"We love you, Anna," he said. "We'll always love you."

"We do, Mom. I love you."

Then he cut into his pork chop. I cut into mine.

He lifted his fork. "Oh, well," he said.

"It's all right, Pop," I answered. "It's going to be all right."

THE NEXT PRIMARY WAS in New Hampshire. Henry Bonwiller was returning to Aberdeen West now to confer with his aides and practice his new speeches for there and for Florida, which followed. This was mid-February now. The Senator's speeches were generally written by different men in the campaign, including a couple of professors from Harvard that June Metarey would pick up every Friday morning from Boston, in Aberdeen White, and drop off again on Monday; but I

happen to know that some of his most famous words were written by
Liam Metarey himself. One afternoon I came into the library and
found him sitting at his portable typewriter by the window, looking
out over the land. I went about restocking the liquor cabinet. "What
do you think of this?" he said, glancing up at me. "We live alongside
too many canyons of failure." He cleared his throat.

"I like it, sir."

"We live alongside too many canyons of hate." He cleared his
throat again. Then he smiled, a little sheepishly. "Now is the time to
cross them. Now is the time to cross them, on bridges of hope."

That line, of course, became Henry Bonwiller's famous "Bridges of
Hope" address, probably the most stirring speech he ever gave, delivered in a husky baritone to a crowd of fifteen hundred antiwar
marchers in Manchester, New Hampshire, on a damp, windy afternoon a little more than a week later. He had a cold that day, and it put
a thread of exigency into his voice that sounded like Roosevelt or Jack
Kennedy, or even Martin Luther King. A perfect note of restrained
urging in a voice that was sometimes just a whisper. The country's
second primary was less than a month away. *We shall go forward together, over this great land and over these great bridges. We shall go forward together, my friends—we shall go forward as one.* The crescendo
of the crowd rolling over the final words. The hand rising in victory.
It may sound like demagoguery now, but in those days it didn't. Even
from the evening news you could tell that something had changed.
And I'll say, too, that it was the first moment I let myself believe that
we were going to win.

After that, when I came into the library with firewood or the newspaper sticks or a bottle of Scotch, I would sometimes find Mr.
Metarey at his typewriter. He'd look up and read me a line or two of
his prose. He was no doubt proud—I think he somehow always
thought of himself, despite his station, as a farmer or a mechanic—
and he was probably also amused at the odd turn in his life; but I also
like to think that he was trying to show me that someday I too might
be capable of such invention, that I too might write the words a for-

midable man would utter. That I might even live in such a world, in fact, on my own merits. Even in the midst of the most frantic, hopeful month of the campaign, I think that this was at least a tiny measure of his thought. In the living room, where two dozen full-sized armchairs had been set up in rows, he made a point of calling me in now to sit among the advisors, mock audiences who listened to the Senator go over his lines. Sometimes Henry Bonwiller practiced them a dozen different ways in succession, changing the inflection here and there, or the order of the phrases. He was an actor, like all politicians, but he was a poet, too—he understood the melody of words.

After Iowa, the campaign had grown in size: the new staff were defectors from other candidates, mostly from Humphrey and Jackson. The Metareys rented fifteen more rooms for them at the Excelsior Hotel in Islington, and I was driving there now sometimes five times in a weekend. Every time I turned into the entrance drive of Aberdeen West, I nodded at the Secret Service agent who was now sitting there on the other side of the road in a dark Mercury Montego, and after I let out the new staff at the circle and parked the car in the garage, I glanced up to the staircase landing to see if a second agent was posted at the tall Palladian window that looked out from the center of the house over all the grounds. This meant that Henry Bonwiller was inside.

It had also become a regular part of my job to make sure that the south library was prepared for his meetings. That room, with its laddered shelves and high, tightly paned windows, had the prettiest wintertime view of the entire grounds—much of what later became the Shelter Brook Set-Aside, cast in the varying shaded layers of deep snow among hills. The south library was where the inner circle liked to convene now for their weekend conference—Liam Metarey, and Larry O'Brien from the Democratic National Committee, and Morlin Chase's brother Clarence, and Tom Watson, Jr., and Dorner Flint from IBM, and Branch Martin from Lockheed, and sometimes Glenn Burrant or a couple of the other trusted reporters. Once I even saw Vance Trawbridge himself, leaning steeply forward in an armchair a good distance outside the circle, sipping bourbon and writing in a notepad that his face nearly touched. The Senator himself sat in the center chair, his jacket off and his tie undone and his long legs stretched out before him. Every Saturday I brought up a bag of sandwiches from the kitchen, and I restocked the liquor.

The news had just come out that the country's budget deficit was going to be the biggest since World War II, and now the Democrats had something fresh to take at the president. On evening news shows all across the country, Henry Bonwiller let Nixon have it. He intoned from the steps of the estate while forty reporters sat in folding chairs on the lawn in front of him, taking notes. Lights from the network cameras cast him in a steely shine that looked forbidding if you were standing in the yard but warmly domestic—as though he were speaking in front of a hearth fire—if you saw it on TV. The plan that week was that the Senator, no matter which questions he was asked, would make the same two points over and over: that the economy was drifting with no helmsman in sight; and that the new budget numbers—$25 billion in deficit—would in no uncertain manner bring the country to its knees.

The polling men liked it. So he said it all again the next week in Portsmouth, New Hampshire, then in Manchester and Plymouth and Whitefield. Nixon announced that he planned to end forced busing in the schools: the Senator countered that this would doom the legacy of Abraham Lincoln. It was not just a choice about schools but about the ethical bedrock of the culture. This, too, resonated. He said it in Concord and Conway and Newport, and then again the next morning in front of the news cameras that were hooked into the power feed from a utilities trailer that was parked now permanently on the stone patio behind the work barn.

And in Keene and Walpole and Ossipee, Edmund Muskie was doing the same thing. And on the courthouse steps in Pierre, South Dakota, and in every hamlet north of Nashua, New Hampshire, so was George McGovern. The newspapers reported it everywhere. So did the TV: Nixon was vulnerable.

Three weeks before New Hampshire, John Mitchell resigned as attorney general and took over the president's campaign. That's when we first heard rumors of what would become their attack campaign in the weeks before the election: *acid, amnesty, and abortion*. There was a flurry of activity at the estate and an all-day meeting. Aberdeen White was taking off now every morning. I heard some of what was said. The plan was changing. Senator Bonwiller was to ignore the president now and focus on Muskie. The president had every Democrat jabbing at his flank, but we had only one rival we needed to think about. Muskie was the man we had to beat. After that, we would take advantage of what the others were doing to Nixon. I heard that again and again as I moved in and out of the rooms, carrying drinks and newspapers and telegrams: "Focus on Muskie," they said to one another. "Focus on Muskie."

THE SPEAKER-SENTINEL, like all local dailies, gets a good share of its leads from tips. Some come by letter, some by e-mail—although these days even senior citizens are savvy about their Internet anonymity—and most, just like in the old days, come by phone. It's a quaint aspect of a small-town newspaper office, that the phone still rings all hours of the day and night. In the morning, I'm the one who logs the messages. Partly because I'm the first one in, and partly because I still hate the thought of missing anything big. *Esther Harnett is using Burdick's dumpster for her trash.* That's the kind of tidbit I'm usually writing down in the tip book with a cup of cooling coffee in my hand. *Are you aware how many parking tickets Gene Short hasn't paid?* Now and then we get a few more interesting ones, but they usually don't pan out. *Officer Stanley takes money from business owners— you'll see if you follow him.* (We did: he wasn't, at least not that we saw.) *Blue Crest Hills doesn't have grip bars in their bathrooms.* (That one was true. Our reporter found any number of violations.) *Brent Nasser from Roosevelt is going to be an NFL placekicker.*

This last one, with a front-page picture of the kid in his silver and green Loggers uniform, produced our bestselling paper of the year.

That's the fight we face.

We also subscribe to the wire services, just like any other paper; but if the story's within a certain radius—which for the moment still includes Albany—we cover it ourselves. You won't find many local dailies that still do that. Most of our board thinks this gives the chains an economic leg up on us—and it very well might; but the alternative is worse. The circulation we hold against Gannett and McClatchy and Murdoch wouldn't be half of what it is now if our own reporters didn't get the bylines. People in Saline want to see the names they know.

And our sources would dry up, too. That's the other part of it.

Because Henry Bonwiller is from the area, we still get two or three calls a year about him, as well. I've got to think that most of these callers are pranksters. But nonetheless I've also got to think that they're a fair barometer of the residual anger that to this day the man continues to stir. I suspect the ones who take the time to phone are part of the steady trickle of tourists who still come through Carrol County to see the landmarks of a senator's downfall. In fact, there are a couple of B&Bs now that do well enough just housing and feeding these pilgrims. Maybe they're only history buffs.

Of course, I would have thought most of these tourists would be his critics, but to my surprise I've found that they aren't. Far from it, in fact. The first one I ever spoke to was sitting in a pickup on Route 35 about a mile north of where the Metarey driveway used to run. This was on my way home from work one evening, maybe ten years ago. He was stopped on the shoulder, leaning back in the driver's seat, a burly man with a flushed look on his face.

"Do you need any help?" I called out.

He sat up and rolled down his window.

"Hear this is where the girl died," he said in answer, setting a map on the dashboard. A New England accent: Vermont, maybe. A dissipated expression. "It's what they say."

"Yes, sir. They do."

"Don't know about you," he went on, "but I'm a Democrat myself— every election since Stevenson. Whole family's that way. Dad. Granddad." He unfolded the map, and I glimpsed where he'd marked it—just about the point where his truck was parked. "You know—was all the Democrats who died in that car. All went into that ditch, right there." He pointed. "My old man used to say that and I have to agree."

"I suppose I do, too, sir."

He pointed again. "I figure he ended up in those woods about there."

"He might have. Nobody's ever proved it."

He only glanced at me. "Must have panicked," he said. "The whole boat going down under him. Everything he'd ever done. That big house, too—up in Islington, is it? Going there next, as a matter of fact."

"Well, sir," I said, "it's twenty minutes or so." I pointed. "Straight north from here."

Of course, *The Speaker-Sentinel* did a story on it. I had my reporter stake out the site, and in a month he'd interviewed a dozen others. And nine of them were Democrats. You'd think it would be those who were angriest at the man before it all happened—the legions who despised him—who would have made the trip to mark his downfall. Or at least to stake out their claims of conspiracy. But from all I can tell, the ones who still come are the ones who *loved* him. They're the ones who are still reeling.

I DON'T KNOW whether my father waited for some reason to send it, or if he just found it one day that winter after he'd started cleaning the house himself. It was still sealed in its envelope, with my name, in her firm handwriting, across the back.

> Dearest Corey—
> I'm writing this on a beautiful warm day in September with all my ripe tomatoes outside the window to pick. Heavens there are some times so many of them I can hardly keep up.

I will put up 10 gallons this year if the temperature stays like this! (But why do I keep planting so many cucumbers? Your father is starting not to like them anymore, which is strange don't you think for a man who loved them all his life.)

I think about you many times during the day. Right now its 11 in the morning and I just cleaned the kitchen from breakfast, these days its hard to keep a schedule and there's really no reason to anyway as long as I'm ready by lunchtime. From your schedule I see you are in your first period English class (is that Mr. Burrows or is he history?) now. How lucky you are. I liked English when I was a girl (even though this letter is hard for me now, you have to keep in practice!) and would have liked to have been an actress (can you believe that? Me? The shopkeeper's daughter?) I wonder if you have read any plays yet. I used to think Tennessee Williams was the best writer who ever lived when I read The Glass Menagerie. I know your chuckling but don't. Goodness knows there are plenty of Irishwomen on the stage before me, the Maureens (O'Sullivan and O'Hara) come to mind first even though their sons might have chuckled at them too and it took quite a pretty day for them to be discovered, remember.

I can imagine you becoming something great like a lawyer who defends the just or a doctor who takes care of the poor or a union man like your father. I hope that you keep such ideas in your head and follow them.

Heavens its almost noon and I have to clean the kitchen for your father's lunch, I'll be right back.

Oh, look what happened. Its three days gone now! (I'm teaching your father a little bit of basic cooking and he likes to make his own lunch now which is a lot more work for me of course like having a toddler in the kitchen.) And I've been just so tired from all the canning (12 gallons so far, I was wrong!) and I have a headache.

I just read this over and see that I haven't gotten to what I meant to say, which is wherever you are and whatever occurs please know that I am with you. When you face difficulty think of what I would say. Work hard. Keep your sense of justice and kindness and loyalty about you. Be generous and treat people fairly and stand by them when they need you even if it doesn't always come back to you. At least not right away. I can tell you it will.

I'm not sure whether I should say the rest but I think I will and will write you another letter anyway to send. This one I'm putting in the drawer with instructions.

I think I'm not long now. You just know. I hope I'm wrong but I don't think so. Now it all just seems different. I guess you will know for certain if your reading this. There's nothing Doctor Leary can do and I've asked him to be quiet about all of it and Mrs. Janeway (from kindergarden remember?) even took me up to Buffalo and they said the same thing. A hundred miles for that! (Thats why I didn't want to ask your father.) You'll wonder why I never told you but one day when you have your own children you'll see. You're at school now, and its a wonderful school and a wonderful chance and you have the benefit of your father's great good character and Mr. Metarey's now too that I know will always serve you. Both of them. And I will too. Always.

I only wish I had more time to see all the good things that happen to you and even some of the bad and above all what you become and what kind of father you make. There are so many things to say but I'm tired now and what I want to say most is that one day you will understand why I did it this way, and I love you Corey and I will be with you always and always.

I'm not afraid. Don't you be either.

Love,

Mom

SIX

I

Then President Nixon went to China.

He left on the 21st of February, just two weeks before the New Hampshire primary. The White House was calling it *a journey of peace*, and that night in the library we watched John Chancellor turn solemnly to the camera and go even further: *an unimaginable act*, he called it. No president had ever dared.

The next morning, the front page stories hit. And then the pictures. Nixon with Zhou Enlai. Nixon in the Great Hall of the People. Nixon before the Red Guard. And the rumors followed quickly after. A trade agreement. Full diplomatic relations by the end of the week. When I carried the newspaper sticks up to Mr. Metarey's office now, he would close his eyes for a moment before he reached for them. Nixon on the Great Wall, smiling in a fur-lined overcoat. The president and Mrs. Nixon, hand in hand with Chairman Mao.

And suddenly the Democrats had to fight just to make it into the papers. Suddenly, nobody was there to hear the Senator on the front porch of the house. They weren't there for Muskie, either. Nor for

McGovern. And not for Humphrey or Wallace or Jackson. Just for Nixon. The president in the Forbidden City. The president at the Ming Tombs. The president smiling through a pair of chopsticks crossed into a V above his plate.

It was sobering how fast it all changed. Now at Aberdeen West we couldn't be guaranteed more than a few reporters at a briefing. Liam Metarey arranged for Henry Bonwiller to be there himself instead, whenever he could, rather than just one of the press spokesmen; but that hardly helped. Two weeks before, he'd drawn fifteen hundred people in an icy drizzle in Manchester, New Hampshire. Now, ten days before the primary, on a crystalline winter day, there were a total of three reporters at his news session. The next morning *The Union Leader* showed Muskie with a twelve-point lead and McGovern even with us. The house had grown quiet. If we didn't win New Hampshire, or come very close, we weren't going to last beyond it. The money would vanish as fast as the reporters had. At dawn on Washington's birthday, I drove down to the Excelsior to give up our new block of rooms.

I remember coming into the library later that morning to wish Mr. Metarey goodbye before I caught the train back to Dunleavy. He was in a chair pulled close to the TV. On the tiny screen in front of him, the president was sitting next to Zhou Enlai, watching a ping-pong match in Peking. Zhou's long, aristocratic face was recognized now all across the country. The crowd was perfectly behaved. Clapping as one. Silent as one. In the center box, smiling magnanimously, the president leaned over the railing and applauded. It was an extraordinary sight, even to me. If I were a voter sitting at home, I realized, I would vote for the man sitting there with the people of China. I remember turning away from the screen in the midst of a long rally, the ball being kept in play by the American from deep behind the table, and telling Mr. Metarey that I would be back the next weekend, to help Senator Bonwiller win New Hampshire.

"I just hope it's not the last time we need you," he answered.

"I'll be here either way."

"I know you will," he said. "I know you will."

I turned to leave, but he touched my arm. "Look at that," he said, pointing. On one half of the screen, the American had just lunged to make a save, and on the other half the camera had zoomed to Premier Zhou, who had his hand on Mrs. Nixon's arm. The Chinese player somehow missed the return, and Zhou smiled and bent to whisper something in her ear. She laughed, a little uncertainly. Zhou turned the other way next and whispered something to the president, who looked back at his wife. Then all three of them laughed together.

"He's giving advice about the primaries," I said. It was the first time I'd ever tried to be funny for Mr. Metarey.

He laughed. "Fo-cahs ahn Mah-skie," he answered. He looked around, sheepishly.

Then I laughed, too, and it struck me later that this was a different kind of moment than we'd ever had together.

"But it ain't over yet," he said suddenly, snapping off the TV and turning back to his work. "Politics isn't a baseball, Corey. That's the damn thing about it." He opened a notebook, shaking his head. "It's a *foot*ball," he said, and turned the page. "That's the thing you have to remember. You never know how it's going to come back up."

ONE DAY SIX YEARS AGO, a few weeks after our oldest daughter had headed back to college, I realized I'd only thought of this from Henry Bonwiller's point of view. Our daughter was at Colgate University, in Hamilton, New York, and in mid-October my wife and I and the two younger girls went up for a visit. We arranged to meet at a coffee shop close to campus. I was just parking the car when I looked up and saw Andrea emerging from the rust-colored trees, carrying her books in one of those leather schoolboy straps out of a French movie that are popular again with college kids, wearing blue jeans and a light-colored blouse that looked a little too thin for the weather. You can imagine how that felt. There was still a touch of summer in the air, but not much. She paused before crossing the street—she still hadn't seen us at the opposite curb—then proceeded just ahead of a couple of bicyclists and an old VW Beetle looking for a parking space; and I must say, watching her walk out of those trees, like some creature of the forest, out into the main avenue of businesses, where the cafés and clothing stores and antiques shops were doing a brisk commerce and students and families and groups of businessmen in suits with their cellphones out were filling up most of the narrow sidewalk, I was struck with such a feeling of tenderness that I nearly broke down.

I guess that in my years with the Metareys I was too caught up in Henry Bonwiller's hopes to think of it from any wider view. JoEllen Charney was only in her twenties when it happened.

I've spoken to plenty of people about it over the years. Understandably, it's not a rare topic of conversation up here, even now. Some of the details are known. But even these details have been sketched and resketched in barbers' chairs and grocery lines, some of the conjecture random and innocent, and some of it, I think, not. Most of it, to this day, remains a mystery.

They met, I think, at a fund-raising function. It is some time in mid-May. All the trees are in bloom and that feeling is in the air. A luncheon to raise money for one of the causes her family has probably never heard of—the preservation of the local streams and woodland, which her father doesn't have the money or the inclination to give to, even though he likes to hunt. He's a working man, operates a forty-five-ton crane for Harburg-Shrewsbury. Her mother is a secretary at an elementary school south of Buffalo and a regular at church. JoEllen is the first to have gone to college, and she's made some friends there with ambitions. Maybe she has ambitions, too—she's not sure. When she won the Miss Three-Counties pageant she had to sing "Danny Boy" to beat a prettier girl from Fredonia, and for a few months this has given her some kind of boost and made more of her old friends interested in her again. She's had boyfriends but she's never thought of herself as any kind of beauty. So she's been riding just a little high. Still, she's a plain girl at heart. She's been invited by one of these girl-friends to this fund-raiser luncheon and is nervous and slightly con-fused to be there in the Elks Hall, finally, where she knows nobody else and which has been set with rented tables and plastic flower arrangements in oversized vases. She's not wearing anything fancy, just her blue jumper and a peach blouse and black flats from work. Then Senator Henry Bonwiller arrives, and for some reason she's thrilled enough just to stare outright at him. He's standing in a small group of older gentlemen near the stage, talking to this one and that, gesturing with his large hands at all kinds of comers and goers; and when his eye falls on hers for a moment, then goes on—then comes back—she blushes and turns away. *He knows I don't belong.* She takes a couple of steps toward the punch bowl and makes a distracted effort with a plastic cup, but when she turns around again he's still looking at her. He makes a little nod and a half-smile in her direction.

The next day, it's her girlfriend again who calls to say that the two of them have been invited to another event. *Invited!* It's a speech the Sen-ator is giving up in Morrison, more than fifty miles away. She chooses the red dress this time, the short-skirted one she sewed herself for Miss Three-Counties. It has a trace of gold thread that shimmers in the fab-ric and she probably shouldn't but she does. Well, why not? They bor-row her girlfriend's brother's car, a Camaro with leather seats, and drive up to the college auditorium where the Senator makes a speech about water rights and the urgent need to enforce the new antipollution laws, and she listens so carefully she can quote the statistics back to him later when they run into each other by accident in the parking lot near her car. He says, "Nice to know someone was listening."

All she can do is blush.

A few days later, she's called at her own apartment, by one of his aides. "This time," he says, "don't bring your friend."

THERE'S ANOTHER INCIDENT I should mention, a small one. A Saturday night. Late February, near the middle of that crucial time. The weather had been warming, but that evening a front had blown in, and Gil had called me over to the Metareys' after dinner to knock down the rafts of icicles that were hanging over the patio from the porch eaves. I was sweeping the last of them into the snow drifts when Mr. Metarey himself appeared. "Don't tell me we have you working all night around here now," he said.

"I'm pretty much done, sir."

"Then maybe you'll keep me company for a minute or two."

It was dark, maybe eight o'clock. When I paused in my work the cold stung my throat, the particular metallic snap of an old-time Lake Erie winter that I remember so well from those years; the perfume of the cedar trees just a bitten hint in the air.

He walked down next to me on the brick. "I've been thinking about you," he said. "How are you faring?"

I looked up. "Fine, Mr. Metarey. I miss my mother, though."

"I know you do, Corey."

"But I'll be okay. Just makes me a little sad, talking about it."

"I'm sorry," he said, looking over. "I know. It must."

I stood and leaned on my shovel. In front of us a rabbit leaped out of the brush and made a swift path across the yard. He set his hand on my shoulder, then lifted it and pointed out at the woods. "Great horned owl," he said. "Listen."

I heard it in the distance: *hoo, hu-hu-hu, hoo.*

We walked down together to the edge of the terrace then, which looked out to the north of the casting pools. The ice was glittering where it had been swept.

"Exquisite in winter," he said, "isn't it? Not so much a painting anymore. More a drawing."

I'd never seen it in that way. The snow was deep all around, and another dusting had fallen that afternoon, so that in the distance the moonlight lit the line of treetops.

Presently he said, "You're not hurt, are you?"

"Sir?"

"In the woods that night. You didn't get hurt, did you? In the car? I realized I never asked."

"No, sir. Not a bit."

"Good. Good," he said. "Would have been terrible if someone had been hurt."

"I'm fine."

"When I was in the service," he said, "ended up in a little scrape in a Willys jeep myself once. Didn't feel like much then—but on nights like this the old neck still likes to remind me of it." He craned his head around. "Almost thirty years later. Just a twinge when it gets bone-damp. Just a little hello."

The owl's shadow suddenly swooped across the snow; a moment later, we could see its profile in one of the close oaks, high up near the top. Its claws were empty. We stood there, looking at it against the crisscrossed limbs.

"Utterly without mercy," he said softly. "That's what nature is." He cleared his throat. "And we somehow expect it not to be. Or pretend it's not, maybe. The source of man's unease, I'd say. If you had to put your finger on it."

"Sir?"

He turned to regard me. "You read Upton Sinclair yet at that school of ours?"

"No, sir."

"Well, you'll like him when you do." He tossed the remains of an icicle, which broke on the crusted snow. "Even if you never eat sausage again." He chuckled, but I saw his expression change. He set one foot on the stone pillar in front of him, like a cowboy at a fence, and leaned forward, shaking his head. He did that when he noticed a view. You'd think he was just a visitor to that property rather than having lived on it all his life.

"We're going to start bombing again," he said suddenly. "Haiphong and Hanoi and everywhere else. We told them we wouldn't do that."

This didn't become public news for a few days: he must have heard about it in the campaign. It turned out to be a prelude to the well-known Christmas bombings, which occurred later that year. The first sign of the ruthless tactics we'd use before we finally withdrew.

"Roust the North before they can mass on us," he said. "That's the theory, at least. They've got two hundred, maybe three hundred thousand soldiers on the border. We're talking twenty divisions, ready to go. Minute we leave, they overrun the South. A big mess." He stood up. "That's why we're going to do it. Only way to get the hell out of there now. Except it's completely out of our goddamn control. Shouldn't have ever gone in in the first place. That's the saddest part. Everyone's coming home now, too." He knocked another icicle off the stone railing. "Everyone except And, that is."

"He's at a hospital," I said. "Christian told me."

"Yes, he is. Had him at one on an island base till yesterday. But now he's going in-country. That's all they'll tell me. Going to be busy now."

"Christian said you might have done that for him."

He looked at me.

"Got him assigned to the hospital, I mean. The medical post."

He looked away again. It occurred to me I'd overstepped.

"Point is who got him sent across in the first place."

I turned back to the land, where the icicles I'd swept glinted in the snowbank. "Sir?"

He didn't answer, but now, of course, I realize he was referring to the president. I've read the history: for months we'd been pulling our soldiers out. Troop strength had fallen from half a million in 1969 to less than a fifth of that now. But Andrew was being reassigned the other way—to an encampment near Quy Nhon, as we later found out.

"Thing is, our guy's not even the front-runner yet," he said. "So this is either just a warning shot or—" He stopped.

"Sir?"

He looked at me. "What I'm saying is that this could be good. A good sign, I mean. For us. A good sign for the campaign. At least we've got that to think of." He grimaced. "It's good news for the campaign."

The moon hid again in the clouds. Everything receded—the yard, the slope, the glinting ice. Not until I'd had my own children would I understand what he must have been going through.

"I hope Andrew's okay, Mr. Metarey."

"So do I, Corey."

"I think he will be."

"Thank you. I appreciate your words." He stepped down from the railing and looked behind us at the house. Almost all the lights were off. "You know," he said. "You raise your kids the way you know. You take what your folks did, you try to add what you think of as your own corrections—things that hurt you, injustices, all that kind of thing—and you try to bring these blessed objects into the world so it doesn't do them any more harm than it has to. At least not too early, anyway. And then one day you realize that they're not all that different—I don't know—they're not all that different from some wild animals you could have just found out there in the woods. And you have about as much influence over them as you would over animals. One's fierce, maybe. One's calm. But probably because it's frightened. One's always got its eye on the horizon. That's And—damn him. Then one day you realize how silly you've been. There's nothing you can do but let them all go. All you can do from your end is pray. I'm not a religious man—far from it, Corey. But I pray anyway. For my children—that's all. All parents do."

"Yes, sir."

"You know what I'm talking about?"

"I think so."

"When I was in the service I spent a little time on a medical base myself. A forward station, up near the Nakdong River. Did you see *MASH*?"

"Elliott Gould," I said. "Saw it when it came out."

"That's right. And Donald Sutherland and that TV actor—what's his name?—Robert Duvall. He's good. Like one of those places in

MASH where Robert Duvall is stationed, but up front. Called it a Battalion Aid Station. BAS. For *Bad Ass Situation*. Just a mess of blood and guts in the worst way." He turned away from me. "I'm talking about the Korean War, Corey. Same as in the movie. The *real* Korean war. The darkest part, too. Didn't have the F-86 yet and the MiGs were doing a number on our airmen. Soldiers as crazy as Duvall. Or almost. My seventh year in the service so I wasn't so low down in the order of things anymore, but even then, I'd see two, maybe three hundred men come through in a battle. Believe me—everyone helped. We all learned to do plenty we were never trained for. Saw things that still wake me up at night. Arms hanging the wrong way. Legs broken clean off. And burns, too. That's where we learned how to use napalm. Most evil thing ever invented by man. Or vying for it. And not just soldiers. I'm talking about the population, too. Mothers and children. Everybody. Burned all over. Something like two million people died in that war. We did triage. You know what triage is?"

"No, sir."

"Deciding who's in good enough shape to even try to save. We sent those ones on to the MASH."

"Like in the movie."

"But it wasn't a funny thing. Let me tell you. And it's probably what And's doing right now. Not funny at all. Not the kind of decisions you really want to be making about your mates, you know? Decide who gets sent on to the hospital where the real doctors are. The rest— well—what could anyone do?"

"You let them die?"

"*Let* them—that's the word, all right. We were doing them a favor, believe me. Shot them up with morphine and sent them off to the other side, may they rest in peace. We had Chaffee tanks then, before we got the Shermans. Light tanks. Got 'em from Japan because they were close. But the other side had all these big new T-34s coming over from Russia. Couldn't do anything against any of it for a while. Felt like you were on the losing side in a bad, bad football game. South Koreans sent their men in with the wrong-size bazooka, too. M-9s—we

were the ones who gave 'em to 'em, by the way. Couldn't scratch the
paint on a Russian tank. Thing would sit there, up on a hill, firing
away all afternoon. Our guys trying to hide in the trees down below.
Just sit there. Firing. Reloading. Firing. Then their buddies would
bring the worst ones in to us, half the time not even on stretchers. On
their own backs."

"And you would do triage."

"One thing I'll never forget—we called them *ping-pong* eyes.
Those tanks had eighty-five-millimeter guns. That's what gave them
the name. They were T-34–85s. Big shells. Some of our boys would
come in with their helmets stuck halfway through their skulls. Had to
pick out the pieces just to get a look. But they weren't even the worst.
There were these others who came in looking pretty much like nothing had happened except maybe they'd been *scared* to death. They
were just carried in like big sacks of rice and you couldn't tell why. I
remember the first time I saw a guy come in looking like that except
for his eyes going back and forth in his head. Back and forth. Just like
that. Not a scratch on him. Not moving a muscle anywhere else, either. Just lying there on the gurney with his chin up and his eyes
going side to side across the tent. Like he was stunned to find himself
back with other GIs and just wanted to get a polite look at every corner of the place before he said anything wrong. Or maybe he thought
he was in heaven. Sent him on to the helicopter to be saved, of
course. And they sent him right back. Didn't even make it onto the
pad. Eyes still going back and forth. 'That's *dead*,' my MC lieutenant
said. 'Ain't taking chopper space for *that*.' And I said, 'What? Look at
his eyes.' "

He turned to me on the terrace, moving his gaze from side to side.

"He was dead?"

"No. But *good as*. After that I saw a few more like that. They were
internal wounds. Bleeding in the brain. Body looked fine. But when
the eyes were moving like that—ping-pong, ping-pong—you had to
let them go. That's one of the things I learned. Hard as it was. There
was nothing else you could do for them. Morphine was our only

choice. *God's own drug*, my MC doc called it. Truth was they probably didn't even need *that*, but you had to figure they were better off
that way. Numbed up and dead." He stood and looked off into the distance. "Ping-pong eyes," he said. "Sounds like something funny."

"Sounds terrible, too," I said.

"It *was* terrible, Corey. So was letting them die. But it was the only
thing we could do."

He waited for me to say something. Now, all these years later, I
think he wanted me to say that he did the right thing.

I said, "I can imagine, sir."

He smiled at me, almost apologetically, and then a dark look came
over him. He turned to the railing and was quiet. We stood there together, watching. A breeze had come up, and I could see the owl
swaying a little on its high perch. I think Mr. Metarey was waiting for
it to fly. From beyond the trees came the whistle of the coal train making the bridge at Saline. At last, he said, "Andrew volunteered."

"Sir?"

"He volunteered, Corey. He wasn't drafted—wasn't even going to
be. Same reason he never finished at Dunleavy. Didn't think it was
fair." He leaned his head back then and looked straight up at the sky.
"That breaks my heart, you know?" Then, in a firmer voice, he said,
"But I'm also proud of him. And I know he can take care of himself.
Always could. When he was seven he broke his arm in those woods."
He pointed. "Know what he did?"

"No, sir."

"Made a splint from a stick and walked back home. Not a tear on
his cheeks. Arm broken in three places. Tied with twigs. He came in
to show us the splint."

"I like Andrew," I said. "I always have."

"Everybody does, Corey. That's his gift."

"It's your gift, too, Mr. Metarey."

He looked over at me. Then he rested his hand on my shoulder.
"Thank you," he said. "And yours, too. We've always appreciated you
around here." He looked back into the woods. "And by the way," he

said. "You don't have to keep calling to see if there's work. Gil says you're calling every day when you're home. There's always work, as far as I'm concerned. For you, I mean, at the Metareys'. If you want it." He paused. "Always."

"I like to work, actually."

"I know you do. So do I."

"Thank you, Mr. Metarey."

The rabbit broke from the brush again and made a darting path across the snow. I looked at the top of the oak.

"Tell you something else," he said. "I'm with Henry Bonwiller because of every one of you kids. I'm doing this so he can end the war for *you*, too. Not just for my own son. You understand that?"

"Yes, sir."

"For the NVA and the Viet Cong, I mean—them, too. Just like the North Koreans we treated, girls and boys, half of them. But soldiers, too. Just as long as they found their way to us. That's also who I'm talking about—you don't think they're just as godawful terrified? Every single man, woman, and child in that country. Not just our friends in the South. I'm talking about every one of them out there in the jungle scared half to death. Looking up at the same moon we're looking up at now. Every one of those kids in harm's way."

At that moment, the door opened and Churchill came bounding down from the porch. He ran straight to the edge of the terrace and pointed his nose into the woods, barking. I don't know if it was the rabbit he sensed or the owl, or something else, but Liam Metarey simply walked over and placed his hand on the narrow white head, which was shining in the moonlight like ivory. The dog quieted.

"What do you see, pup?"

He stood next to him like that, his hand on the quivering head, while all of us looked out onto the land. At the top of the oak the owl turned and we saw its second pointed ear against the sky.

"Henry Bonwiller might not be perfect," he said then. "But with some very important things he does what's right. That's what counts. He's going to stop the war, for one. Doesn't matter what else he does."

He paused. "It's the greater good I'm talking about. A hundred thousand lives."

"Do you think he has a chance?"

"Of winning?"

"Yes, sir."

"Don't know the answer to that, Corey. Used to think so. Sure. Certainly. And I'm thinking it a little more again just now. But Muskie's going to be tough from here on out. That's for certain. And the president's doing all he can for McGovern, out in South Dakota. I wish our man hadn't done a few things. But he's done 'em, all right. But yes," he said. "I think we can still win. Long as a few breaks roll our way."

The owl called again—*hoo, hu-hu-hu, hoo?*—and somewhere behind the house another one answered—*hoo, hu-hu-hu, hoo-hoo*.

"I'm giving all this land away," he said then.

"Sir?"

"My friend Bob Jenkins, over at the Nature Conservancy—he helped me do it. The place'll be untouchable. That's the right thing to do." He pointed up, a short way into the distance over the first stand of oaks. "Already did it, as a matter of fact. Gave it away yesterday. Officially." He was pointing at what later became the Shelter Brook Set-Aside, where my father and I walk now in the afternoons.

Then he went on. "Not all of it," he said. "Not the house or the land close in. That's for June and the girls and And, to do what they want with. Turn it into a carnival if it suits 'em." He gestured around him. "I'm talking about all the watershed to the east. That's my dad's original piece, all the way down to the quarries and the mine. He walked on it till the day he died. All the oaks and the brook and the cedar swamp. All that," he said, one hand still on Churchill's head and the other pointing toward the hills beyond the flood berms. "Preserved till eternity when I go. I gave it all back."

II

THE ELEVATOR WAS OLD but elegant, with a sliding iron grate instead of a door. Lamps and hallway tables slid into view as I rose, then slid away again, and at the top floor there was another flight of stairs. The apartment had been added on to the roof. A metal door opening onto a tarred deck holding a few trees in pots next to a railing that looked out over West Eighty-sixth Street. Then across a hodgepodge of antennas and water tanks to a tiny slice of the Hudson. Above it, the dim lights of New Jersey. From the front door, I could see a crowd.

The main room was small, and so was the deck, and both were filled. So were both tiny bedrooms and the even tinier kitchen, which I passed through as I searched. But I couldn't find Christian. A door connected the bedrooms so that the whole apartment made a loop, which I circuited and then circuited again to be sure, sidestepping my way through. The walls were hung with small, colorful quilts that looked South American and a number of unframed oils that might have been done by art students—maybe painters were her new friends. Finally I gave up and poured myself a glass of bourbon from a bottle that was on a table. I'd worn a tie and a very nice wool coat Holly had bought me in a secondhand store in Bryn Mawr. I was overdressed.

I loosened my collar, then made my way outside and found a place near a bench at the railing to take off my coat. Sure enough, a couple of art-school types pushed through next to me, talking about a Mondrian show at the Guggenheim. I listened to their conversation: it made me want to move to New York. We were all so close to one another that anyone watching would have thought I was part of their group; but really, I was just looking out across the river, resting my foot on the bench, wondering why I'd come.

A voice from behind me said, "Oh, the tie again."

I turned. It was Clara.

"I thought I'd have better luck with it this time," I said.

"Well, I guess that's not asking too much."

We hugged. I remember it well because I wasn't sure what would happen. The last time we'd really spoken was at my mother's service. That was two years ago now.

She said, "I'm afraid Christian's not here."

"She's not?"

"Sorry."

She stood there. She was wearing a gray cashmere sweater, like one Holly wore. Slightly overdressed herself. Perfume, too: orange petals. I took a drink of my bourbon.

"That's kind of an unusual way to give a party then," I said. "Isn't it?"

"I suppose so." She shrugged, not unkindly. "And you came all the way from Philadelphia."

"I had to be in New York anyway," I said, "for something else." I tried to think of what that might be. It's possible I was blushing. I turned and gestured over the rooftops. "So—I guess this isn't her place then?"

"It's *ours*. We share it."

"Kind of small for two, isn't it?"

"Not if you knew the rent."

We were pushed up close by someone moving behind. "Small for two hundred people, anyway," I said.

I didn't really want to be talking like this. That's what I realized at that moment. She'd been generous to me at my mother's funeral, and that was the one memory I'd kept, somehow—her steady presence next to me with a plate of crackers and a glass of iced tea. I decided to be quiet. To wait a few more seconds before we started again. Just then a fire engine turned on its siren, and we stood there as it rumbled by, shaking us all the way up on the roof. I wonder if she was thinking the same thing. She was quiet, too, until long after the engine had passed. We both looked out. It was an interesting silence, like the middle page of a book.

When she finally did speak, her voice was different. "She's had a hard time lately, you know."

"I do. I can imagine."

"Parties especially. They're the worst, naturally. With everything. She hoped to be here tonight. If she'd heard you were coming, she would have, I'm sure. But I don't think you RSVP'd, did you?"

"I don't think so. Sorry."

"She never knows how she's going to feel, anyway. It might not have mattered. Sometimes it's one way, sometimes it's the other. She was happy to see you, though."

I looked at her.

"At Linden's," she said.

"Oh, that! I was happy to see *her*."

She smiled. "But a little nervous."

"Is that what she said?"

"She told me you were there with your girlfriend."

"I guess I was."

She raised her eyebrows. "Although you didn't admit it."

"Ah," I said, nodding. Somehow, my glass was empty.

"Actually, I think she thought that was sweet." She sat down on the arm of the bench. "I think she was flattered."

She looked up then, her sweater lifting slightly at the ends of her collarbones. I think another fire engine might have gone by. I didn't answer. She just kept looking at me. Neither of us moved. Finally, she knit her brow. Then she turned to the railing again.

"She's had a hard time, Corey. Like I said. You might not recognize her if you talked to her."

"I know. That's how she was at Linden's. I *didn't* recognize her. Not at first, anyway."

"Dad used to say, 'If you begin in certainty, you end in doubt.' "

"Which means?"

"Just what it says."

To the west, the river was a gap in the necklace of lights. Down Eighty-sixth Street, I could see a black slice of it. "And Christian began in certainty?"

"I think she did."

"Then what happened?"

"She takes everything hard, I guess. So did I. But I guess she took it harder. Christian's always been that way. It's in our family, you know, the kind of thing she's going through. I still cry all the time. But my sister—it's a lot worse. She hasn't forgiven any of them. I guess she's ended in doubt."

I heard the elevator grate rattling. Inside me, the bourbon stretched out its arms.

"Or maybe not ended," she added. "But that's the way she is now."

"Actually," I said, "*you* always seemed to be the one who began in certainty."

She stood again and leaned on the rail next to me. "Is *that* what you thought?"

The bourbon stretched again. "Well, at least," I said, "I was always, you know—well, afraid."

"Of what?"

"Of you."

"Since when?"

"Since you jumped in. In the middle of Lake Erie."

"Oh, I see—that." She touched her throat. "I wasn't sure you'd seen."

"Of course I saw. I was watching."

Again we were silent. I heard the short, down-turned warning yaps of a hundred cabs on Broadway.

"Actually," I said, "I thought you were ferocious."

"Thank you."

"You're welcome."

Now the distant, geared rumble of some kind of street machinery. The subway's screeching stop.

After a time, she said. "I know you did, Corey." She shook her head, still looking over the rooftops. "And you were right. I *was* ferocious. I guess I *felt* ferocious. And I wanted everyone to think I was. It's strange to say, but I wonder if I always knew what was going to happen. Like I was getting myself ready."

"I'm sorry," I said.

"Don't be sorry. In the end, it's what kept me alive. I was going about it all the wrong way. But that's the thing that ended up saving me. I guess. When everything stopped."

She turned and looked back at the deck. There was no ring on her finger.

"It's a funny thing to say," she said, "but that's how I think of it now. Everything *stopped*. And my sister and I just kept hurtling on."

"I truly am sorry."

"I know you are. So is everybody." She lifted her arm and waved at someone in the crowd. "But let's not be so gloomy." She waved again. "I *did* start in certainty," she said. "I was certain you'd jump in after me."

"Fall in, maybe."

"That would have been fine."

"I was afraid to go near the side."

"That's why I was standing there, you know. I thought you'd get over it."

"I was holding a pie."

"You'd already put it down."

"Had I?"

"Yes. Strawberry-rhubarb. Not too sweet. Your mother was a good baker."

"Thanks, Clara."

"Just the right amount of butter."

"That's quite something to remember."

"Oh, I can still picture it perfectly," she said. "You set it on one of the coamings. Father saw that and moved it into the cabin. It was getting sprayed." She wedged around to face me. "I started in certainty, and now I've ended in certainty. Is that one of the combinations?" She knit her brow again. But after a moment, her look softened. "Actually, I like you in a tie, Corey," she said. "Do you know that? It's really very nice."

THE ANGRY CALLS WE GET at the paper aren't all about Henry Bonwiller. We get them about JoEllen Charney, too. And there was a new rash of them, believe it or not, soon after the Senator's funeral. Last week, a woman wanted to speak to me.

"You want to know where the little tramp's body is?"

"Who's this?" I said.

"In the stone quarry."

I knew it wasn't a local. A faded accent—Georgia maybe, or the Carolinas—and the wrong words. For some reason nobody around here calls it a stone quarry. It's either lime quarry number one or two, or the granite mines.

"Whose body are you speaking of, ma'am?"

"You know what I'm talking about. Henry Bonwiller's cheap little thing."

That's because there's been a rumor around for years that JoEllen's body was never found. The rumor's not true, of course. She's buried in North Hall Cemetery, near Pinewood, underneath a white marble marker with two doves and a tiny flag etched on it, and after she was found but before the burial her body was in the morgue in Islington for ten days. Some people wonder about that many days in the morgue, but we're a small county and our medical examiner happened to be away when she was found. There was an autopsy at the end of that time, too—whether or not you believe what it concluded. And I know plenty of people who do.

ON THE AFTERNOON of February 26th—I know the date because I've read the history—I was in the downstairs atrium putting together position sheets for the statewide papers when I heard a whooping shout from the upstairs study. It sounded like Henry Bonwiller. And a moment later, Mr. Metarey. Presently the door opened and the Senator leaned out. He came to the hallway railing, next to where the Secret Service man sat reading the paper, and looked down. When he saw nobody but me he said, "Well, shoot! Get on up here, boy, right now!"

"What is it, sir?"

"Got some good news. Get up here, before you miss it!"

That morning I'd taken the bus home from Dunleavy, fearing that this weekend with the campaign was going to be my last. I'd begun to steel myself to finishing out the year, too, using my weekends to get ahead on my classes until it was warm enough for soccer. Henry Bonwiller now trailed Muskie by thirteen points. Aberdeen West was at a fraction of its normal capacity, and the bustle of all the reporters, which had given the house a constant air of anticipation, had dwindled to almost nothing. Mrs. Metarey was gone; so were Christian and Clara, and most of the campaign staff had driven north to Nashua and Manchester for a final push before most of them, no doubt, would switch, to Muskie or now maybe McGovern. The marble entrance halls echoed.

I climbed the stairs and entered the library. There was no one there but Mr. Metarey and the Senator. On TV, Walter Cronkite was talking about the trial of Angela Davis that was set to begin in California. "Change the station," the Senator said. "It's got to be on one of them by now."

Liam Metarey did. First he turned to ABC, where Harry Reasoner was speaking outside a banquet hall in Peking.

"No, no. That's not it."

"I know that, Henry," said Mr. Metarey. "I'm looking."

"It's Muskie," the Senator went on, turning to me. It might have been the first time he'd ever addressed me outside the car, other than to give an order. "We just got a call. Some dinky newspaper ran a piece about his wife. Says she smokes and drinks—"

"It was *The Union Leader*," said Mr. Metarey from the TV. He changed the channel again. "The Manchester *Union Leader*."

"They say Jane Muskie smokes and drinks and tells dirty jokes. Ha! Ha! Ha!" He bumped me on the shoulder with his Scotch glass, then took a drink. "Well who doesn't?" he bellowed. "And now look at what the guy does." He turned to Liam Metarey. "You found it yet?"

"Still looking."

On the screen now, a commercial was ending. Then David Brinkley came on. This was NBC.

"Jesus Christ almighty God," said Henry Bonwiller, and he pulled me by the arm until I was right next to him in front of the TV. "Watch this, boy."

The picture is muffled by snow—not by static, but by real snow, which is falling heavily in Manchester that day. Edmund Muskie is standing on the bed of a truck in front of the *Union Leader* offices, where, as the snow swirls around him, he proceeds to defend the honor of his wife against William Loeb, the paper's publisher.

"He's talking about the drinking and the dirty jokes," Henry Bonwiller said, bumping my arm again with the glass. "That Loeb's a son of a bitch, all right. Worse than the rat-fuckers who feed him. But if I know Jane Muskie, he'd better talk faster."

"Shhh," said Liam Metarey. "Here it comes."

Then in the middle of it, as David Brinkley begins to narrate, Senator Muskie suddenly appears to break down. In the thickening snowfall the picture is hard to discern. The camera moves in closer. He's recovered now and is shaking his fist in the air, but then it happens a second time: he convulses for a moment, and at this point there's no doubt—he's crying.

On national television.

"Come on!" Henry Bonwiller nearly shouted. "Did you see that? Did you see that?"

"Yes, sir."

"He does it again, boy. Keep watching."

And he does. One week before the primary.

"Get the Scotch, Liam! The good stuff!"

"It *does* look promising for us, Henry," said Mr. Metarey.

He turned to me. "*Promising?* That horse been rode hard and put to bed wet. That's the end of him, son. Right there." He ran his finger across his throat. "Period. End of poem." He rose and slapped Mr. Metarey on the back. "Let's have a drink to this fine day of hunting. Give the boy a drink, Liam." He pulled a bottle of Glenlivet from the cabinet and poured a glass. "Here!" he said. "Do not go gentle into that good night!"

"I don't think Corey's ever tasted Scotch."

"Nonsense," said Henry Bonwiller. "It's all I drank at his age!"

"To President Bonwiller, then," said Liam Metarey.

"To President Bonwiller," I repeated, holding up my drink.

"Oh, I like that!" he roared. He raised his own tumbler of Scotch to the ceiling, then followed it with his eyes, like a man having a vision. "To President Bonwiller," he said softly. Then he lowered his arm, and at that moment—as though instead of a glass in his hand, he'd been holding a wand—phones began ringing all over the house.

THAT NIGHT, after I'd finished setting up the chairs for the morning press briefing—even though I suspected most of them would go empty—I came outside to fetch my bike and found Liam Metarey in the garage. He stood leaning forward under a solitary lamp, grinding a set of skew chisels on a pedal wheel. It was late, probably close to midnight.

"You warm enough for a ride in the snow?" he said without looking up. "Take one of the riding coats. If you want."

"That's okay. I'm used to it."

"Well, be careful then."

I stood by the door for a moment. I was feeling bold. "I guess the football bounced our way," I said.

"Oh, it did," he answered. He began to pump the pedal underneath the machine and the sharpening wheel started up, rising to a steady note as it gathered speed in the quiet garage. "It did, all right," he said. "Bounced right up into old Henry's hands. Things are looking a little better from here. You get those chairs out?"

"Yes, sir."

"Going to need a few more tomorrow, I'd bet. Or day after tomorrow, at least. When they get back from Muskie's funeral."

"I hope so."

He dipped one of the chisels in water and took its measure against the whirling stone. "Funny thing is," he said, still not looking at me, "our men didn't do that."

"Do what, sir?"

"Plant that baloney story about Jane Muskie," he answered. He pressed the chisel into the wheel and sparks flew away into the dark garage. "The president's men did that," he said. "Looks like somebody on their side's working for *us* now."

A QUIVERING, LIGHT-INKED HAND:

Oh, Corey. You probably think I'm crazy, inviting you like that and then not showing up. (But you didn't even call!) (Oh, I don't know, even if you did call I can't say what I would have done.) Things! Things! Things! Things are just so stupidly hard for me. I wish I could just shrug them away like everyone else. But instead I'm stuck in a bowl of glue, thrashing all around.

But you, especially you—you must understand. How long did it take you to get over it all? Or have you? I don't think I ever will. Who are all the lucky people who can control what their minds think? Are you one of them? Who are all those lucky people with their hand on the switch? You're probably sitting there in some smoky coffeehouse with someone special and have to hide this note. Sorry! I probably shouldn't send it. (I guess you'll see I did! Beware good intentions.) But at least I wanted to say sorry for not being there after you took the trouble to come up. Clara said she was out on the roof with you looking at the city. I love that view. It reminds me of Paris with all the gardens and water towers on the roofs. Then felt I like some watcher of the skies! Remember? She said you looked nice.

Please give me another chance.
Xo,
—C

HER FIRST MEETING WITH THE SENATOR is at a nightclub. In Hapsburg. Thirty miles away. She doesn't tell her friend about it this time, and this time she takes her own car instead, a white Gremlin that she washes and vacuums and fits with an air freshener before she leaves.

She brings three minis of vodka to calm herself; she has one in her driveway and the second, followed by a breath mint, just before she gets to the club, where she finds him waiting for her in his car in the lot. Of course it's a Caddy. They never go into the building. They drive around instead and he's friendly and calm and authoritative—not as formal as she thought a senator would be—telling her about the rock mines that used to be in these hills and the possibility that IBM would be coming up here to build a plant on the old site. Then they come out on a reservoir and he stops the car. It's a warm night and it's a convertible but he doesn't open the top. She wouldn't want him to anyway. But he takes a flask from the glove box and offers her some, which she takes even though she's had the two minis already, and then he takes a little himself. This is a senator, sitting across the seat from her. He has a wife—she's looked it up.

"Sing 'Danny Boy,'" he says softly.

Well, how did he know that! But when she finishes she's almost sure his eyes are wet, and think how that feels. He moves across the seat and half-sings "the summer's gone and all the roses falling" himself, in that voice that might as well be coming out of the radio, it's so honey-colored where it plays in the lower registers. She adds the harmony.

"You're good," he says. "They teach you that in Optimists' Chorus?"

"How did you hear about that?"

"A little bird told me."

It all feels like a bubble she's watching glint in the sun. She doesn't have the last mini until she's driving home.

After that, they meet a few more times, for rides like this usually, with a stop at the end at a motel; and soon they give up the rides and just start meeting at the motel. She drives the Gremlin. Mostly it's a place called The Pines, a set of hideaway cabins in a grove off the road near Islington. He arrives an hour or two later in various different cars and sometimes now he has a driver with him—she can see him through the slit in the shades, a tall Negro in a chauffeur's cap half-sleeping five feet from their window. There's always something to drink, either Scotch whiskey or wine, and he likes to bring a sandwich with him and eat it when they're finished, even though she never has anything herself. At this point she still can't imagine eating in front of him.

Then there's a day, maybe three weeks into it, when he says to her, "That bastard Leftwich is going to run for my seat." When she looks it up later she can't figure out how to spell the name but she gathers her nerve and asks the librarian: Louis Lefkowitz is the Republican attorney general of the state. And sure enough, she starts seeing his name in the paper. She starts seeing it all the time—*New York Attorney General Louis Lefkowitz*—and it's a funny thing but she feels like she has an enemy now. The surprise is that she likes it.

Their enemy.

After that Henry Bonwiller starts talking to her about all kinds of things, about who's going to get money for a shopping center project and who's going to be indicted, about what the teachers' union is going to get in their new contract and about remodeling Kennedy Airport for a new kind of superplane. And he stops asking her to sing. He does his talking when he first arrives, pacing back and forth in the little motel cabin as though he's trying to walk and talk his way from one world into another. She lies on the bed listening carefully. After a while he sits down next to her and has another drink. Then he reaches up and loosens his tie by yanking it.

Right after he's climaxed, he has a habit of falling asleep. But only for a few minutes. When he wakes up, he eats his sandwich, gets dressed, and goes. Once the driver had to knock on the window. He had a vote in the Senate the next morning.

A vote in the Senate!

Then comes the day he tells her he's thinking of something big. Later, after he's dressed, he says he's not just thinking it, he's going to do it.

"What?" she says.

"Be president."

"President of the *United States*?" It slips from her mouth before she can stop it, like a dog running out the door.

But he laughs! He thinks it's charming. "No, president of the choral society," he says, and takes her hand to swing her around in a little jig. When they sit down finally on the bed his mood changes and he tells her an extraordinary thing. She can't decide whether it's just a speech or something he really feels. Something he tells *only her*. He says, "I'm doing this for the black man and the Latino man and the American Indian. For the working people like your father and all the other fathers who send their boys to Southeast Asia for no reason anybody can explain to them. Just out of their goodness and their faith in the country. For the unwed mother in Chicago who's raising her sister's kids, too, who gets by on a welfare check and five swing shifts a week at the Uniroyal plant in Gary. Those are the people I'm going to help. Those are the people I'm doing this for. Those are the ones."

He's a hero, she decides. Takes his strength and gives it to the country. Those strong arms and that voice and that mind that turns her around on a string sometimes like the mobile in the dentist's office. *He hasn't said this to anybody else yet.* That's what she decides. And he looked at her face right after he finished saying it. *Her* face. He turned to her as he sat on the bed. She remembers that so clearly— because this was really something he should have been saying standing up, that's how good it was—and something changed in his face as he knotted his tie and jerked it straight in the collar. Was it her own look? She's tried and tried, but for the life of her she can't remember whether she smiled.

III

SOME TIME AGO, not long after September 11th, I decided to look up JoEllen Charney's parents. I can't explain the relation between these two things, other than that the first one finally motivated me to do some of what I'd been meaning to do for years. On an errand in Buffalo I stopped out to see them—Eunice and George Charney. The house was in the scrub country between Albion and the Niagara River. A small, vinyl-sided ranch with the cab of a big rig parked out front and a couple of pieces of earth-moving equipment sitting in the tall grass of the side yard. I'd called in advance. Told them I'd known their daughter.

They received me in the backyard, where George was whittling duck decoys from hunks of cedar that had been cut with a chain saw. We sat down at a set of plastic lawn chairs around a rusted table. They both seemed to be doing okay for their age, and when Eunice rose to shake my hand I had a brief glimpse of a certain, inviting melancholy in her eyes—the same, down-rounded lids that had been made briefly infamous thirty years before. George had the puffed cheeks and grayed skin that you see after a life of beer and cigarettes, but there was still something hard in his features. He turned and spit onto the lawn.

"Now, tell us how you knew JoEllen," Eunice said.

"Let me explain myself," I answered, "just so I'm clear. I used to work for Liam Metarey."

George Charney put down his whittling.

"But you have to understand, I'm not coming on anyone's behalf. That job ended thirty years ago. And I haven't seen Senator Bonwiller in almost as long."

"He's not a senator anymore."

"No, he's not, Mr. Charney. You're right."

"He's just a son-of-a-bitch lawyer."

When he stood, he knocked one of the cedar decoys off the table. He limped across to the side yard where the machinery was and picked up a whittled cane, whose handle was also carved into a duck's head. He stood there leaning on it, looking back at us, the carved eyes staring as blackly as his own.

"Go on, young man," said Mrs. Charney.

"I wanted to come out because I have children now," I said. "A daughter myself: *Daughters*, I mean. Mostly grown. And I guess I didn't want to do anything but give you my condolences. I know it's late. That's all I wanted to do, Mr. and Mrs. Charney. Say I'm sorry for what happened."

"Thank you," said Eunice. She reached across the table and took my two hands in hers for a moment.

"Your pop's Grange Sifter, ain't he?" her husband said from across the lawn.

"Yes, sir."

He took a couple of steps back toward us. I could see now that he wasn't doing as well as I'd thought. One leg lagged behind and he had to swing it around the cane. He was breathing hard. "Your pop and I worked together on the Corney Flood Dam."

"Corney Dam," I said. "I remember it. Must have been 1968."

" 'Sixty-nine. Right before I did the leg." He yanked out the chair and sat again. "Never could get the control gate on the sluice to close right. Still not sure it wouldn't lie down like a drunk dog if a whole lot of water hit it."

"We think about JoEll all the time," said Eunice.

"I know you must."

"She's in heaven, we believe."

"I do know that."

She looked into my eyes. "Is there anything you meant to tell us?"

I glanced over toward the back of the yard, where on the other side of the machinery a thin woods started. Then back at her. "No, ma'am. Just that I'm sorry. I wanted to pay my respects. Long overdue."

"Then, thank you."

"Well," I said. "I don't mean to take up your day."

"I liked your old man," George said. "Everybody did."

"Thank you. He spends his time at the new community center these days. Plays cards and that kind of thing. He's okay with it."

"Oh, yeah. They're all over the state now. Wouldn't mind one ourselves."

"Used to be the Y. Now it's called Bright Horizons." I laughed. "Outside Saline."

"Is that right? Built that place, too, for God sakes. If I remember. Had to bring in beams to get the roof up to code. Thirty-six-foot long."

"I've seen those beams. They're big."

"Big is right."

"Thank you for coming by, Mr. Sifter," said Eunice.

We stood then, and Mr. Charney approached us again, shaking my hand finally and then walking me slowly out around the side of the house to the car. A mongrel dog joined him, staying close to his cane. "What do you do?" he asked, as I was about to close the door.

"Newspaper business."

"Oh," he said. That seemed to stop him. "Where at?"

I rolled down the window. "A paper called *The Speaker-Sentinel*."

"Don't read much. Not around here, though, is it?"

"No, not really. South of here. Fifty miles. Islington-Steppan-Saline."

"I didn't build it, anyways."

"It's a distance."

I started the motor.

"What do you do for them?" he asked.

"I'm the publisher."

"The publisher."

"Means I run it. Least at a place our size."

"That right? Grange Sifter's boy runs the newspaper?"

"I guess he does."

"Ain't that funny?"

"Ain't it, is right," I said.

He patted the dog, then leaned down and rested his arm on the door. "You not planning to write anything about my daughter now, are you?"

"No, sir. That's not why I came out."

He looked in at me and I saw his eyes run over the seats, the dashboard, my jacket hanging by the rear window. Then he stood up and said, "Of course I'm sad about JoEllen. If that's what you want to know." With a bit of effort, he crossed his arms and leaned back on his hips the way my father and all his workmates used to do, to ease the effort of standing. "I got no idea why you come," he said, "but I'm sad for my daughter every day, if that's what you want to know. I miss her all the time." He leaned in closer again. "You think it goes away?"

"No, sir. I don't imagine it does."

"Son of a bitch killed her. Me and Eunice know that. Is that what you're asking yourself? Why don't her father do something about it? Is that what?"

"No, sir. That's not it at all."

"That's what everybody wants to know. But what the hell are we going to do about it?" he said. "What the hell are me and Eunice going to do about it now?"

"What was he doing on the tractor?"

"What was who doing?"

"Liam Metarey. You said he went out on the Ferguson. That afternoon in the snow. When Henry Bonwiller was up in his office. Sleeping off his drunk."

"I have no real evidence he was drunk."

"Sure was drinking a lot of coffee."

"You listen very carefully."

"I'm a reporter," she said, smiling. But she kept her eyes on me. "And the tractor?"

"How should I know?" I said. "It's a huge piece of land."

"But you told me he went out on the tractor. You noticed it and you told me. Is it normal for a man to take a tractor into the woods in a snowstorm?"

"I just saw him head up the driveway. I don't know if he went into the woods. He could have been heading into town, for all I know."

She raised her eyebrows. "On a tractor?"

The next day, just as Henry Bonwiller predicted, Muskie began his slide. His swift and famous descent into oblivion. And a week after that, in New Hampshire, he finished fourth. Even McGovern beat him. And Henry Bonwiller, who in January had been down by seventeen points, finished first. I heard that news, too, in the commons lounge at Dunleavy. This time Mr. Clayliss shook his head.

The week after that, in Florida, he very nearly did it again. He'd been given almost no chance at all there, but it took a last-minute push by Governor George Wallace—governor of the state next door—to eke out the win. By less than a point, as it turned out. And Wallace had spent nearly all his cash doing it. On top of that, Henry Bonwiller beat him soundly in the counties around Miami and Palm Beach, where the real money was. That Monday, phone calls went out across the area. Mr. Metarey got him on the cover of *Life*—in overalls and work gloves, sitting on a bright green sawhorse that I'd painted that morning and then roughed up with engine oil and a chain. McGovern was starting to make his case by then—he was known around Aberdeen West as a dogged campaigner—but his opposition to the war wasn't yet as well known as the Senator's and he finished well down in the pack. There was talk of him throwing his support to Bonwiller in exchange for the vice presidency. But I don't think the idea went far. "Man's got the charisma of a turnip," I heard Senator Bonwiller say to Liam Metarey one afternoon as I was leaving the library. Humphrey, for his own part, ran dismally in Florida. There was talk now of Muskie finally giving up, as well.

Back in Saline, once more, hotel rooms were not to be had. The campaign had rented every bed again at the Excelsior, and at all the roadhouses between there and Steppan, too, but now there was no stopping the number of political operatives who wanted to join us. The campaign hired a man just to interview them and furnished a room in the basement just for him to do it. Even on the weekends, there might have been seventy-five aides on the estate, and those of us who had been around longer than a few weeks began to exchange nods in the halls.

On the 21st of March, in Illinois, he won again, this time overwhelmingly: 780,000 votes. No one else even came close. The general election was a little over seven months away. Planes were landing at Aberdeen West from Washington and New York and Boston and Albany, and now the talk had shifted to a new subject: how to beat the president in the fall.

AND THEN WHAT HAPPENS to her? What does this extraordinary moment with a United States senator finally do for her? The next morning she feels a little pit in her gut. Nothing big. Maybe just needs a
little breakfast; that's all. Coffee. But afterward it's still there and as
she sets the cup on the counter to dry, she feels it again. This time a
little stronger. A tiny little stone. Resentment. That's what it is. Clear
as day. What's the matter with her? She's tried to help people all her
life, and so has he. And what could be wrong with that? But it's there.
She feels it again as she waits for him that night at The Pines, watching TV until almost eleven-thirty, when she finally hears his tires on
the gravel. That's what it is now: a cold little stone low in her belly. She
hopes it won't show in her face. When she hears the car door close she
smiles at the mirror and goes to answer the short-short-long knock.

It disappears when they make love. The stone melts. It goes back
into her veins.

But in the morning, still at The Pines, she stays in bed a little
longer than she should, reading the paper, and it comes back. It starts
in the front of her mind and she can make herself think of something
else, but soon it's there again even when she's not thinking about it; a
little sour flicker just before she starts another article, just before she
turns on the hot water in the shower, just before she gets out of the
Gremlin at McBain & Sweeney for work. It's there when she says
"good morning" to Mr. McBain and even when she smiles at the jan-
itor she likes with the war limp, a Negro man like one of the ones
Henry Bonwiller wants to help. It's there again when she waits at The
Pines that night.

*I'm doing this for the black man and the Latino man and the Amer-
ican Indian.*

So why does that upset her? But it does. And it panics her, too. Because it won't go away. And she doesn't understand. Why should it
sour her that he wants to help all those people, those people in need?
Louis Lefkowitz wouldn't do anything for any of them. And she hates
Louis Lefkowitz. So then what is so bitter in her that this is what she

feels whenever Henry Bonwiller says his brave and extraordinary things? But it is. This chilly little stone attached inside her. People must see it on her face. It's not there every minute exactly but it comes right back as soon as she is called upon to produce anything from inside herself, a word or a smile or even a hand on a shoulder—the bitterness comes out alongside it like some foul glue stuck to everything. At the worst times—mornings, usually—speaking is actually starting to become a trick. Speaking normally and not showing what's inside her. She checks her expression in windows, in car mirrors; she checks it in her compact while pretending to remove a new ream of typewriter paper from the bottom drawer. Driving, she makes up little conversations. "Hi," she says. "Good morning." "Good morning to you."

One afternoon at work she hears a client in Mr. McBain's doorway say the name *Bonwiller*. She draws up straight, slips a piece of paper silently into the platen of her Selectric. "That *slime ball*," the man says. She stiffens. Pretends to study the letter she's about to type. "How a guy can be in everybody's pocket at once, I don't know. The niggers and the unions. And the oil companies. What a combo."

"Well, I don't know about that, Frank," Mr. McBain says in his skillful voice, from inside the door.

"Yeah?" the man says, "Well why's nobody trying to help *me*?"

That's *it*, she thinks. She rolls the paper into the platen and begins to type. And for a few moments, at least, she's cured. Why is nobody trying to help *her*?

MY FATHER WORKED till dark on the weekdays, so it was Gil McKinstrey who picked me up at the bus depot in Islington now, every Friday. And he would take me straight back to the estate, rather than to Dumfries Street, which I liked. When I was in Saline I still slept in my own bed, of course, but it probably isn't hard to see that I preferred Aberdeen West to my own house; in fact the truth was that I might even have been trying to avoid my father now, even though I knew that in our new circumstances we needed each other more than we ever had. I'm not proud of that reaction, but I suppose it's common.

There was a return bus at dawn on Monday that got me back to Dunleavy just in time for my first-period class, so sometimes I slept at home on Sunday night as well. I'd have spent both days at Aberdeen West, doing whatever was needed—sometimes working on the land but more often running errands for the campaign. My father cooked breakfast and dinner for the two of us—he was getting better at it— and on Sunday evening I'd do my laundry in the machine on our back porch, then take my two shirts and my two pairs of pants upstairs to iron. Dad was usually in his bath.

One evening in March, not long after the Senator's watershed win in Illinois, I was standing at the ironing board in my room when a seagull flew down and landed outdoors on the sill across from me. It perched on the wood and looked in. Gulls don't often come so far inland around here, and especially so early in the season, but this one had. It cocked its head and stared at me, appraising with its curious eye.

"I can do a shirt in two minutes now," I said.

It raised its wings and showed me their gray undersides, like a dove's.

I sprayed water on the collar and ran the iron up to the seam in tiny quick strokes. "See?" I said.

It flew then, and I went to the glass to follow. When I found it, it was down on our fence, perched on some stalks from one of my mother's tomato plants that were still twined through last year's cages.

"You'd be happy about the ironing," I said. I moved back from the window and in a pair of quick strokes finished one of the sleeves.

You're getting better at it, Cor.

I flipped the shirt over and did the other one. After a moment, I said, "Mrs. Metarey *does* scare me, you know. You were right."

She's like Clara—you told me.

"They both scare me, Mom. It's like they know something, or they know that *I* know something. About me, I mean." I turned the shirt inside out and did the button side now, pulling on the tail with my other hand so that there was no crease. "I think Clara thinks I'm trying to sneak my way into their family."

Maybe that's what she's afraid of.

"Or maybe it's what you said."

Are you in love with Christian?

"I don't know, Mom. She's wonderful."

Does that mean you love her?

"I'm not sure. There's still something about her that sort of disappears when you look at it. It's like she goes away a little. Sometimes when I'm at school I have a hard time just remembering her. I remember that I like her and that I love being around her, but I can't say much more."

Clara's not like that.

"Clara's the opposite. She scares me even when she's not around."

I think I understand why. Clara feels things deeply. Maybe like her mother does.

"And you were right about Mr. Metarey, Mom. He *is* trustworthy. Even with everything he has to take care of, he thinks of the people around him. His kids, especially—but me, too. That's a comfort."

It is to me, too.

"There's some kind of rivalry between Christian and Clara over him, I think. That's all I can figure out. They both want him to notice them. That's why Clara does all those crazy things. And maybe Christian, too—why she does all those nice things. Sometimes I think it's all they see in me. That I'm a way to get to their dad."

I finished the shirt and folded the arms neatly into my duffel. "There," I said. "That's more than I've ever told you."

GLENN BURRANT, to his credit, was one of the few liberal columnists who treated Muskie's fall with skepticism. He wasted no time in questioning the rumors of Jane Muskie's debauchery; and a month later he was the first to question a letter to the editor, which had appeared in *The Union Leader* shortly before the New Hampshire primary, saying Senator Muskie was biased against French-Canadian Americans—who numbered close to a million in the New England states. These bits were only a small part of his column, but sitting in the Dunleavy library the week after Henry Bonwiller's second win, in Illinois, I read them with uneasy attention. The letter to *The Union Leader* about Muskie had been signed by a man named Paul Morrison, of Deerfield Beach, Florida, and Glenn Burrant had actually taken the trouble to look for him. His article ended with the words, "Paul Morrison, of Deerfield Beach, Florida, as far as this reporter can determine, does not exist."

That week, I wrote Glenn a letter—the only time I ever did. I wanted to tell him how much I respected his work, but I also wanted him to know that I'd taken to heart the words he'd said to me when we first met: on my bus rides home from Dunleavy that spring, I'd taken it upon myself to read *A Mencken Chrestomathy*. So I ended my letter with a quote that I thought he'd like, especially in regard to his latest column. "A national political campaign," I wrote, "is better than the best circus ever heard of, with a mass baptism and a couple of hangings thrown in."

A week later there was a card in my box at school:

Every man is his own hell, was all it said.

ONE SATURDAY MORNING later that month I arrived early at the estate to find the parking circle empty. It was a weekend, but even at that hour there should have been a dozen cars already lining the drive. I walked up the side steps to the house and two Secret Service men opened the door.

"Name," one said.

"Sifter."

"Sifter what?"

"Corey Sifter, sir."

He didn't bother to answer. He was looking at a list on his clipboard. "All right," he said. "I don't see why—" He looked me in the eye. "But go ahead."

I glanced at his partner, who nodded. "Have to search you, son."

Inside, the rest of the staff was gone. Something was going on in the upstairs library. I had a strange feeling as I walked around on the lower floor. Already all the doors were shut, and it was not yet seven in the morning. And at the top of the stairs, in a folding chair blocking the landing, another Secret Service man sat scanning the hallway below. He wasn't the one who usually sat there. I set myself up in the workroom off the kitchen and began unloading a box of new phones, then assembling them. The first floor was completely empty of activity except for two other agents who one at a time kept coming into the room where I was working, then going back out. They kept a continuous pace through the house and the grounds, walking briskly, one of them always inside the building and the other one always out. There were no cooks in the kitchen.

The week before, just as Liam Metarey had feared, the North Vietnamese army had crossed the demilitarized zone, and within days they'd pushed twenty miles into the South. Nixon had responded on TV, from his desk in the Oval Office: America would not back down. So had Kissinger, from a podium outside the Rose Garden. B52s were sent to the 20th parallel. Then all the way to Hanoi. Haiphong Harbor was mined. It looked as though the war was changing into exactly what Mr. Metarey had feared: all-out combat, to be followed, just before the election, by a peace treaty. More strategists were flying in to the estate, but nobody needed to tell us the obvious: the endgame was being timed to favor the president.

Later that morning, while I was working on the phones inside the deserted house, I heard a percussive beat in the air. I went to the window. From behind the barn a helicopter suddenly appeared. It lifted up, joggled its tail rotor, then dropped again below the roof. It was a military chopper, like the ones we'd been seeing on the news. I stepped out onto the porch. Another agent was out there.

"Back inside," he said.

"What's going on?"

He pointed into the house. "I said *back inside*."

AT HIS DESK, Mr. Metarey opened a newspaper on its stick and pushed it across the leather blotter. "Have a look," he said. I'd been stacking firewood.

I picked it up. The *St. Louis Post-Dispatch*. National section, April 8th, 1972.

"Bottom left," he said. "Small. With the car ads."

I looked again, and there it was. Fourteen-point headline over an eight-line filler:

SENATOR TIED TO FATAL ROAD INCIDENT

Islington, NY—Senator Henry Bonwiller (D-New York) has been questioned in connection with the highway death of a local woman near this well-to-do vacation community along the eastern shore of Lake Erie, according to sources. The Bonwiller presidential campaign has not issued a comment, and police have termed the investigation simply a precautionary measure.

"Not a bad poker face, kid."

"Sir?"

He picked up his pipe from the ashtray and puffed on it. "You read it?"

"I did, sir."

"And what do you make of it?"

"It's awfully small."

"Small, yes—but it's there."

"And his name's not in the headline, sir."

"True."

"And it's strange," I said. I set it back on the desk.

"Why do you say that?"

"Well, the *Post-Dispatch* is a liberal paper, isn't it, sir?" Even in those days I knew which editorial pages favored us—the *Times*, the *Post*, the *Globe*, the *Post-Dispatch*—and which didn't—*The Wall Street Journal*, the *Tribune*, *The Union Leader*, *The Dallas Morning News*, the *Boston Herald Traveler*. "St. Louis is one of the friendly ones, I think. Right, Mr. Metarey?"

"That's right, Corey."

"But it's the same article that ran in the *Tribune*."

He didn't answer. Instead, he turned and looked out the window, where a few spring flurries were drifting under the long soffits of the roof.

"At least I think so, sir," I said. "If I remember."

"That's exactly right, too," he mumbled, still looking away. "February sometime. The national section." He opened his desk drawer and pulled out a file folder, then fished in it till he found something. He glanced in at it, puffing again on the pipe. "Not a word different," he said.

"Except for the headline."

"That's right, Corey. You noticed that, too. They left out the name but the headline's still a damn sight worse. It's that one word."

"*Fatal*—"

"And *that* was Colonel McCormick," he said. "*This* is the *Dispatch*."

"What's happening, sir?"

"Wish I knew. Could be they're still trying to protect us."

For years, as it turned out, I was left to think about what he meant by this. He drew on the pipe again, but it was nearly extinguished. "Could be a message, too," he said. "A word to the listening."

Was he talking about the president? Or about the newspapers? For a long time I assumed that the Bonwiller family—and perhaps the Metarey family as well—had simply reached out with its iron hand to quell the news, wherever it rose. But I don't know now if that's true. It could have been even more corrupt than that.

On the other hand, to be fair, it could have been less. In my job since then I've seen plenty of leads die quietly on the vine, of their own accord. Lack of proof. Lack of trustworthy sources. The public forgets that the worst thing a newspaperman can do is publish a rumor. That's still true, and still a boon to any politician who needs only to weather a single storm. But whatever happened, whatever Liam Metarey was referring to, it's still impressive to me that for so many months, so little was revealed. Was it in fact worse than I knew? Had Henry Bonwiller paid off the newspapers? Was it in the end that crude? Was that what he meant? Or was it Nixon's men, finally, playing this long and thorny hand? Is that what Mr. Metarey knew?

At the desk, he drew once more on the pipe, hard, then turned it over and tapped it into the ashtray. Something came over his face as he did—a look of sudden, deadening fatigue—and for a moment, as I stood watching him, I actually thought he was close to tears. He pinched off a fingerful of tobacco, refilled the bowl, and struck a match. In all the time I worked for him, he never told me what he knew about all of it, of course; but at that moment, I think, as he held the flame over the bowl and sucked for several seconds on the nib— as though he needed some time to compose himself—at that moment, he came the closest to doing it. I can't explain how I know that, but I do. I remember it clearly. His face looked as though for a moment he'd taken off a mask.

"Well, Corey . . ." he said, around the pipe.

But then the mood passed. The bowl came to flame and his face reconfigured itself. "We've got a whole new set of enemies now," he said briskly. "That's part of it."

"Yes, sir."

"But not all."

He was referring, I now realize, to nothing more than what had just occurred in the race. After Illinois, Henry Bonwiller had been transformed into the indisputable front-runner. And he was polling well in every state that mattered from here on out: in Pennsylvania and Massachusetts, which would vote at the end of the month, and in Ohio and Indiana, which would vote not long after. McGovern was still alive in the West and parts of New England, but everyone—at least everyone in the Bonwiller campaign—considered him a long shot. And despite what had happened in Florida, Wallace was hardly mentioned at all. Humphrey was hanging on, too, but it was understood that this was only for influence at the convention. And in every region now except New England, Muskie was all but dead. Just that week a couple of editorial writers on the East Coast had called Henry Bonwiller the nominee. This, of course, worried Liam Metarey.

"Faint rumble of armies," he said.

"Sir?"

"Faint rumble of armies."

He tilted his ear toward the window. I turned in that direction, but all I saw through the glass were the snowflakes, dancing upward in the eddies of the eaves.

SEVEN

OF COURSE, IT'S PREDICTABLE what I found out about Eoghan
Metarey: the history of riches is always sordid. And if it weren't, we
would make it that way. That day in the Haverford library, as soon as
Holly had left, I opened one of the books I'd hidden under my notepad at the desk. *The Age of American Barons*, by Geoffrey Morris. I
flipped to the index and found the entry: *Madarey, Eoghan J.* Earlier
that morning, I'd stumbled on it: I'd been looking for the wrong name.

Later, I discovered that the spelling had been changed by Eoghan
Metarey himself, sometime around the turn of the century. His younger
brother Rupert split with him around that time, keeping the Madarey
spelling but setting off for Canada. In fact, a whole band of Madareys
still populates southern Ontario, and even if the name differs, the two
halves of the family clearly share the same fierce inheritance: today, you
can't drive twenty minutes anywhere between Ottawa and Montreal
without passing a Madarey's Restaurant, and—as everyone from Buffalo to Belleville knows—you can't turn on your radio within a hundred
miles of Toronto without hearing a jingle for Madarey Cadillac.

The type was small, and I carried the book to a spot near the window to read. I felt my breathing change. Sitting down in the empty hallway at the back of the stacks, I copied the passage by hand into my pad:

One of the most aggressive of this second wave was Eoghan Madarey, a Scottish iron and coal miner, and later a rail pioneer, who had come to New York State from near Dundee in 1881. Like his hero and fellow Fife immigrant, Andrew Carnegie, Madarey was a self-made millionaire, and where he had sought his fortune first was in the carboniferous basins of northern Nova Scotia. He was a driven man, sometimes brutal, who maintained separate houses for his various concubines during his long marriage. He was also said to have kept a riding crop in his pocket, which was not for use on his horses. His home was principally in Saline, New York, close to the eastern shore of Lake Erie, but he owned estates throughout northern New England and Nova Scotia as well. He was also well known for throwing lavish parties at his Hudson River manor, named River Glen, attended by the likes of John D. Rockefeller, J. P. Morgan, and Vincent Astor, and for keeping in his employ a local English teacher whose only duty was to help cleanse his speech of its Scottish brogue.

Coal was the first source of his significant wealth. By the time he was 22 years old, in 1898, Madarey Mine #1, near Westville, Nova Scotia, was employing over 300 men, who were paid between 90 cents and $1.80 per day, and possibly half that number again of boys, who were paid 75 cents. This was before the wide advent of compressed air drills and well before the invention of longwall mining, and picks and wedges were the only tools used to work the seam. The rooms were first holed across the middle; then the sides were sheared and wedged. It was dangerous, dirty work, as it remains today, but the millions of tons of coal lifted to the surface each year by pit ponies and later steam hoists formed the basis of Canadian and much of northern New England's heavy industry, as well as provided readily available fuel for the widening network of electric power in the region.

Eoghan Madarey's first claim had been a sizeable strike along the Acadia seam. This strike produced the harder, purer anthracite, which was suitable for steelmaking, rather than the softer, less pure, bituminous coal that dominates the region. Although the Madarey seam was thinner and more expensive to mine than the vast, neighboring Pictou fields, the higher grade of extract fetched a superior price, and Eoghan Madarey was a substantially wealthy man before the age of 30. (Thornfield estimates his fortune at $28 million by 1911.)

But not long after Madarey Mine #1 was in full production, trouble struck. During a thunderstorm on the night of May 11, 1900, a lightning bolt came to ground along an iron rail at the surface of the mine, and the charge carried down into the working chamber, where it exploded a pocket of methane gas and coal dust. The shaft collapsed and 14 miners were trapped inside. A line was sunk and voices could be heard. Families gathered at the mine head.

As it happened, Madarey Mines had been engaged at the time in a tense standoff with the Provincial Workman's Association, the miners' union that later became the Amalgamated Mine Workers of Nova Scotia. The dispute was over wages. No strike had been called but one seemed imminent. Miners had been staying home from work in increasing numbers, and armed guards had been called in to patrol the company land. But after its initial successes in the preceding two decades, the union was now weakened by declining membership and limited funds. At Madarey #1 and several other local mines, many of the recalcitrant workers had already been replaced by scabs. Tempers were short on both sides.

It is not clear who was caught in the collapsed shaft, but it is believed to have been unionized miners. Madarey management allowed fresh air to be pumped through the life-line, but they refused further access to the site to attempt a rescue, citing safety, and at the same time also refused the union's request to postpone wage negotiations. Stewards of the PWA found themselves in the position of negotiating with Eoghan Madarey while 14 PWA members were trapped 500 feet under the earth. When union observers attempted to widen the life-line to deliver fresh water, Madarey guards prevented them, again citing safety and pointing out that the trapped miners had access to the pit ponies' drinking troughs, which were at every landing. The union countered that the trapped men might not be able to reach the landings. Management then refused to allow food to be delivered, perhaps as a negotiating tool. The following day, in a gesture of "goodwill," Eoghan Madarey himself at last consented to the delivery of water. And the day after that, subsequent to a union wage concession, rescuers were allowed to lower a minimal amount of salt cod and bread into the mine. But still no work on a second shaft was opened.

On the morning of May 14, 1900, three days after the collapse, workers tore down a fence and succeeded in opening a wider life-line from a shelf still standing in a neighboring shaft at 250 feet, through which they passed food and water and clean air to their mates below. Families gathered again at the mine head but were driven off by Madarey guards, claiming private property. This time, equipment was commandeered by the union from nearby sites to attempt a full-scale clandestine rescue. But in the middle of the night of May 16, 1900, while a small clan of miners dug in secret along the neighboring shaft, apparently with the cooperation of a few Madarey guards, another explosion was heard. The full contingent of company guards then drove off the rescuers, and in the papers the next day Madarey again pointed to danger at the site.

By morning, the wider life-line had somehow disappeared, either damaged in the explosion or, as unionists have long believed, intentionally closed off by the company. Contract negotiations proceeded, and as part of an agreement a few days later in which the union consented to the small wage increase offered by the mine owners, Madarey at last agreed to a rescue attempt. Here, nine of the miners from one pocket of the shaft were brought out alive. But by then the five from the neighboring pocket, who were unable to reach the pit ponies' water, had perished. The incident became a rallying cry for the unions, which once again strengthened their positions in the years that followed. Today, the five lost miners are immortalized in the lyrics of several songs, including "Westville Number One" and "The Dark Sixteenth of May," as well as in a nursery rhyme still sung in Canadian preschools. . . .

I set down the book and looked out the window. It was spring. Holly would be coming back to the library in the afternoon to study with me. Outside, students were riding bikes and throwing Frisbees and lounging on the steps, and it struck me again, the way it had just begun to do in those days, how diligently privilege had to work to remain oblivious to its cost.

I'm speaking of myself now, too, of course.

BY THEN EVEN A BOY LIKE ME understood the capricious headiness of politics—I'd already watched once as Nixon had stolen everything from us with his visit to China—but you couldn't be around Aberdeen West in late March and early April of 1972 and not realize that something powerful had changed. It was around then, I think, after the wins in New Hampshire and Illinois, and with the new polling coming out in Wisconsin and Massachusetts and Pennsylvania, that Henry Bonwiller underwent a critical change. For the first time, I believe, he began to imagine himself as President of the United States.

Think of that moment. One of the hallmarks of our politics now is that we tend to elect those who can campaign over those who can lead; it's an obvious point but because of my history I've spent a fair amount of time pondering what it might have meant for Henry Bonwiller and Liam Metarey. For a man on the rise in politics, power first comes through character—that combination of station and forcefulness that produces not just intimidation, which is power's crudest form, but flattery, too, which is one of its more refined. After that, power begins to grow from its own essence, rising no longer exclusively from the man but from the office itself. And this is where some balance must be found between its attainment and its allotment, between the unquenchable desire in any politician to rise, and the often humbling requirement that one's station must now be used to some benefit. And here, of course, is where corruption begins; for power contains an irresistible urge to further itself: there is always the next race. But when finally there isn't any more, when at last there is no more ambition to quell, no more inchoate striving to follow as a guidestar, then a politician must make a transformation that he may have no more ability to make than he has to grow wings and fly. He must change his personal ambition into ambition for his country. This, I believe, was where Henry Bonwiller stood that spring, as he first began to actually imagine himself as president. It's luck of the draw, of course, who can make the change and who can't. I imagine he was wondering himself.

I have no more knowledge than what I've recorded of the strange events earlier that month on the estate, but I can't help considering now that the army helicopter that touched down behind Breighton's barn the week before was carrying an envoy of the president. John Ehrlichman, maybe, or H. R. Haldeman, or even John Mitchell. The presence of the Secret Service even makes me wonder if it had been Vice President Agnew who made the visit, arriving in secret and to this day unreported. And if I had to guess about what took place that morning, I'd say that it's important to remember that Henry Bonwiller had not only recently become Nixon's probable November opponent but that he remained at the same time a pivotal force in an overwhelmingly Democratic Congress, the great barrier to Nixon's ambition, at a time when the public was crushingly weary of the war. And one must also remember the techniques the president was already using. The Watergate break-ins hadn't yet occurred, but the first would take place in less than a month, and the plans were undoubtedly already in the president's mind and probably in the minds of Ehrlichman and Haldeman and Mitchell, as well; and the president in his own conception of himself might have just recently crossed the line of decency that he would soon obliterate. What might he have wanted with Henry Bonwiller and Liam Metarey under those conditions?

I wouldn't be the first to guess that JoEllen Charney herself was working for the White House. It's an old story, as old as Samson and

Delilah, and an old theory about Henry Bonwiller, too, that's based on fifteen years of cocktail party whispers, indiscriminately amplified by fifteen subsequent years of webpages. But from what I've come to know since then of the Charney family, I don't give it much weight. And on balance I don't believe that Nixon had any sort of privileged knowledge of what had happened between JoEllen and the Senator, either. But I do know that George McGovern had just begun to re-assert himself after his early showing in Iowa, and at the same time that Nixon had just witnessed the wildly successful fruition of his henchmen's strategy to destroy Edmund Muskie. Was the president now completing the next step in the hand selection of his own No-vember opponent? Most historians would tell you that Henry Bon-willer, with his New York ties and his New York money, would have been vastly more effective than George McGovern in a national race. Was there a deal being made? At the time, Senator Bonwiller and Senator McGovern were the two most outspoken voices in the coun-try against the war in Vietnam, and Nixon in his inherent shrewdness would have understood that this would have made the two senators not so much allies against him as bitter rivals themselves. More bitter rivals with each other, probably, than either of them was with the president.

What I've finally concluded is that Nixon might have sent an envoy, in the guise of legislative diplomacy, to give Henry Bonwiller early knowledge of the escalation he planned that month in Viet-nam. It's not a particularly sensationalistic theory, but that's part of the reason I allow it credence. The escalation, which included night-time air raids against the civilian population of Hanoi, would no doubt have deeply angered the Senator; but what Nixon must have known is that advance news of it would also have flattered him—the second skill of powerful men—because it meant that for the first time Henry Bonwiller was being treated as a possible president. It also would have given the Senator an advantage over McGovern among their congressional colleagues. Naturally, I have to assume that there was at least one mole in the Bonwiller presidential campaign, so it's not a stretch to imagine that word of the new majesty in Henry Bonwiller's bearing might have reached the White House. Nixon probably rejoiced.

But this is conjecture, and thinly supported, I admit, and I get beyond myself. What's more important to record is that early that spring Henry Bonwiller began to refashion his public bearing. He began withdrawing to the upper rooms of the estate rather than ambling in his garrulous way among the staff; he began sending minions again to the press briefings instead of appearing himself; and he began to stay away from the daily campaign-wide meetings in the downstairs offices or the speech rewriting sessions in the living room. A new order of access had appeared among the staff as well. Clarence Chase had set up a desk in the anteroom at the base of the stairs, and anyone who wanted to see Henry Bonwiller now, or even Liam Metarey, had to go through him first.

It was under these new conditions that at the end of the month the campaign threw a different kind of party. It was a two-day affair this time, and the guests were fewer in number, but the preparations were more painstaking than I'd ever seen; even a boy like me understood that the men and women who arrived for it were not just the ordinary, moneyed supporters who'd been at the other events, but the particular few that the candidate was considering for jobs in a new administration. In my time at the Metareys' I came in proximity to any number of famous and powerful figures, but I'd never been among so concentrated a group of them as I was over those two days. George Meany was there, and Carl Stokes, and Averell Harriman, and Senator Kennedy and Senator Mansfield and even Senator Humphrey. So were Arthur Schlesinger and Betty Friedan, and the famous young journalist David Halberstam, who'd just written a book called *The Best and the Brightest*, which Glenn Burrant had told me to read. G. V. Trawbridge was in the crowd, too, and I assume now that both men must have agreed to take everything on deep background. I saw Daniel Patrick Moynihan and Shirley Chisholm, also, and even though now I can remember all these names and faces so clearly, the truth is that on the afternoon itself all but Trawbridge and Humphrey and Kennedy had to be pointed out to me, either by Christian or Glenn Burrant or Mr. Metarey. But I can also say that without any prompting I sensed instantly that there was a new sort of stature in the room. And I must also say that I've never been, and I don't think I'll ever be again, among any group at any time in which every hope and ambition is heightened to such an extent by the proximity of such an exquisite victory.

But again, that's not why I tell this bit. Because of our location near two great lakes, the spring rains around Saline are famously torrential, and that was what they were as the gathering approached. On Friday evening the sky turned gray to the northwest and proceeded to empty itself unrelentingly all that night and the next day. It was as heavy a downpour as I've ever witnessed in my life. Gil McKinstrey and I had to open the drain culvert on the fly ponds so that the water wouldn't crest the berm onto the lawn, and we'd gone out at night to rescue a whole flock of sheep from a neighboring farm who'd climbed to the higher ground around the Lodge Chief Marker. But the rain wasn't a particular problem for the campaign party itself, and it even lent a certain air of excitement to it, with the vast thunder rumbling in over the water and the many vivifying flashes in the night. The only one who seemed to mind was Breighton, who could be heard whinnying and stamping in his stable until Gil McKinstrey went out to put something in his feed. For most of the visitors it was nothing but a regional oddity, and I suspect it only added to their striking impression of the Senator's home country. Most of them were sleeping at the Excelsior, anyway, and being driven around in limousines hired from Buffalo, and the event itself was really a series of dozens of smaller meetings, all of them held in the row of rooms at the end of the downstairs hall of the estate, or occasionally in the library. One hardly even had to carry an umbrella. But on Sunday at noon Henry Bonwiller was scheduled to give his closing speech under the outdoor tent, and when I showed up that morning to prepare the chairs for the audience the rain still sounded like a bucket of gravel being poured out onto the roof of the work barn.

How much of all of this—of political power, of personal fortune, of the outcome of a life—can be attributed to chance, I'm in no more position to say than anyone else, but around eleven that morning a scrap of silvery light appeared over the lake to the west, and a short time later—at the exact hour, in fact, that the Senator was scheduled to make his way into the crowd under the tent—the clearing migrated over the property. Sunshine filled the air and the lawns sparkled suddenly like beds of jewels. You could sense a feeling of awe then, even among this educated and powerful crowd, and you could sense something more, too—a particular feeling that we had all been chosen. There were giddy remarks and plenty of jokes about it—God was a Democrat, and so on—but really, you couldn't help thinking it signaled something. Henry Bonwiller ending up speaking to an afternoon that looked like the world's first afternoon, and sure enough, as soon as he finished, when he was still moving among the small groups in the parking circle and on the front porch of the estate, the clouds moved in again from the west, the hole of light closed, and the rain poured forth once more.

Later that evening, long after the last guests had departed, I decided it would be a good idea to check the drainage pipe behind the fly pond, to make sure it hadn't silted closed. The light had just gone down, and as I was crossing the short, earthen dam there in the steady rain I came across what I took to be an injured animal lying in the mud at the bottom of the berm—my mind went to the flock of sheep Gil and I had found earlier on high ground. As I reached the middle of the crossing I saw it more clearly in the darkness and heard it grunting quietly. At first it lay still, but when I turned on my flashlight it began to struggle, kicking its legs as though it was stuck in the deep swale of mud and making a harsher sound, as though I might be a predator; and it was only as I came closer down the steep side of the hill and trained the beam on it through the thick rain that I realized it was something else, not a sheep at all. At first this was all the sense I could make of it.

It's easy to come up with reasons why I later became a journalist. I wasn't raised in an educated family but I was privileged with a fine education myself, and though my parents had little learning they both respected it, the way they respected any endeavor that required discipline. I was mentored by a man with unparalleled access to the world but who still somehow retained a sense of justice, and whose life was in large part measured by his gifts to the community—both traits, really, that define a journalistic career of a certain kind. Or I could say that Holly Steen, with the hunger and ambition of her learning, had something to do with my own commitment to a life of words and paper. I could list all those reasons, or I could as easily list the writers I first read at Dunleavy—Dickens and Upton Sinclair and Mark Twain—or the ones at Haverford—Hegel and Marx and Robert Coles; but the simple truth is that it's more likely because of the moment that followed, in which I climbed down the waterlogged slope and saw that the figure at the bottom was not any animal but a man; and then, in another moment, that the man was G. V. Trawbridge. If I'd had time to think, I might have gone to fetch someone, but instead I pushed my way through the ankle-deep mud and lifted him in my arms.

Years later, reading his memoir, I found out that Vance Trawbridge was born with a deformity but that as a grown man he was struck with multiple sclerosis as well, and I read of all the difficulties he faced in his life—near the end of his career, he fell nearly every day and his hands were so weak he had to dictate everything with his failing voice into a tape machine. Though he doesn't mention this incident at Aberdeen West at all, he does write that this was the period when the multiple sclerosis was first taking hold of him, and I imagine it was horrible when it happened. He must have slipped at the top of the berm.

By the time I found him he was completely encased in mud, and his thin limbs were shivering. But even soaked he was remarkably light, not much heavier than a child, and when I lifted him he laid his head back in my elbow the way a child might. His dark features looked up at me imploringly. He seemed only half conscious, and the cold of his body worried me.

I set off back up the slippery footing of the berm. It was hard to tell he was even clothed, so uniform was the mud that covered him, but as we walked the rain continued to fall steadily, and by some strange miracle it began to wash him, so that by the time we reached the surer footing of the gravel I could see his face and his oversized glasses, which still clung to their strap, and then the stripes of his seersucker suit, and by the time we were on the back lawn I could clearly make out the white of his shirt and the red of what I feared was a wound on his neck but that under the porch lights turned out to be his bow tie, pulled halfway around his collar.

It was June Metarey who met us on the steps. "My God," she exclaimed. "What in God's name—"

"I think he slipped."

"Vance, are you all right?"

"I'm okay, June. Okay."

I hadn't, I realized, thought to speak to him.

"Thank you, Corey," she said. "Bring him inside to the downstairs guest room and run and get my husband." Then she took his dripping hand, and I'll never forget what she said next. She said, "In the eyes of God, Vance, all of us are crippled."

His head rose in my arms. "Thanks, June," he said. "But *I'm* the crippled one. That's the truth of it."

By the time I got him through the door, Mr. Metarey and a couple of the maids were already in the atrium with towels, but probably none of them realized that I had found him nearly buried in mud, or that when I picked him up he was in as squalid a condition as I have ever seen a human being. By now, he was merely drenched. They probably saw him as unfortunate but also as a bit comical, the seersucker cloth clinging to his chest now and his large head made smaller and more timid, somehow, the way a dog's is, by water. If anything, the event may have looked more like a blessing or a baptism than the shameful degradation that it must have been for him and that for some reason it will always be for me.

And yet somehow, I also think back on this moment as one of the essential turns of my life, that the shame of holding the great man in such a state transmitted a kind of duty and honor to me also, and that it committed me in my own far slighter way to follow in his path. And although it might sound far-fetched, I believe that something passed between the two of us in those moments, some acknowledgment of station and consequence and human obligation that is impossible to explain but that still has hold of me today.

He was taken to the guest room, and Mr. Metarey thanked me profusely and then sent me across to one of the cottages to shower and change into a set of Andrew's clothes. But that night before I left I was called into the house again, where Mr. Trawbridge stood now in a newly pressed suit in the entranceway, looking as he always did, leaning on his canes next to Senator Bonwiller. I saw Clara in the dining room.

"So you're the young man," Vance Trawbridge said, when Mr. Metarey introduced us. "Thank you. You might have saved my life. I won't forget your kindness."

I was terribly self-conscious, in part because I could see Clara watching us, but I was still excited from what had happened and was only searching for something to say. The proper answer would have been "You're welcome, sir" or "Very glad to help." But instead I said, in my father's affable way, "Consider it a gift from the campaign."

There was laughter all around.

SOMEHOW, THE POST-DISPATCH STORY, like the *Tribune* story before it, failed to spread. I saw it nowhere else. Not in the *Times*, all that month. Not in *The Washington Post* or the *Courier-Express*. At the estate, I checked the *Chronicle*, the *Examiner*, the *Post-Intelligencer*, the *Herald Traveler*, and *The Dallas Morning News*, too. At school, I continued to check the *Post*, the *Globe*, and the *Courier-Express*. It wasn't in the *Speaker*, or *The Sentinel*, either, and it wasn't followed up in the *Post-Dispatch* or the *Tribune* themselves. It wasn't in any paper I looked at—and I looked at a lot of them.

"They were waiting for the killing moment," said Trieste.

"How do you mean?"

"They wanted to make sure the dagger went into the right man." She was putting on the duster, getting ready to leave on a rainy evening.

"Oh, I see," I said. "You're presuming a lot of conspiracy."

"Or not presuming enough, maybe. It should have been everywhere. Overnight."

"Things were different then, Trieste. There were no computers. There was no Internet and no e-mail. Reporters used the phone. And teletypes. I don't know if your generation understands that. I don't know if your generation even knows what a teletype *is*."

"Of course we do. Or *I* do."

"Then you're unusual." I went to the window, where the rain glittered in the streetlamps. "Editors felt they had to verify stories," I said, looking out into the dusk. "*Before* they ran. There was a whole filtering process. Interviews. Witnesses. Sources. Checks. Rechecks. And the question—is this relevant? Is this *news*? It was still asked." I turned back to her. "Believe it or not."

"You don't think it was relevant?"

"Of course it was relevant. But in those days all the papers had their own reporters. Not just the *Times*. They sent them out to do their own stories. It took a combined effort. And a combined effort takes time."

She buttoned the duster and pulled the collar up around her neck. "So that's what you think it was, Mr. Sifter?" she said finally. "Editors checking their own reporters' sources?"

"As I said, Trieste—there was no Internet then. No Matt Drudge. No Daily Kos. No Andrew Sullivan. No blog-world."

"Blogosphere, Mr. Sifter."

"Thank you."

"And that's what you believe, sir? That's what you think happened? It didn't make it out because there wasn't any blogosphere yet?"

"Truly," I said. "I don't know."

"Sir," she said, pulling on her hat, "I don't think you're presuming enough conspiracy."

THE FEELING IS GONE, thank God, even if she knows inside that it's just a temporary respite. For a day, she's fine. But the following evening, sure enough, when she locks the three office doors and sets Mr. McBain's outgoing mail in the box, it's back. The stone. He might be meeting her that night or he might not. He's going to call around eight from a pay phone. That's all he'll say. She goes home and heats up a can of tomato soup. At eight she turns on *Mannix* and watches halfheartedly. Then cleans the apartment. At midnight, finally, she goes to sleep.

That week, in desperation, she tells her mother: she's seeing someone. A *married man*, she says, as if that's the biggest part of the secret. They're at a bakery where you can drink tea from a full pot. Her mother, who's driven in forty miles by herself, is holding her cup and saucer up near her chin, the way she does, but when she hears this her breath catches and she sets them both down hard in the middle of the tablecloth. The spoon jumps. She says, "You have to gather your strength, JoEll, and leave him."

JoEllen knows her mother is right, even if she hasn't heard half the truth. Even if she hasn't heard a tenth of it. *Gather your strength and leave.*

But that's not what she does.

Two nights later, she's in the cabin at The Pines, and he's finishing his sandwich. She says, "How come we don't ever go someplace nicer?"

He sets down the sandwich and looks at her. She has surprised even herself.

The next day someone calls and tells her there's a room for her at Morley's Inn, in Saline.

In the afternoon she drives over. The room has a king-size bed with a bedcover striped in maroon and tassels that hang from the corners. There's a chocolate on each pillow. She eats hers and takes his to give to him later as a surprise. This is more like it. A dark wood desk in the corner with pretty stationery in the drawer and a silver ice bucket sitting on a red leather coaster. This is much more like it.

But again that night he doesn't show up until after eleven. By then, she's nearly given up. He's got to get home right afterward, too. She's got nowhere to go herself, so while they're still lying in bed she says, "How long can I stay here?"

"Long as you want, honey." He stands up and pulls on his trousers. His shirt. Straps on his watch. "And you're going to be part of the campaign now, too," he says.

"I'm going to be what?"

"You're going to be working on the campaign, from now on. Come to some of the meetings. Be seen with the staff. Out in public. You'll get paid a little, too."

She frowns at that.

"For the campaign work."

"What will I do?"

"We'll figure that out." He pulls on his coat. "Someone will call."

And that's the way it proceeds. Someone does call. She goes to a couple of meetings in Islington, at a restaurant on the pier called The Swan. He sits across the table from her. Half a dozen other people are there, and a few others come and go. He smiles at her, nods, but that's all. Someone gives her a steno pad and that's what she does. She takes notes while they talk. It's just dates. A speech at the Hilton. A speech at the Harvard Club. A ribbon-cutting at a horse track. She draws out a calendar and marks them all. But nobody asks to see it.

The stone's not exactly gone from her gut, but almost. Sometimes she still feels it, not as bad, just a prick of cold somewhere in the center of her. But if she laughs a couple of times she can get it to go away. Back at Morley's the room is always ready now, too, under the name *Annabelle English*. Now and then she thinks of her mother. *You have to gather your strength and leave him.* She's not sure if she's gathering her strength, but she doesn't think so. Sometimes she'll go to a campaign meeting, then come back into Saline to spend the night alone in the big bed. In the morning she gets a beauty treatment next door. That helps. The view from the window helps, too. The tree leaves and the fountain. The strolling couples. So does the bottle of Scotch in the silver bucket. They refill the ice when they make up the room. Then one day, putting away her coat in the closet, she finds a pair of new dresses hanging there—that's a nice surprise—and when she opens the drawer she finds some new underthings, too. Pretty ones. That's pleasant enough but the week after that she opens the closet again and there's a fur stole on a hanger.

Well.

She's not sure what mink looks like. There's no tag but it's lined with black satin. She slips it on, the satin cool on her neck. She lets it hang over her shoulders and runs her hands over the fur, then quickly touches her breasts underneath. In the mirror, she says *Annabelle English*. She's pretty. It almost surprises her.

And for a couple of weeks, it gets her through. That and the name and the underthings, the way she looks with one shoulder wrapped in fur. The Scotch, too, and the campaign meetings, and the hotel staff who move noiselessly about their chores. There's a dignified quiet to the place and an evening light, like a nunnery. The desk clerk uses the name once himself—*Evening, Miss English*—before he stops saying anything to her at all. On the corner of his lapel he wears a tiny crucifix. Then someone calls at the apartment and says she shouldn't check in anymore, just go straight up through the restaurant. There's a stairway off the bar. It's a steakhouse, and he's meeting her there every Tuesday and Thursday, lunch with two other aides who show up late and sit at the table with them for a little meeting before he gives her the nod and she goes back up the rear steps to the room. Sometimes it takes him another hour. She sits at the edge of the bed, listening for his steps on the carpet. Practicing a certain kind of smile.

Daytimes he's rushed but talkative. Nights, he's quiet.

One of those nights, maybe two weeks later, they have more to drink than usual and she puts on one of the new dresses, but all of a sudden there's the stone again inside her, bigger than it's been—she tries to give a little laugh but it doesn't work—and abruptly she lets the stole drop from her shoulders. "This feels so dirty," she says suddenly. For some reason she thinks of the desk clerk. His folded hands. "I feel like I'm doing something wrong." She can feel the drink pulling her along. A string around her wrist. "It's not wrong what we're doing," she says, moving up close to him, "is it?"

"That's silly, honey. We're just doing what human beings do."

"Any human beings?" she says.

"Yeah."

He's tying his shoes. The fur is near him on the carpet and he gathers it without sitting up, hangs it over the chair. Then double knots the laces.

"Or *us* especially?" she says. "You and me?"

He looks up. "All right," he says. "You and me."

"Mmmm," she says, moving next to him.

"I'm going to have to be traveling a lot coming up." For some reason he says this now. "That's what happens in a campaign."

TWO SUNDAYS LATER, the cover story of *The New York Times Magazine* was written by G. V. Trawbridge. The first paragraph:

THE GREAT PRESIDENTS have won the job not so much by campaigning well as by appearing at the right moment in history.

Abraham Lincoln arrived in a capital city soon to be threatened by
Stonewall Jackson's advancing artillery. Franklin Roosevelt arrived
in one littered with the burned tatters of the routed Bonus Army.
Henry Bonwiller, as powerful a figure as has ever sought this great
office, seems poised to arrive in one worn nearly under by the sad
tide of Vietnam.

The cover itself was a photograph of the Senator in his Washington
office, standing halfway in front of the flag.

The title: "A Bonwiller Presidency."

One of the new hires, not knowing Liam Metarey, tacked the picture up to the bulletin board in the downstairs library, and I have to
say it was a proud moment for me. But I also knew Liam Metarey well
enough by then that I had a good idea of what he would think when
he saw it. And I was right. I wasn't standing very far away when he
walked past, yanked it down, and crumpled it loudly in his fist. And
on the way out the door he dropped it into the trash can.

You can imagine what I was feeling. At that age I would have followed Liam Metarey anywhere on earth, but when that article appeared I'd felt, for the first time since the campaign had begun,
somehow significant, as well—that I'd done something that not just
any kid from Saline might have done. I secretly understood that my
actions had had bearing on those salutary words being written by
G. V. Trawbridge, and that I'd finally made some contribution, however indirect, to Henry Bonwiller's campaign for president.

In the evening, as I was straightening up the downstairs foyer, I
plucked the crumpled sheets from the trash and stuffed them into my
pocket. And at home that night I smoothed them flat again and
folded them to fit my wallet.

"AND DIDN'T THAT BOOK change your opinion about the old robber
baron?"

"About the what?"

"About Eoghan Metarey."

"Oh. Most people wouldn't call him that, Trieste. Not around here, at least."

"Actually I thought I was being charitable. I've heard a whole lot worse." She was smiling again. This time, the secretive one. The unopened bud. "And I've known that story all my life."

"You knew about the mine accident?"

"Yes, sir."

"I guess you're hanging around at different lunch counters than I did at your age."

"We make our own lunches, sir. We don't go to lunch counters."

"Well, my dad and I used to. And at the ones we ate at, you weren't going to hear that kind of story. At least not when I was a kid. If my father knew about Eoghan Metarey's history, he certainly wasn't going to tell me. And I seriously doubt he even did. That accident happened in Canada. Those were Canadian miners. Folks in Saline didn't read newspapers then. Certainly not Canadian ones."

"It's not the accident I'm talking about. It's what he did after."

"I know that, Trieste. But I don't think people heard about it here. It was 1900. They couldn't just turn on the TV."

"But Saline's a union town, Mr. Sifter. Canadian miners are the same as American miners. Dead ones, at least. Word would have traveled, and it seems to me it should have been a story."

"It wasn't a union town *then*, Trieste. The Wagner Act wasn't till the thirties. It was *Liam* Metarey who let the unions in. The old man himself never would have. Probably still turning in his grave over it. And Eoghan Metarey was the one who founded the *Speaker*, too. Remember that. Used for his own purposes, of course, but founded nonetheless. Don't imagine it was a story he'd cover in his own paper."

"Freedom of the press is guaranteed only if you own one."

"That's Liebling," I said. "Very good."

"You're surprised."

"I'm surprised anyone your age remembers him."

"I don't *remember* him, sir," she answered. "But I've read him. Would *you* cover it now?"

"Of course I'd cover it now."

"Hmm," she said. She took a bite of her muffin. "But didn't it change what you thought of the family?"

"It was their *grand*father, Trieste. Clara and Christian's, at least. It was nobody I knew."

"And you had a lot to be grateful to them for."

"Yes. And I still do, Trieste. I still do."

I TOOK THE TRAIN NORTH from Philadelphia again, reading Camus. It was April of my senior year at Haverford. A perfectly blue spring sky and the trackside shacks and dives beginning to vanish into forest. At Penn Station, throngs of commuters rushing the platforms. I buttoned my coat and turned uptown to walk the fifty blocks. The midtown edifices like statues behind washed glass. The crowds like crowds of emperors.

At the top floor, Clara answered. There was still no ring on her finger.

I saw it then. I saw it in the subtle smirk on her mouth as she went to fetch her sister; in the way she sat primly, her knees together, on the ottoman, while Christian and I shared the couch. I saw it when she insisted Christian and I spend the afternoon without her.

So we did. We went to Linden's again. Sat at a small table in back. By then Christian looked better. Her hair had grown in. She wore a sundress, though it was chilly for it.

"What are you studying?" she asked.

"English. A history minor."

She sipped from her mug.

"Mother says you've become quite a good student."

"I guess. I guess I have."

That was what our conversation was like. She'd been an art history major at Columbia until she'd left school. Now she was figuring out what to do. Before we finished our coffee, I asked if she'd rather go for a walk. We made our way, hardly speaking, along the edge of the park, pointing out the sights to each other. A mulberry tree. What looked like a policeman on roller skates. The gingkos coming shyly into leaf. But after a while we were silent.

Back at their apartment, Clara met us again. "Coffee?" she said as soon as we walked in.

"Just had some," said Christian.

"I'll take another."

Clara disappeared into the back and Christian sat down on the couch. I took the chair across from her. After a moment I said, "Might as well go check on the coffee."

I rose and went into the kitchen. Clara was standing at the counter with her back to me, shaking the grounds into a filter. After she set the filter in the pot she turned around again, leaned back against the counter, and looked up. We hadn't spoken at all, but I saw it there again. She knit her brow, as though to remind me. I nodded my head. She was wearing a short pearl necklace and a sweater whose neckline almost touched it.

"Well, Corey," she said finally, "Church would say it's time to do something about it."

EIGHT

SOON SHE'S READING about him all the time. *Senator Henry Bonwiller (D–New York) introduced legislation today to require congressional approval for.* . . . *Reached for comment, Senator Henry Bonwiller (D–New York) said he supports any measure that would bring an earlier.* . . . She looks for his name and for Louis Lefkowitz's, too. Their enemy. The newspaper is a living thing, waiting quietly at the end of the hotel desk. She folds it quickly and carries it up to the room. In November, the first big headline: EARLY POLL: BONWILLER A FACTOR IN IOWA. They're seeing each other twice a week now, maybe three times. But she's spending whole days at Morley's on her own now, too, eating meals and never seeing the check. Dark glasses. The paper spread in front of her at the table. Her friends have vanished. Then, a couple of months later, another headline: BONWILLER CLOSING ON LEAD AS FIRST TEST APPROACHES. That night they meet again. She's had a vodka tonic by herself in the bar. It's snowing just a little.

He doesn't even get there till almost two in the morning. Wakes her up when he comes into the room and she has to do her makeup again in the bath. More drinks. She can feel the string again, tugging her. But then he asks her to sing for him. "Bonnie Kellswater" and "Red Is the Rose." He sits in the chair with his Scotch, eyes closed. Then "Johnny I Hardly Knew Ye," and for that one he joins in on the chorus with his velvet bass. That does something to her. Always has. They make love in the big bed. He's got a certain energy. Afterward, while he's reading something that's stapled together, she leans out from the mattress and opens the window shade so she can watch the flurries in the lamplight. The brook is frozen and the falls are a shimmering icicle.

"Close that." He takes another drink.

A little dart of hurt.

"I like looking." She's pulls up her slip, refastens her bra. Out on the square, a couple is walking, arm in arm. It's so late for anyone to be out, but there they are. They stop under a lamp, the snow drifting down around them like a desk toy.

The light goes off behind her.

"Close it."

He pours another.

But after she does, she pulls back the corner again and peeks out. The string again, tugging.

Finally, he sits up. "Okay, then," he says, slapping down his reading on the bedspread, "let's go out then."

"Really?"

"Really."

"But wear the dress."

She smiles. "Which one?"

"You know which one."

She has to take off the slip again to do it, but she doesn't mind. She likes that dress. He watches her pull it over her head and shimmy in. The tight red cling. She does it nice and slow, and when she's done he steps behind her and she feels something tap up the back of her spine, ahead of the zipper. Fingers.

Maybe kisses.

They take his car. She likes that, too. Usually she has to drive her own and this is nicer. She ducks in the seat as they pull out of the garage, but once they're out of Saline he says, "Screw it, it's a beautiful night." She has no idea what time it is. He slows down on the outskirts of town and takes a long drink from the flask in the glove box. Near the highway, the Esso station's still open. Or maybe it's already opening up for the morning—who knows how late it is? He pulls in there but he waves off the boy who comes out of the building clapping his hands in the cold. Doesn't need to fill the tank. Just wants to use the bathroom. While he's inside she takes another nip at the flask. When he comes back out he's combed his hair.

There's something sweet about that. Boyish.

He gets in again and takes his own turn at the flask, and she takes another, too. Then he pulls something from the glove box and reaches to snuggle her under his arm. "Listen to this," he says. It's a book. A little tiny leather-covered book no bigger than his hand. "The sniff of green leaves and dry leaves," he says in that certain voice, "and of the shore and dark-colored sea-rocks, and of hay in the barn . . ." And on he goes for a little while in the melancholy way he gets sometimes until finally he sets the book down and turns the ignition so that the heat comes on again. He says, "That was a poem. Walt Whitman. You should read Walt Whitman."

"I will," she says. Nobody's ever told her anything like that. She'll get it from the library in the morning.

Now she's right up next to him. The radio is tuned to a jazz station, big band, and she lets her head rest on his shoulder. They cross back onto the road, and just before they reach 35 he pulls over, unlatches the clips on the windshield, and lets the sky open up above them. Big and black and clotted with stars though there's still a few flakes drifting in it. He takes another drink and pulls back onto the highway.

"You're going to freeze me," she says, giggling.

She wraps the stole over her neck and moves up closer. But actually the Cadillac's big heaters are more than enough, blowing waves of warm air over them. It's so cozy! Like hiding under the covers.

"Okay, then, we can freeze together," he says back. He shouts up at the sky: "We're going to freeze!"

But they're not; the heat is blasting. It's the most wonderful thing. And here and there a snowflake, a delicate crystal on her dress lasting just a moment in the light. At the bend, there's another car approaching.

"I have heard what the talkers were talking," he begins to recite now, in a slow half-whisper with his eyes on the horizon. "The talk of the beginning and the end." He puts his arm around her, pulls her in tighter. "But I do not talk of the beginning or the end." He glances down. "That's more Whitman."

"It's nice," she says. "It's pretty."

"There was never any more inception, than there is now," he goes on. "Nor any more youth or age, than there is now; And will never be any more perfection—than there is now."

She hooks her thumb over his seat belt and burrows in close. Rubs her cheek on his shoulder. Then lets her fingers drift down.

"That's nice, too," he says. He takes a heavy breath. She likes that moment, the way it stirs something.

"Oh," he says, in another kind of voice.

She sees the gold threads standing out in the red fabric of her dress now, shining lightly, and another snowflake that lands and then winks out on her leg. The other car's headlights must be on them. For a moment she can feel him shift lower in the seat—just a little. But then he sits back up tall. She moves her cheek down to rub his chest. Moves her hand lower, too. Lets her fingers start their work. "Oh, honey," he says, a rough murmur now as they head into the wide turn before Silverton Orchards. "Mmm, honey." The other car's lights are coming at them from an angle through his window now, sweeping across her door as they reach the sharp part of the curve. He's driving too fast—that's what she realizes—and she jerks her head up, her mind clearing for an instant to see, of all things, her mother, setting down her cup and saucer, saying *promise me you'll always carry money for a cab*.

FOR THE MOST PART, I've left our daughters out of this story. I have my reasons, even though the principals here have come back now in all of them. The revelation, no matter how often it comes, is always a surprise: that our pasts are remade like that, in pieces and shadows. Our girls' names are Andrea, Emma, and Dayna. I won't bring them up except to relate a single incident.

We'd taken them on a family boat trip to Alaska. The Inside Passage. This was August, five years ago. Andrea is the oldest, the one at Colgate, and I suspected that this might be our last chance to travel with her. In September, she was starting her senior year. She was twenty then, and she had a steady boyfriend in Boston, and Emma had just graduated from the high school that Dayna was about to enter. I haven't taken many vacations in my life, but I knew this was the time.

Clara did the booking and found a cruise that left port in Seattle and made its leisurely way north, past Vancouver Island, through Queen Charlotte Sound, and circuitously through the Alexander Islands to Juneau. The boat was small, by cruise standards, and was fitted more for scientific research than luxury. This was fine with all of us. There was no swimming pool but every few yards along the walls of the bridge there were high-grade binoculars hung from hooks. The library was as large as the dining room and displayed an enviable collection of birding manuals and drawn renderings of all of North America's wildlife, from grizzly bears down to plankton and mycelia, as well as the usual books by Jack London and Farley Mowat. The rooms were simply finished in a maritime way, with bunks bolted to the walls and grab-handles along the bulkheads. Clara and I shared one berth and the three girls shared another.

From the first morning out of port, we stopped two or three times a day, at the mouths of rivers, where eagles and ospreys circled, and off-shore of any number of tiny islands, which the boat's passengers were encouraged to visit on launches that were lowered on a boom and boarded from a low deck off the stern. I must say, I haven't felt many pleasures in my life that could equal the feeling of sitting at the back of a six-passenger rubber dinghy as the ship's crewman next to me steered it through the swells, the salt spray dampening the faces of my three daughters and my wife, while in the near distance the arched spine of a gray whale's tail slapped the water and dived. When the launches idled down and sat bobbing off the beach, otters appeared.

We were half a day north of Cape Scott, at dinner our second night, when a man my own age appeared at our table. He introduced himself as Millar Franks, from Vancouver, Canada. He was traveling alone, and of course we invited him to sit with us. He turned out to be quite an interesting companion. He was a naturalist, a self-made multimillionaire in business, and now a social agitator by avocation. After retiring from the flash-memory card company that he'd founded, he'd set to the task of improving the lot of women in Canada. This was very interesting of course to Clara, who works for the League of Women Voters now, but it appeared to be even more so to our daughters. Millar Franks had started a foundation that granted money to all sorts of projects—initiatives in women's health, in women's education, in the plight of women in prison. About all these things he spoke fervently, gazing keenly at whichever of the girls had asked a question, or at Clara. More than once, he even seemed to forget he was eating. On top of that, he was able to identify every gull and plover that was circling the panoramic, shoreward-looking windows of the dining room, looking for scraps. You can imagine the reception he received at our table. I liked him enough myself. Though

I had my reservations, he was exactly the kind of worldly, knowledge-able friend one hoped to find on a ship.

The next day, north of Port Hardy, the boat dropped anchor in the sound, where a pod of Dall porpoises could be seen off the seaward side. All species of storm petrels and auklets filled the sky. As we were waiting to fill the launches, Millar Franks joined us on deck. Just as our family reached the ladder off the low boarding deck, though, we realized that our own boat wouldn't have room for him; but instead of saying goodbye to Mr. Franks for the day, Andrea stepped out of line and offered to accompany him on the next boat, which at that mo-ment was being lowered on a pulley from the overhead boom. There was no time to consider it: down the ladders we went, and the remain-ing four of us took our places together in our family launch. As we sped across the calm sound, I looked back at Andrea and Millar Franks trailing us. I was trying to concentrate on the sea, which broke here and there with surfacing seals, but from the side of my vision I could see him talking to her, gesturing with his arms at the shore and at the carousel of birds that circled the flotilla. She was leaning to-ward him from her perch at the edge of their boat. He was my age, as I've mentioned. And Andrea had a boyfriend in Boston, whom both Clara and I liked, and whom, as it turns out, she would later marry.

That night at dinner, he sat with us again and ordered some very nice wine. Clara doesn't drink, for reasons that should be clear, but our own kids seem to be able to handle it well enough that we en-courage them to make their own decisions. Even Dayna and Emma were given a glass, and we didn't say anything when Andrea poured herself a second one. Soon, somehow, Henry Bonwiller's name came up in a story Millar Franks was telling.

"Do you know him?" asked Clara.

"I do," he answered. "He's a great man. A great hero of mine. The last champion of liberalism. Or at least of what you Americans call liberalism. It's what we Canadians take for granted."

"He's not so popular anymore in the States," I said.

"That's because you're prudish."

"Prudish?"

"Yes," Andrea joined in, seeing the look in my eyes. "We Americans have always been prudish about our politicians."

"Since when have you been such a student of politics?"

"Dad—"

"The man did some very questionable things," I said. "In fact, he did some deplorable things."

"You don't know that," said Clara.

"I have a very good idea about it."

She was staring openly at me.

"Doesn't matter what he did in his private life," Millar Franks said, and thankfully, he was not the kind of man who noticed anyone else's reaction at the table. "Henry Bonwiller was brilliant. He was idealistic. He was compassionate. And, as you Americans say, he could play hardball. He was the only powerful progressive politician you've ever had."

"That's not the point," I said.

"Yes, it is," said Andrea.

I looked over at her. In a few months, she would be leaving us. I took a drink of wine and reconsidered. I suppose this is the real reason I didn't say more. Not to spare our dinner, or our new friendship with Millar Franks, or to avoid the disapproval that had just appeared without the least disguise on the face of my wife. In truth, the reason I didn't say anything was simply that Andrea would probably never again come with us on such a trip. She might never again sit at a dinner like this, might never again join our conversation so guilelessly, might never again submit to the gentle enchainment that we no doubt were to her now. I swallowed my wine and swirled what remained in my glass.

Millar Franks was going on about American liberalism, but even as I looked down I knew Andrea was aware of me. She was also gazing with obvious interest at our guest.

Andrea is like her mother. Devoted. Fierce. Willful. There is an unexpected trustworthiness in such a character, though, just as there

is in Clara. When she was growing up, Andrea was the one who embarrassed us at dinner parties. One night when she was five years old,
as her great-aunt Helen sat eating dessert at our table, Andrea said
simply, "You're as fat as a cheese"—an expression that has remained
in our family since then; and at nine, a normally well-mannered age
for girls, she still had no compunction about saying, in her tin-
soldier's voice, "I don't like you," to any grown-up blithe enough to
fake affection toward her. She's always seen right through that one. As
a father, I have to say, I take some comfort in it.

And of course I know where it comes from, too. It's the thing that
most scared me about her own mother from the time I first knew
her—that same abiding and prickly truthfulness. I first saw it in the
days when I was a newcomer to the Metarey family, the days
when—no matter how diligently I worked or what I told myself
about my new station—I was most obviously an interloper in their
world, both in Clara's eyes and in my own. Clara saw that for what
it was; but she also knew—well before I did, I suspect—that what I
longed for was not the earthly comfort of that world but all its possibility.

And I'm sure Andrea would have treated an upstart like me the
same way. The Metareys set out to make a president. If I asked Clara
now what she saw in me, a boy who first spoke to her with a shovel in
his hand at the bottom of a sewer trench, I believe that she'd say character; by which, I think, she'd mean discipline—which is the most
basic thing her father must have seen, too. It's a quality of my father's,
as well, expressed for him in the clean, narrow ring of silver between
every pair of copper fittings he ever sweated, in the true vertical of
every laid-out pipe in every basement he ever plumbed, and in the
meticulous, brush-swept floor of every work site he ever left for the
day. In another world this would have meant prominence or fortune,
and in his own it meant respect, from the men he worked with and
the men who hired him.

That's the firmness Clara saw. And it's the firmness I see now in Andrea.

My wife, though, probably saw something else in me, as well. I sometimes think that her view is still colored by the great, deferred reverence that she's finally found for her father. And of course by any daughter's regular longing for him. I have no doubt that if Liam Metarey had been born in my own house he would have worked as hard as I did and moved just as far as I did from my own beginnings; and it's also clear that Clara and Christian competed for their father's benedictions more solemnly than even most sisters do, if a bit more circumspectly. That's part of it, as well. I still believe that in some way I'm only his stand-in. Liam Metarey was a man who sowed his worldly attentions at a distant reach but turned his private ones halfway inward; and certainly, to his children, this must have made them all the more prized.

And thus I am the recipient of those attentions once again, twice reflected, from his grandchildren. Andrea doesn't often stop to talk to us now, but when she does it's with perfect honesty. Clara was openly skeptical of me from the day I met her until the day I wept, standing on her lawn, for my mother. Evidence of an intrinsic understanding of what Mr. Metarey—in a different, darker submission—must have understood himself: that the heart can't be denied its timing, whether terrible or graced. The afternoon of my mother's service, Clara moved charitably in and out of my conversation, her hand on my back, reminding me every few moments that she was standing there—a wall I'd always known was solid but that now, suddenly, I could lean on. She did the same thing on our wedding day, not ten years later.

And now it's Andrea who does it. She's not the most voluble of our children but she's certainly the one who's always provoked the fiercest expression of loyalty from her friends, from girls who used to stay up half the night with her on whispered phone calls, and from boys who'd regularly climb the spindly cedar beside our porch to try and break her queenly resolution. Which I don't think many of them did. Like her mother, she isn't afraid enough of anyone to be duplicitous. And like her mother, she won't let you in until she's decided to. She's been that way since she could talk.

That night on the boat, the sea was rather rough and I was sleeping lightly, but I woke shortly after midnight, seemingly without prompting, to find a figure standing in the dimly lighted doorway of our stateroom.

"She's not in the cabin," Dayna said.

I sat up in bed. "What? Who's not?"

"Andrea. She's not in her bed. I wasn't sure whether I should say anything."

I switched on the light above my pillow. My first thought, truly, was not Millar Franks.

"She was there when we went to sleep," she said. "But now I woke up and she's not."

I didn't bother to wake Clara. Above ship, the decks were slick with dew, and Dayna and I walked their full length, glancing aside into every portico with its two-seat bench and brass-cased running light, and through every porthole into the library and the lounges and the anteroom behind the bridge, from where passengers sometimes watched the crew at work. She was nowhere to be found. I looked over the railing. We were three days north of Vancouver, under a harvest moon. The dark water glinted as it rose in the wake of the prow. I knew Millar Franks was staying on the upper deck, where two penthouse suites stood on either side of the hallway, around a corner from the captain's quarters.

We walked there. I knocked at his door. No answer. I didn't knock again. Not out of decorum, really, but because I realized that if Andrea was in there I didn't want to force her to emerge. Her sister and I waited a few moments in the covered hallway, then returned to the deck.

Dayna is our careful, observant one. Unlike Andrea, she'll wait out a stranger, quietly, like some bird in the grass, and unlike Emma, she'll lie down on our living room couch the same evening and report to Clara and me every thought and feeling she's had that day, as if we were indeed her friends and not, as our Emma seems to believe, her jailers. She reminds me sometimes of my mother—of the way she was just before she died, at least—inquisitive and insistently conspiratorial, and at the same time, I suspect, ceaselessly private. And her laugh, when it comes—not all that often but not rarely, either—is as clear as water. Of course I hear Christian in it.

Emma is our reticent one. She has in her much of her maternal grandfather, in fact. Much of Liam Metarey's modest grace and affable, generous view of the world, and much of his guarded, quiet solicitude, too. And strange as it may sound, she has grown up touching me on the shoulder, just as her grandfather used to. How is that possible? When she wakes me from a nap in my leather library chair, it is with a hand rustling my hair, and whenever we part for any length of time, first she hugs me and then, stepping away, she reaches back to touch me on the shoulder. She was no doubt sleeping untroubled back in the cabin.

But here was Dayna, fourteen, worried with me about Andrea. She was no doubt more sophisticated than her peers by virtue of having two older sisters, but she was still not at the age when I could assume she knew exactly what was on my mind. I suppose that was prudish of me. In retrospect, it seems particularly so. But that night as we made our way down the penthouse hallway back onto the misty upper deck, I had the feeling of standing delicately between the two of them, of trying to protect my oldest and youngest daughters at once.

Of course, I was also still thinking of the sea. We walked the loop of gangway again, where I could feel the sickening heave of the boat, the full-length tilt and countertilt from the swells that were moving southeast against us as the vessel labored north along the coast. I moved to the railing, pretending to look out at the moon, but really to get a glimpse of the water, to see just how formidable it was. There was a steady wind but not a stiff one. No whitecaps about. I took a pair of binoculars from one of the hooks behind us and pointed it out at the featureless dark. Was I expecting to see her head bobbing somewhere off the stern?

What I did see, in fact, when I suddenly had an idea and leaned over the rail to swing the lens down toward the boat's waterline, was her shoulder and the back of her hair, and her elbow over the railing alongside a bench on the low deck where the launches were stacked at the stern. Then her cheek, smiling and nodding. I waited. After a moment, a man's arm, gesturing and pointing out at the water.

"Look," I said, aiming the binoculars for Dayna. "Land ho!"

"Oh!" she said. "Who's that with her? Is it Mr. Franks?"

"That would be my guess, too."

"They're going to catch cold, Dad."

"Only if we're lucky, sweetheart."

After I brought Dayna back to the girls' cabin, I emerged again and went for a walk alone on top. The swells still canted the deck in their sickening cadence, and as I moved between the handholds I realized the wind had grown stronger, too. In front of the captain's bridge the weather vane's cups were whirling furiously, and there was a low humming noise from somewhere in the rigging. If Clara had been awake, I knew, she'd have asked me to leave our daughter alone.

When I emerged from the inside staircase onto the low deck, though, Millar Franks didn't even pause in his elocution. He was facing me when I appeared out of the steel hatch, and he nodded but kept on talking. The boat rolled slowly and I found myself looking down at the black water, then back at the horizon. Andrea's back was still turned to me as she sat at the railing, watching him. She was leaning in his direction. I have to say my heart fell. He continued with his speech, still pointing over the sea at what from this low vantage and in the running lights off the stern I suddenly realized was some kind of baitfish school, roiling the engine's wake. He even reached out at one point and touched her on the arm.

That's when she turned.

As I said, Andrea is very much like her mother. That's why, I think, she drew herself up when she saw me, gathered her resolve into a pose of defiance that even in the dim light I recognized. She gazed directly at me.

"Oh, Daddy," she said. "You can go to sleep now." Then she added, more softly, "I'm fine."

For a moment I had a remembered fear of what she might do. But then she merely turned and refocused her attention on Millar Franks; and after another moment I turned as well, and went inside to bed.

"OKAY, BUT DIDN'T YOU also think of what it *meant*?"

"Of what *what* meant?"

"You know what I'm saying, sir. What it actually *said*. The *fatal road incident*."

"I was sixteen."

"And I'm seventeen. But I know exactly what it meant."

"You have the benefit of hindsight."

"And didn't you, sir?"

"And three decades of skeptical journalism."

"Maybe."

"But, yes, Trieste, I did." I stood from the desk and went to the window. "But there's something that happens—I've seen this since—there's something that happens when you're involved in an affair like that. Involved in a lie like that."

"You start to believe it's true."

"Well—yes."

"If I wrote that, Mr. Sifter, you'd say it was a cliché."

"Well, yes I would. Possibly. But really, it's something I learned for myself. And something I know for myself. First you tell the lie. With fear, or something like it. I guess, at sixteen, what I felt all the time was more like excitement. That's right—maybe more like excitement than fear. Or maybe the fear caused the excitement. That could be it. And you tell it like that for a while. Everybody told it like that for a while. Liam Metarey. The staff. I'm sure Henry Bonwiller, for that matter. I'm talking about a few days. Maybe a week. But if you keep telling it—if for whatever reason it's discussed and discussed, and the lie is what you tell, and what everybody around you tells, then at a certain point—and it's really damn quickly, that's the other thing—at a certain point you just *do*. You believe it."

"How can you believe it?"

"I guess it just becomes the truth." I looked out at the sun, which was about to set. "At least you store it in that part of your brain that stores the truth. The calm part. It loses its power. The destruction that you were afraid of. It sits in there like an old letter you've read a hundred times."

"But there were those articles. Two of them."

"Two small ones. They didn't matter. We *made* them not matter."

"And people have talked about it for thirty years."

"That came later. And a lot happened in between."

She looked at me skeptically.

"And it doesn't matter, anyway," I said. "I'm talking about *then*. When anybody might have said something. The thing about it—and here's what's interesting—I did know that something bad had happened. I *did* know that. All right, something dreadful. And I also knew that I was involved with it. For a few days I tried to figure it out. But remember—there was nothing in the news. Almost nothing. Not for a good long time, anyway. And even then, I don't think they got it right. It wasn't until I was out of college—I was working in New York—it wasn't until I saw for myself some of the workings of the world that I think I understood what had happened. Maybe I should say, some of the workings of *people*. It just came to me eventually. You get to a point when you can figure things out. Intuition. So for a while I was aware again that I'd been close to something that was illegal. Big deal. I wasn't going to say anything then. A hell of a lot of time had passed. And for another thing, I didn't have anything to say. What? That I'd changed a couple of quarter panels with Liam Metarey?"

"That a girl was killed."

"How was I supposed to know that? And *you* certainly don't know what happened. Nobody does."

"Do you believe that?"

"Yes, I do. But the thing is, that was easy enough to live with. There were always shady dealings. Show me a politician who doesn't have them. And it's what I said—I was aware that I'd been involved with something that was—well—*terrible*. But it wasn't until we had Andrea—she was our first—it wasn't until we had Andrea that it just broke over me. That I'd been involved with something—not that I *did* something, but that I was involved with something—something *unforgivably wrong*."

IN PHILADELPHIA, on a warm Sunday afternoon in the mid-spring of 1972, Henry Bonwiller addressed the largest crowd ever to have gathered for an American presidential candidate. Fifty-five thousand people, according to the *Inquirer*. And all of them there because of the war.

I sometimes try to imagine it from the Senator's point of view. The faces. The shimmering rows of packed-in bodies, swaying. The rippling mumble of a horde that runs from Independence Hall, choking every side street and flowing around the corner until it fills Washington Square. And from there stretches on. The police setting up last-minute barricades. Radios. Waving arms. Shouting. A sea of caps and jackets. The hand-lettered signs and the blue-and-white hats; the blue-and-white Bonwiller streamers; the long, two-posted, blue-and-white union banners, printed by the campaign for all the tradesmen's locals, floating above. Dories on a harbor. Peace symbols. Flags. Singing. The waves of sound bouncing off Old City Hall and Congress Hall and Philosophical Hall and coming back to Henry Bonwiller even inside the entranceway as he makes his way to the portico. The chest-swelling charge of the growing chant as he reaches the steps and opens the door. Crosses to mount the stage. Frightening for a moment, all that sound, like a fighter jet overhead—it's really that loud, swooping down as he emerges into the bright air—frighteningly loud till suddenly he understands it, and almost as suddenly knows what it means. A chill splits him. What it all means! And then not frightening but bracing. Then—as he reaches the double aisle of security men and steps through them onto the stage-rear bleachers, climbing to the top where it comes at him now from every side: calming. That's what it is. So deeply calming. *Bon! Bon! Bon!* He takes a breath and raises his fist over his head. Then opens it.

You didn't have to watch the news or read the papers to know. Gallup and Harris and Princeton all showed it, too: his momentum was unstoppable. The same kind of throng in Boston the next night, and in Columbus the night after. But all you really had to do was watch him in a crowd; all you had to do was drive a mile with him in the open-topped Cadillac; all you had to do was walk a block with him on any street, anywhere in the country. Men called out windows. Traffic stopped. Policemen saluted. I can imagine how it must have felt.

But Liam Metarey—I wonder how it all must have felt for *him*, too. To be carried so high on a wave of acclaim, which was intoxicating even in the puny examples I'd seen of it—yet to know, all the time, what killing menace lurked behind. To ride such a cataclysmic surge. To let yourself be taken upward and upward despite all of it. All that you know. To fly so high the ground disappears.

A man who seeks such office surely must crave public acclaim as sustenance; yet, paradoxically, he surely must also be immune to doubt. That, I think, is why Henry Bonwiller was the candidate and Liam Metarey only the strategist. Perhaps Henry Bonwiller simply erased from his mind all that had happened and all that any reasonable man would have suspected was going to happen in response. But I don't think Liam Metarey was capable of that. Not of either one.

By Easter, strangely, the house had quieted again. Most of the staff had moved down to Baltimore and Atlanta for the races that were approaching in the South, and at Aberdeen West there were no more than a dozen campaign workers about. Liam Metarey, for whatever reason, was one of those who'd stayed behind, even though this was the hour of his candidate's triumph. I don't know whether he'd fallen out of favor—I never saw it, but I have to assume an unrelenting battle for influence was always being played out close to the Senator—or whether it was merely that he'd not been needed in the new territory. He didn't, by his own admission, know much about the southern states. More likely, though, I think he knew what was coming. He'd been kind to me in nearly every instance of our association, and I can only take from his actions that he was a person who could feel what another felt—which is why, if you follow the idea to its conclusion, he took so strongly to heart his standing in the community. Perhaps that's why he stayed at home.

But it's also important to say that in all my time at the Metareys' and in the campaign, I never enjoyed more than an outsider's view of the proceedings—even if I was almost always a welcome one. I saw only the house, and only those rooms that I was asked to enter. I never explicitly heard strategy. I never witnessed a struggle among the principals or even any significant words of derision or contempt, although certainly the campaign must have been rife with them. Whenever the house emptied, as it did a few times even in the flurry of the early battle days, it seemed to me that the campaign itself had come to some kind of early close, when of course it had only just moved away temporarily, to Iowa or New Hampshire, or to wherever the next engagement lay. There were probably other Liam Metareys in the effort and other Aberdeen Wests, too—all across the country, for all I knew. And certainly other Corey Sifters, as well. The war of primaries was new in those days, and I suspect the campaign's tactics must have been changing at every turn. Those were the years when the modern strategy was first being made into what it is today. But all I ever saw were the mostly peaceable workings of policy, the constantly genteel meetings in the upstairs rooms of the estate, and the staged appearances before the press, in which Henry Bonwiller stood before the cameras framed against the west acreage's never-ending expanse of trees. I can't say I ever truly understood what was happening behind it all.

What I do know for certain, though, is that it was not until after the Senator's crescendoing victories in Wisconsin (44 percent), Pennsylvania (47 percent), and Massachusetts (51 percent), and his overwhelming poll numbers in Indiana and Ohio (48 and 52 percent), that it was not until after we had exulted in five states and then confidently turned our attention to Tennessee and North Carolina and

West Virginia—it was not until after all this occurred that, one warm morning in late April, the telephone rang in Mr. Metarey's upstairs office, where I was opening the casement windows for the breeze. He listened for a moment, nodded, and hung up. Then he appeared next to me at the glass.

"Well," he said. "They're here."

"SPEAKER-SENTINEL," I said again. "Sifter."

Again there was silence. I waited. I checked the caller ID: the number was familiar, but barely. Finally I hung up.

"Nothing?" said Trieste. She was working at the desk by the door, writing up the county board of supervisors meeting and the arrest blotter. Next to her a reporter was on deadline for page one.

"Wrong number," I said.

"Or second thoughts."

"Right. Or second thoughts."

A moment later the phone rang again.

"*Speaker-Sentinel*. Corey Sifter. What may I do for you?"

Again, nothing.

"Sometimes they'll do that," I said, hanging up.

"What?"

"Wait for someone on this end to say more."

"Or less."

A minute later: a third time. I picked it up but didn't say a word. On the other end I heard rustling, then breathing. "Yes?" I finally said. "*Speaker-Sentinel?*" I heard a scratching sound, like somebody moving a fingernail across the mouthpiece. Then tapping.

"*Speaker-Sentinel*," I said. "Yes? May I help you?"

More tapping. The breathing was quick and rasping. That's when I realized whose number it was.

"Oh my God," I said. "Stay there—"

<u>NINE</u>

I

On the porch outside 410A Dumfries was a note:

NEKS DOR

When I ran over to 410B the first thing I saw through the open door was the phone off the hook on the rug. Then Mr. McGowar in the chair. It wasn't until I got inside that I found Dad on the couch next to him. He was lying there in his work clothes with Mr. McGowar holding his hand.

"Did you call 911?" I said, taking Dad's other hand. Mr. McGowar nodded his head vigorously.

Dad looked like he'd been severely frightened. Or at least half his face did. The eye on that side was wide open and the mouth contorted, and his hair was disheveled everywhere. But the eye on the other side was calm and seemed to be staring reasonably ahead, and the mouth on that side was set the way it used to be set in the morning when he went to work. He turned toward me and I didn't know which side was him—the calm and reasonable one or the one that was wild with fear. I looked from one to the other.

"It's me, Dad."

"What's the fuss?" he whispered.

"You tell me."

There was a tap on my shoulder.

FEL OVR

"He did? When?"

DONO

"Dad, what happened?"

"Oh, Christ."

FOND M OTSID

With one arm Dad was pushing down sort of lamely on the cushions—pushing down and then giving up, then pushing down again—and after a moment I realized he was trying to sit up. One of his arms wasn't working.

"Well here, then," I said. "Let's help you."

We raised him, with Mr. McGowar at one shoulder and me at the other, and moved him into the chair. One arm dangled, and when we sat him up his whole body listed. He looked up drowsily. That's when I noticed the smell of urine. I went into the bathroom for a towel, and Mr. McGowar found him another pair of pants. Dad looked okay, actually, after we managed to get them on him. Not as bad as I'd first thought. He tried to stand up on his own then—he was stable enough once he got his legs under him—but I still wasn't happy with the look in that one eye, so I got another towel for a cushion and we sat him back down in the chair. By then I could hear the sirens. Mr. McGowar

pointed to the phone. When I picked it up I found the 911 operator
still on the line.

MR. METAREY AND I STOOD LOOKING out the office window at the
corral, where Breighton was nosing the new crocuses that had parted
the grass. We both just stood there for a time. There was something of
such balanced majesty in that horse's posture that even Liam Metarey
was stilled.

"Hard to stop watching," he finally said. "Isn't he?"

"He is, sir."

I turned back to straightening the room.

"No. Stay a second. You work too hard. Have since the moment I
met you. Just look at that beautiful animal for a minute." He opened
the curtains wider.

"He's a good horse, Mr. Metarey. Calm, too."

"Utterly content is what he is. I thought June was crazy to get him.
I really did. Now I'm grateful she didn't listen to me. Sometimes I
think he's just here to mock our paltry endeavors."

We stood watching again.

At last, he said, "I need you to get everybody up here for a meeting."

"Sir?"

"Would you be kind enough do that? Everybody who's still around,
at least. In my office." He went back to his desk, pulled out the leather
planner from the drawer, took a long breath, and began circling on
different pages. "When the rest of them get back up north, we'll have
another meeting—in the big library, for that one. For everybody.
They'll be coming in all day, I presume. Make it nice," he said. "Nice
wine. Tell Gil to decant the Bordeaux—he knows which one. Nice
food, Corey. Don't spare anything. Might as well."

"Yes, sir."

As soon as I left him, I took the station wagon from the work shed and headed off to town. There was a lot to do. At Burdick's a line of women waited at the meat counter, but it wasn't long before Ren Burdick himself came out from the back and stopped next to me.

"Hear you'll be needing a truckload from us, eh?" he said in his sly, French-Canadian voice.

"We're having a meeting," I answered, as quietly as I could.

"So I just heard."

He took me to the back, where one of the butchers was already wrapping foil around a pair of steaming beef roasts. He pulled out a couple of cooked ducks, too, and three good-sized whitefish that had been deboned and decked out on planks with parsley and cranberries. "You could buy the wine from me too, eh?" he said, wrapping the parcels in butcher paper. "You know?"

"Mr. Metarey said to get it from McBride's."

"Fair enough, eh? What'd you say it was for again?"

"I don't know, Mr. Burdick."

After that, I drove to Cleary Brothers Bakery for rolls, just as the youngest of the portly, cheerful Clearys was pulling them from the ovens. On the way home, I stopped at McBride's for the cases of white wine that Gil had asked for, to serve alongside the Bordeaux. By the time I got back to the estate, it was early evening. The windows of the station wagon were steamed from the roast beef. I pulled up next to the service kitchen to unload.

In the pantry as I was closing the door of the walk-in refrigerator, it was Gil who stopped me. "Guess you ain't heard," he said.

"Heard what, Gil?"

"Why the shindig. From the looks of you, at least." He was sitting on the big Manitowoc ice maker, bouncing his boot heels back and forth against the side. I realized I had never seen him idle. "Article about the girl," he said. "Is what I hear." He shook his head. "Comin' out in the paper."

"What?"

"On the front page, I guess."

"Which paper?"

"Can't say I know."

I ran upstairs. When I reached the landing, I could see Mr. Metarey sitting in the chair in his office, leaning forward with his head on the desk between his arms. I didn't knock, but I waited at the threshold, and after a moment he looked up and waved me in. "Sorry, Corey," he said.

"I just heard."

"I should have said something. I should have. To you especially." He stood and looked out the window toward Saline. "You've been all over town, I hear." He let out a mild chuckle. "I got people calling about a celebration. I should have told you before you went."

"Where's it coming out, sir?"

"Well, where would be the worst possible place?"

"It's not—"

"It is, Corey."

And the fact that I never said G. V. Trawbridge's name, and that Liam Metarey never answered with it, only confirms in my mind that, despite the turmoil of a campaign and despite our nearly impenetrable common lie, both of us had long known what was going to happen. What had to happen.

"When?" I said.

"Day after tomorrow. Sunday. Not sure how he kept it secret this long."

"What about his other piece?"

"Well, I'm not sure what you're asking, but if you're talking about the one in the magazine, the answer is I don't think he was setting us up. I think he believed what he wrote."

He looked at me.

"It's okay, Corey," he said. He put his hand on my shoulder. "This too shall pass."

"What about TV, sir?"

"Well, they've got their dogs on the scent already. I'd expect we'll have till sometime Saturday night to enjoy ourselves, before they get full hold of it."

"Is it bad, sir?"

He looked at me closely. Those dark eyes of his. Those dark eyes of his father, and of his daughter. At that moment I was acutely aware, somehow, of the silence we'd long shared, of the particular morality that had made our trust—his of me, mine of him—a matter of such long-standing assumption. And I understood—perhaps it's more accurate to say, *I promised myself*—that this trust would remain intact.

"Well, that's what I'm trying to find out," he said finally. "Just how bad it *is*." He shook his head and turned away. "Just what it is he thinks he's found out. And from whom." He turned around and looked at me quickly. But it was only that, a look. "Or at least, how much." He went to the window. "Got my own men working on it already, but got to give 'em credit down at Times Square—they've circled the wagons. Won't say anything to anybody from our staff. Vance won't even call me back. But from what I gather—yes, it's bad. Bad indeed. I've got lawyers on it but they've got lawyers on it, too. For a lot longer, I might add. Pretty damning all in all, from what I'm told. More than damning," he said. He turned from the window. "Killing."

"What does the Senator say?"

He let out a low laugh. It sounded, in a way, relieved. "The Senator's practicing for the convention, Corey."

That evening, the estate began to fill. And late that night, as I was finally getting back to my own house, I heard the thunder of the campaign jet returning from Chattanooga. The next morning Henry Bonwiller began a series of meetings in the guest quarters. I spent that day the same way I'd spent the one before, hurrying all through the kitchens and the barns and the cellars, and all over Saline and Islington. But now I understood what I was preparing for: a strange kind of event that never seemed to start and never seemed to end but that lasted all that day and the next, men getting drunker and drunker, standing around the tables of roast beef and whitefish, moving from meeting to meeting. I drove to Burdick's again for baked hams and wheels of cheese and more roast beef, then to McBride's for more Scotch and bourbon and wine, and every couple of hours to any number of hotels in Carrol County to ferry back surly-eyed advisors and aggrieved-looking managers of statewide races. I recognized a few operatives from other campaigns, too. The same brusque McGovern aides who'd visited after Florida, and a woman—the only one I saw— who'd been at the house that same week in March, now wearing a small blue-and-red Wallace pin on her lapel. And as I was walking at the far end of the downstairs hallway, a door opened abruptly into a side room and I think I glimpsed Glenn Burrant in there—but just as abruptly it closed again. The meetings lasted through the morning.

Early in the afternoon, news came that the next day's campaign stops in North Carolina had been scrapped.

That night, after I'd parked the car in the garage, I emerged to find Henry Bonwiller himself walking alone along the rim of one of the fly ponds. By that point I was exhausted—everybody was—and though ordinarily I wouldn't have stopped to watch him, this time I did. It was late, close to midnight. He'd been in meetings since breakfast. Here he was, this close to the presidency, if he could just survive one more salvo. His silhouette was imposing against the still lighted rooms of the house. He was moving slowly—strolling really—pausing to skip rocks across the long ovals of ruffled water that shimmered under the high moon.

"Young man!" he suddenly called out, and when he turned in my direction I approached a little closer.

"Yes, Senator?"

He looked away from me, back over the water. "A fine night, isn't it?"

"Yes, sir," I said, moving nearer again. "It is."

"On this fine night," he said, so softly that I had to move all the way up behind him, "they're making their final plans to destroy me. Are you aware of all this, Corey?"

"I am, sir."

"Because of what I've done for poor people," he said. He glanced back over his shoulder. "And working people, Corey. That's why they're doing it. You can say what you want about the rest." He reached down and picked up a stone from the path.

"You've done a lot for the country, sir."

"I know what I've done," he said. "I know it's not all good." He turned and threw the stone, and it skipped, almost magically, all the way across the water.

"Nice one, sir."

He turned and studied me then, the way he never had before. "But you know?" he said. "I've had a dream of justice, and it's a dream I've always followed. That's the truth about me. That's the truth I hope is written someday, even with all the rest."

Standing there under the moonlight, he reached out his arm then, and we shook hands.

Then he turned and walked up the path toward the house.

I stayed there, next to the water, and I remember wondering at that moment what it was like to be a man like him. At the time, I saw his life only in a boy's grandiose terms. His strength. His ambition. His array of mortal enemies. Vanity is so often considered the essence of anyone who is stained with it, but I think now, partly because of my experience with Henry Bonwiller, that it's actually a secondary quality, more on the order of wistfulness or mirth, and that it's in our best interests to recognize that it comes so often twinned with the greatest attributes we ever produce. I've seen it more than once yoked to an exceptional empathy, for example—a paradox, perhaps, but the way I think it was in the Senator's particular case. A peculiar ability to see everyone, even one's own self, as both a stranger and an intimate. Henry Bonwiller was no doubt driven by self-manufacture, by a greater and greater need to enlarge himself in the reflective eye of the populace, but I also think he had some inchoate knowledge of what it was like to be the dregs of that populace. The excluded. The illiterate. The poor. JoEllen Charney was not half his equal in achievement or class, but she was a hopeful girl driven incessantly to make the best of things, not by decision but by character, and carried by a current of determination that some might call delusional; and in that light I think she was much like the man who killed her.

DAD HAD HAD A STROKE, and after that we moved him into a place called Walnut Orchards, just outside of Saline. Assisted living. So now he's spending his days among the men and women he's known since kindergarten. But Mr. McGowar, the one he would have preferred above all the rest, wouldn't come with him, at least not permanently. He did come with me to see Dad off on his new life, on the morning he was transferred over from Islington Lutheran Hospital.

Later that afternoon, when it came time to go home, I took Mr. McGowar aside. "Really," I said, "you can move in here if you want. You absolutely can. You understand? We'd cover it. Be near Dad. It'd be good for both of you." I studied his cactus of a face. Implacable as ever. "Clara and I will pay for it. Really—it wouldn't cost you a thing. I can even watch the house."

He didn't have to write his answer. He just flipped a couple of pages back in his pad and turned the sheet face out:

FIN AT DUMFRIES

So Dad is here on his own now, in the end. I visit every Monday, Wednesday, Friday, and Sunday, and maybe every fourth time I'll stop by the old neighborhood to pick up Mr. McGowar, too. At ninety-five, he still insists on walking out to the bridge to meet me, at the same stop where for fifty years he met the quarry bus. But sometimes I'll surprise him at the house, just to check on things. A new family's rented 410A, but every evening Eugene still comes over from 410B to watch the news with them, and there are still plenty of rocks for him in the garden. In other words, he remains remarkably spry, despite his years and his lungs, or whatever it is. Maybe he wasn't wasting energy on anything else.

He and Dad are two fine examples of the human species. That's what I've come to appreciate. When I bring Mr. McGowar over to Walnut Orchards, the two of them will head out together onto the grounds for a walk, and neither one can be deterred from fixing things. Rock out of line on the garden border? Mr. McGowar will wedge it up on his boot toe and shimmy it back into place. Snapped branches hanging over the walk path? Out comes Dad's pocketknife. And even if Mr. McGowar can't quite use the pry bar the way he used to, nothing's ever going to keep his eye from a stray lump in the soil. He's like a dog that way. Nature is nature, I suppose. When I was a kid he looked like he'd already been powdered for the coffin, but thirty-five years later he still looks the same. The only thing that's changed are his teeth, which are closer now to the color of old newspaper. The rest of him is still the color of rock dust.

Dad, on the other hand, has become quite a different person.

His second day here, I arrived in the afternoon to check on him. Didn't want him to accuse me of coddling, so I'd left him alone for the morning. When I came in, he wasn't in the room. I must have sounded agitated when I asked at the desk, because the young woman there said tersely, "Assisted living, not prison." She smiled then a little, maybe to show me she hadn't meant it without humor. "We don't keep track of anybody, sir," she explained. "We just provide meals and services."

I walked most of the grounds before I found him. He was in the library.

"What are you doing in here?"

"Am I not allowed?"

"I just didn't know you were interested. I've been all over the grounds."

"Next time call first."

This, of course, was a change—since the stroke.

"All right, Dad. I will."

"Look at this," he said, pointing to the walls. "This is unbelievable. Someone told me it's as good as a college library."

"It looks like a nice collection."

"A professor left it. And there's a group who's going to put on a play next week." He pointed to the desk.

"*Hamlet*, I see."

He nodded vigorously. "I've been trying to read a few of the classics," he said. "It's hard. But it's good."

And that's what Dad's done. He's begun, the way I did at Dunleavy, to read.

Dr. Jadoon, who is the house doctor here, tells me this is not a typical "post-event change." Dad still has the physical reminders of what happened—the left arm has shrunk a bit and much of the time just stays in his pocket, and he's still got a little of the frightened look in that one eye—but if you saw him dressed and from farther away than across a table, you might not even know that anything's different. It's the brain that's been transformed. The personality. He spends a good part of his day now with books. And I don't mean *Pride of the Yankees*. I've seen William Manchester and Howard Zinn on his table. When we drive out to visit Mom's grave, he'll sit there in the car with a library hardback, until I've parked, unlocked the doors, and gotten out. That's no exaggeration.

The other part of his new personality is his unfaltering politeness, which seems to be—well, gone. Not all the nurses are fans of his; this in itself is a change.

Dr. Jadoon doesn't think all of it is physical.

"The bodily symptoms," he said to me on my first visit to his office with Dad, "we can expect those. The upper extremity. The face—which you can still see a bit, no? And you say his character is different."

"He used to be the politest man in the room. Unfailingly."

"That could be the stroke. No question. A little loss in the frontal lobe. A pinch of disinhibition, you know." He pulled on either side of his bow tie. Dad was in the next room, getting dressed. "Just prying the lid off the box. A bit, perhaps. You see, even with all our imaging studies, in the end it's hard to know what's going on—or what's *gone* on—inside a brain." He shook my hand, holding my elbow with his other one. "As for the remaining changes, Mr. Sifter—what I think, if you'll allow me, is that he might have been wanting to. All along, you see." His smile was a genuine one. "*Read*, that is. *Learn*." He opened the door, steering me forward in his genteel but efficient way. "Now he simply has the time."

"SPEAKER-SENTINEL."

"Is this Mr. Sifter?"

"It is."

"*Corey* Sifter?"

"Yes, ma'am."

"Eunice Charney, Mr. Sifter." She paused. "JoEllen's mother."

I drove down to meet her at Cleary Brothers, which is now run by a chain from Burlington, Vermont. It features a four-spigot Italian espresso machine at the bar and a half-dozen sienna-colored awnings out back. She was sitting under one in a flowered hat, and I had no trouble recognizing her, even though she didn't look as well as the last time. She still resembled her daughter, though, strikingly. The eighty-year-old version of a famous beauty.

As soon as she saw me, she said in her soft voice, "Thank you."

"It's the least I can do."

She looked out from her hat when I said that.

I sat down. "Sure is hot out here," I said. "For this time of year."

"You're thinking why did I call you up."

"I was glad to hear from you, Mrs. Charney."

"George is fishing on the lake, over nearby. Near enough, anyway. Still can do that, glad to say. One of his pals got a boat—didn't do what George did with his money. Call me Eunice. If I was the one watched the money, we'd have *our* boat, too." She brought out a large purse and began rummaging in it on her lap. "You work," she said. "I'll get to the point."

"No need to rush. Can I treat you to something else?"

"I got my tea." She pointed to the cup, then lifted it to her lips. Held it close up against her chin and took a sip.

"These are some pictures," she said. She rummaged in the purse again and set a packet on the table.

They were clippings. Senator Bonwiller alongside Hubert Humphrey at what appeared to be a state fair. A forty-year-old newspaper. Yellowed. Senator Bonwiller in a rodeo hat in front of a crowd in Saline, speaking at a stand-up mike. The grays and blacks migrating toward a single dark tone in the center of the page and the ink fading off completely at the sides; but still a little newer, I could tell. She flattened the crease and set out another. Senator Bonwiller waving from the front seat of the Cadillac. Same evening, it looked like. I leaned in to get a closer look.

"That's what I thought," she said.

I lifted my face.

"Let's see it again." She moved aside her hat and looked me over. "Recognized you the minute I took them out."

"I was in high school."

"I figured about that."

"Mr. Metarey hired me to work around his estate. My Dad worked for him, too, like everybody did around town. I drove people, that was just one part of the job." I pointed. "That's the Senator's Cadillac. I must have been driving it when the picture was taken."

"So you were his driver?"

"Senator Bonwiller's?"

She didn't answer.

"Sometimes I was, Mrs. Charney. But not all that often."

She took another sip. Held the teacup close to her chin again as though she needed it to warm her. Then another sip. Let it settle. Looked over at me from under her hat. "JoEll loved singing," she said.

"Is there something particular I can help you with?"

"She had a voice, too. The voice of an angel. She used to sing 'Danny Boy' down in the cellar before she went out at night with her friends. Nice kids, all of them. She was good that way, before she gave them all up for him. Had her room down there in high school—that's the way she wanted it, don't ask me why. Even though we had a nice one for her upstairs. A plenty nice one. But she wanted her independence. Always did. I'd hear her singing up in the kitchen. Got used to it, though. Hate to say that I didn't always remember to think of it as the miracle that children are. That's what she was, too. A miracle. So beautiful."

"I can imagine, Mrs. Charney."

"Of course you can. You got daughters. How many did you say?"

"Three."

"How old?"

"Grown now. Gone from the house."

"I had *one*," she said. "*Have*."

"Mrs. Charney, I don't know any more than anybody else."

She set down her cup in the center of the table. "Don't you?"

"I wonder about it just like everybody else does, ma'am. There's no one alive who knows for certain—I'm convinced of that. I drove Senator Bonwiller every now and then but I wasn't driving him that night."

She looked up. "Which night?"

"The night it happened."

"Why do you say it happened at night?"

"Mrs. Charney, that's what everyone says."

She looked away. "Nobody's ever proved anything about it," she answered. "Nobody's even proved she was in the car. If they can't prove that, what are they ever going to prove?"

"I don't know, ma'am."

"They say she froze to death. That she'd been drinking. That my daughter'd been *drinking*. Somehow ended up in those woods *by herself*." She sniffed. "Those woods are a mile from the nearest corner, Mr. Sifter. Or were *then*."

I waited.

"Was she in the car?"

I didn't answer.

A quiver began under her eyes. "Mr. Sifter," she said evenly. "I'm her mother."

"I don't know for certain, Mrs. Charney." I looked away. "But I believe it's possible she might have been."

"That's the kind of stuff they can tell for certain in an autopsy. I know they can tell something like that, right?"

"An autopsy was performed."

She looked at me sharply.

"I'm sorry," I said softly. "Really, I didn't mean to worsen any of it."

"Did you know my daughter?"

Next to the table, a web of moss was spreading between the paving stones.

"Did you know JoEll?"

"No, ma'am. I didn't."

"Never met her? Not in all the time you drove him?"

"No."

"Well, she was a beautiful girl." She glanced down where I'd been looking. "And kind. And she liked to sing like that. But she never did have airs. Even after Miss Three-Counties—won the whole thing, too. Didn't affect her one bit. She told me once she was involved with—a married man. A *married man*. That's all she said. No airs at all. Never went on any more about it than that. Never told her friends, either. All those nice kids who might have helped her out of that situation, or warned her. Or even noticed when she didn't come home that night, when she was lying out in that field"—she bit down on her lip—"by herself." But she drew her posture up. "And I suppose *he* must have been the one told her to keep her mouth shut."

"I think you might be right."

"And he was the one arranged everything after, too."

"Possibly."

"The autopsy."

"I don't know, ma'am. I really don't."

"You know, George has never cried for her. He doesn't want me saying that for whatever reason of his." She shook her head sadly. "Men, I guess. But I know it's true. Refuses to shed a single tear until someone does justice. Does justice for JoEll, Mr. Sifter. My husband has vowed to be the last one standing. Tell you the truth, that doesn't mean a thing to me. But it means a lot to him, for whatever reason. Only more torture for George, in my opinion. But it matters, all right. I wish he *could* cry about it. Might help him some."

"I can imagine how he feels."

"Can you?"

Now she looked closely at me. And it was as though a lifetime of manners just slid right off her. She regarded me up and down. Her eyes at last stopping and looking straight into mine with no acknowledgment at all of what she might be seeing there. As deep and distrusting a look of scrutiny as I've ever been given in my life.

Finally, she turned. Spoke the rest of her piece quietly, looking over the fence into the courtyard of the lunch place next door. "Been a Democrat all my life," she said. "George, too. But what did he want with my daughter?" She touched her hat. "Married, too. A big shot. Could have had anything he wanted. Movie star. Model. And he wanted JoEll. I ask you why, that's all. What would a vile man like that want with my sweet JoEll?"

DAD'S BEEN A PHYSICALLY ASTUTE MAN all his life, and of course it's no different now that he spends his days the way he does. He practiced three different trades on the crews of Liam Metarey and could well have practiced a fourth. Not only was he a plumber and a stand-in electrician and a skilled layer of concrete—not so easy a job, nor quickly learned—but he was also a half-decent carpenter, from his own knockabout days as a teenager. In those times, in this lumber mill country, when you wanted to build a shed or a piece of furniture, you first cut down your own tree. He knew how to rough-size the timber with a two-handled saw, to smooth it with a set of heavy jointer planes, and to spike it all together in a pattern of framing that you still see in some of the older houses around here but that went out of use with the arrival of plywood. All this is to say that I can understand, if not actually approve of, the way he is behaving at his current quarters.

For example: one recent morning when the floor aide, Mrs. Milton, went to open his window and found it stuck from the humidity, Dad jumped from his bed—on which he'd been reading an anthology of high school poetry—and set to work helping her. Clara and I had come to escort him on our twice-monthly visit to Mom's grave, which he always resists—I sometimes wonder if he's embarrassed by the plainness of the headstone—and when the window stuck, he seemed to see his opening. He hurried to Mrs. Milton's side and took hold of the sash.

Fine enough, and what you might expect from a man of his generation. But this window wasn't the double-paned, smooth-sliding, molded-vinyl device you see in most nursing homes but an old double-hung with a wooden screen and storm. Walnut Orchards, unlike most other places with such names, actually did start out as an orchard—not just of walnuts, but of cherries and pears, too—and the wing where my father sleeps used to be the cannery. It's a green-roofed, white-clapboard building half the length of a football field, with Dutch rafters and a row of those old-fashioned windows, trimmed in black. The length and number and low set of the panes give it the look of a particularly long, luxurious, and beautiful horse barn. But such windows, when stuck, are nearly impossible to open.

Not for my father, however, even at eighty-one. He tested it a few times, then proceeded to hit the sash, first with the open palm of his good hand, then with his shoe, then with the poetry anthology, and finally with a paperback of Norman Mailer's *The Time of Our Time*, which caused the frame to emit a cracking sound but not quite to move. At last he resorted to the metal leveling plate that until he took out the eight-in-one tool from the pocket of his pajama pants—I was as surprised as anyone—had been screwed to the foot post of his bed.

He used it to pry off the stops on either side of the casing, and at this point the window fell gracefully backwards into his hands. But we were now in direct communication with the outside air, and this somehow caused Mrs. Milton to give up on her kind demeanor and go straight to the alarm cord, which at Walnut Orchards activates a revolving light outside the room door, like the one on an old police cruiser. A bell goes off, too, in the office, some distance away. I think she might have thought he was trying to escape.

The alarm bells are presumably intended for medical emergencies, and I made a note to ask the manager how much could be expected of the nose-ringed young man who arrived a few minutes later, wearing red Converse high-tops and a shirt that said QUESTION AUTHORITY? By that time, Dad had removed the rest of the trim and was retrieving a broken sash cord from inside the frame. The orderly merely sat down indolently in a side chair, next to where Clara was standing, to watch him. Dad pulled on the broken sash cord, and up came the rusted old iron weight at its end, like an eel out of a slough. It was a hot day and within a few moments the heat from the open window had overpowered the room's air-conditioning, but Dad was like an old lizard waiting to be warmed. He began to whistle "Whiskey in the Jar" as he retied the knot.

"That's a strangle snare, honey," I said to Clara, matter-of-factly. It seemed we had all accepted his task at this point, and we could all also see that he was doing a perfect job.

He stopped whistling. "No, it's not," he answered irritably. "It's just a simple noose, for Chrissake." Then he added, "Boy, my knuckles are stiff."

"It is *not*," I said. I turned to Clara. "It's a strangle snare." It was. A simple noose uses a single loop. Dad taught me all this.

"Cor," Clara said.

I should add that lately his memory has begun to worry me. Even more than usual. Not that he's forgetting things—everybody around here seems to do that—but that now it appears impossible to correct him with the truth. There seems to be a tiny homunculus of pent-up annoyance running free in his brain now, which is not at all how he used to be when I was young. Until the stroke, in fact, I doubt a single day of his eight vigorous decades had been marked by anything but hard work, personal reserve, and courtesy.

"Lord," he said, after a few more minutes of fiddling with the knot and the weight, "a *strangle snare*?"

"You taking the medicine Dr. Jadoon gave you for your fingers?"

"Lord," he said, louder. "A *strangle snare*?"

I had no choice: "I told you, Pop," I said, "a simple noose only uses one loop."

"Cor—"

"God damn you to hell."

"Cool," the orderly said.

"Dad," I said. "How do you plan to get the trim stops back in?"

"Fuck," Dad answered, and reached behind him, as though the hammer might be there on the floor.

The slackness was gone now from the orderly's features, and he was leaning forward in the chair like an honors student. I realized he was imagining his own situation, wondering if the current standoff with his own father—judging from the nose ring and the shirt—was destined, as mine appeared to be, to last out a lifetime.

But I'm not going to record any more. All I'll tell you is that the rest of what Dad said was heated. After a few minutes I tried to disengage, a trick that, thankfully, has become easier as I've grown older, but Dad spit out another diatribe. This one was aimed at the quality of modern lumber, the thinned-down hardware available at big-box retailers, and the greed of the facilities executives at Walnut Orchards. When the orderly chuckled here and there at his asides, my father took him quickly as an ally, and I was left to stand there until Dad finally tired—first of his own conversation and a few minutes later of the window, which he finally set back down against the wall.

By now it was almost too late to make the trip to the cemetery, but I didn't say anything. It was unsettling to see him like this, but I knew that if I set the window back in the frame and tried to move him along I might never hear the end of it. I'd also planned to tell him some news that Clara and I had heard, but I realized now that this, too, would have to wait. It was news about Aberdeen West.

THAT SUNDAY, *The New York Times* ran its famous article—the one that would eventually win G. V. Trawbridge his second Pulitzer Prize. It came out on page one, above the fold. I saw the paper at the breakfast table in the guest house, brought in by Liam Metarey himself and placed next to Henry Bonwiller's black coffee and toast. By then, there was such a feeling of stunned reversal at the estate that I simply walked up and read the opening of it over the Senator's shoulder. After a moment, he stood, moved to the window, and began tossing a marble egg in his hand. He was looking out at the land. At the far end of the horse pastures, Gil McKinstrey was driving a tractor over the berm, and as Henry Bonwiller watched the machine disappear behind the hill I had the feeling he was watching his ambitions vanish, too. Nobody looked at me. Nobody spoke.

> BUFFALO, N.Y., April 23—Allegations have come to light in re- cent weeks about the death of JoEllen Charney, an Islington, New York, legal secretary who is believed to have been in- volved at the time of her death in an extra-marital affair with front-running Democratic presidential candidate Senator Henry Bonwiller of New York. Miss Charney, who disappeared in De- cember, was found dead shortly before the Iowa Presidential caucuses, encased in ice in an apple orchard that shares a bor- der with the campaign offices of Senator Bonwiller.

A New York State Police investigation earlier this year re-
sulted in no indictments, but sources have confirmed that the
case has been re-opened by the Buffalo office of the F.B.I., and
that Senator Bonwiller is a person of interest in the new investigation. An indictment, if one is coming, would be expected
by summer.

Later that morning, the Senator left. I was in the driveway when
the campaign jet rose steeply over the house and banked to the south.
The boom of that plane always startled me, no matter how many
times I heard it, and in its aftermath each time the particular silence
of that place seemed to begin all over again, as though the land were
cleansing itself. First the sound of the birds returned—it was impossible to know if they'd stopped chirping or if my ears had only stopped
hearing them; then came the distant putter of the tractor; then the
clap-clap-clap of a hammer and the rising triplet of Churchill's following yap. Last, always, came the mumble of the wind, high in the
sycamores, the shivering of those giant leaves that to me is still most
emblematic of that land and those days. I stood under the bur oak,
wondering what was coming.

Later that day, I was questioned again. I must have been the first
one they approached, because the agent came in just a few moments
after I'd parked his black Mercury Marquis in the garage. I was filling
a bucket with soap to wash it when he appeared at the door. He held
out a panel fold. "FBI," he said. "Got to ask a couple of things."

"Yes, sir."

I dipped the sponge and lathered the hood.

"Just a couple things, Corey."

I was young enough to be surprised that he knew my name.

"Yes, sir."

"How about puttin' that down?"

"I'm sorry, sir." I set the sponge back in the bucket. A half-dozen
sawhorses were stacked next to where he was leaning against the wall
by the door, and I pulled one out and took a seat across from him. He
was a big man, and a laundry soap smell came from his dark blue suit.

He adjusted his pants, which seemed uncomfortable, and took out a small pad from his breast pocket. "The Senator, Senator Bonwiller," he said. "Now, you say he was a good driver?"

"Was he a good driver?"

"In your opinion."

"I guess I never saw him drive."

He wrote.

"What's his mood been like then?"

"Same as ever."

He looked at me.

"Optimistic," I said.

"That's good. Optimistic."

Again, he wrote.

"You ever see him drink?"

"Did I?"

"That's what I'm asking. I heard you never saw him drink."

"No." I looked ahead. "I didn't."

He smiled. "That's good, too, isn't it? You never saw Henry Bonwiller take a drink." He snapped the pad closed. "That's all I need then. At least for now."

He set the pad in his breast pocket, then rose and moved to the door, hitching his pants on his hips. "You can get back to the vehicle," he said.

As soon as he was gone, I set to work again with the bucket and sponge. Then I brought out the wax. I vacuumed the seats and the carpets, and on the visor I clipped a new booklet of toll coupons. Then I went outside to the top of the driveway and scanned the grounds. From there I saw him in the side pantry, his blue suit in a chair now next to the window, across from Gil McKinstrey.

When I returned I went through the car. There was a badge in the glove box. It said *U.S. Secret Service—Department of the Treasury.*

Later in the afternoon, I walked over and stood below Liam Metarey on the front steps of the house as we watched the newly shining Mercury make its way up the driveway into the trees.

"Flashlight and a wool cap in the glove box," I said. "Some antacids. A badge. Secret Service."

From the top step, he glanced down at me. "Secret Service?" he said. "Is that right? Not FBI?" On his face a rueful smile flickered.

"No, sir. No papers, either. Nothing about you or the Senator. Coffee cups and receipts and that kind of stuff under the seats, that's all."

"Thank you, Corey."

"Just the spare in the trunk," I went on. "Couple of flares."

He looked back up at the entrance road, where a spot of light from the windshield was all that was visible now, moving through the trees. Then he touched my shoulder. "Well," he said, "good job, anyway."

He looked at me solemnly.

And even now, I have a clear memory of the insignia on that badge—five points surrounding a hexagon within a hexagon, and the script in blocks. But it wasn't until almost two decades later, when I was writing for a paper in Boston, that I came across a fact that I should have remembered from high school: the Secret Service works for the president.

FROM THE ROAD one afternoon on the way out to visit Dad I saw that the cranes had finally begun to move.

"Great," he said, when I arrived. "Let's go see."

"I'm talking about the cranes over at the Metareys', Dad. Over at Aberdeen West. What I told you about the other day on the phone. They're building a mall out there. Remember?"

"I know what you're talking about. Let's go have a look."

Even driving there was a challenge. There's traffic in that direction now starting two hours before the afternoon whistles, made worse by the repetitive shoring and widening of the highway, which of course only brings in more traffic. At the Steppan-Saline exit, we pulled off the road. A Starbucks drive-through sits there now next to a Comfort

Inn, and a truck plaza with a Hardee's at one end and a Mobil, a Citgo, and a BP at the other. When I was a kid, there was just one station in town, the Esso. I stopped at one of the new ones to put in a few gallons and to give Dad a little time to acclimate. He sat in the car reading his poetry anthology.

The rumble of idling big rigs filled the air. In front of us was the orchard where they'd found JoEllen Charney's body, not all that long ago; but now you couldn't see anything to tell you that fruit trees had once stood there or that a beautiful woman had come to her end among them. All you could see were parked cars and beyond them parked trucks. The boulders that Mr. Silverton's great-grandfather had hoisted out of the ground with a horse team and chain so that he could plant his Spartans and McIntoshes—stacking the great slabs upright in his own, small Stonehenge—had long since fallen over or been knocked flat and dragged away.

Over the trees, the crane booms were close in sight, foreshortening and then lengthening as they turned. There were two of them, both working at a good pace but neither one moving steadily enough to be swinging a wrecking ball. To stall a bit, I tried counting the traffic on the cloverleaf behind us, but this was futile. I counted just the big rigs instead, and even that number was overwhelming. In the old days, the Metarey property reached all the way to the road here, ending at the trees and the apple stand, which was financed by a cash bucket hanging from a post. Now the highway tolls are counted by an electronic eye, and the interstate shoots past a half-dozen towns, some of them small cities, that weren't even plowed when I was a boy.

We drove the last few miles in silence. As we approached the turnoff to the Metareys' drive, Dad finally put down his book and said, "You can't argue with the logic," as though he'd been paying attention since we'd set out. He swept his hand across the suburban panorama.

"No," I said. "You can't." There was a new traffic light for a subdivision across the highway, and we waited to turn. "But get ready anyway."

"I'm ready," he said.

We came up the driveway, which had been thickly graveled for the heavy machinery, drove beneath the sycamores, and emerged between the familiar stone gates.

"Oh, God," he said.

I swung the car sharply over onto the shoulder.

"Jesus."

Everywhere on the property, the oaks lay across the grass.

The cranes were swinging back and forth above them, gray shapes dangling from their grapplers like the severed legs of elephants. On the ground, front-end loaders were using scoops to roll gigantic sections of tree up the sloped lawn into pinch harnesses, where a pair of men would fasten the hooks and the safety, and then the crane would roar and lift into the air.

"Oh, God," he said again.

"Oh God is right."

The booms took turns skimming their cargo over the front porch and then the grass lot where I used to park cars, and finally up the old driveway toward the stone gates where Christian and I used to sit in the mornings. Beyond us, trucks were idling in a row and another crew was guiding the wood down into them. Two trunks took up the width of a flatbed, and three filled its length. The drivers then lurched into gear and drove out beneath the sycamores.

"I thought you said he preserved it."

"He did, Dad. Not all of it, though. They sold this part years ago, before Clara and I were married. You know that."

"Sold it to a preservationist, I thought."

"Guess the preservationist must have sold it to someone else."

The air rumbled with diesel engines and whined with chain saws, which other men in lift buckets were using on the limbs that remained. I'd guess there were at least fifty oaks down. But dozens of others were still standing. Workers were heaving the smaller branches into a chipper, and the chipper was spewing its waste into a covered dump truck that in a few minutes sped off down a different driveway, this one through the woods to the east. I could trace its path from the cloud of dust hanging above the trees. In a moment, another had pulled up.

"I'm sorry," said my father.

"Mr. Metarey used to check the bark on every one of them. Some of them were twelve feet around."

He closed his window.

"He treated them like people," I said.

"I know," he answered. He glanced sideways. "I remember digging underneath the big one."

I closed my window, too. And I must say, for a moment as we sat there with the hellish scene taking place almost quietly before us, I actually felt a return of the place's magnificence. Without the sound, the balance of the battle seemed to change. The great house still stood, though the paint on the trim was coming off in long strips and a breach had appeared in a corner of the porch roof, below Mr. Metarey's old study—probably from one of the cranes. It was strange to see the long south wall in such unvaried light, its face deprived of the stippled shade that had cooled it in three different centuries; but the fact remained that the house was still there. I don't think I'm exaggerating to say it looked defiant. And with so many trees down, the land around it looked only more immense, as though it could absorb this insult, too—just a passing turn of luck—and still prevail.

"All things must change to something new," Dad said then, "to something strange." He shook his head. "I just happened to be reading that."

"Who is it?"

"Longfellow."

The great dappled sycamores over the barrier drive still hadn't been touched, nor had the deep woods around them except where the new construction road had been cut; these woods were maple and Scotch pine, and the Scotch pine still hid the interstate. The cranes roared and the shadow of their swinging arms crossed over the knoll in front of us, the lifted trunks casting their own dark gashes as they

glided above what had been the wide, bluegrass lawn where Henry
Bonwiller had held his press conferences. My father had only a stony
look on his face—I couldn't tell whether it was his old reserved feeling or his newfound anger—but I myself had to wipe my eyes. I'm
well aware that the world must change. But I had to wipe them anyway. Dad looked away. Behind the house a trio of skid-loaders was
making fast work of the long berm that had once shored the fly pools.
And as I watched, a bulldozer crept up to Breighton's dilapidated
horse barn, where Christian and I had first kissed more than thirty
years ago. It tested it with its shovel—a strangely delicate gesture—
and then pushed it over in a heap.

I drive a new-looking Camry, and of course in a few minutes one of
the foremen approached. I think I might have recognized him—a kid
from a year ahead of me at Roosevelt—and I think he might have recognized me, too, but with the tears on my cheeks and with what was
taking place before us, both of us were embarrassed. I lowered my
window.

"I guess you know you can't sit here," he said quietly.

SENATOR ACCUSED! That's what the *New York Post* said.

The *Daily News* was pithier: BYE-BYE, BON!

The *Times* followed its own scoop with BONWILLER CAMP STUNNED
BY REVELATION. And *The Wall Street Journal*, whose headline writers
would never have been mistaken for friends of the Senator, was already
looking ahead: DEMOCRATS SCRAMBLE TO REPLACE BONWILLER.

BUT HENRY BONWILLER WASN'T going to let them. The next afternoon, he put out a statement:

The recent press allegations about the tragic death of a devoted worker in the Bonwiller for President Campaign, Miss JoEllen Charney, are a fiction. When the facts are known, Senator Bonwiller will be completely exonerated. In the meantime, Senator Bonwiller continues to fight for working men and women, women like Miss Charney herself.

Then he threw a party.

He chose May 1st—the eve of the votes in Indiana and Ohio and Washington, and three days before a rack of southern primaries would begin. "International Workers' Day," he said to Liam Metarey. "They can't miss the symbolism." The two of them were sitting in a pair of willow rockers on the porch outside the Senator's guest cabin, two tumblers of Scotch on the table between them. I was straightening up inside.

"It's May Day, too," said Mr. Metarey. "That's what they'll pick up on."

The Senator glanced at him.

"The distress signal, Henry. Mayday."

"I don't care. The unions will come out for me. Every worker in the county'll be here. Make it good. Good as the first one. Real down-home stuff."

"With all due respect, Senator, what they need is a press conference. Not a party."

Henry Bonwiller burst out laughing. "I guess that's why I'm the Senator, Liam, isn't it? Because I know that what they want up here is a party. Reporters included."

"Okay, Senator. Well, I suppose we can do it, if you want."

"I do. And I want a big one. Ray White again. Just like the first time."

"I'll see if he's available."

"He'd better be available." He emptied his glass and pulled a cigar from his breast pocket. "After what I've done. You can remind him."

"Senator," said Mr. Metarey, "I think most people in the country—

certainly everybody in the press corps—well, Henry, let me put it this way: they'd have to be fools not to know the odds on what's coming."

"Liam," the Senator said, "leave this to me." He stood, leaned to the window, and squinted inside to where I was sweeping the floor. "Corey!" he said gruffly, "how many we feed and water at the one before?"

"The first party, sir?"

"Damn it," he growled, "how many?"

"I think a thousand, Senator—a thousand guests. More or less. If I remember."

"But you're wounded now, Henry," I heard Mr. Metarey say. "If you don't mind my mentioning. All the papers were calling you the front-runner then. With all due respect, sir—look at what they're calling you now."

The Senator disappeared from the window.

"Pricks are calling for me to pull out."

"That's right, Henry."

"Blood's in the water, all right. You're certainly on the mark about that." I'd paused in my work now and was watching them. He was smelling the skin of a cigar, rolling it in his fingers. Then he bit off the end. "But I'm the one bleeding," he said tersely. "Not you."

"Yes, sir. But—"

"And I'm the one who's gonna stop it." He spit the tip. "Corey!" he called again, "How many'd you say at the first one?"

"Roughly a thousand, sir."

"Thank you," called Mr. Metarey.

"Blood in the water. Yes, yes. Scandal, all right. Papers all over me. Sniffing like hounds. Nasty as you can imagine. In that case," Senator Bonwiller said, flicking open his lighter, "I'd plan for *two* thousand."

"Senator," Liam Metarey said, "I'm obliged to tell you, I believe you're making a mistake."

II

"SHE NOTICED YOU said it happened at night."

"She did."

"And how *did* you know that, sir?"

"Trieste, you're going to make a good reporter."

"Thank you, sir." She smiled. "And you're going to make a good source."

I had to laugh. "But the answer is that everybody assumes it. If it happened during the day, someone would have seen it."

"Possibly."

"Probably, Trieste. Almost certainly."

"But then she let it drop?"

"Trieste, her daughter—her only child—died. Thirty years ago. In her shoes, what you'd want to do is find peace. I really think that she only wanted to hear something nice about JoEllen. That's all. That's why she was talking to me, Trieste—not to investigate something. She'd found those pictures of me driving. That means she was looking through all those things again from those days. She must have just wanted to hear something about JoEllen again. That I'd heard her sing or maybe that I liked her. Maybe that I met her during that time and that she was happy."

I saw her then, JoEllen, sitting in Morley's in her hat and dark glasses.

"Happy," I said, turning to the window. "At least, when she was with him. That's what would have meant something to her mother."

ONE AFTERNOON A COUPLE OF MONTHS LATER, I set out with Dad and Mr. McGowar to visit Mom's grave. It was late October, and the tapestry colors along the parkway were giving way to the winter vista. The drawing and not the painting. At a distance through the thinning woods we could see the glint of Little Shelter Brook where it turns toward the river, and beyond it the full reach of the gray and white subdivisions that now cover most of the hills between here and Buffalo. Dad had put down his book, maybe because Mr. McGowar was in the car. It was *Let Us Now Praise Famous Men*. South of town, where the two yellow cranes still stood above the horizon, he said, "Let's go see if they've made any progress."

"I thought we were going to see Mom."

"She's not going anywhere," he said. Then after a moment, "Sorry."

"That's okay, Dad. Why do you want to see it all again?"

"I just want to."

"It's going to be worse."

"Of course it will. It's getting cold. They'll want the foundation down and the utilities closed in before winter. Eugene," he said, "is it okay if we don't go see Anna today?"

The pad appeared.

FIN

By the time we reached the approach drive, the sun was low over the trees. Through the bare woods on the other side of the road, I could see our old neighborhood, the dark brick façades and the steep gambrel roofs. Dad and I rarely look that way anymore when we pass on 35, and for some reason we never talk about it. The houses are lived in now by the temporary employees of the big electronics assemblers that have moved in along the parkway. And by Mr. McGowar, of course, too. That afternoon I'd picked him up at the old bus stop.

At the gravel entrance to the Metarey estate, pickups turned in ahead of us and behind us. Every hundred feet or so on the shoulder there was a no-trespassing sign, and a union restriction placard next to every gate in the fencing. Still, I knew we wouldn't have a problem: there's not a plumber or electrician in the whole county who wouldn't cross the street to say hello to my father, and not a construction crew who wouldn't let him onto a job.

Sure enough, there was a guard at the main entrance, but Dad hopped out of the car and ambled up the hill to greet him. Through the window of the shack I could see them laughing together.

The pad appeared:

STIL A TAWKR WEN HE WONS TU

As soon as he returned, we set off up an incline that hadn't even been there the last time we visited—a mound of earth squared off and angled by the heavy graders at just enough of a slope to hide the entire site from the road. I think we were still in the vicinity of the old iron gates, somewhere near where the asphalt used to give way to river stone. The huge portico of sycamores was gone, and the dirt rise we were climbing suddenly smoothed into an embankment of gravel thirty yards across.

"Six lanes," Dad said. "Not bad."

We could hear the big machinery now.

"Okay, Dad, Mr. McGowar—I'm warning you."

Then we were at the top.

In a moment, Mr. McGowar's hand appeared between us.

WOW

"That's what I meant."

A whole new settlement, out on the plain before us. Stores. A low, rambling cluster of them. Complete down to the dark tile roofs and glass entrance arcade. Dozens in varied succession. All joined together in a single, stretching edifice that rose and fell along different rooflines like an Amsterdam street-front but that was still one unending building, maybe a third of a mile across. We sat looking down on it.

"Silent," said my father. He took off his Yankees cap and set it on his lap. "Upon a peak in Darien."

Around it, where I think the east woods might have run, was the parking lot. Room for a few thousand cars and a half-dozen feeder roads snaking in a careful, symmetric geometry that was apparent from above. The whole thing probably a quarter-mile deep and twice that long. Half of it still gravel. From this height we could see a handful of paving crews scattered across the expanse, like wagons on the prairie, trailing dark swaths of new concrete. And beyond them, on the far side of a narrow, excavated creek, the houses. Rows of them, staggered into the hills toward the orchard.

"There's nothing left here, Dad."

"No."

At the center of one of the courtyards was a concrete-walled pond, and from the summit we could see water in it that had been dyed aquamarine and a fountain that as we watched began to spout. From a maintenance hatch off to the side, a couple of men were adjusting its controls. I had an inkling they were standing where the fly-casting pools used to be. Beyond them the pavement turned to gravel again, and one fleet of cement trucks out there was carrying the work forward to meet another team on the far side that was carrying it back. A loading dock was already finished.

I heard a page flip.

OPN BI THANGSGIVN

"My God," Dad said, "we were just here—what was it?—some time ago. They were just cutting the trees."

"Six weeks ago, Dad."

MAB CRISMUS

"He's fast," Dad said. "I'll give him that. Working on a Sunday, too. Wonder who he is. Union job site, so he's paying for it, at least. City Irish, a quarter on your dollar. From Buffalo. Ruthless."

DOLR HES A SCOT

"Okay, you're on."

"There's nothing left," I said. "It's gone."

"Completely."

A pair of twenty-four-wheelers pulled up behind us, shaking the earth, dust rising from their tarps as they climbed past in low gear and started down. They moved along the ring of access roads until at a certain point they both swung onto the lot and opened their under-hatches. Pale lanes of new gravel appeared behind them.

Mr. McGowar's hand moved to the front seat again, pointing.

NOT CMPLTLE

"Not completely what?"

GON

He pointed again.

OK TRE

I looked. Sure enough, a quarter mile to the east, where the main entrance road widened to what looked like a river delta of asphalt— and where, I was beginning to realize, the house had once stood— there it was.

The bur oak.

Leafless. But still standing.

By the time we reached the ring road, it had disappeared behind the buildings. But we followed the drive around, circling the ever-changing roofscape and the packs of parked pickups, only here and there catching a glimpse of it until I wasn't even sure it was what we thought it was. But then we came around a turn and there it stood again, its crown stretching over the entrance circle.

"Dad," I said, when we got out. "Mr. McGowar. You knew."

"It's nice," Dad answered. "You have to admit. Stately."

The trunk stood at the center of the circle so that incoming traffic had to part beneath the limbs.

"A union job," Dad said. He nodded at it with his chin. "Mostly, at least. More work than it looks, I'll tell you that."

"It looks like plenty." I saw now that it was slightly smaller than life-size, but from a distance you wouldn't have known.

BRONS

"Stiffened with concrete, Eugene. Cellular concrete." He gestured up toward the lowest boughs, which shone dully like caramel. "Came all the way up from Pittsburgh with the equipment. That must have been a tricky one."

"It's quite a monument," I said. "But to what?"

"That's a philosophical question, son."

"Yes, it is."

"Well, you're the philosopher. All I know is that it's one fancy construction treatment. Don't see it much around here. No local bids— you can bet on that. Lighten it with air, I guess. Boy," he said, shaking his head. "Didn't do anything like that when I was in the business."

SHUR DDUNT

"Set in molds," he went on. "Special rebar, not even forty-grade. Long lengths. Probably built it by computer. Only reason for the concrete is to hold the rebar, if you ask me. And the rebar just holds the bronze." He tipped his ball cap. "But nobody did."

"Nobody what?"

"Asked me." He smiled. "Lady up in Vermont made it. Trucked the steel all the way out there so she could bend it. That's right, Eugene—a lady. Don't know how she did it, but she did. One branch at a time. Only part that wasn't union, by the way. Brought down like that, too. Don't know how much concrete in the branches either, but plenty in the trunk. And it's got roots, too." He took off his cap and held it to his chest, like a ballplayer waiting out the anthem. "Had to or it'd fall."

"No leaves, though."

"Doesn't need 'em."

"And you knew all about it."

"Everybody knows about it, at least where I live. The rest I heard about fifteen minutes ago. From the guard. He's Murph Mills's boy."

I looked at him. "Murph Mills's boy?"

"Got his union card. Working his way up."

I looked at him again. Nothing on his face.

"This is the fall of our culture, Dad. This is the end of a way of life."

"Oh, come on."

"It's a fake tree."

"It's a statue. A bronze monument."

"This guy is merciless, Dad."

"He is. You're right. Merciless. A hack. A thief. An Irish pirate." He cracked his knuckles. "But I see two hundred men out here."

I thought about that.

SCOT

"Double or nothing, Eugene," said Dad. He lifted his cap and ran his hand through his hair. "But it takes a lot of men to do something like this. A lot of men working. And a lot of bronze in it, too."

"And?"

But he didn't seem interested in pursuing it. "Well," he said. "You have to admit, it sure looks heroic out here. The lone holdout."

By now, it was nearly dark, but in the distance the pavers were still at their task. The concrete trucks were stirring their loads and adjusting the mix, and now and then the sound of the gearing would rise as they pumped. We started across the street to the arcade. The crews were working in pairs, leapfrogging each other so that the finishing team could float out one load while the pouring team spread the next. They were good. Even I could see it. I watched one of them cover at least five yards in the time it took us to walk half the length of one wall of stores. Mr. McGowar led the way, bouncing along in his high-kneed style.

Here and there as we moved along the façade, a piece of blackout paper had come free from a window and we could see into the building itself, where more fountains were running under the glass-roofed atrium and a series of footbridges arched over what must have been an artificial stream. Out on the lot, a row of sodium lamps blinked on.

"What do you two think of all this?" I said.

"Looks like they're tight on a deadline."

AL FAK
NO GRANITE

"Good, Eugene."

"No, I mean *this*. What they're doing."

"What do I think?" Dad said, stopping to look at me. "I don't know what I think, to tell the truth. That's the way progress is. It's always half criminal. Greeks said it about their mall, too—the whatever-it's-called."

Further along the sidewalk, where it broadened at the entrance, we came within reach of the lamps and I saw that the paving here had been flecked with something to make it glitter. In front of us were bicycle racks and iron benches and mini courtyards with raised planters in their centers. Maple saplings stood in pairs, held true by guy wires. A slant of land to the left caught my eye and I had the sudden feeling that we were walking on what used to be the dirt ring of Breighton's corral, just south of the main house and a hundred yards up the low slope that ended at the flood berms. The casting pools had been cut diagonally across those berms, so that they wouldn't face the rising or the setting sun. I saw now that the courtyard had been planned the same way.

"But tell me," he said quietly, "what did you *used* to think?"

"What do you mean, what did I used to think?"

"Well . . ." he said. "You know . . ." He swept his hand across the expanse. "What did you think when all this belonged to one man?"

We walked on.

"It did, Dad," I said after a time. "I know." I paused. "But there was a public trust then. Eoghan Metarey took care of a whole town. Liam Metarey planned for the next generations."

"Yes, yes. But still—that's a hell of a lot of land for one family."

"It was conserved for public use."

"Part of it. And never mind what Hobbes would say about that." He turned to me. "But all this"—he gestured again—"this was sold straight to the builder. Fair and square."

We walked in silence again.

HUZ HOBS

After a few moments, Dad said, "A philosopher, Eugene. A dismalist. But a realist." Then, to me, "In case you hadn't noticed, I've been catching up on that kind of thing."

"I *had* noticed."

"And at least this way everybody gets to use it," he went on. He stopped abruptly. "The *Acropolis*," he said. "That's it. I read that the Greeks thought it was an abomination. Or enough of 'em did."

"You think this is everybody using it?"

"No, it's a scandal. But I just think about it sometimes." He resumed his pace. "In my old age."

Something happens to him these days if he's out around sundown, a primitive kind of wilding, followed by a bout of wordless melancholy, and I could see now that it was upon him. Dr. Jadoon has warned me about it. I've witnessed it myself a couple of times, and I probably should have taken both of them home right then. It was almost dark already and beginning to get cold. But in the eerie light of the sodium lamps, Dad looked particularly brittle: I don't know why that stopped me. He stepped around a sawhorse and started off across the darker surface of yesterday's pour, and when Mr. McGowar realized that I wasn't going to do anything, he hopped right over the sawhorse, too. All I could do was follow. Next to Dad, Mr. McGowar seemed to be loping along. There was a lane of unpaved gravel to the side of us, and Mr. McGowar was scanning it as he walked. Maybe it was the contrast, but behind him I could see Dad more clearly than I wanted to: the loose sleeve of his shirt around the bad arm and the gaunt pinch of that shoulder. The pants bunched at the belt. The stiffened gait. I didn't like watching. Proud men have a force field.

At a bench at the far end of the lot—soon to be a bus stop, I thought—Dad finally sat down; but when he looked back I saw only a contemplative stillness on his face. Mr. McGowar took the spot next to him.

"Fine looking," Dad said to him. "Isn't it?"

PRIDY

I have to admit, it was. The dusky stars, just now appearing. Steam swirling above the mixers. The two distant encampments of concrete pourers, glowing in the void. The glinting bronze limbs of the oak, hovering in the dark behind them.

"I've always thought that what we did was beautiful, Eugene," Dad said then. "You know that? In a really profound way. The clarity of it all. Granite. Tin. Silver. The physical undeniability. Lead. Antimony. Heat it right, keep it dry, slope it—and it works. Figure the load, pour the slab—and it works. Know the span, size the beam. Bang, the whole damn job. Bunch of stiffs like you and me, putting up our great pyramid. You couldn't stop us."

IT WZ OK

"It *is* beautiful, Dad. It's very impressive."

"Good way to have spent a life. Building things."

"It was. It is."

The two of them sat looking back over the work.

"Anyway," Dad said abruptly, "I was thinking of taking up painting."

TO MUCH PREP

"Oil painting, Eugene." He pointed at the eerily lit crews. "Art," he said. "Beauty. It's what you're left with when your joints give out."

"Okay, Dad."

"And Gaelic. I've always thought it might be worthwhile to learn Gaelic. In case I go back."

"Gaelic, Dad. Okay."

His look darkened. "Well, why the hell not?"

That's when he took his cap, set it on the bench between them, and, turning to support himself with his good arm, slid off stiffly onto the ground.

I was the first to reach him, and by the time I had him under a shoulder Mr. McGowar had him under the other. But all Dad said was, "You're in my light." He shook himself free. "Both of you."

"Dad, what are you doing?"

"Someone should tell him his mix is too wet."

He had his key ring in his hand. Mr. McGowar had gone back to the bench.

"Dad, what exactly—"

"I used to want to kill those damn kids." He rose on all fours and nodded toward the crews. "Waiting for me to go home. The Duffy boys. Vic Connors. Waiting till I gave in and went home to eat supper. Those no-good Blair brothers. Pack of wolves, all of them. One of the reasons I gave up the trade." Laboriously, he undid a key. "But now the little bastards are the ones out here working."

For the record, I didn't watch.

But Mr. McGowar did. He sat there on the bench, smiling.

And whenever one of the mixers quieted, I could hear the scratching.

In the distance the silhouettes of the crews moved about the work. The shovels. The long bull float. The high rubber boots. In front of me, Dad's dark shape like a man praying.

When the scratching finally stopped, Mr. McGowar and I stepped over. Dad was cleaning the key. From a chain on his neck he brought out a tiny flashlight, which didn't surprise me, and shone it on the surface:

> *Philosophers have only interpreted*
> *The world in various ways.*
> *The point*
> *Is to change it.*

"What's that?"

"A saying."

Mr. McGowar was grinning like a monkey now.

Finally, Dad leaned over and scratched out, with a last flurry of work:

> *—September 1971—*

"Dad?" I whispered.

He was struggling to push the key back onto the ring. "What?"

I set my hand on his shoulder. It was chilly under his shirt. "Is everything okay?"

He didn't answer, but he rose to his haunches, like a catcher, and presently I felt something settle over the back of my fingers. Like old, cracked rope, but surprisingly warm. It might have been that Dad was just holding on so he wouldn't fall over. It probably was, in fact. But I stayed like that anyway. Mr. McGowar turned away.

"You *have* been reading," I said. "That's Marx, isn't it?"

"Yes, it is," he answered. "And yes, I have." Then he added, "I can see why you like it."

"ALMOST LOOKS LIKE AN INDIAN VILLAGE," Mr. Metarey said, quietly.

It was May 1st, early morning, and I'd just unhitched a pallet of folding chairs from the hay hook to carry out for the Senator's party. "Sir?" I said.

He tilted his head. "Out on the plain."

He pointed. On the lawn beyond the house, the main pavilion tent was being raised, and the poles were pushing the canvas into a row of peaks that looked like a village of tepees against the sun. Smoke from the roasters hung over the horizon, too, and in the long shadow of one of the oaks, where the pigs were turning on spits, spears of flame were jumping. It was an arresting sight.

"Come to take it back," he said.

"Eerie looking, Mr. Metarey. I see it." I came up next to him at the door. "Good thing we're living when we are."

"I suppose you could say that." He took a step into the barn but caught his foot and leaned heavily against the post. I moved past him to unhook the pallet of chairs from the gable wire.

"Still a few Indians here when my father had it, you know," he went on. "A few dozen, anyway. In the hills to the east. Tonawanda

Seneca, if I'm not wrong. From the old Iroquois Confederacy. Men the government didn't know about. Living the old ways."

"When was that, sir?"

"Eighteen ninety-six, I think. If you can believe that." He looked down. "That's how long we've held it between the two of us, Corey. Seventy-six years. My dad and I. I have to say, that's not so bad. Great Law of the Iroquois said that in every—what was it?—every *deliberation*, you had to think of what it meant for the seventh generation." He shook his head. "And so far, we've had three generations here on this piece. Four if you count my granddad." He pointed behind him. "Lived in Gil's shed for a couple of years till he died. That was before the house was built. Still, though—I think we've been pretty fair with it."

"It's beautiful land, sir. I imagine there's nowhere like it."

"Thank you, Corey. You know, when my father came over from Fife he was six years old and his own father was something like twenty-three. You know what my granddad did for a living?"

"No, sir."

"Back in Tayport he was a blacksmith, but here he was a bonded servant. You know what that is, don't you?"

"Not exactly."

"Not teaching that kind of thing at Dunleavy, are they? A good thing to learn on May Day, I guess. It meant he was in debt to the man who paid their passage. Seven years, just working off the trip. But evidently Granddad used to say it was the best deal of his life."

I could see that he was watching the driveway now, where the first cars had begun to arrive. At this hour, they still carried only the day's workers, the drivers heading down the two-track and parking a few hundred yards behind the garage so that there would be room for the invited guests closer to the house. Mr. Metarey was quiet, but I was rooted there by the hope that he was going to say more. He'd never spoken to me about his family.

He turned from the driveway. "And my own dad was part of the deal," he said finally. "On top of it. We're talking about 1881. Worked full-time starting at the age of six. For their benefactor. Besides all he did at home because my grandmother was still back in the old country. Did he get an education? Not a dime's worth. He was a son of a bitch, all right—but I remember him reading Greek when I was a boy and practicing English elocution. Kept an English teacher around with him when he was older, too, just for his speech. Never quite could banish the brogue, though." He shook his head again. "That's what those men were like, you know. The best of them, at least. Hell bent on self-improvement."

"It's impressive, sir."

"It is, isn't it? He tried his damnedest to be American."

"I'd say he succeeded."

"Their obligation was paid when he was thirteen, Corey, and inside of a year he and Granddad had opened the hardware. Sold farm equipment to the other Scots and Irish who were coming into the country around then. I mean mechanized farm equipment. New-world stuff. Geared run-behind threshers and steam plows. You could still use some of it today." He looked up at the pulley on the hayloft gable. "I guess I still do," he said, "don't I?"

"No one's come up with anything better, Mr. Metarey."

"That's one way of putting it." He laughed. "And that same year they sent for my grandmother and my uncles. In less than a decade they had an oil well, up in Saskatchewan. And the anthracite mine down in Cape Breton. Did it all in Canada. Soon Rockefeller was taking them out on Long Island Sound on his boat. John D. Rockefeller, I mean. A five-masted schooner, I've seen the pictures. In 1901, I think that was. And in 1921, my father was the one who convinced a young state senator to run for governor of New York. He was always a Democrat, my father. Never forgot his past. Doesn't always work that way, does it?" He looked up the driveway again. "You know who the state senator was?"

"No sir."

"Franklin Roosevelt."

At that moment, as if on cue, Henry Bonwiller's dark Cadillac appeared. It emerged from between the sycamores and made its way slowly up the center of the entry lane. The top was closed, but as the car passed a group of workers winching tight the guy wires of the main tent, the Senator leaned out from the back window and waved, keeping his hand up as though there were a crowd there even after he had rounded the long curve and the men had turned back to their task. Carlton Sample was driving. He kept a stately pace, but as soon as he pulled over in front of the house he hopped out, went briskly around to the far side of the car, and opened the door. Next to me, Mr. Metarey stiffened. I'd only seen Mrs. Bonwiller one other time, on the day the Senator announced his candidacy, and now I only saw her dark coat and the back of her pushed-up hairdo as she moved quickly to the steps with Carlton Sample and disappeared into the house.

Then Henry Bonwiller emerged, stretching his arms and waving again before he turned and strode up the stairs himself, as convincingly as if this were the day he'd been elected president. I was watching Mr. Metarey's face now. If I had to put a word to it, I'd say he looked afraid.

"And he walketh about," he said softly, "seeking whom he may devour."

"I'll finish getting the chairs out."

He turned back to me. "I know all this," he said, "because I've read about it. You know what it's like to read about your father in a history book?"

"I imagine it'd be nice, sir."

He glanced over at me and laughed again. A short, surprised chuckle like the knot coming untied on a balloon. Then he tousled my hair. "You're right. It should be nice. Let's get those chairs out."

I leaned down to slide the pallet away from the hay pulley, and it was then, when he reached to help me, that I smelled the liquor.

It was the first time ever. I might have paused for a moment.

"They're all coming," he said, "because they think Henry Bonwiller's going to drop out of the race today."

I took a chance. "He's not going to?"

"No, he's not, Corey. He's been up all night writing a battle speech. I know because I've been on the phone with him since three o'clock this morning. Thought I could convince him this time, but no. Thinks he can tough it out. We're going with the original plan."

Another whiff of liquor reached me.

"They're all here for the hanging, Corey."

"Sir?"

"Our guests. Henry's right about one thing, at least. If I know anything about human nature, we're going to get a rather capacious crowd."

"I can bring out the chairs from the north storage."

"And he's gone again and hired Ray White, too, just like he said. Lord, it should have been just a goddamn press briefing. A short speech and a typed statement and then he should have been with his lawyers. But now we're roasting pigs. Bought out every bottle at Grant's and McBride's, and Gil's gone into Islington for more." His expression slackened for a moment, but then he brought it firm. "Well, I guess we could use it, right? Either Henry's on the money about the nature of late-twentieth-century man or we're going to have the largest bill in history for a press corps lynching set to rhythm and blues."

"Ray White knows what's going on, too?"

"Everybody in the country knows what's going on, Corey. It's all wrong—wrong as can be. Henry doesn't understand what's about to happen. He thinks a good ol' time for a bunch of reporters is all it's going to take."

"Maybe it will turn out all right."

"Of course it will, in the end. That's about the only comfort I can take."

Just then, two campaign aides came hurrying across the lawn to speak to him, and this ended up being the last thing Mr. Metarey said to me. I went back to the pallets of chairs, and within a few minutes, the buses had begun to arrive. And after that they continued to appear out of the trees all morning, dropping off their riders at the parking circle and then rolling down the long driveway to park in the lowland behind the berms. The AFL-CIO sent in a load of rank and file from Rochester, and the Teamsters arrived in their own caravan of big rigs, blowing their air horns as they made their way down the turnaround. The Mine Workers and the UAW sent good-sized contingents, too; and even Council 82, the policeman's union, showed up in uniform to help direct traffic. Shortly after that, the journalists began arriving in buses that had been sent up to Buffalo Airport by the campaign. That's how many of them made the trip. And their support trucks followed soon after, idling their engines while the television crews rolled camera carts onto the western lawn and the on-air reporters began rehearsing, turning their made-up faces away from the sun. And even as the hundreds of ordinary guests were streaming from the parking lots into the tent, the local hires were still carting cases of drinks from the back of the maintenance station wagon onto blocks of ice behind the garages; a man I'd never seen before was driving Gil McKinstrey's car, and he would wait only as long as it took to unload one batch of supplies before he headed up the drive for another.

By eleven in the morning, Gil and his crew from town had set up half a dozen bars under the main tent. The common citizens and the union rank and file gathered in clumps around them, while on the other side of the great lawn, under a smaller canopy where waiters moved about with trays, the politicians and the organizers and the union leaders mingled with the reporters. Liam Metarey walked among this crowd. So did Milton Shapp, the governor of Pennsylvania, and Roy Wilkins from the NAACP—later, I heard that Jimmy Hoffa had been there, too—and several of the judges and out-of-state advisors that I'd been seeing around the house. It was an impressive group, but certainly not the most impressive I'd ever seen there.

By noon, the whole tent was full and the crowd had spilled out onto the slope behind the stage. A good part of it was press, maybe three hundred in all, and maybe that number again were political operatives and campaign workers; but the rest were either supporters, or union members, or just townspeople from Saline and Steppan, whom the Senator had invited to swell out his support, and they were pressing in around the spits of roast pig and still clumping around the bars.

I had to agree with Liam Metarey: it was all wrong.

At one point, when I went into the house, I found a man in the living room, picking up the carved turtle ashtrays and examining them, and another man standing in front of the great stone hearth, trying to gauge its height with his arm. Two women were in the downstairs hall, eyeing the rows of photographs on the wall and the long Persian runner on the floor. I doubted that anybody from Saline or Steppan would have been so forward, or even anybody from Islington, but there was another group loitering in the entrance hall under the grand portrait of Eoghan Metarey, and I think it was only his stare that kept them from coming the rest of the way into the house. An unspoken point of decorum seemed to have broken down.

After the pig roast, the plan was for a few local politicians to warm up the crowd—waiters would be circulating with drinks—and after that for the Senator to take the stage. He would talk for twenty minutes, addressing the allegations but then turning quickly to the war, and during his talk the staff would distribute a statement. There would be no questions. This, I understood, was the Senator's own decision: as soon as the speech was over, he would depart for Chattanooga, to give the impression of a normally functioning campaign. And the next day, he hoped, he would wake to find that *The New York Times* and the Nashville *Tennessean* and the Hearst newspapers and the Ridder newspapers and the three evening news shows had all softened their stances against him. Once he'd left, Ray White was going to play, and the crowd would be invited to stay into the night.

To this day I'm a student of politics, and it never fails to surprise me that journalists, and politicians, and all the people whom my profession now calls *opinion makers*, can still be swayed with just a few of the right gifts and the right trips, with just a few of the right drinks and the right singers and the right last names, and that the citizenry, in turn, by the millions and millions, can still be brought in line behind them. And it's only grown worse. Henry Bonwiller has disappeared now from the public eye, and I know, for example, that not many young people the age of my daughters even know who he was anymore. Or that he was instrumental in getting our troops home from Southeast Asia. Or that he funded the environmental protections that cleaned up Lake Erie and Lake Michigan. And the health laws that still allow a pregnant woman in our state, even if she doesn't have any money, to get some of the best medical care in the world for herself and her child. And I suppose nobody rises to a position of power without cunning. But it still surprises me to see, as I have now time and again over the years, the mixture in a single person of such public idealism and such personal ruthlessness.

As lunch was ending, one of the Senator's aides asked me to dolly a split case of vodka and bourbon and a box of mixers upstairs to the south library. This meant that a meeting was planned for later. I wondered what that implied, since the Senator himself would be on his way to Tennessee. Would some of his staff be throwing their support elsewhere? Was a betrayal being contemplated? At this point in the party plenty of liquor still remained, and I put together a case of mixers and a tray of appetizers from the pantry. As another of the state political speakers took the stage, I carried them inside on a kitchen dolly. As I entered the library with it I let the door swing shut, and when I turned to set down the liquor I saw Mr. and Mrs. Metarey on the couch across from a man I didn't recognize. He was sitting in a chair with a small pad open on his lap.

"Hello, Corey," said Mrs. Metarey.

"Excuse me, I didn't know anyone was here."

"Corey," said Mrs. Metarey, "this is our friend Joe Campbell. From the Federal Bureau of Assassination."

"June—" said Mr. Metarey.

The man looked at me briefly, then back at Mr. Metarey.

"He's just having a lovely time at the party. Aren't you, Mr. Campbell?"

"June."

I opened the door and wheeled the dolly back out. As I pulled the knob closed behind me, I heard the man say, "We're offering you the choice, sir."

Outside now, there was a raucous edge to the conversations that spun around me as I wedged and pushed my way through the knots of bodies toward the bar. I had to tell someone. I thought of Christian and even Clara, and for a moment when I glimpsed Governor Shapp in a nearby crowd, I even considered telling *him*; but it was Gil McKinstrey I finally stumbled on, spinning a blender of ice.

"Something's going on," I blurted.

"What is it?" he answered with annoyance, flicking the blender switch to clear the blades.

"Mr. Metarey's upstairs in the south library." I lowered my voice. "I think he's with the FBI."

He turned the blender on and left it running. Then he leaned over. "Two things," he said. "One is that Mr. Metarey can handle anything that comes his way. And two is keep your mouth shut." He nodded toward the thicket of reporters on the other side of the bar.

People pushed past, pressing their way closer to the drinks. What choice was Liam Metarey being given? Was he being asked to force the Senator out of the race? Was that the equation? Was he being coerced to turn against him? To speak as a witness in exchange for immunity? And if he chose not to, was he going to lose that immunity himself?

At that moment something changed in the sound of the crowd, and when I turned I saw Governor Shapp making his way to the front of the tent. Milton Shapp was popular with the unions in those days, and in four years he would run for president himself, so there were a multitude of hands for him to shake as he moved down the aisle toward the stage. Mrs. Metarey and the girls had taken seats in the front row now, and I could see Christian's rose-colored dress and the top of Clara's dark hat. Next to them were two teenage boys, and I recognized Senator Bonwiller's sons. Governor Shapp stopped to shake their hands, too, and Christian looked beautiful when she stood; but as soon as he turned she sat down again. I think she was embarrassed. Flashbulbs were going off around them. I suppose I would have been, too.

Governor Shapp then climbed the stairs to the podium; but when he got there he didn't make any kind of speech. He merely gripped the microphone, introduced Henry Bonwiller with a couple of sentences, and stepped aside before the Senator could shake his hand in front of any cameras.

This, I suppose, was as grave an omen as we would ever receive.

The Senator in the meantime had entered through a flap at the back of the stage, his wife beside him, and now the two of them crossed to the front, holding hands, while Milton Shapp climbed quickly down the stairs; when the Bonwillers reached the podium they raised their arms to the crowd, squinting into the commotion of flashbulbs. Mrs. Bonwiller was a tall, thin-boned woman a few years younger than the Senator. She came from an old southern political family—her father had been an ambassador in the Johnson administration—and I could see the game attempt she was making at composure; but what I remember most from that moment was not her stymied grace or the faint flinching of her jaw but the fact that I saw, as they held their clasped hands up between them, that she looked a little like JoEllen Charney. It was the eyes and mouth.

The applause went on for a long time. I remember being struck by the length of it—and even heartened for a moment, when I looked around the tent and saw that it was being sustained not just by the union rank and file, who filled the better part of a quarter of the seats, but also by the crowds of townspeople from Saline and Steppan, who filled probably another quarter, and who were massed outside on the lawns, as well. The sound hadn't even died out by the time an aide appeared to usher Mrs. Bonwiller off the stage, and then the Senator moved to the podium and had to quiet it with his hand. He proceeded to deliver the speech that Liam Metarey had warned me about.

Judging from the reaction of the several dozen members of the press that I could see, it must have come as a rather steep surprise. Before he was five minutes into it, reporters were already moving toward the teletypes in the garage. I made my way over to the entrance turnaround myself, and by the time he'd finished, raised his arm to the back rows, and strode powerfully to the main door of the tent, I was standing a few steps away from Carlton Sample and the Cadillac. Flashbulbs followed him up the drive. When he reached me, he stopped and turned to the cameras to shake my hand, as though I were a newly convinced voter from the local precinct.

"Underestimated," he whispered.

"Sir?"

"Had to be twenty-five hundred, if there was a person."

"At least, Senator. Maybe three." I lowered my voice. "Sir, Mr. Metarey's—"

"Oh, I like that!" He was smiling broadly while the cameras clicked away. He whispered again, "Three thousand people in a town half the size of a pair of flea's balls!"

He turned to where Carlton Sample had opened the door for him, and I saw then that Mrs. Bonwiller and their two sons were already in the back. "Can't stop the voters," he said. "Can you?" Then he pulled off his suit jacket, rolled up his shirtsleeves, and while the flashbulbs burst in a dizzying crescendo behind him, climbed into the passenger seat and raised his hand one more time to the crowd.

It was only after Carlton Sample had driven away with them that I found the sheet of paper. It had been run over on the gravel.

Later on, of course, I heard that he'd paid a good many of those people to come, thousands of campaign dollars, as it turned out; but lest we forget all the parts of him—lest we recall only the recklessness and the almost metallic vanity, lest we overlook the great, democratic urges and the commanding idealism—lest we lose sight of what kind of man he was in his entirety, here is what that piece of paper said.

Remember his splendid voice:

Ladies and Gentlemen. Members of the press.

Today we find ourselves <u>mortally</u> engaged in one of the <s>preeminent</s> <u>struggles</u> of [DEFINING]
our time. Do not miss the import of these days. We are <u>mortally</u> engaged.
Not only in the jungles of southeast Asia, but here at home.
Across our <u>towns</u>. Across our <u>cities</u>.
(POINT) Across our <u>countryside</u>.

We struggle to <u>rekindle</u> the <u>fire</u> of American <u>democracy</u>.
To <u>build anew</u> on the <u>genius</u> of <u>Thomas Jefferson</u> and <u>James Madison</u>.
To <u>revive</u> again the <u>compassion</u> of <u>Abraham Lincoln</u>.
(QUIET) And the hard-minded <u>decency</u> of <u>Franklin Delano Roosevelt</u>.
To <u>rediscover</u> the courage of our <u>frontiersmen</u>,
Like the <u>courage</u> of my friend and mentor, John F. <u>Kennedy</u>.
To make our own vision as <u>grand</u>, and <s>imposing,</s> and <u>egalitarian</u>, [COURAGEOUS]
as the vision of <u>Lyndon Johnson</u>, and The Great Society.
I repeat: The Great Society.
(SLOW) Even as we struggle to end our <u>tragic war</u> in Vietnam.

Yet as I speak, there are some in power who endeavor to change forever
     —Forever—
The <u>terms</u> of <u>decency</u> that have always marked our way forward.
To negate the <u>struggles</u> and <u>abidances</u> that have been the <u>touchstones</u> of
our past.
     (WAIT)
And will be the <u>touchstones</u> again, of our future,
As we make our way to <u>peace</u>.

My <u>friends</u>. A young woman has died <u>tragically</u>. <s>Many of you are</s> aware of the news. [You are all]
An <u>intelligent</u> and <u>virtuous</u> young woman who I knew from my campaign.
A woman who worked <u>tirelessly</u> for the causes she <u>believed</u> in. For the
causes we <u>all</u> believe in.
Fairness. Peace. Justice.
I stand before you, my fellow citizens,
And I ask that we take a moment to remember her.
(WAIT)
Ladies and Gentlemen, I have been accused of having played a role in this
tragedy. <u>But I had no role in it</u>.
I am accused by rumor and whisper. I am linked by hearsay and innuendo
to a tragedy that, if I had <u>any</u> part in, I would have resigned immediately
from my office, and from this race.
That is what the people of this country have a right to expect.
Ladies and Gentlemen, I am aware every day of the trust you place in me,
I am aware of my obligation to sanctify that trust and make it the stalwart

That's all I have.

I suppose that most people now would take the entire speech as nothing more than self-serving oratory. But with what I know of Henry Bonwiller, finally, I suspect it was more than that, even if it was delivered at such a desperate juncture and filled, as I believe it was, with lies. I think it was in fact the expression of a certain fundamental conviction that he always did maintain—that deep-held sense of what it was like to be excluded from the bounty of this country—which was as essential to his character as to Liam Metarey's own, even if neither by rights deserved to feel it, and even if in the Senator's case it was draped in such perverse and churning narcissism. His speech went on to appeal to the voters to look past his difficulties, and then it turned to a litany of accusations against the president of the United States. He went on almost twice the length Liam Metarey had planned, accusing Nixon of scandalous manipulations of the political process. I saw several reporters shake their heads skeptically—no one had heard yet of Watergate—then down the ends of their drinks. And I realized at that moment that they were not going to spare him.

But on from there he went, extolling his proposals for ending the war, for building a system of nationalized medical care, for offering college tuition grants in return for national service in parks and cities. And at the end, in a steady, quiet voice, came his affirmations that he would never bow to the manipulations of his political enemies, that he would never end his work for the causes of justice and equality and peace, and that he would never drop out of the race.

A few minutes after Carlton Sample had driven away with the four of them, the boom of the campaign jet spread over the land, and in a moment the shining fuselage climbed steeply past. Then it leveled off and banked to the south, toward Chattanooga. If things went well in the press, I knew, he would head to Raleigh-Durham the next day; and if that went well, to Charleston, West Virginia; and then on to Omaha, Nebraska, and Lincoln. Ray White had just taken the stage with his saxophone, and as the plane slanted off into the late afternoon sky he watched it through a flap at the back of the tent, shading his eyes in something like a salute. Then he dropped his hand and blew the first, quiet notes of "Overcome," which in a moment were filled out by a drummer and a bassist and then by a rhythm guitarist, and at last by a piano player, each taking the stage in turn and adding a part until by the end of the song, when the rhythm changes to flat-out bayou R&B, a good part of the crowd literally could not hold itself back from stomping.

It was a bracing moment. Even the reporters, who were lined up for the teletypes the radio booths and the camera setups, couldn't help turning back and listening as the great man played his tribute. It's important to remember that at that point the Senator had probably done more for the causes of civil rights and labor than anyone in congressional history. But then the song was over, and Ray White went into a slow ballad version of "Evelyn Brown," and the reporters continued to leave. Surprisingly, the townspeople began to depart, too, perhaps because they were taking their cues from the press or the political operatives, many of whom would be getting on buses now for the overnight ride to Tennessee. And when that song was over, Ray White looked out at the steadily exiting crowd, raised a hand to still his band, switched his alto instrument for a tenor, and went into his own mournful rendition of "America, the Beautiful."

That's when Clara and her mother moved to the side of the stage. They were conferring about something, and then, as Ray White was still winding up the last, chilling high notes of the final verse, Clara climbed the steps, crossed confidently to the middle of the platform, and whispered in his ear. He nodded, and as soon as she'd stepped back he launched immediately into a foot-pounding rendition of "Curly Dog Eats." I assume she had told him to pick up the tempo, but even as Ray White bent double over his saxophone and his drummer sent a spray of sweat arcing around his set, the crowd continued to make its way out. They filed up the sides of the tent, then into the drive and down the two-track to the waiting cars and buses, and as I watched them I could feel the dwindling of my very last hopes. Dozens of cases of liquor remained in the barn and three more pigs were roasting on the spits. The band played another up-tempo tune. Then another foot-stomper. Then another. At last, sensing perhaps what it all meant, they segued into their great, sad elegy, "Goodbye, Goodman Joe." He was a proud man, Ray White.

The forgotten of this country have a consistent history of turning on their champions, and I suppose the way working men and women have forsaken the very politicians who could help them most speaks of the primacy of emotion in politics. Perhaps the great decline of FDR's party, which was beginning in Henry Bonwiller's time, didn't come about because Democrats favored a logical argument over a moral one, but simply because they clung to the idea that either one mattered at all. Onstage now, as Ray White blew the last slow notes of "Goodbye, Goodman Joe," which die merely to breath, I watched the drummer lay down his sticks; then he set them in their case, looking out dolefully at the shrinking audience. A moment later, Ray White set down his own instrument, nodded his head in farewell, and walked off the stage.

If I learned one thing over my time with Henry Bonwiller, it's that mass politics is an emotional struggle above all, a primal battle that is more charismatic and animalistic than either ethical or reasoned, and as I watched Ray White climb slowly down the steps in front of all those emptying rows of chairs, I had an inkling, well beyond my years or understanding, that I was watching the fall of more than just a single politician. No more than three hundred people remained now, scattered through the tent and lawn.

And by the time the hired boys began cleaning up, perhaps a half hour later, the grounds were nearly empty. Soon the tent workers arrived for the poles and the canopy, and as they waited in their flatbed truck for the chairs to be cleared, Carlton Sample pulled around them and parked the Senator's Cadillac in front of the house; then he emerged in his green chauffeur's jacket and to my surprise set to work with the cleaning crew. He picked up a plastic garbage bag and started walking among the tables, collecting empty cups and dirty napkins. I'd never seen him take part in such a task before. The sack swung from his shoulder and knocked open the flaps of his coat, and he kept glancing back at the house. At one point he even walked over to the car again, let the bag down from his shoulder, and used his cap to shine the door handles. But then he returned to collecting trash. I felt ashamed, somehow, watching him. I suppose he knew the future.

I suppose I knew it, too. And I began to clean up as well. All the seats had to go back to the barn, and I started breaking them down and stacking them on the rolling pallets. By now the weather had evolved into a hot and unpleasantly damp stillness, and for the first time in my life, as I tried to move methodically through the rear of the tent, kicking in the back legs of the chairs so that they fell flat onto the ground in rows, I felt that I didn't have the energy to do my job. I was daunted. I filled two pallets but left the other chairs lying on the grass and set off with a single load toward the house.

I have to admit, I think I was looking for Mr. Metarey. He'd never spoken to me as intimately as he had that morning, and even with what I'd heard later in the library, I think I hoped, with a child's fool-ishness, that I could re-create that earlier moment with him—even if I knew now he'd been drinking. I was hoping he might confide in me again somehow, or at least treat me in the familiar way he had—not necessarily about the episode in the library but about what had happened in its entirety. About Henry Bonwiller's fabulous rise and then his fiery defense. And now his probable fall. About everything that was happening so openly, and yet so mysteriously, in front of me. But it was Mrs. Metarey I found instead, coming around the corner of the house.

"Oh, Corey," she said, stumbling to a stop. "You surprised me. I see our guests have other parties to get to."

"We're all cleaning up."

"Oh, don't," she said. She let out a peal of laughter. "For God's sake, just go enjoy yourself. That's what *I'm* going to do now. God only knows I did what I could. There's nothing else left to do."

"Mrs. Metarey, is everything okay?"

She looked at me.

"With Mr. Metarey," I said.

"Oh, Lord!" she answered, and she nearly shrieked with laughter. "Please go enjoy yourself now."

Please go enjoy yourself. I must say it seemed even stranger from a woman who had comported herself the way she had in the library just a short time before, with what I assumed was the FBI. But I think she must have somehow felt the same lapse in decorum that the rest of the crowd had. To tell the truth, so did I, and this was what at last allowed me to leave off. I moved the pallet of chairs against the side of the porch and walked inside the front door of the house. I also suppose that I knew then without doubt that it was all ending.

Inside the entry, the great capitalist and his canary gazed down at me from the wall. Their two sets of darkly reconnoitering eyes. I tilted my head and stared back. I'd never bothered to look at the whole canvas, I realized. On the table next to Eoghan Metarey's elbow stood a glass of ice water coated with a glinting skin of condensation—the painter's fabulous skill evident in the tiny shining droplets that were nothing more, I saw when I moved closer, than perfectly executed half-moons of gray. I noticed for the first time, as well, that a handful of coins lay almost invisibly among the knots of the table, and that the mantel in the background held an ornately prepared fish on a china plate.

But what was a strangely acute disappointment at that moment was that it had all become commonplace for me. I thought of the onlookers I'd seen earlier in the day, who'd been staring in frank amazement.

For some reason, then, I decided to go upstairs. I'd climbed those steps a hundred times, but now I tried to do it like a newcomer. Like a man fingering the heft of one of the sculpted ashtrays. Christian's room stood directly at the top of the landing, and when my knock wasn't answered I went in and closed the door behind me. I looked carefully around. The bed was covered in its sea-blue Turkish spread, stitched in gold, and on the ledge of the wainscot sat her row of votive candles and her pair of carved African figurines, of a man and woman kneeling. Through the panes of the French door I looked out at the stone porch where we'd kissed a few times, under the limbs of the great pin oak whose spring leaves were newly unrolled—small, pale versions of the elegantly tipped hands that in the summer tapped her window. I crossed finally to the glass and opened it. My memories seemed so distant.

It was from there that I heard the sound of Aberdeen Red. First the revving of the engines, then the softening, then the second revving as it made the turn onto the runway; in a moment the double wings appeared above the trees. They leveled off and then banked to the west, heading toward the lake. There was something elusive in June Metarey, I realized, just as there was in Christian; something that fled when you tried to understand it. But Clara was nonetheless her mother's daughter, just as Christian was her father's, and I had the first inkling then of what I know now from experience—that not only are our parents buried cryptically inside each of us, but that we are buried just as cryptically inside each of them, and that we may look in either direction to see the secrets of our children and of ourselves.

The plane was heading out over the Shelter Brook woods, the wings so low over the hilltops that here and there they vanished into them completely. She was making a line for some distant landmark. How did such freedom not confound a person? If I were Mrs. Metarey, where would I go? To New York City? To Montana? To Canada? Of all the privilege I'd encountered in that house, and of all the magnificence of that world, this was the purest, perhaps, and the one that has remained the most thoroughly foreign to me. There was nothing stopping her from anything. There was nothing stopping any of them.

Soon the fuselage was only a dark hash mark in a wafer of white sky at the horizon. But there, just where it would have disappeared, it banked suddenly upward, then leveled again, and I stayed at the window long enough to understand that it had turned back. Now it was heading toward us again. All along the contours of the land, the woods had come into leaf, and the canopy was a sea of pale green darkened only by the undulations of the hills and the long, leading shadow of the plane. I realized that I'd never seen it fly this late in the afternoon.

I stepped back into the hallway. It occurred to me that I didn't know what kind of family June Metarey had come from, and as I glanced at the long rows of pictures hung on the walls there it came to me that she might have been heading back to her own people. This might have been where she was going, until she'd changed her mind at the horizon and turned the nose toward home again. As I made my way down the corridor toward the library, I looked carefully at each one of the photos—photos that I'd passed dozens of times on my trips upstairs with newspaper sticks and drinks and firewood. What I saw now was that they all seemed to be of the Metarey clan; I found none of June Metarey herself as a child—I was searching for what might look like a ranch out west—and none of what might have been her own family. I remembered suddenly her words in the library about Eoghan Metarey—who was her relation only by marriage—words of such fierce reverence that until that moment, I realized, I'd thought she'd been speaking of her own father.

I don't know how June Metarey felt about all that had just happened with Henry Bonwiller. She was ambitious—that, I know. I would say that she was even more ambitious than her husband, and that because she was so finely tuned to that kind of yearning she understood better than anyone else its perils. But she was also not one to give up. She seemed to have lived, for reasons I will never know, so close to desperation for so long that I suspect its shade seemed not like the coming of night to her, as it must have seemed to Mr. Metarey, but merely the condition of the earth. Henry Bonwiller had overcome difficulties before. He had a formidable army of supporters: he could overcome them again.

But as the father now of daughters, I don't think it would have been possible for Liam Metarey—whose girls were at the age my youngest is today—to be as sanguine.

At the entrance to the library, I paused, aware that Gil McKinstrey was probably wondering where I was. But still I wanted to go in. It was why I'd come inside, of course: to find Mr. Metarey. And to help him. But the tall, hand-carved double doors stood closed before me, and for the first time in all my days there I was afraid of knocking. What if he was still in there with the FBI? What if under duress he'd turned on the Senator? Or showed a side of himself that he never wanted me—never wanted anyone—to see?

It was my desire that stayed me. My desire to talk to him again. If an agent was in there, maybe Mr. Metarey would pass something on to me, to tell his wife or the Senator. Or perhaps he would say something outright about the situation. On the other hand, if he was alone, as I suspected he might be by now, and if he was relaxed enough even after all the events of the day, then maybe I would get to have another conversation with him. Perhaps he would say something about what had happened.

But sure enough, I became aware then of Gil McKinstrey's muffled voice: "Corey!" he was calling. "Corey Sifter!"

I looked out the staircase window behind me and saw him on the gravel drive to the side of the hay gable. "Corey Sifter!" he called sharply. "Where in God Bless are you, boy!" He smacked his hand against his hip the way he did calling Breighton. Then he disappeared into the barn.

I knocked quickly on the door of the library, and when there was no answer I pushed it open. The room was empty. This was a disappointment, of course. But as I glanced through the windows at the hired hands moving all about the lawn, I was unprepared for how deeply the combination of disappointment and my own uncharacteristic evasion of work—as well as the fact that in the last few minutes I'd somehow understood the true magnitude of the family's impending failure—I was unprepared for how deeply these things would strike me. I actually had to sit down. I pulled a chair to the center table.

On the blotter in front of me were a couple of used lunch plates and their wineglasses, and instinctively I began to gather them to take downstairs. Next to the plates was a pile of books. For some reason, I spread them on the table.

I became a newspaperman, as I said before, for reasons that most profoundly had their effect on me at Dunleavy and Haverford. At both places, I'd simply fallen in love with books—first off, with Mark Twain's. But soon with Dickens's and Dostoyevsky's and even Hegel's, and later with A. J. Liebling's and James Agee's and Jacob Riis's and H. L. Mencken's. And I think when I found these later ones I was hastened to them out of my powerful memories of both Glenn Burrant and G. V. Trawbridge. Yet there's more to it than that. As time passed and my generation quieted, my acquaintances at Haverford eventually became businessmen and lawyers, just like their fathers; and some of them no doubt began to contemplate running for the statehouse then, or for Congress, or even for president. None of which I could ever imagine. I found out earlier than most about ambition— about real ambition—from my time at the Metareys'. And that's another reason why I do what I do.

At the table, I began looking through the titles. As I did, I heard Gil McKinstrey call again. The sound of my name was faint but there was no mistaking the irritation now in his voice, and I rose and crept toward the window until I saw him standing beneath the hay pulley again. He was hitching up a pallet of chairs, and he called out another time, but he was looking the other way, toward the tent. At that moment, Aberdeen Red appeared above the trees, and I watched it bank above him and turn in the direction of the strip.

When I stepped back from the window again, to hide from Gil, I happened to notice that one of the books on the table was *The Jungle*, by Upton Sinclair, which Mr. Metarey had mentioned to me. And of course this only quickened my desire to see him. So I pushed aside the rest of the stack and picked it up in my hands—the very copy that now sits in my office, next to Mencken's *Newspaper Days*—and then

I moved across the back of the room toward the stand-up reading desk by the door. I only wanted to impress him. Or to be friendly with him somehow. To show him that I was in fact worthy of some portion of the generosity he had shown me. I opened the leather binding against the platen, and—just for a few moments—I began to read.

My back was to the window, then, when it happened, and I didn't see it. I only heard it.

But I know now that such a sound is unmistakable.

First the quick, accelerating roar of the engine; then the mallet blow. The desk shook. Then: silence. The impact occurred in the second stand of oak and larch on the far side of the corral, a quarter mile short of the landing strip. I ran to the window and yanked it open. The plume of smoke was instant. A nefarious black twister surging straight up over the windless field. In a moment the spell of stillness lifted and was replaced by a soft crackling. And in another moment, by a pair of rapid explosions, one and then the other. Now the billowing cloud churned higher, broken suddenly by two leaping towers of flame that shot above the branches. "Gil!" I shouted. "It's Mrs. Metarey!" I ran to the east windows and thrust them open. "It's Aberdeen Red! It's Aberdeen Red!" Then I ran the other way, out the door and down the stairs through the house, calling out. I could hear others shouting as well, but there was no answer, only more calls and the sound of the servants' running feet, then one of the maids in the hallway saying she thought Mr. Metarey had gone into town. She picked up the phone on the wall and tried to dial but seemed to be overcome and collapsed into a chair. I ran into Mr. Metarey's back-porch study to look for him, and into the first-floor conference room. Then I sprinted down the stairs toward the woods, shouting his name.

How do each of us come to understand what is never spoken? By what constellation of gesture and avowal, by what detail of comportment or tone do we discern the dark, inobvious intent of those around us? The earliest real words Liam Metarey ever spoke to me—"work will set you free"—returned to me with a shock when I came upon them again, six years later, on my first trip to Europe, and only suggested once more that our worlds—our lives—are not at all what they appear. That all of us, no matter how difficult this may be to accept, are merely marking a course set early in our days. June Metarey's political shrewdness had carried her—had carried both of them—so very far, but her dismal prophesying, which seemed so basic to her character, was what turned out to be the truth.

The black plume was already spreading over the land. Within a few minutes, the lone fire engine from Saline sped through the gates, but when it drove down the embankment onto the wooded flats we found that the two-track was not wide enough to let it through. The firemen clamped all the hoses together into one and ran it through the woods. But still it wouldn't reach. They shouted into their radios, even though it was obvious that nothing they could do would matter: by the time they reached the clearing, the plane was a roiling mass of flame and acrid black smoke that billowed over itself and flooded the sky. In the spreading gloom, the twin leaping spires of orange sent shadows dancing against the trees. The smoke kept pouring. A human being couldn't even approach it—I know because I tried to. The oaks near the impact had been immolated, and the stinking cloud bellowed horrifically now from the center of its own clearing. Around it stood a circle of larches with their needles burnt off.

I stood thirty yards away. The smoke kept rising, a whole black mountain now that struck a ceiling above us and spread across the sky. The stench of gasoline and charred rubber was foul in the air. The light had already grown dusky, and soon it was like night. Every time I looked I knew I was seeing Mrs. Metarey's obscenely hellish grave but at the same time I could barely turn away my gaze. There is no approaching that kind of horror. The scene seemed to be taking place behind a window of warped black glass, and in the throng of confusing figures and fleeting light I turned left and right. I think I was looking for Christian and Clara. I say I think because I really don't know. It had occurred to me that my job now was to help them, but my mind had trouble seizing on a single fact, especially one like that. I just kept turning back to the roaring, churning center. That's how a person reacts, I discovered. Or at least, that's how I did.

For some reason I decided then that I needed a tool for clearing away the brush, and with a strange concentration I began to look for something. More fire trucks had arrived by now, and when I found a hatchet leaning against the wheel of one of them, I picked it up and brought it back down to the edge of the clearing. The fire spurted lower tendrils now but was still dazzlingly bright in the darkness, and the smoke still poured skyward. The brush and grasses had caught in a hundred places, too, and webs of low flames crisscrossed the uphill paths in a shimmering maze of red and orange, like lava emerging from the earth. But these burns were petty affairs: some of the firemen even walked right through them. Of course I knew a hatchet was useless. But still I stood with it in my arms. I was actually aware now that my mind wasn't working properly but I seemed to lack the discipline to do anything about it. I saw Christian and Clara in every dark-suited figure moving in the shivering light, and I saw Mr. Metarey every time someone ran down the hill. At one point I even looked into the horrific mass and saw June Metarey's black skeleton suspended by its shoulder belts over the cockpit; a moment later I saw it climb out over the wing between low licks of blue flame and jump to the ground. I shook my head to clear it. I'm sure I was in tears.

It was obvious that nothing would even be recognizable by the time it finally burnt out, and at this point Gil McKinstrey came down from the shed on the Ferguson with a cart full of chain saws and set to work with the firemen cutting a break, farther out among the smaller birch. In a moment I joined them, and I have to say it was bracing to finally do something. My mind cleared a bit. It was not difficult to stay out of the smoke, which still raced upward but didn't spread until it had overreached the trees. We notched the trunks so that they toppled away from the center, and in a short time we'd cleared a rim. At that point there was not much else to do but stand

and watch. A wreath of flickering blue flame now snaked around the dark nucleus. Several maids were standing near the barn, and when I looked up I saw in the revolving glow of the engine's lights that they were weeping.

I turned back to the woods. At that moment Gil McKinstrey abruptly dropped his chain saw and took off up the hill. A second later, I saw the lights of the Chrysler coming down through the front gates. And that's when I began to cry in earnest. Like a child who manages to restrain himself until his parents come home. And though I'm ashamed to say it, I wanted badly—for some child's reason as well—I wanted badly to be the one to tell Mr. Metarey. I started to run toward him, even though now I could hardly make out anything through my tears. I was trying to get ahead of one man to tell another that his wife had just been killed. But Gil's distorted shape was already over the nearside berm, and after just a few steps I stopped and simply stood at the edge of the trees, wiping my eyes so that at least I could see him as he sprinted across Breighton's corral, jumped the fence, and then slowed to a trot on the upper drive where the car had come to a halt. He leaned up to the windshield, and suddenly his hand went to his face. He had to grab hold of the hood. Carlton Sample emerged from the driver's seat, and a moment later the back door opened and first Christian, then Clara, and then June Metarey stepped onto the gravel.

And my question is: How did I know, just an instant before?

I think sometimes of his last moments. He would have felt the wind, seen his broad sea of oaks approaching. Then their limbs. He would have noticed their new, pale leaves. All of them fluttering in the approaching wake. Is he looking at them? Are his eyes open? I think they are. I see him moving down through their shivering embrace, their tips first brushing his wings, then folding over them. The leaf of the red oak divides at its margins into lobes that end in a point; the same lobe on a white oak curves to a rounded edge; and the leaf of the black oak is distinguishable from the red only by its variegated size. The great mysterious work of God. I see his arms out in the open cockpit. I see him parting the air with his outstretched hands. Is he shouting? I don't think so. I think he's quiet, actually. Quiet as the greenery comes loose and rains in every direction around him. Quiet as his worries are jettisoned first in the heave and then in the snap of the first great branches. Quiet as his father's land with its frail meadow of sprouting acorns reaches up to take him.

TEN

As we reach level ground, my father laughs suddenly, shaking his head. Then he says, "The Oaks."

"Yes?"

"That's what they're calling it."

"Calling what?"

"The new place. The mall."

It's a little easier for him to talk now because we're out of the hills. We're coming down from our regular outing in the Shelter Brook Set-Aside, the land that Liam Metarey preserved. Every week, we take a meandering hike up the short slope that looks over the last stretch of undeveloped terrain between the old Silverton Orchards and Saline.

"Well," I say, "I guess there's nothing I'd put past them. Just surprised I hadn't heard about it."

"Don't worry." He turns up his boot sole to pick a stone out of it. "You're only a newspaper guy."

He rubs his hands, then leans them on his knees to rest.

"Last to know," I say.

"Last to be told, at least." He grins from his bent position. Then he stands. "That's just how they do it now," he says. "Build the whole thing in secret. Guys on the job can't even talk. Not if they want to have a job in the morning. Just deliver a wrapped package. At Christmas."

We start to walk again. He's still in reasonable shape, but recently the hills have been tougher for him. We used to do three or four of them. Now we do two, or sometimes one.

"That guard told me on the way in," he says. "You know, he's Murph Mills's boy."

"I know, Dad," I say. "You already told me." We're near the parking lot now. He's looking down as he walks, the way he does these days, not watching anything in particular. A peaceful expression, really, in the low afternoon light. A little sleepy, maybe. A touch of consternation. "Dad," I say, "how old would Murph Mills's boy be now?"

"Hmmph." He pulls off his Yankees cap and scratches his head with the bill. Then, as though finally remembering, he mutters, "Christ."

"Maybe you mean Murph Mills's grandson."

"What's the goddamn difference?"

And for the rest of the way we walk in silence.

AUTOPSY REPORT

NAME: Charney, JoEllen Marie   AUTOPSY NO: A72-11
DOB: 1/19/45   DEATH D/T: 12/16/71-12/24/71
AGE: 26   AUTOPSY D/T: 1/27/72 @ 0930
SEX: F   ID NO: 37GH24
PATH MD: Fitzpatrick   ME/MEDREC#: 0172-37924
TYPE: M.E.

FINAL DIAGNOSIS:

    1) Hypothermia
        A. Vitreous Glucose 84.5 mg/dL
        B. Wischnewski ulcers
        C. Diffuse erythema
        D. Acute pancreatitis
    2) Head Injury
        A. Scalp abrasion/contusion, right temporal area, minor
    3) Muskulo-skeletal injuries
        A. Fracture, left 5th finger, distal phalanx
        B. Fracture, left 5th finger, proximal phalanx

Toxologic studies:
Blood alcohol: 0.14%
Blood toxic substances: none detected

CLINICOPATHOLOGIC CORRELATION: Cause of death of this 26-year-old white female is accidental hypothermia secondary to alcohol-induced ataxia and fall.

                    By

Clyde R. Fitzpatrick, MD
Pathologist

bsc/1/27/72

IT ISN'T UNTIL A COUPLE OF WEEKS LATER, as we're driving home from another outing, that Dad says, "Then how come you didn't ask me about the date?"

"How come I didn't ask you about what date?"

He's looking out his window, showing me only the back of his ball cap. "The one I put in the concrete. I know it's not 1971."

We're near Walnut Orchards. The terrain is really quite beautiful here, a run of shallow, overlapping hills that are staggered from the glacier's first track through the basin, the low horizon striped by the shadows of their intersecting valleys.

"I have to admit," I say, "I was a little worried."

"Then why didn't you say something?"

"Same reason, I guess."

He thinks about that. Or seems to. He's still looking out the window. We're at the edge of the Shelter Brook Set-Aside, which is a surprisingly large piece of land, even for the Metareys—the largest single conservation in the western half of the state. The north edge runs from the end of the old Silverton Orchards all the way to within a couple of miles of where Dad lives now. And some of the retired farmers who own the parcels adjoining it have given sections, too, or have allowed paths to be built on the acreage they'll own until they die, so that today if you walk every inch of the winding, gravel paths you'll cover something like 350 miles. You cross Little Shelter Brook now on arched footbridges made of timbers, and you can relieve yourself in bathroom huts hidden at the sides of the trails and rest on iron benches at the hilltops. From a few of those benches, you can see the red-tile peak of the Target store and the wavy blue NABO of the CINNABON sign at the Oaks, and from the ones at the north end you can hear the trucks on 35; but from others you can look thirty miles into nothing but meadow and hilltop, and along the pastures you can watch whole families of deer not twenty yards away, standing on the grassy banks like girls in heels.

He still hasn't turned from the car window. "You and Dr. Jadoon," he says evenly.

"What about us?"

"You're always trying to trip me up." He lowers the glass partway down and tosses out the stem of the crab apple that he's picked up on our walk. "Both of you together. I know how you work. Every chance you get, you test my memory. See what the old man can do. I'm not senile, you know. You think I don't see it?"

"Well, I guess this time I wasn't."

"Wasn't what?"

"Testing you."

"This morning," he says, "I was reading the *People's History of the United States*." He turns. "Howard Zinn. Is that good enough for you?"

"It's good, Dad. It's very good."

"You know what that date was?" He bites into the tiny apple now and makes a sour face.

I think about it for a while. "No, I don't," I finally say.

He looks over at me, rather smugly. "It's the last time we were together."

"I don't get it, Dad."

"The last time we were *all* together." He takes another bite and makes another sour face. "*All* of us. It was the seventh. September 7th, 1971. The day you went off to—to whatever the name of that school was. I told your mother it was the end of our lives together. That day."

"Dunleavy," I say.

"I said to her you were leaving us for good."

"I wasn't, Dad. I wasn't at all."

"I didn't want you to go, you know. But your mother thought it was some kind of great chance. God rest her soul."

"You didn't want me to go?"

"No sirree. She was the one who did. Wanted to give you the opportunity. We argued like hell."

"I never would have guessed."

"I know you wouldn't have. That's why I'm telling you now." He raises his eyebrows. "For the historical record." He takes another bite and purses his lips. "It went on for weeks. I thought it was the worst thing you could do. But it doesn't matter anymore. That's one of the things about life, isn't it?" He chews deliberately, his skinny throat bobbing. "These things aren't so bad," he says, holding out the chewed core, "once you get used to them. Dunleavy—that's it. I can never remember that name. It was a Monday, I think. September seventh. Or it might have been a Tuesday. That's right. You might have started on a Tuesday, for whatever reason. Maybe because of Labor Day."

"Ironic."

"Yes, it is."

He bites again.

"There's a guy on my hall," he says. "Leo Something—he can tell you the day if you give him the date. It takes him about thirty seconds. We'll ask him when we get back."

"You didn't want me to go?"

"No, I didn't, son."

"But you told me you did."

"Did I? As far as I was concerned, you were going to the other side."

"And did I?"

He looks at me. "Well, I don't know," he says after a moment. "I really don't." Then he laughs and adds, "But that's the way the world works, isn't it? When the guys started using PVC instead of iron, I was going to quit the trade. But I went over to their side, too, in the end. And I loved it." He lifts his shoulders, the weaker one lagging behind under his shirt. "Might have saved my joints if I'd done it earlier."

"Dad," I say. "What do you think about me being a newspaper-man?"

"Me?" he answers. "What do I know? English was never my subject."

"Did you even take English?"

"No." He flicks a tiny apple seed off his pant leg. "They didn't offer it to kids like me."

"How much *are* you reading these days, Dad?"

"A lot."

"How much?"

"Well, you know something—I found out I'm good at it. Who would have thought it? Your old man. Fast, I guess. Never would have known. A couple of books a week, maybe—seems about natural to me. Not bad for a plumber, huh? Never took English class in my life."

"You read two books a week?"

"About."

We're at Walnut Orchards now, and I turn into the lot. "Wow, Dad," I say. "Why now?"

"Why now?" This seems to stop him. "Well, for one thing, my schedule's not what it used to be." He kicks the Camry's footwell, leans forward, and picks the loosened bits of dirt from his boots. A look appears in his eyes. "But I guess it's also what they always say—because there are a lot of books."

I stop the car in front of the door to his hall, but he makes no move to get out. He pushes the dust into a little pile on the floor mat instead, then sweeps it into his palm, his fingers shaking a little. "And all this reading *you* get paid to do," he adds, opening the door finally and dropping his handful of dirt onto the asphalt. "It must be quite a life."

"It is, Dad. It is."

"Well, it must be." Then he offers, "But I still miss you."

"I'm right here, Dad."

"I've missed you ever since you went off to your new life." He shrugs on one side. "You were always ambitious, you know. Your mother encouraged it. I couldn't stop it, I guess. And now I'm glad I didn't."

"I don't think of myself as ambitious."

"Oh, but you are. It's just the way you've always been."

He's raising himself now on the door handle, and it takes him several moments to wrestle himself free of the seat. But I know not to offer to help. "And when you get down to it," he says, standing up at last on the lot. "Mr. Metarey wasn't even the one who sent you to Dunleavy."

"You and Mom had to have a part in it, too—I know."

He leans back down to the window. "Actually," he says softly, "that's not what I'm talking about." His hands are shaking a little more. "What I'm talking about is Eugene McGowar. Him and his men and all the men like him. I hope you haven't forgotten that they're the ones who really sent you."

"Oh, I see what you mean, Dad. Yes, I know that."

He looks down at the floor of the car. "Mr. Metarey gave you things I couldn't, son. I understand that. He was a better father than I could be."

I shut off the engine. "Dad—is that what you think?"

"It's what I know, Cor. And it's okay with me. We've all come out better for it, haven't we?" His eyes rise to mine. "And I know you did things for him in return—for Henry Bonwiller. For both of them, I'm talking about. I know you did things—I don't know exactly what." He stands again and turns.

"What, Dad?"

"Well," he says, looking back for a moment just before he walks away, "Henry Bonwiller was the best friend the working men of this country have ever had."

BY THE FOLLOWING SATURDAY, when Mr. Metarey's funeral was held, a high fence had been built around the crash site. The NTSB had arrived within half a day of the accident, three men in a government car who spent a couple of hours with their Polaroid cameras in the acrid-smelling wreckage and then drove back to Buffalo. Later that morning, Glenn Burrant showed up, his flip-back reporter's notebook in his hand. From the barn I saw him sitting on a toolbox next to the destroyed plane as the hired carpenters nailed in the last of the fence boards in front of him. Then he straightened his tie and walked back to the house. He was still pale when I opened the door of the Corvair for him that afternoon, as he was leaving. "Never thought it would end like *this*," he said softly, climbing into the driver's seat. He looked as ashen as any of us.

"Nobody did," was all I could think of to answer.

That day there was all kinds of somber activity on the estate, and I, like the rest of the staff, had come in to help. But I don't think it was until that evening that Gil looked up from a box he was taping shut and said, "You know, has anybody seen Churchill?"

I think of that dog, too. I think of Mr. Metarey's hand on his eager head.

I think of Liam Metarey who had no training in aviation but could build an engine from parts. I think of Liam Metarey who had directed the great instruments of his father's fortune, who had lifted the weight of that fortune into the next realm of influence and station. Of Liam Metarey who could break a horse and use a tap and dye as well as any man in Carrol County, who could rebuild a set of valves and pistons in his barn. Of Liam Metarey who had given me a good many of the great gifts of my life and to whom I shall remain indebted forever. He was a man—like his father, I now believe, and like his younger daughter—a man for whom the poles of grandiosity and despair had come loose from their yoking. Like many other men of such achievement. Yet he was unfailingly kind to me. No matter what happened.

His generosity foreshadowed his end in a way that seems obvious now—for who else gives away so much? And I like to believe that his last moments were not shot through with fear but with calm, even if they were darkened by the fierce calamity of his intent. I don't think

Henry Bonwiller, or JoEllen Charney, or anything about the turn of events were the causes of his demise but merely the tools of it, which, as I consider him, I realize he had always sought, at greater and greater altitude, with all the energy of his mind, over all the days of his reign. Such a great man was he for tools.

I think of him all the time. To this day.

Henry Bonwiller, of course, spoke at the funeral. And I think it was this large but plain gathering, more than any understanding of his own deeds or any flight from the brutal turn of the campaign, that prompted him finally to do what he did. He was a monstrously ar-mored man—how could he not be?—but that does not mean he was impregnable. The service was simple. Four men to bear the coffin— Gil McKinstrey, two of Mr. Metarey's cousins, and Andrew, who had flown home again on leave—and just two speakers, the minister and Henry Bonwiller, who had gone on from Chattanooga to Raleigh-Durham the day after the crash, but then canceled the trip to West Virginia. He stood before the assemblage at Trinity Episcopal Church in Saline and bowed his head.

The nave was full to standing and still dozens of rows of folding chairs were lined up outside the open doors. He lifted his tired face to the crowd and spoke about how long he had known Liam Metarey, and what a trusted friend he had been. I know some of those in the audience were reporters—they were not officially wel-come, but they came anyway, Glenn Burrant among them. My fa-ther was there, too, of course, sitting beside Mr. McGowar—the second time in my life that I'd seen them together in their suits. So were hundreds of townspeople. Henry Bonwiller didn't go on for long, and he was so moved—or perhaps he was just so expert a showman—that he abandoned his oratory and merely spoke in a gruff monotone into the microphone, barely above a whisper. His voice carried out through the nave and onto the grounds where I was standing. I wanted to be behind everybody, for some reason. To see them. Or maybe so that they could not see me. Andrew and Christian and Clara sat together with their mother at the front, and even from outside the church I could see them lined up in the pew. I had to turn away.

Henry Bonwiller finished his eulogy by taking a folded sheet from his breast pocket and reading aloud the Auden poem "Museé des Beaux Arts," which I still read now, every year, on Liam Metarey's birthday.

About suffering they were never wrong,
The Old Masters; how well, they understood
Its human position; how it takes place
While someone else is eating or opening a window or just walking
                                        dully along;
How, when the aged are reverently, passionately waiting
For the miraculous birth, there always must be
Children who did not specially want it to happen, skating
On a pond at the edge of the wood:
They never forgot
That even the dreadful martyrdom must run its course
Anyhow in a corner, some untidy spot
Where the dogs go on with their doggy life and the torturer's horse
Scratches its innocent behind on a tree.
In Breughel's Icarus, for instance: how everything turns away
Quite leisurely from the disaster; the ploughman may
Have heard the splash, the forsaken cry—

He looked out at the audience. Many of us were weeping. Presently, his lips clenched, he nodded, turned to the coffin, and saluted it. Then he returned the folded sheet to his coat pocket and spoke the rest from memory:

But for him it was not an important failure; the sun shone
As it had to on the white legs disappearing into the green

Water; and the expensive delicate ship that must have seen
Something amazing, a boy falling out of the sky,
        had somewhere to get to and sailed calmly on.

For a moment he stood straight, as though to gather himself. Then he leaned down to the microphone and whispered, "I shall seek no higher."

Even the reporters, I think, thought it was just another line in the poem.

ELEVEN

I DON'T KNOW EXACTLY WHEN it happened, but sometime during the winter of my senior year at Dunleavy, Glenn Burrant disappeared from his job. The summer before, after Mr. Metarey's accident and the end of the campaign, I'd stopped reading the paper, nearly altogether, and I didn't start again till my last semester was almost over. Once more I was rooming with Astor, and I was still going back to Saline occasionally on weekends—to be with my dad, mostly, even though he said he didn't need me. Frankly, the events of the preceding months had shaken my resolve, and any number of times that year I felt that I might quit school. It was only my loyalty to my mother and my gratitude to Mr. Metarey, I think, that kept me there.

And yet at the same time, and especially with my mother gone from the house on Dumfries, I'd also begun that year to think of Dunleavy as my home. Or at least I'd begun to feel as comfortable there as I did on my weekends back in Saline. I didn't have as many friends as Astor did, but I wasn't an outsider anymore either, and I found that there was something at school that I enjoyed now each day: soccer, European history, singing, the long Friday evening meal when the freshmen performed their skits for us in the dining hall. In November, Nixon had been reelected by the second largest landslide in history.

Other things about me were changing, too. My grades were still good, but I no longer felt the need to be at the very top of my class. I slept in now till seven-fifteen, waking when Astor's alarm went off and hurrying to class with him, and at night I sat around sometimes with a group of our friends instead of going by myself to study. I watched TV for my news, whatever glimpses I could catch between the cartoons and sports that were always playing on the set in the commons. In my desk drawer, I still kept my well-creased copy of Vance Trawbridge's "A Bonwiller Presidency," but it wasn't until the waning days of March, when the new grass was making its first push through the winter blanket, that I found myself in the library stacks again, standing, for the first time in a long while, at the rack of newspapers.

It was a Wednesday, and Monday morning's *Courier-Express* had been placed neatly on the top shelf. I didn't really have much desire to read Glenn's work anymore, but I opened to the editorial page anyway, out of some old habit. His column wasn't there. That stopped me, somehow. The library kept only a month's supply of back issues, and I went to them; but it wasn't in any of those Monday papers, either, and it wasn't in any of the other days'. That's when I realized he'd been fired.

"Why do you say fired?" Trieste asks.

"His column was gone."

"He could have just gone on to a bigger paper."

"But he hadn't," I say. "I just knew it." We're in the newsroom, late on a fall evening, and she's getting ready to leave again. This has become the time we talk.

"If *I* said that I just *knew* something, Mr. Sifter," she answers, taking the duster from its peg, "you'd send me home."

"But I did. I just *knew*." I look over my glasses at her. "Call it reporter's instinct."

She examines me. Then she says, "Which is, of course, merely say-ing that you thoroughly understood the issue."

"Maybe."

"Was he fired because of what he knew?"

"That's all I can guess."

"Come on. You told me the *Courier-Express* was such a liberal paper."

"Henry Bonwiller was a liberal candidate."

"Why didn't Glenn Burrant just publish his story somewhere else?"

"Because things were different then. He couldn't just put it up on his blog. And he wasn't the kind of guy who could just walk into any newsroom and get a job. He smelled like a dill pickle."

She laughs at this, but only for a moment. "But they knew his rep-utation, didn't they?"

"They knew it up here."

"And too many people up here are grateful to the Metareys. Is that it, Mr. Sifter?"

"And too many were in the Senator's pocket."

She closes the buttons on the duster. It's a fine evening, but as the nights have grown colder now she's taken to wearing it every day, rain or shine. "What do you think he *knew*, then?" she says.

"I don't know the answer to that. I don't know if it was something about Anodyne or something about JoEllen." I look at her. "Or even something about the president. But I think he knew something. I think he'd gotten inside somehow. He was a very good reporter, you know. Not just because he did his research, but because he had the ability to imagine what it was like to be his subject. Remember what he wrote me? That every man is his own hell?"

"That's Mencken, too, sir. I looked it up."

"Very good, Trieste. The thing is, I don't think he meant it about himself. I think he meant it about Henry Bonwiller. Or sometimes I think Nixon."

She's standing at the door now. "Or Liam Metarey."

"Possibly."

We're silent while she finds her bicycle key in her waist pack.

"Either way," I say, "it shows that he could put himself in someone else's existence. That's the way he worked. What he found out about those faked letters to *The Union Leader*—that was even before Woodward and Bernstein."

"And *that's* why he was fired?"

"It's all a guess. The Bonwillers' reach was long. But the president's was long, too."

"Have you tried to find him?"

I consider whether to answer this. Finally, I say, "I *have* found him, Trieste."

She sits down again, at a desk by the door. "You have?"

"He's living in Ottawa. He's a retired high school history teacher."

"Have you gotten in touch with him?"

"No. He knows who I am and what I do. If he'd wanted to get in touch with me, he would have done it a long time ago."

"I see," she says. She rises again.

"Nothing will bring JoEllen Charney back."

"Yes, I know." She looks at me. Then she steps through the door, walks slowly down the stairs, and is gone.

That spring at Dunleavy, I wrote Glenn another letter, but it was returned as undeliverable. And at Haverford, whenever I was in the library, I took to reading newspapers again—the bigger ones, like the *Globe* and the *Post* and the *Times*—hoping, as some small part of my thinking, that I would one day find his byline. But I knew—I just *knew*—what had happened. And years later, when I was a newspaperman myself and the Internet was first emerging, when news reporting had begun its tidal shift, I began to look again, this time through search engines. But it wasn't long before I understood that these, too, would turn up nothing. Whatever Glenn Burrant knew—whatever he'd discovered about JoEllen, or Anodyne, or Nixon himself—whatever it was, he'd decided to walk away with it.

THESE DAYS CLARA STILL SPENDS a fair amount of time trying to re-habilitate her father's name. I have to say, I admire her perseverance but for a long time was surprised by it. She's methodical at the task. Every time the question of Liam Metarey's part in the scandal is dredged up, she'll write to *The Plain Dealer* or the *Globe* or the *Inquirer* proclaiming his innocence, and whenever a new book comes out, she'll write again, this time to the literary supplements, and she'll visit the author lectures in Cleveland and Buffalo and sometimes Albany to make her points in the question-and-answer periods afterward. She goes to all the fund-raising dinners for the state Democratic Party and makes the rounds there in support of her father's reputation, as well. It's not what you might have predicted.

If a man shall begin in certainties, he shall end in doubts. That's the accurate quotation: it's Francis Bacon. I happened upon it recently in a history of Enlightenment Europe. But Clara if nothing else proves the obverse: for she hasn't ended in doubts. How was I to know that the girl who burned her father's toolshed and jumped off his boat, the girl who seemed to be trying her best to derail his fortunes and interpose herself into the most serious of his aspirations would then devote the material energy of her middle years to bestowing an unlikely knighthood on his name? How was I to know that my wife would be the most fervent defender of a family that she had mocked and bucked against so much of the time I knew her?

Or perhaps I did know. Perhaps we both did.

Liam Metarey remains a mystery to me to this day. I knew him for what he seemed to be in the eyes of a sixteen-year-old boy who had never even earned a living on his own. In retrospect I understood almost nothing. Was he kind to me? Always. Was he honest with me in his dealings? Overwhelmingly, yes. The miscalculation he made was a miscalculation principally of loyalty, I think now, less to a man than to a cause, and when he made it I can only think that he was envisioning the greater future for many more than just himself. And there is the matter of his own past, too, which was an entirely foreign thought to a boy my age then. What was it like to have taken the mantle of that great family, taken it from a man as vicious and single-minded as his father? A man not poor and then rich, but both together at the same time, rich and poor, all his life, just the way Liam Metarey was. But unlike the son, the father was merciless all through it. Was the mercilessness the lesson the son finally took? The lesson that in the end failed him?

That is just a guess on my part, of course, but it is a guess that Clara agrees with. Her grandfather died before she was born, and so I will never know the true nascence, the story of the ruthless American pioneer, the man who brought forth such a powerful family the way one brings forth a machine, a lever that multiplies its force as it swings into the new century and the new world. This new world was the America of coal and electricity and the great steel railroads, where hard work and tightly lashed ambition and what today we might call unchecked avarice created the first royalty in a new land. That's the lineage Liam Metarey was born into, and it's the lineage that produced that one decision, I think, made in some kind of panic perhaps, but nonetheless made, one snowy afternoon thirty-five years ago.

It's also the lineage that our own children will carry. And I wonder all the time how this will play out. I see it over and over again in my wife's letters to newspapers and in her unflagging arguments at dinner parties. There it is again, the reach of families like hers, the solid wall against the onslaught. But I must say I respect it—I respect it greatly—in Clara, and sometimes I think it is evidence of the very wound that makes me love her.

I wonder sometimes what she might ever have seen in me, a boy who in another life might have strived for nothing more than a living wage and weekends. But I suppose the answer to this, again, is that I am like her father. Which is in a way saying that my own father was like hers, and that this is how we recognized each other. Her family produced the great patriarch, and now with each generation, as Trieste might say, we regress closer to the mean. How wistful it makes me feel that I cannot see our girls' futures. How I long to know they'll be all right.

Francis Bacon, I might add, was no stranger himself to this kind of longing—this yearning to know the future that's long been the alchemy of the educated class. It was his tough-minded obsession that finally pulled England into the Scientific Revolution, after all, and his methodology that still guides us today. But I doubt he was any more in love with the physical world than Liam Metarey himself was, nearly four technological centuries later; and this remains a testament to the man I knew. It was Liam Metarey who pointed out to me that the squirrels eat the acorns of the white oaks as soon as they find them, but that they bury the acorns of the red oaks to dig up for winter. A wonderful bit of fact, and one I've never found anyone else to know—although if you stand in a field like one of the Metareys' old ones for any length of time in late autumn, you'll see immediately that it's true. Liam Metarey had noticed it entirely on his own, simply by watching. And I'm grateful that my children have in them the history of a man like that. Francis Bacon—the first scientist—would have liked it, too.

I suppose Bacon meant what he said in terms of human inquiry—his revolt against Aristotelian logic, England's general religiosity, and the suppositions of the early investigative scholars—but it applies to human beings, too, doesn't it? *If a man shall begin in certainties, he shall end in doubts.* It explains my wife; and Christian, too, probably; and Liam Metarey; and my father, for that matter. I never got the chance to find out about my mother, I suppose; but it probably explains me, as well.

Not long ago, Clara decided to invite Dad, Mr. McGowar, and Trieste over to the house for dinner. She's good that way, her sense of social groupings, and though I wouldn't have foreseen the combination myself, I realized as soon as all three of them were in my car that she was right. For one thing, there aren't many dinner parties outside of Manhattan or a nursing home where not a single guest drives. So they had that in common, at least. In the backseat of the Camry, Trieste took out her own pad—her *Speaker-Sentinel* reporter's notebook—and wrote out questions for Mr. McGowar. Though as far as I know he can barely even read, this delighted him. I'm not sure how she knew to do it, other than her eccentric gift for people, and I imagine she had to keep the words simple; but if I know Trieste she managed to ask about half a century of cutting rock, about his childhood in Carrol County, about the Great Depression, about the first set of indomitable years for the Yankees, and about the ins and outs of water-cooled saws—all in the time it took us to drive from my old neighborhood to my new one. And that was only a start. In the mirror I could see Mr. McGowar's grin like a slice of yellow melon. And Dad was obviously enjoying the fact that the two of them were conversing behind him; it left him alone next to me, in this case to make some progress on A *Tale of Two Cities*.

And for me, too, it was a pleasurable silence as I drove along, broken only by the sound of turning pages. Like my own childhood on Dumfries Street, only with Trieste in place of my mother and Sydney Carton instead of the ball scores.

At the house, Dad greeted Clara in the foyer with a bow, then a handshake, then a kiss on the cheek. Despite the changes in his personality, he has remained unfailingly polite with her—the "primacy of long-term memory," says Dr. Jadoon—and he proceeded to introduce Trieste. Trieste then proceeded to charm my wife, I think, with the peculiarly feminine aspect of her gaze, despite her boy's clothes.

Our dining room happens to hold the old oil portrait of Eoghan Metarey from Aberdeen West, and Clara, possibly because she wanted to sit next to Trieste herself, decided to seat Mr. McGowar across from it. I realized midway through the soup that this had been a mistake. He wasn't eating. He was looking up at it instead, shimmying his head from side to side as though to avoid bats swooping in the air.

"Everything all right, Mr. McGowar?" I said.

He pointed.

THE IS
THA FOLO YU

"Oh that—you're right. They do. Just a trick of the painter's, though. That's all it is. So do the bird's. Always did something to *me*, too, I have to admit. Used to hang in the entrance hall when Clara was growing up. Can't quite describe it."

We looked together. It still amazes me, actually. The skill of it. The dark gaze that you would swear moves. The iridescent yellow plumage of the canary, too. And the shining water glass. The way the man himself still seems every bit a part of this world.

At the other end of the table, Clara said, "You knew him, Mr. McGowar, didn't you?"

He stiffened.

HU MAM

"My grandfather. Eoghan Metarey."

YES MAM I DID

"There aren't many alive who can say that."

"Eugene's been in the granite mine," Dad said, "since—since when was it, Eugene? 1921?"

MAYS RUTH
YANKEES GIANTS

"That's 1921, all right. Good, Eugene." He winked at me. *Sports pages*, he mouthed.

GUD SERES

"I hear it was, Eugene."

By the time we'd reached the main course, Trieste was in on the questions, too. In her mind, I could tell, she was working on a story. "Mr. McGowar," she said, as soon as Clara had served the chicken, "when you went into the mine, did you start right out on the saw?"

Mr. McGowar set down his spoon.

GOSH NO
TUK 20 YERS

"How old were you when you went in, then?"

~~ILEVUN~~
ULEVIN

"Isn't that kind of young, Mr. McGowar?"

NO OLD

"Plenty started at eight or nine," said Dad. "They're small at that age. Don't have to cut the shafts as wide."

Trieste looked at me, I think because at that moment she was reluctant to look at my wife. She may not be tactful, but she's sensitive. "But—" she said, "But—but what about labor laws? Isn't that child labor?"

"Child labor laws weren't written till the Depression," said Dad. He smiled. "That was FDR."

Now Trieste put down her fork. "Now isn't *that* interesting."

Mr. McGowar took the opportunity to pick his own utensils back up and start eating. I was still watching him, of course. It's difficult not to. He's one of those people so purely himself, so thoroughly unlike anyone you've ever come across, that when you're with him you're constantly suppressing a chuckle of admiration for the fact that someone has turned into exactly what he has. Indomitable, I suppose some would call it. And at a table you can't help looking at him, like a museum piece eating soup in the chair next to you.

And for his own part, he kept looking up at the painting behind Clara.

"Isn't what interesting, Trieste?" said Clara.

"That it was then, in the worst of times," she answered—I could hear her composing a lead—"when the national economy was at its low point of the century . . ." She tapped the table with her finger. "That *that's* when we wrote the child labor laws. That *that's* when we showed the most care for our children." She picked up her reporter's pad and made a note in it.

I thought Dad and Mr. McGowar would approve of the observation, but Mr. McGowar had another funny look on his face. I could tell that he wanted to keep eating, but he picked up the pad instead.

MEN JST WANTD THE KIDS JOBS

At this, Dad let out a snort.

It was followed by silence.

"Well," Clara said, rising to pour the wine. "I guess that settles that." Another silence.

"Mr. McGowar," I said. "Willie Mays wasn't even born in 1921."

Dad was still grinning triumphantly. "Carl Mays," he said.

PITCHER

"Good, Eugene."

Trieste said, "Well, what was Eoghan Metarey like, then?"

I'd never seen Mr. McGowar blush. But he did. He lifted his fork to his mouth and blew on it, to stall for time. He turned one way and then the other. Only when he started writing did his stony color return.

FAR AND ONST

Clara looked at him.

"Fair and honest," I said.

"Thank you, Mr. McGowar," said Clara.

"Did you know him, Mr. McGowar?" asked Trieste.

And now he actually laughed. A two-part hiccup that sounded like a seesaw with a tight hinge.

FIFT YERS
SAW HIM ~~UNS~~
WUNS

It was a short evening. By eight I could see both Dad and Mr. McGowar settling lower in their chairs, and I know how the two of them can be when the sun goes down. So we left before dessert. But on the drive home, Dad was reading *A Tale of Two Cities* again on the seat next to me, and I heard a good bit of energetic scribbling going on from the back. Presently Trieste's pad was passed up to the front. Dad wrote something and passed it back. It wasn't until I'd pulled over at the quarry bus stop to let Mr. McGowar out, however, and he'd reached forward to shake my hand, that Trieste said, "Did you see the painting, Mr. Sifter?"

"Which one?" I asked.

Mr. McGowar withdrew his hand and I could hear him feeling for the door handle in the dark.

"The portrait. Your wife's grandfather."

"I mean, which Mr. Sifter?"

"You, sir."

"In that case, yes I did. I know that painting as well as anyone does. What about it?"

There was more shuffling from the back.

"Tell him," said Trieste.

Now Mr. McGowar was rattling the door. I unlocked it for him.

"It's okay, Eugene," said Dad. "You can go ahead."

I turned on the light. In the mirror, his cheeks were red again.

"Come on, Mr. McGowar," said Trieste. "Go ahead. Tell him what you noticed in the painting."

His blush deepened.

"Please, Mr. McGowar," I said. "I'd like to hear."

I heard pages flipping. Then after a moment his head appeared between Dad and me.

COD

WOTR

MUNY

~~CUNR~~

~~KUNAR~~

BURD

He looked away.

"Go on," said Trieste.

MINERS

"I don't get it," I said.

CLEVR ARDST

"Old man probably never really looked at it," Trieste said glee-
fully.

Dad chuckled softly. "Got one over on him, at least." He closed his
book. "Painter must have been a union guy."

"I don't get what you're talking about."

"It's Westville #1," said Dad. "That's what it's a painting of. Don't
you know what Westville #1 is?"

"It was the mine in Nova Scotia."

"That's right. The canary and the money and the water. It's what
you call an allegory."

"My God."

"And the cod," said Trieste. "That's what he let them eat."

"Painter risked everything for it," Dad said. "But he's probably still laughing."

"The blindness of power, sir."

Dad was the one who started the singing, too.

> *On the dark sixteenth of May,*
> *Oh, down by the shores of the Westville—hey!*
> *A dark, dark breach in the dark, dark—hey!*
> *Oh the dark sixteenth of May.*
> *Hey!*

In the tinny shine of the Camry's dome light I watched him and Trieste belting out the short verses while all three of them clapped their hands. Trieste was beaming, and after a while, so was Mr. McGowar. When they finished I looked over at Dad, who was holding Dickens between his knees.

He shrugged. "Ingenuity of the American working man," he finally said.

IT DOESN'T TAKE MANY YEARS of fatherhood to think you finally understand your own parents, and I've long since arrived at that point with mine. And like most everyone else, I've grown more grateful for the things they gave me and more respectful of what must have been admirable courage as they watched me go—in my case, to a life utterly different from their own. And as I've watched our own girls move away now, too—first to sleepovers, then to summer camps, then to college and boyfriends, then to jobs and husbands—as I've watched them one by one walk their own ways, I can only hope that they too arrive at this same juncture, that they too come to see us for what we've always *tried* to do for them, even if it's not always what we've succeeded at. Maybe this is nothing but vanity. But I wonder how we've fared with them. I wonder which of our idle words have wounded them and which, years later and a thousand miles away, have buoyed them; which of our hopes have lifted them over the daunting obstacles in their lives and which have pressed back against their own ideas of themselves. I think I know my children, know all three of them, yet I'm certain from my own childhood that of course I don't.

Not long ago, on a cool, rainy Friday, a man walked into my office at the paper. He was average height but slight, dressed in a thin raincoat, not threadbare but almost, and a pair of loafers whose soles were stained with mud. His hair was damp from the weather, and so was his face, but he didn't seem to notice. The drops fell on the desk as he shook his head to refuse the chair I offered him; he spoke to me instead from beside it, gripping the rail. He set down a tattered briefcase on the seat.

"Mr. Millbury?" I said.

"Very good."

"I recognize the face."

"I'm here about Trieste."

"Trieste's a wonderful girl. A wonderful kid."

"She had supper at your house."

"Yes—she told you. With my wife and my father. A very nice evening."

He looked at me with what seemed like annoyance, as though my words were a minor riddle that he had to solve in order to get to his business. He lifted the briefcase and set it on the desk. It was wet from the rain, too, and I could see drops spreading onto the wood.

"We don't want it," he said softly.

"Want what?"

"Charity." He unlatched the briefcase, opened it, and emptied it onto the blotter.

"Oh, it's nothing," I said. "It was on sale. I got it for almost nothing. I thought Trieste could use it. Keep her warm in the winter."

"Thank you but we don't want it," he said again, still softly. "I don't want it, and neither does she. She's fine with what she has." Then he stood, closed the briefcase, and walked back out the door.

MAYBE LIAM METAREY NEVER FOUND ANYTHING on the afternoon he took the Ferguson out into the snow. He never spoke about it. Not to me, at least. And I can only try to piece together what happened in that apple orchard from what I think he might have been trying to tell me, cryptically, on another night.

This is how I imagine it:

He's been with Henry Bonwiller all morning. Throwing good, dry walnut on the fire in the study, hoping it will help the Senator sober up. Warming the place enough to get him to stop shivering. He's never seen him quite like this, three sheets to the wind, wet, and mumbling since he came in practically at dawn. Took off his shoes but his pants were soaked to the knees. Mucking around in the snow. Or falling. But he won't change his clothes. Won't take them off.

The drinking. For the first time, Liam Metarey understands it's going to be a real problem. For the campaign. This thing he should have seen long ago, the way Clara did. Should have had it vetted by the lawyers. The outlandish flaunting of the rules. Barely made the stairs to the study this morning in the dark. One arm up under his shoulder. And he's seen him that way more than once. In public. The night June smashed the pole barn, for one. But others, too. Like he wants to throw it all away.

Something to keep an eye on—more than an eye on. Make it a point from here on out. Keep the reporters away from it, too. A mile away.

Now Henry's in the chair, nodding off. Still shivering. Liam Metarey can smell the booze.

He makes a pot of coffee.

Sends for Gil. Instructions: His cousin, in Toronto. The dealership. Out-of-town press hears he smashed the car—a month till Iowa—it's over before it's started. His cousin can send someone across the border with the parts. Simple thing.

He makes more coffee. Takes his own cup black and gives it to Henry the same way. Tilts it to his lips for him like feeding a baby.

Not until they've drunk down two pots between them does Henry wake up and say, "Shit, where's she?"

Slurring.

"Where's who?"

An ashen look on his face.

"Abbles."

"Who?"

"Ab-bles. Silverdon's."

This is all he needs.

By the time Liam Metarey's halfway up the driveway he thanks the lord for the Ferguson. Real snow here. Six inches on the ground and maybe twice that much still to fall. And not too cold yet, either. Still warm enough for plenty more. The storm growing over the lake. Better not have left her out here.

With a start, he turns back. Leaves the Ferguson running outside the back door. Takes the stairs to the library two at a time.

"Did anyone see?"

"Anyone what?"

Shakes him in the chair. "Did anyone see?"

"No."

"You sure now?"

Shakes him again.

"Henry!"

"Gas. Stobbed for gas. Peed."

"The boy see you?"

"The boy?"

"At the gas station, Henry."

"Well, yeah, might've."

Back on the Ferguson now. As fast as it'll go, through the trees. Could be anywhere in all the goddamn woods. Miles and miles of it. Glittering shell already smooth behind him. Erased. Or pretty close.

It's more a sense than anything. Two faint furrows. Shadows. Not much more, running down the driveway: the Cadillac's tracks. Wandering side to side. Good and drunk. Good and goddamn drunk.

He follows.

Light's already bad. Clouds and winter and trees, late afternoon. But it brings out the shadows. Two gray slivers in the pale crust.

He's out near the orchards now. Out from under the big canopy and into the heritage trees. Cragged, hundred-year-old Macintosh and Spartan in rows. He can see half a mile either direction.

The tracks stop.

He slows. Backs up.

There they are.

Then they're gone.

A stiff wind riles the branches and he looks up to see the snow sweeping in from the lake. A moment later he's in it.

A blizzard.

Out between the rows now. That's where they must have gone. Out between the bending trunks. Deeper now over the softer ground, which slows him. But harder to lose. The ruts still there but not for long. Has to shield his eyes to see. Swirls of moth-sized flakes careening berserkly in the gusts. Northwest toward the orchard house and the highway.

The turn.

He kicks it up to third, cuts north and makes a diagonal across the land, the Ferguson's huge wheels shattering the drifts. Here and there, downed branches cracking under the axle. The low, sucker growth snapping.

In the boulder meadow, he has to zigzag in the massive rocks. Dozens of them in their crazy pattern, looming like ghosts. He turns tight around them. Looking left and right, his fingers parted over his eyes to clear the snow. Left and right. Making his way toward the S-curve where the road comes in tight.

At the end of the field, near the bend, he comes out from behind the last rock and something glints in the snow.

He climbs down: a flask.

Plain. No marking. Still something inside. He tilts it: bourbon. For some reason then he sets out to look for the cap. But that's crazy. He can't see more than ten feet through the thicket of white.

He climbs back into the seat and sets the flask in his pocket, and when he leans over the shifter to start up again he sees them in the snow on the other side.

The black pumps.

A fringe of red.

Hair.

His gut comes up.

Off the tractor. In his own tracks, around to her.

She's face down. He brushes the snow. Fur coat, up over her shoulders and head. Red dress under it.

He lays his palm on her back.

It rises.

He rolls her over and she's a bag of rocks. The face white from cold and snow stuck all over it. Fur pasted down. Bruise on the forehead. Dark blood. Dried or frozen. Eyelids glued shut. He looks away. Looks back.

With one finger he brushes off the frost. Carefully. The bulge of the eyeballs under his glove. He stops. Pulls the lids open.

Jesus!

They're moving: back and forth.

He lets go and the head rolls sideways.

Doesn't want to touch her again. And he sees something else now, in the crease of the neck. Just for a moment. Did he see it?

"JoEllen."

A jump and a flicker. Under the skin.

But the eyes: he saw it.

Touches her arm. "JoEllen."

Shakes it.

"JoEllen!"

Slaps her face. A woody hardness like the rind of something.

Takes off his glove. Touches the cheek.

Is that warm?

He opens the eyes again: back and forth.

Hardly older than his daughter.

Christian.

Back and forth.

He looks toward the road. Bile in his throat. The snow, the snow. Gusts whipping it like a curtain closing. Dark in an hour and a freeze coming in. A week of it. Hard freeze and another foot or two still to come. He looks up. Three, maybe. Dry snow. Drift snow. Still sweeping in from the lake.

And all the wind.

He climbs up into the seat. Drives a few yards. Then shuts it off and climbs back down.

On the ground he moves a few things. A branch. A rock. Brushes out his boot prints.

Lifts her by the hard handles of the frozen fur, doesn't want to touch the skin again. Even with his gloves. Turns her back over and the head drops forward into the white like a sinker. Kicks snow over it. Half covers the body.

The sack of rocks.

Back in the seat now, his throat pinches. He leans out and a gash blooms in the white. Spills steam. He leans out farther. Another gash and the steam again.

But in a minute, no steam.

Then nothing.

Reaches into his pocket and pours a little bourbon down his throat. Pours so the flask doesn't touch his lips. Syrupy from the cold. But it quells it.

Carefully then, he leans out again from the seat. Aims. Throws it so the uncapped neck stays upright. Soundless when it hits, right beside her. Below the crook of her arm. A perfect shot. The hole closing.

Starts up the Ferguson.

Follows his own tracks back to the driveway. Shuts it off when he reaches the big trees and looks back. All the marks rounded off now, too. Already. Starting to disappear. It's a blizzard, all right. Lord's sent a blizzard to help them. And the wind still keening.

Blow everything flat by morning. That's what the Lord will do. Not for him but for everyone else. Turn it all into a desert of ice. Covered till spring.

Nothing he could have done.

It was meant to be. Maybe that's why.

Nothing he can do for her. But plenty to do for the others.

I understand.

To save his son.

To save a thousand sons.

All that wind and snow. The great heavenly blanket. Just a bump he can make out now in the thick of it, vanishing already as he watches, the red dress blinking into white.

"COME ON, DAD," I say. "Let's go see Mom."

"Why should we do that?"

"Because you want to."

He's struggling with his shoes. They're still steel-toed Red Wings, twenty years after his last job, worn nearly through. And he doesn't like me to help him with them, even though some days it takes him ten minutes to get the laces tied. He's got pain in the shoulders, pain in the knees, pain in the hips, and now and then pain in the knuckles. His plumber's pension, as he calls it. But more than anything else, I can see that he doesn't want to go. Sometimes I wonder if all the pain is a convenience.

"Come on," I say. "We missed going two weeks ago."

"We did?"

"Yes. Remember? We went to the Metareys'. And we missed it two weeks before that, too." I point. "Remember the window?"

I can see him thinking.

"That's right," he finally answers. He lets go of the bootlaces and sits upright on the bed.

I face him. "You remember the window, Dad, right?"

"Of course I remember the window."

"You pulled it out," I say. "And Mrs. Milton called the orderly."

"Thank you. I remember fine."

The laces are through the eyelets now, and as he climbs stiffly down to the floor, then rises on one knee to pull them tight, I see him for a moment in overalls and a wool cap, at our back door in dawn light.

But he can't quite get the left one the way he wants.

"Here," I say, "let me."

"No."

"How're the fingers today?"

"They're okay." Then, "Stiff."

"I can do it for you. Really. It doesn't mean a thing."

"I said no."

Half an hour later, when we turn in at Greenhaven Cemetery in the Camry, he's still working on the knot, leaning forward in his seat. Huffing and puffing. But midway up the long entrance road to the cemetery plot, where the headstones start in their temperate rows, he finally decides he's tied it well enough. He sits up then and lifts *David Copperfield* onto his lap, though we have no more than a quarter mile to go. When we arrive, I get out and stand in the grass while he finishes a chapter. Then we walk over together.

Behind Mom's grave is a marble bench, a gift of the Metareys. The monument itself is a slab of limestone, long and squat, rising no more than six inches high but running almost the full length of the seat behind it. A low wall. Mom didn't put her head high but she was obdurate. The same, really, for Dad, even though now he seems to be lifting his brow a bit into the wind. We like to wander for a few minutes when we come. But today he leans down right away and picks a handful of the daisies that grow in profusion along the paths here. He does this every visit, and then, as always, he begins to join their stems with square knots. The work involves two hands, and I can see the right one having to wait for the left, but he's strangely patient with it, the way he is with his shoelaces. The daisies are oxeyes, and the bare heads have long gone to seed so that the tying is easier. Before long he's made a length of chain as long as his arm. Then he takes off his hat and walks up to her.

"She'd be sorry about what's going on over at the Metareys'," I say, moving next to him.

He looks down at the stone. "You never cared much about them, my love."

"She did, actually," I say. "You did, Mom."

"Then you kept it to yourself, my love."

I think about that.

He begins to tie the daisy chain then into the particular knot he likes. It's called a sennit, and he used to tie it for me when I was a boy—a long intertwining braid that looks in the end like two bodies joined by arms, wrapped round and round each other. His fingers are slow but they're surprisingly limber when they're warmed up.

"She was a good woman," he declares finally, turning. He says this to me nearly every visit, and has for all the years we've come together, but each time it's as though he means it anew. Longfellow and Shakespeare and William Manchester, and I guess Marx and Zinn and now Dickens, and even a stroke—they haven't changed all that much about him. He holds the crown of knotted stems next to his chest and closes his eyes for a moment.

When he opens them, he says, "You never expect the way your life is going to turn out. Do you? And you never get to find out how your children's turned out, either."

"You don't, Dad. I wonder about the girls all the time."

"And I used to wonder about *you*." He smiles, a little sheepishly. "Not all the time, maybe, but I did. I thought that when Mom went, it was a blow you'd never get over. That I'd never get over, either."

"But we did," I say. "We both did." Then I add, "We love you, Mom."

"Don't be sorry, Cor. She would be glad."

He holds out the daisies in his two hands in front of him, examining them in the light. They tremble on his palms.

"Dad," I say. "Did you know it was going to happen?"

"Did I know what was going to happen?"

"What happened to Mom. Did you know back then? Did she tell you? That she was sick, I mean." I turn to him. "That she knew she was going to die."

He doesn't look up from his task. "What kind of crazy question is that?"

"I don't know. It occurred to me."

"Of course we didn't know. That's ridiculous. If we'd known, we would have done something. She wasn't sick a day in her life."

I look at him. He's already thinking of something else, I can see. He leans down and sets the knotted daisies alongside all the others, a carefully arranged stack of plant stems turning to transparent strings on the ground beside her.

"I've just always wondered," I say.

"Well, that's a silly thing to wonder," he answers, and stands. "Okay," he says after a moment. "I'm ready."

And then we head up. Over the long, low slope running from the cemetery to the top of the hill, where the stone foundation of an old Dutch fire lookout still stands. It's a primitive square of weather-beaten stone set in the dirt at the apex of the ridge, but if you stand on

it and turn to the west you can still see thirty miles over the long shadows of the last unspoiled moraine in the county, the one that traverses
its lowest valley. The valley where the Millburys live. At the far end a
slice of Lake Erie glimmers. This is where Dad and I always come
now. Perhaps for the way it brings up the memory we both have of the
way this whole territory used to be. The land isn't flat anywhere in
Carrol County—you can hardly find a stretch of level ground large
enough for a ball field—but the rises are barely taller than the houses
that sit between them, and for now at least, the builders have left the
hilltops alone. The farmer's ethic of hiding from the wind. If you
climb sixty feet vertically—as Dad and I do now, slowly, while the sun
reaches its peak above us—and if you confine your gaze to the west,
the way we do now, as well, you can still look out as far as you can see
over land that you'd swear has been empty forever.

THE SENATE HEARINGS ON ANODYNE ENERGY, as some remember,
didn't start until the end of Jimmy Carter's tenure in Washington,
more than two full presidential terms after Mr. Metarey's death. And
even then the investigation was overshadowed by other events. Henry
Bonwiller wasn't the only one to appear before the panel. So did
twelve members of Wyoming's state House, four of North Dakota's,
and two from former president Nixon's Atomic Energy Commission,
along with United States Representatives Kyle Stennart of Wyoming
and Madeline Blank of New York and the heads of half a dozen energy and resource corporations in the Midwest and Canada. To name
only the first week's witnesses. The proceedings, like the financial
dealings themselves, seemed to have been designed to be confusing.

Late in the afternoon on Friday, November 2nd, 1979, in the waning hours of the week's news cycle, Henry Bonwiller took a seat at the
witness table in the Senate chambers to be questioned by a roomful
of his colleagues, many of whose careers he had helped build as

chairman of the Appropriations Committee. He was only in his sixties then, but his arms shook a little as he lowered himself into the chair. A new network called C-SPAN had trained a camera on the proceedings, but I remember that even in the offices of *The Patriot Ledger*, in Quincy, Massachusetts, where I'd been hired for my first reporting job after college, I was the only one watching.

For an hour I listened to the Senator being questioned about a mystifying array of transactions. He'd been brought in as an investor in Anodyne Energy a decade before by an agent of another entity, the Buffalo office of a Canadian holding company that itself seemed to be mostly in the business of creating other, smaller companies, many of them offshore, to manage profits and losses on its books. Henry Bonwiller's wife and sons were the owners of stakes in various drilling operations represented in those books, and in fact the family had apparently made a good bit of money from them. But the stakes turned out to be futures options granted retroactively, a clearly profitable but probably illegal arrangement that Senator Bonwiller seemed to understand only at the moment Senator Russell Long of Louisiana explained it to him, as the prelude to a question. "Senator Long," Henry Bonwiller answered, chuckling in his basso undertone, "if I understood the details of that kind of stuff, I'd be working on Wall Street."

To which Russell Long, chuckling himself, replied, "So would I, Senator, so would I."

That was the last question of the afternoon, and two days later a mob of Iranian students stormed the American embassy in Tehran, taking ninety hostages. After that, I couldn't even find the hearings on C-SPAN.

But the Democrats by then were in the waning days of their legislative power, anyway, and there was a feeling throughout the nation that their nearly thirty-year lock on both houses of Congress was ending. People believed that President Carter and his concern with human rights had weakened the United States—the hostages would spend another fourteen months in captivity—and though the hearings ended without a censure, Senator Bonwiller's stance against the

military and in favor of the unprotected classes at home was beginning to fall under the shadow of a new, darker mood that was spreading across the country.

Dear Mr. Sifter,

I've been meaning to write for a long time to say sorry for
what my father did, and also to thank you again for all the
things you and the Speaker-Sentinel have given me, which, as
I look out over the Yard (my father would cough loudly right
now) seems just about exactly the thing he was afraid of. (Oh,
well.) And the thing *I* was afraid of, too—at least, before I
found myself on these strange but really sort of mild shores. I
can finally sleep at night, in other words, which is a relief since
my first few weeks in Boston I felt like I'd stumbled into an
all-night boxing and car-honking match. But now I look out
my window and it all seems normal. I've also realized that all
the other freshmen in their fall sweaters are as harmless as I am
and probably no less confused (or scared). I believe that's
something of a long lede, sir.

First: my father was only trying to do what he thought was
right. He had his own taste of fancy colleges when he was
young (PhD, chemistry, Johns Hopkins, 1974) and fancy
offices after that (E. I. duPont, 1975–1990) and fancy clothes
for a while even, and for his own various reasons he's still afraid
of all of them, at least as far as his children are concerned.
Which is to say, he's an eccentric man but in a lot of ways a
privileged one, and he was only trying to save me from a world
whose false enticements he knew very well.

So here I am, staring down the same road he took, just
about exactly. I do miss the duster, though, (when it's not
raining here it's snowing, and all) and I even thought of asking

you to mail it out to me but I know my dad would find out
about that and take a trip down to your office. So we'll skip
that, shall we?

I'm pretty busy, naturally. I've been in town a good part of a
semester now and am still waiting for the impostor police to
knock at the door. Just like everybody else, I guess. The last
thing Dad said when he dropped me off was that the brain isn't
the salve for the heart that I evidently hoped it was (his words).
Well, that was a nice send-off, wasn't it? (Be gentle, sir, when
you part with your daughters.)

But we Millburys are a tough bunch (if nothing else), and as
far as I can tell (from my first semester's seminar reading, at
least) Dostoyevsky and Virginia Woolf seem to agree with Dad.
I've already come upon the fact plenty of times myself, in all
the girls at the T stops in their black makeup and ripped jeans,
not to mention in the glass of every darkened shop window in
the rain. I used to take a secret pride in believing I was above it
all. Gone. Gone, all of that.

I'll keep this short. I hope it will be only the first of many
letters, even though I know that's presumptuous on my part
and naïvely optimistic—naïve optimism, however, being a trait
I've learned to respect and strive for.

That's all for now.

Thanks always. You have meant a great deal to me.

—Trieste

THE MORNING AFTER LIAM METAREY'S FUNERAL, it fell to Gil
McKinstrey and me to remove what remained of the plane from the
patch of burnt ground where it lay. The small fires in the fields had
reached all the way to the drainage gullies, and a few had actually ex-

tinguished themselves in the gravel paths around the fly pools. Though it had been less than a week, green sprigs were already rising amid the stubs of charred grasses. Merciless nature, as Liam Metarey might have said. The plane itself was unrecognizable. Three broad, misshapen ingots of steel lay where the fuselage had been, and a few uncovered struts poked from the tip of a wing that had come to earth beyond the firebreak. A few other smaller shards lay here and there amid the black. But that was all. Gil looped the largest slabs inside a chain and used a block and tackle to lift them into the long cart behind the Ferguson. I went around collecting the smaller pieces and throwing them in. I was thinking of Mr. Metarey again, of course— he would have melted the salvage and cast it again as something useful. It didn't matter if he could have bought a new plane to replace it—it didn't matter if he could have bought a hundred of them. He would have done it himself: he would have read about it, or talked to an old-timer, or just invented the technique on his own, some way to make use of what had been left behind. It was one of the aspects of his character that in the end I most admired. We were both quieted, Gil and I, by the swiftness with which all of it—the man, the plane— could disappear.

"Humid out here," I finally said.

"Barely keep my reefer lit," Gil answered.

Then we were quiet again, working in the hot sun.

He didn't speak again until the end of the morning. "Guess you'll be spending the summers elsewheres now," he said.

"You going to stay on?"

"Not up to me," he answered.

He tipped his cap and went back to working. That was all we spoke for the rest of the day. I had wanted to say something to him, had wanted to for months, ever since the night I had teased him from the hood of the wrecked car in front of Mr. Metarey and Senator Bonwiller. He and I were more similar than different, without a doubt; but I noticed he wouldn't let me guide the heavy blocks of burnt metal up into the cart as he stood in the flatbed and cranked the grip-ping chain with his wiry arms. Perhaps this was a mark of his respect for me; but more likely it was his dismissal of a callow boy who had once belittled him in public. Instead he leaned over the outrigger and steered the harness himself—he was doing the jobs of two men rather than permitting me to help him.

I let him. There was a divide between us now that I could no longer cross.

And of course it only widened again, a year later, when I graduated from Dunleavy and was accepted at Haverford. It was then that I dis-covered that Mr. Metarey had left a fund for my college education. My mother had known about it for quite a while, it turns out—a com-fort to me now—but had decided not to tell me. I learned of it in a let-ter from Mr. Metarey himself, in fact, written right around the time JoEllen Charney died. My father gave me the letter at my Dunleavy graduation dinner, along with a wrapped package that contained, in accordance with Mr. Metarey's long and carefully drafted will, his leather-bound copy of *The Jungle*. The timing of the letter, and the odd wording at the beginning, only add to my wonder:

> December 20th, 1971
> Dear Corey,
> I have asked your mother to give this to you on the day you pass from the world you've known into the world beyond.
> I envy you because you are going your way with a clear eye, having seen so much of what is noble in our own small sphere and also so much of what is venial and a little of what is mortal.
> I've told your parents that we are adding a gift to your education. When my own father sent me away to school he said one thing: "The rest is up to you."
> So perhaps that is how I should leave this, as well.
> As Ever—
>   L.M.

Mr. Metarey's financial gift didn't cover everything, as he easily could have; but it covered a good deal, and often over the next four years as I worked at the circulation desk of the student library to pay off what remained of my tuition, I thought of him, speaking to me from across the years. He would have told me that work is good. He seemed to have absorbed the lessons of every class, of my own then and of the one I am a member of now, and of his own, as well, which is beyond what I or even our children—his granddaughters—will ever know. He would have told me that it is perilous to be given too much, that fortune of all kinds weakens the spirit. He would have told me that a man cannot overcome his past but that he cannot not try; that, with care, the wounds of one generation are diluted in the one that follows, and again in the one after that, so that, if we are lucky, we can bring forth in our children the things for which we have strived ourselves. But we cannot make them want what we want. They, too, will strive.

And I suppose that I would have told him other things in return. That Henry Bonwiller was eventually brought down not by JoEllen Charney, as I imagine Liam Metarey feared, but by Anodyne Energy. Anodyne Energy because in the mind of the public, that accusation— which, even after the hearings, remained ill understood—never needed to be proved. The shady drilling leases, the backdated options, the shell corporations—not many people comprehended these things, but they served, finally, to fell a man whose country had turned against him. In 1976, he won his Senate seat for a fifth term, but he lost it in the midterm elections that followed. We were in a new political era then, and the whiff of what Anodyne represented, the old-school horse-trading and unvarnished arithmetic of personal gain, had become a killing weight to any politician who still pulled it.

The stories about JoEllen Charney would surface and resurface over all the years since then, but the Bonwiller family—aided, of course, by loyalists like my wife—would through sheer reach of its power simply tamp them down. Over and over again. Henry Bonwiller had her murdered for what she knew about Anodyne—it wasn't long before that rumor was whispered over Scotches at Albany cocktail parties, and it wasn't long—although I'm sure it's not true— before it became the most widely believed of all. But there were a half dozen other versions as well, more minor but more damning: he ran her over with his car when she told him she was pregnant; in midwinter he got her drunk and left her in the woods; his wife had her poisoned and then dropped in the snow. And there's even one I've heard lately that's got my own attention again: that he didn't lose control of the car at all but was intentionally run off the road by his enemies— but my mind stops when I consider it. If Liam Metarey were alive he'd have heard all of these conjectures by now, thrown about with what I consider a troubling lack of authority, and I must say I miss the possibility of what he might eventually have told me. I know I wanted—I still want—to tell him that Henry Bonwiller survived the whole affair, and that he himself would have survived it, too. But I can only guess, in the end, if this would have made a difference.

I am tied to that family and will never be untied. And now and then I see my own past—my past with my own parents, in my own house, among my own people—now and then I see my own past as being so distant it has nearly disappeared. Sometimes that seems like an unfathomable loss. But what is there to do about such feelings?

Clara and I live near Masaguint now—the old Dutch Downs—not far from the Millburys' blueberry marsh, and in the evenings after dinner we can sit on the screened porch and not hear any cars. At least for the time being. We're ten minutes from the border of Carrol County and a little less than an hour—without traffic—from Saline. Clara works full-time these days for the League of Women Voters, a position that puts her in contact with almost all the Democratic officeholders in this part of the state, and she still writes her letters to the editors of the *Courier-Express* and *The Times Union* and *The Plain Dealer*. And now and then she gives me an inkling that she plans to run for office herself. Around here that means a counselorship and then, if that works out, perhaps the statehouse. Whatever the case, she seems to like her job, and she works at it long hours, which means

I usually stay at the paper myself till mid-evening, checking the morning's stories and sorting through the piles of tips; when I'm through with that, I'll stop off at Burdick's—it and Gervin's are the lone survivors downtown—and at home I'll fix something with reasonable care for the two of us. Then I'll send off an e-mail to one or another of the girls, and occasionally I'll even write a letter. When Clara pulls up after dark in her Subaru, I'll set both our dinner plates in the microwave to heat. That's our life. We stay in touch fairly well with everyone.

What have I learned? The old verities, mostly: that love for our children is what sustains us; that people are not what they seem; that those we hate bear some wound equal to our own; that power is desperation's salve, and that this fact as much as any is what dooms and dooms us. That we never learn the truth. When you've been involved in something like this, when in your memory there's some marauding creature still alive, some fleeting, nightmarish beast always running up behind you, it's in the nature of all of us, I think, to want to turn and see it, no matter how terrible or how mild it might be. But as in the childhood dream, you can't ever really do that. There it is, spinning one way and then the other, exactly as fast as you do, always staying behind you somehow, always just managing to vanish from your eye.

June Metarey died last year, I'm sorry to say, walking one of Churchill's grandpuppies. Other than the weekly dinners we used to have together, we hadn't seen much of her toward the end, for no good reason, and this still saddens Clara. But she is grateful for the way her mother went, swiftly and without anguish. Christian never married but she has a daughter, adopted from Guangzhou, and the two of them are learning to farm organically, on a small but very pretty parcel near Putney, Vermont. Although Trieste Millbury continues to send me scribbled notes from coffee shops around Boston, I've seen her only once since the dinner at our house: her father made her resign the internship. And I have to say I can understand his view. But she did come by the office in the spring to thank me for the partial tuition scholarship that the Speaker-Sentinel Foundation—with Mr. and Mrs. Millbury's approval, of course—had offered her when she was accepted at Harvard.

Gil McKinstrey has got to be close to seventy, but he's still working as a finish carpenter for a developer who's building some higher-end subdivisions around here. Carlton Sample retired twenty years ago and owns a share in a wine store in the Oaks mall—right beneath the boughs of the great tree, as it happens—and as far as I know, Glenn Burrant is still living in Canada. Vance Trawbridge, as everyone knows, died tragically in a fall, shortly after he finished writing his memoir but before it was published. That memoir shows a courageous man, but also a more melancholy and conflicted one than I think any of us thought. Holly Steen is the only one I've lost touch with completely, although I'm tempted now and then, out of a kind of tender curiosity more than anything else, to try to find her. Astor Highbridge is a professor of American studies at Berkeley, and he still spends a weekend with us every two or three years when he's back in this part of the country.

My wedding to Clara took place twenty-six years ago this month, in a small adobe church in the mountains near Questa, New Mexico— Clara wanted to be as far from home as possible, in every way she could. It was a very small ceremony, just my father and Mrs. Metarey and, yes, Christian, who hugged me at the end, the way, I suppose, she might have hugged her brother.

I can understand why. The fall of my senior year at Dunleavy, Andrew Metarey was killed, in a rescue operation near Phu Cat, when his medevac helicopter came down under enemy fire. Three months later the Paris Peace Accords were signed. I took the train home for the funeral, and it was the last time I saw Christian and Clara before I went off to college. It was almost embarrassing to be there with the family that day, so great was their loss. I think everyone felt that way. Gil McKinstrey was a pallbearer again, along with Mr. Metarey's cousins. Christian, I know, could not even speak.

The relatives of the other soldiers who died in that helicopter still gather at the Vietnam Memorial in Washington each October, and Christian and Clara and I go every year. We have a picture of Andrew over our sink, holding Churchill as a puppy, high up over his head. So we still see him every day, and we see that sweet white dog, too, and the younger version of his wistful eyes. I've never had a brother, so I don't think I can really know how it feels for either Clara or Christian. And I don't see how June Metarey could have lived through any of it.

That covers it, I think.

My father, for his own part, is still at Walnut Orchards, going nearly as strong as ever. Preparing, I sometimes think, to live a century. He's still reading several hours a day, as though he thinks there's an exam coming up. That tickles me. His old friends don't know what to make of it, but it's turned Dr. Jadoon into a believer in something greater than physiology or brain anatomy. Recently, Dad has begun reading to Mr. McGowar, as well, during their afternoons together. Usually Dickens, he tells me, which seems to speak to both of them somehow. Then they'll go out to check on the grounds.

Dad's arthritis still bothers him, and recently we were told his heart is enlarged, but neither of these problems stops him if he wants to do something. Next week, for example, we're planning to go together to a show of hand tools from colonial times, a traveling exhibit that's stopping in the Carrol Fairgrounds on its way down to Cleveland. I'll wear a tie, no doubt, since I'll be coming from work. And he'll wear his Red Wings. That's just the way we are. We'll have a pleasant afternoon together, even though he's showing his cantankerous side more and more these days. With experience, I've learned how to soften it. I just step away for a minute. I'll go use the restroom, or step outdoors to answer a message on my cellphone, and I know that when I return he'll be sitting quietly on a bench somewhere, reading.

One thing I haven't mentioned is that he recently threw a bag of apples, one by one, at a car that was parking outside his window at Walnut Orchards. But it was a BMW, and the logic of it—*his* logic, at least, which I could recognize—made me a little less concerned about him. I suppose I don't know where this behavior is going to lead us in the end, but no matter what happens we still have our regular Sunday excursions together. These never fail to calm him, somehow. Every time we take my car to Greenhaven Cemetery and visit the hills around my mother's grave, he is led back for a few hours to the graceful quiet of his early days. A man can range far in his life, but in the end it doesn't really mean much: now that my wife is so busy, and our own girls have gone their way in the world, these hours with my father are among the most lovely of my week. That's what it comes down to, I guess. We still like to walk in those hills, especially when it's warm, and sometimes now we just stand in them.

ACKNOWLEDGMENTS

I'm deeply grateful to so many for their help in writing this novel. Most especially to my wife, Barbara, who spent almost as much time with it as I did, and to two trusted friends, my editor, Kate Medina, and my agent, Maxine Groffsky. But especially, also, to several others who read the manuscript so kindly and carefully: Joe Blair, Po Bronson, Chard deNiord, Michael Flaum, Dan Geller, Dayna Goldfine, Bill Houser, Jon Maksik, Leslie Maksik, Lauren Reece, and Steve Sellers. I'm indebted to Fred Gerr and Tom Pitoniak, for their scrupulous and exacting work, and to many wonderful people at Random House, including Gina Centrello, Sanyu Dillon, Frankie Jones, Jynne Martin, Sally Marvin, Kate Norris, Beth Pearson, Tom Perry, Abby Plesser, Robin Rolewicz, Jennifer Smith, Beck Stvan, and Simon Sullivan. For assorted tidbits about journalism, dogs, and political primaries, thanks to Neil MacFarquhar, Jane Van Voorhis, and Dave Redlawsk, respectively. Thank you to my mother, father, and brother as well, for their patience and support, and to my children especially, for their long forbearance. For technical advice, I have relied upon the goodwill of two pilots, Kevin Malone and Chuck Peters, and four physicians, Michael Cohen, Marc Diamond, Chris Jensen, and Marcus Nashelsky. All the text's medical inaccuracies, as well as its aeronautical ones, are my own.

—E.C.

AUTHOR'S NOTE

Between the hardback and paperback publications of this book, my long-time agent and friend, Maxine Groffsky, has retired, and her role has now been picked up with care and grace by Jennifer Rudolph Walsh at William Morris Agency. At William Morris, I'm also especially grateful to Tracy Fisher, Alicia Gordon, Eric Zohn, Jessica Almon, Claudia Ballard, and Margaret Riley.

—E.C., October 2008

AMERICA
AMERICA

ETHAN CANIN

A Reader's Guide

A CONVERSATION WITH ETHAN CANIN

Random House Reader's Circle: *America America* is an ambitious novel that embraces the great themes of politics, power, family, class, integrity and love; even the title suggests we are in for a monumental read. How did this novel begin for you personally, and what does it represent for you as a move in your own life as a writer?

Ethan Canin: *America America* began for me as a smaller idea. Originally, it was only the story of Corey Sifter, a working-class boy, who falls in love with Christian Metarey, an aristocratic girl. I'd written about 250 pages of that novel when the attacks occurred on September 11, 2001; and that morning, as it turned out, was the last time I wrote fiction for close to two years. I put the novel aside and didn't pick it up again until 2003. And when I began writing again I found myself much more urgently involved with history and politics and the nature of power. A senator made his way into the story, then a presidential campaign. The novel's evolution began to reflect my own, and that of many others who on that day became more serious about the world.

RHRC: Many have commented on the unmistakable parallels between Senator Bonwiller and Senator Ted Kennedy. In creating the novel's "man of history," did you intentionally draw upon the 1969 Chappaquiddick affair and Senator Kennedy's prominent career?

EC: I was certainly aware of Chappaquiddick as the book took form, but it was far from the front of my thoughts. For me, that incident merely brought up the more general problem of what to do about the great public-minded man or woman whose private behavior is dubious.

I should also say that although the incident in *America America* is in some ways similar to what happened off Martha's Vineyard in July 1969, it's not Senator Kennedy I think of when I think of Senator Henry Bonwiller. It's much more Lyndon Johnson, actually; Johnson, that seismic paradox of public generosity, social vision, and political ruthlessness.

RHRC: Corey Sifter says several times in the novel that he is, in a sense, telling his story for his children. I loved the remark that "children change your past. . . . All one's deeds live doubly" (12–13).

EC: As the novel grew, and even as it became more overtly political, this nonetheless remained the abiding question that drives Corey Sifter: his contemplation of how all his own acts—those acts, as he says, of "honor" and "duplicity" and "veniality" and "ruin"—of how all those acts now "live doubly." As a young man he was able to ignore his own questionable deeds; but now, as a father, and in his case as a father of daughters, he is obligated to reimagine them.

RHRC: *The Washington Post* called *America America* a "masterful feat of literary Photoshop." I loved this observation because it's impossible not to marvel at the brilliant way in which fictional characters are superimposed onto the news of the 1960s and 1970s. Was this difficult to pull off convincingly?

EC: As a matter of fact, the historical background is one of the easier aspects of writing a novel. Far more difficult is dreaming up the smaller, character-based scenes, scenes that rise entirely from one's own imagination. The reason that writing from history is easier, I think, is that historical incident limits the imagination; and although it may not seem obvious that limiting the imagination would help a writer, in fact it does. In my experience, at least, limiting it is the surest way to free it.

One of my favorite ways to find fictional inspiration, by the way, is to browse historical timelines. I also like world atlases—any country with a squiggly coastline seems to inspire me, as do visual dictionaries, those reclusive creatures of the reference shelf.

RHRC: I was delighted by your apparent passion for presidential history, as evidenced by Mr. Metarey's meditations on philosopher Isaiah Berlin's "The Hedgehog and the Fox." Is this a field you delved into while researching the novel, or are you a closet presidential history junkie?

EC: I'm fascinated by political campaigns—which is not to say I'm not disgusted by them, too—but I have to admit that much of the knowledge in that particular scene came from research. I wish I could say it came from memory.

RHRC: Did you ever have the urge to fly a biplane like Aberdeen Red? How did you research the technicalities of flight for the novel?

EC: To research the flying bits I went up in small planes with a couple of pilots who were friends of mine. One of them took me up on a flight from northern Michigan, over the Great Lake, toward Chicago, and when we were well over water he let me take control of the plane from the right-hand seat. It was a cloudy day and I concentrated on keeping the wings level with the horizon. This seemed rather easy. In fact, I was just getting slightly bored with it when he mentioned in his calm pilot's voice that we were in the early stage of "the death spiral." I was too inexperienced to notice the altimeter, which, as he then pointed out to me, was moving steadily downward in the dial. It was an eye opener, to say the least. I thought I'd been keeping us on a level course; I hadn't felt the least hint of the fact that we'd begun circling down toward the water.

RHRC: As your fans might know, you wear many professional hats: not just that of a writer, but also of a teacher and a physician. Which career is most challenging?

EC: I no longer practice medicine, but I can say that for me medicine was easier, and certainly less emotionally turbulent, than writing. In medicine there's a fairly large but still finite body of knowledge that you need at hand for most of your daily work. It takes a few years to learn it, but once it's there, it's there. With writing, on the other hand, every new book—indeed every new story—is a fresh and terrifying reinvention of everything. I don't think you ever fully figure out how to do it; at least, I haven't.

Teaching brings me back to some of the things I most enjoyed in medicine. As a writer, what I miss most about being a doctor is the intimate contact I had with all kinds of people. Teaching gives me back some of that contact—in my own case, the chance to engage with impressively talented, energetic, and devoted students (which is what we have, generally, at the Iowa Writers' Workshop)—students who are similarly embarked (and most of them realize it) on what is probably an un-understandable and certainly an unmasterable endeavor.

RHRC: *America America* is a political novel and a character novel but also in some ways a mystery novel. Yet Corey never tells us exactly what happened between Senator Bonwiller and JoEllen Charney and Liam Metarey, as he might have in a standard mystery. Why does he not reveal everything he knows?

EC: Corey indeed never gives us access to the major dark events of the book the way, say, a detective narrator might have; but to my mind he has nonetheless deciphered most of them. I think he's fully aware of his own role in Senator Bonwiller's dealings, for example, and is also well aware of the role of Liam Metarey, a man whose kindnesses are in large part responsible for the life Corey now leads. To my mind, in fact, that is why Corey can never fully bring himself to tell us everything — out of loyalty to a generous and lifelong benefactor. But just as Liam Metarey has left clues for Corey, so Corey has left them for the reader.

1. This novel makes many assertions about the American political landscape in the early 1970s. What are some of those assertions? In what ways have American politics changed since then? And how does Henry Bonwiller compare to today's politicians, in terms of his political demeanor and beliefs as well as in his sense of both personal and public morality?

2. Structurally, the novel is braided from several strands—the political story, the personal story, the story about economic class and social station, and the story of the town itself. Which of these

stories, in your opinion, provides the novel's bulwark? How does each contribute to the novel's themes?

3. Corey has two father figures in the novel, his own father and Liam Metarey. Despite the differences in their social and economic stations, the men are similar in several ways. How? How do the two of them influence the man that Corey becomes?

4. Very early in the novel, an elderly man hobbles to the grave of Senator Henry Bonwiller, where he breaks down and weeps. Corey says he recognizes the man but never reveals a name. Why not? Who is this man? Why is it important to Corey that he is weeping? Why are we left to discover for ourselves the man's identity?

5. Trieste Millbury, the intern at *The Speaker-Sentinel*, clearly reminds Corey of himself. What role does she play in Corey's retelling of his past with the Metarey family? Why does he tell her his story?

6. At one point in the novel, Corey says: "It struck me again, the way it had just begun to do in those days, how diligently privilege had to work to remain oblivious to its cost." Then he adds, "I'm speaking of myself now, too, of course." What are the costs, both to himself and others, of the privileges that have been bestowed upon Corey? Has he in fact worked to remain oblivious to these costs?

7. Newspapers play an important role in Corey's life—in their pages, he first learns about politics, and during the Bonwiller campaign he becomes obsessed by journalism and journalists; he interacts with reporters like Glenn Burrant and G. V. Trawbridge in significant ways; and, of course, in the end he becomes a news-man himself. In what ways has news reporting changed during the span of this novel—from the time of Eoghan Metarey's rise, through Corey's childhood, up until the present day? In what ways has it remained consistent? What effects have these changes and these consistencies had on our democracy?

8. In a key scene near the conclusion of the book, Liam Metarey makes a gruesome discovery, then a fateful decision, while driving his tractor through an apple orchard in a blizzard. Why, after making this discovery, does he make this decision? The scene is a pivotal one, yet Corey is not in fact present when it takes place. Since nobody has explicitly told him what happened, Corey's de-piction of the events seems to come largely, or perhaps entirely, from his imagination. What evidence does Corey have for what he deduces? Has Liam Metarey attempted to communicate to him what has occurred? If so, when? And what else might he have been trying to explain to Corey?

9. In many ways, the interactions of important characters drive the circumstances that result in Liam Metarey's death. Do you think the principal catalyst for his actions and death was JoEllen Charney? Henry Bonwiller? Andrew Metarey? Or was it some-thing deeper in Liam's character?

10. Corey's description of the relationship between the town of Saline and the Metarey family is one of mutual trust and dependence. How does this relationship change over time, especially with respect to the influence of larger social forces like unionization and the rise of giant corporations? How does the opinion each party has of the other change over time?

11. Though Corey mentions his wife numerous times early in the text, the reader does not learn who he has married until much later. What is the purpose of delaying this information? And why, when Corey finally reveals his wife's identity, does he do it with so little fanfare? What is the significance of the information Corey shares with the reader and the information he omits, not only in regard to Clara but to other plot elements as well? Is it fair for Corey to withhold vital parts of his story? Does he leave clues about them nonetheless?

12. More than once in the novel, the narrator mentions a quotation from Francis Bacon: "If a man shall begin in certainties, he shall end in doubts." How is this idea reflected in the lives of Liam Metarey, Eoghan Metarey, Granger Sifter, Henry Bonwiller, and Corey? Bacon was no doubt referring to the advent of the scientific method during the seventeenth century, but how might his words apply to our current culture?

13. Throughout the novel, Corey remembers and retells past events without adhering to chronological order. How does the lack of a linear chronology influence the reader's experience? Is there a logic to the manner in which he recalls the scenes? Why does he tell the story like this?

ABOUT THE TYPE

This book was set in Electra, a typeface designed for Linotype by W. A. Dwiggins, the renowned type designer (1880–1956). Electra is a fluid typeface, avoiding the contrasts of thick and thin strokes that are prevalent in most modern typefaces.

Join the Random House Reader's Circle to enhance your book club or personal reading experience.

Our FREE monthly e-newsletter gives you:

• Sneak-peek excerpts from our newest titles

• Exclusive interviews with your favorite authors

• Special offers and promotions giving you access to advance copies of books, our free "Book Club Companion" quarterly magazine, and much more

• Fun ideas to spice up your book club meetings: creative activities, outings, and discussion topics

• Opportunities to invite an author to your next book club meeting

• Anecdotes and pearls of wisdom from other book group members . . . and the opportunity to share your own!

To sign up, visit our website at
www.randomhousereaderscircle.com

When you see this seal on the outside, there's a great book club read inside.